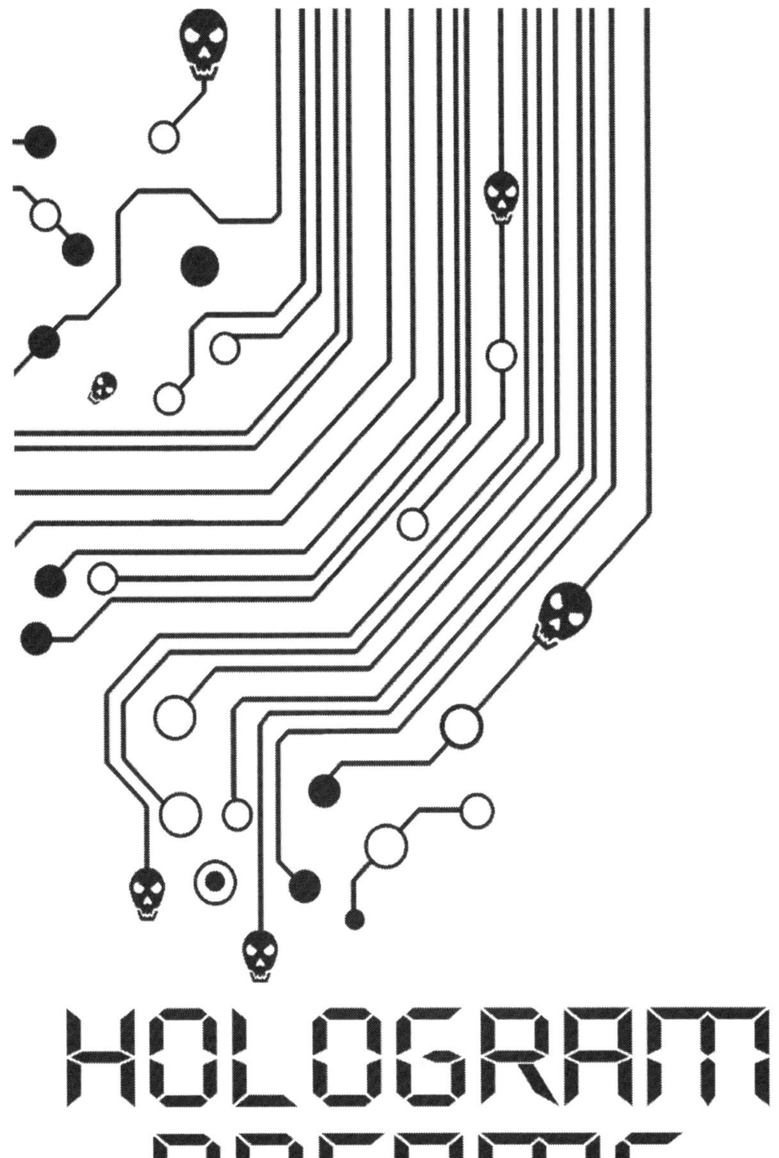

HOLOGRAM DREAMS

R. G. KNIGHTON

Hologram Dreams

Published: 14th Feb 2016

Publisher: R.G. KNIGHTON

This book is dedicated to my family.

Thank you for all your help and patience.

"Imagine a world where you can make nearly every fantasy come true!"

How would you like to walk on the moon, take the leading role in your favourite movie, or maybe you would like to dance beside the world's biggest music stars in a classic video?

Perhaps you have a story of your own that you wish to bring to life; well this is the place to be, and we at the Hologram Dreams Corporation can do that just for you.

Our groundbreaking reproduction will completely immerse you in a fantasy world. Gone are the days of android technology as a means of production. Today nearly everything created will now be a holographic image. Not only that, the characters will also respond to your every move or command, you will even be able to reach out and touch them.

This is all made possible thanks to our exciting new innovation, the image density profiler!

Sign up today and make all your dreams come true! What are you waiting for?

(Advertisement copyright: Hologram Dreams Corporation. MMLXIV)

PROLOGUE

In the early hours of a late-autumnal morn, crisp, frosty air dusts its diamond-white powder silently across the bleak Old Chelmsford Moor, bringing a fulminant chill to the balmy night. Treeless, bracken covered, and a risk to life, this scarred and ancient landscape now looked a little brighter even though it was a very dangerous place. For hundreds of years the wetland had provided the surrounding towns with a rich provision of fuel grade peat, but eventually supplies dwindled and it now lies abandoned. Today the moorland remains crisscrossed with long, steep-sided, man-made trenches, where the majority are half-filled with dank water, courtesy of tidal flow from the nearby river Maldon.

If the conditions are just right, a keen eye could spy will-o'-the–wisp tiptoeing ethereally across this unwelcoming bog. Floating like gossamer ghosts on a gentle breeze, the milky threads dance to a silent rhythm just above the fallen oily rainbows floating heavily on the lagoons of brackish water. Indifferent to the sticky mud on the shoreline, the vaporous plumes tumble end over end before evaporating into the coarse grasses huddled under the thorny gorse that also cling doggedly to the sour cold earth.

Highly unusual for this time of night, the local wildlife appeared curiously mute. Even the mechanical chatter of the nightjar ceased, spreading an eerie silence from a community's sense of imminent danger. The spine-chilling hush lasted for only a few seconds, until suddenly broken by the sound of something splashing heavily into the stinking, muddy water. Out of the darkness, a figure emerges of an attractive, slender young woman in a state of near exhaustion and gasping for breath. She is in a desperate state and frantically attempting to stay ahead of something that for the moment is still out of sight. However, the terror etched across her delicate features showed that it was not too far behind.

Aged somewhere in her mid-twenties and dressed in skin-tight black leather trousers, matching knee-high boots, and a loose fitting white silk blouse, she proceeds to wade waist high along a narrow river tributary, trying to put greater distance between herself and as yet, the unseen horror heading her way.

With aching lungs burning like hot coals and her chest protesting at the massive gulps of achingly cold, damp air, her muscles cramped, fading rapidly from the lack of oxygenated blood. Forced to give in to exhaustion, she concealed herself in the tall reeds growing against the black muddy bank on the far side of a narrow stream. Trying vainly to remain as quiet as possible, but doing a pitiful job, she reluctantly drew deep, ragged breaths, hoping desperately to regain some of her strength. Completely drenched in the near freezing water, the desperate woman shivered as she clawed away the strands of wet hair plastered across her face, and then used the sleeves of her blouse in a very unfeminine manner to wipe away the runnels of clear snot pouring steadily from a very ruddy nose.

Hugging herself tightly, trying to stop chattering teeth, she realised that remaining in one place was a poor idea and prepared to move on, only to halt, paralysed with fear as she stared wide-eyed into the darkness. Not too far distant a blood-chilling howl rent the cool night air, Panic-stricken, the woman clamped both hands across her mouth to stifle an instinctive scream. The fear of the guttural cry produced a fresh spurt of energy and she waded out into yet another pool of foul smelling water. Hoping to reach a ridge of firmer, higher ground sighted not too far away, she hurriedly stepped out of the shallows and waded into an unseen channel of fast moving undercurrent, cutting directly across her path. It was over in an instant, one second she was there and then gone, as her body slipped silently into the abyss lying beneath the inky flow.

Several seconds passed and it looked as if the bog land had claimed yet another victim, when twenty yards further downstream she violently resurfaced, splashing desperately to stay afloat and coughing up gobbets of rank bog-water mixed with bile and mucus, clogging-up and stinging the back of her throat. Completely exhausted and still gasping for breath, she was lucky to drift close to the shoreline and grab hold of a large tuft of deep-rooted, purple moor grass that doggedly refused to give in to this most unwelcome land. Somehow finding an inner, hidden strength, the exhausted woman managed to clamber halfway out onto the bank and lay panting hoarsely in the cold black mud.

She was close to passing out, but still held an awareness of the imminent danger and frantically looked back, scanning the surrounding expanse for any sign of movement through the ghostly mist. For the moment, all was quiet, but suddenly the silence was harshly broken when the blurred image of something large, something very large, splashing through the water less than fifty feet away. Gasping deeply, the terror fuelled an even greater urgency as she frantically clawed and kicked her way up the soft muddy incline until finally reaching the top of the solid riverbank.

Less than sixty yards away in the window of a remote farmhouse, a lighted candle flickered, radiating a beacon of hope for sanctuary. The sight of this spurred a newfound determination and she set off in a broken run towards the welcoming glow. Luckily, the boggy surface dried up as it levelled out into an old abandoned cart track, improving her speed that she hoped would put a greater distance between herself and the creature. Suddenly, without rhyme or reason the young woman stopped her run, crouched down, and held her breath to listen. Her guess was right; the sound of a second set of heavier footfalls carrying on the cold, damp air meant her assailant had made it up onto the same patch of land and was gaining rapidly upon her position. It too stopped and howled again, this time much louder than the first, signalling conclusively that it was now but a few yards behind.

With the advantage of massive three toed webbed feet splaying out on impact over the soft earth, the giant beast had easily followed the feminine scent and homed in on its prey. Setting off once again, she managed to stretch her lead a little, but then foolishly risked an over the shoulder glance to gauge the distance; this was a grave mistake. Taking little care in where she placed her feet, the toe of her boot caught in a cartwheel rut, rolling the foot outwards, twisting her ankle and collapsing the lower leg, sending the poor woman sprawling headlong onto the soft grassy verge. Heavily winded from the clumsy landing, and unable to move, she could do nothing more than silently endure the pain, listen to rapid heartbeats thudding wildly in her ears, and wait for the inevitable.

Several seconds slipped by and she realised that the heavy footsteps had stopped, yet her pursuer was still nowhere to be seen. Fearing that any movement on her part would give the game away, she remained exactly where she fell, trying to remain quiet and still. Seconds turned into minutes and nothing happened, all she could hear now was the sound of her own ragged breathing in the cloying darkness. Terror often plays tricks with the mind and believing that her attacker may now have circled around and was waiting ahead of her on the trail, she made the foolhardy decision to abandon the track and slide back down the riverbank. This took the direct route through the bulrushes where she hoped the assailant would lose track, leaving her the victor in this deadly race.

Semi-submerged yet again, with only the top half of her face visible above the waterline, she quickly realised it was a mistake when she came face to face with thick clumps of reeds considerably slowing down her progress towards the sanctuary of the lone whitewashed house.

Good fortune intervened and the brooding rain filled clouds slowly drifted apart, allowing the light of a full moon to illuminate the surroundings, making escape a little easier to plot. It was also fortunate that the dense reeds were thinning out; leaving a short swim towards a clump of bulrushes nestled in the soft glow coming from the candlelit kitchen window. Setting off with a careful breaststroke, the young woman was almost half way between one safety zone and the next when she spied a thin row of bubbles rising up from the depths. The air trapped within, raised a clear half-dome, each containing an image of the moon before it popped lazily on the inky surface. The bubble trail moved steadily closer and she froze in terror when a large pair of amphibian oculi slowly lifted above the waterline. Unblinking they moved even closer until she could see her own terrified reflection in the vertical obsidian slits mounted inside the rich golden eyes. Taking a deep breath and ready to scream with all her might, she quickly bit her lip and changed it into a silent sob of relief as whatever it was, floated on by, only inches away from her face. Watching intently she ignored the broken reflections on the ripples of the water and even managed to chuckle as an enormous male bullfrog proceed to climb ungainly out of the water then settle onto a large lily pad growing near the bank.

Crying with relief, she turned back to resume with her escape when the silence shattered. Exploding from under the surface of the water, 800 pounds of giant man-eating lizard roared into the cold night air. The eruption caused a mini tidal wave of foul smelling muck and muddy water spreading out in all directions; washing the indignant bullfrog halfway up the nearest bank before sliding unceremoniously on its belly back into the bog.

Squealing in delight, the creature raised its massive nine-foot high frame onto muscular hind legs and roared. Spraying water everywhere, it thrashed its head violently from side to side, announcing to the world of yet another victim.

The lizard's surprisingly beady eyes for such a huge frame, fixed on the filthy petrified face of the young woman as she cowered, quaking and silent against the steep riverbank. She could have tried yet again to escape, but paralysed with fear she remained inert, resigned to her fate. Mesmerised by its menacing behaviour, she stared as its slender black forked tongue lazily slipped out from inside a lipless mouth, tasted her scent, and then flicked upwards to transfer the intoxicating odour into one of its huge flapped nostrils that repeatedly pinched and blew from its own excited, panting breath. Aroused by her smell, the lizard thrashed its massive scaly tail up and down in the filthy water, and then opened its jaw wide to reveal several jagged ranks of sickly-yellow, trilateral, razor-sharp teeth, arranged around the outer rim of a truly cavernous mouth.

For a few seconds the monster stopped and stood almost rooted to the spot, matching its victim's stance. This appeared to offer a speck of hope, but in the blink of an eye, it was all over. With lightning speed, the creature lunged, opening its jaws wide it engulfed the upper half of the terrified woman's torso. Clamping its jaw tightly around her abdomen and effortlessly resuming a standing position, its enormous head tilted to the skies, inverting the body as it cleared the water, leaving only her legs kicking hopelessly back and forth, as they protruded from its mouth. Every time she stopped, the monster relaxed its bite and gulped hard, unfurling the pleated leathery folds of skin around its neck to accommodate the meal sliding wholly and headfirst down its throat. This continued for nearly a minute until the prey completely disappeared.

Once again the creature screamed like a banshee, thrashing wildly in the waist high, slurry, while the shape of the poor woman's form could still be seen writhing around, kicking, and punching in a futile hope for escape from inside its thick, slime covered flesh. Satisfied with the kill, the monster lizard turned away, descended silently below the waterline and vanished into the bog.

"Cut, that's a wrap."

From somewhere in the darkness, banks of spotlights illuminated the scene, revealing a small crew of men and women who had been filming the entire process. The lizard resurfaced, turned around, lowered its head, and appeared to watch as its stomach ripped open from the inside. This revealed the devoured woman who was still very much alive, albeit wet, upside down, and pressed tightly to another very exhausted actor who worked the lizard from the inside. He graciously helped his victim slide out from inside the latex rubber costume, into the arms of a neoprene-suited lifeguard who carried her to the riverbank for a hot drink and a nice warm blanket.

"Excellent Sophie, you're a natural actress." The director exclaimed loudly, fawning excessively over the leading lady, whose money had funded the entire production. The sound fades, and as the camera backs away from the scene, the holographic projection disappears, revealing the production equipment and a barren film set previously hidden from view. The physical representation of the filthy bog was now a network of clear water channels cut into the ground. The lizard creature, now without its colouring and intricate detail had reverted to a simple plain green rubber suit. From stage left, a handsome man wearing khaki trousers and a blue denim shirt walks into shot, turns to face the camera, and addresses the viewer.

"Did you all enjoy that? I know that I did; but did you realise that someday soon the star of the show could be you? Men of the world, I am sure you have wondered how you would feel to be the tough guy hero in an all action movie, or to score the winning goal in a world cup final. Also, you ladies out there, I bet many of you have often dreamed of being the beautiful damsel in distress held tightly in the arms of the most handsome of men and carried away on horseback into the sunset Or maybe a world-class athlete streaking passed the opposition on the final bend to win the champion gold medal. Dream no more people because now you can!

My name is Ted Langton, and as head of production for the Hologram Dreams Corporation, I'm the man capable of making your wish come true. The short film you have just watched is our remake of the final scene from the cult classic film *'The Lizard Creature from Hell'*. We have kindly been given permission from the leading lady to use a clip of her production, to show the world just how exciting all of this can be. Now, I know that you are all probably thinking that this type of recreational fantasy has been available for some time, and can only be purchased by the more affluent members of society. This is true, the expense has always been the result of utilising a combination of real actors, robotics, animatronics, and the painstaking reconstruction of a film set, but not anymore. The advent of the latest holographic reproduction technology means that we've managed to do away with nearly all of that and now for a fraction of the cost, still achieve incredibly realistic results."

The screen behind the narrator disappears and is replaced by a vignette of different images timed to synchronise with the well-rehearsed speech.

"How would you like to walk on the moon, or travel back in time to meet your ancestors? You could star in your very own scene from a movie classic, or dance with your favourite singer in a pop video. If you prefer we can develop any storyline from your own imagination, or from your favourite novel that will be painstakingly recreated to your satisfaction. Not only will we produce a visually stunning scene that will be watched for years to come, we will stimulate all of your senses. Feel the soft crump of freshly fallen snow trodden underfoot, the warm summer breeze caress your face, or the smell of cherry blossom in the springtime. For an all-inclusive price, you can experience a total immersion in your chosen fantasy; we leave nothing out. You will be the envy of friends and family, the limit to all of this is your own imagination."

Each time the narrator describes a different example, the background changes accordingly to emphasise the presentation. While this takes place, the Hologram Dreams contact information scrolls akin to movie credits down the right-hand side of the screen. All of this is informative, but irrelevant, because when the advertisement broadcasts in just over a month's time, everyone in the cinema will simultaneously receive a forced download to their own personal communication device. The additional annoying factor is that the download is impossible to erase until the consumer replays the video in full. This new invention christened LAA, or *'Location Awareness Advertising'* is the latest marketing tool and a bane for nearly every member of the general populace across the globe, as major organisations invest in brand forced messaging onto every wristwatch, mobile phone, tablet, or anything else that happens to breach a law-abiding visual radius of the advertised product.

INTRODUCTION

Fifty years from now, the incredible advance in robotic technology steadily negates the need for human input. For the majority of the first world, working hours have now been reduced by more than half, giving the general populace huge amounts of leisure time. To fulfil this void, the entertainment industry has been quick to respond to demand, creating ever increasingly diverse and interesting pastimes. This idea was initially championed by the movie giants who stepped up to the plate and invested billions in the effort to develop something exciting, and with the equipment they had at hand, fairly easy to produce. For those who can afford it, the opportunity of being able to star in your own personalised movie clip is currently running at number one.

Armed with access to massive collections of old costumes, props, hundreds of film sets and thousands of robotic extras, the major players followed a well-worn path by adapting a portion of their vast studios into composite film production units as a way to supplement income from cinema audiences who now prefer home entertainment. Comparatively different to the majority of these leading players, is the company way ahead of the rest of the field, the Hologram Dreams Corporation. Not based inside an old film-studio like its contemporaries, this recently developed organisation boasted a customised entertainment franchise, built from the ground up by the genius of Philip Sanderson, majority shareholder, CEO, and creator of the company.

Originally, he had little interest in the entertainment industry, concentrating more on the world of finance. However, an idea blossomed following his invention of a cheaper and more efficient holographic trading technique. Implementing this new feature into the entertainment industry, slashed costs, thus allowing massive discounts given on what were previously multi-million dollar productions. Instead of selling this concept to the highest bidder, Sanderson decided to raise capital on the value of his discovery and create a studio of his own.

Within weeks of this announcement, it appeared that half of the world wanted to be a star and now anyone who could afford the average price of a two-week foreign holiday had the opportunity to fulfil a dream.

HOLOGRAM DREAMS

CHAPTER ONE

In a cloudless lazuli coloured sky, the fierce heat from a midday sun beat down relentlessly onto the deck of the *'Orion'*. The craft, a charter hire from Black's Marina of Portsmouth had been organised and paid for courtesy of Neil Wickham, one member of a close-knit group of eight university friends who had all agreed to accompany him on a luxury break to celebrate their graduation. The only other resident on board was the ship's captain Kristy Black, an experienced sailor, navigator, and recent acquaintance of the young holidaymakers.

The yacht in question was one of the best in its class. It measured over one-hundred and twenty-five feet from bow to stern, contained ten well-appointed cabins, sauna, spa bath, and even a home cinema, everything you could wish for the perfect holiday. The problem was that this one-hundred and eighty ton triple steel masted luxury schooner now lay becalmed and drifting close to the tropic of cancer, somewhere in the middle of the Red Sea.

Neil, at the age of twenty-nine was by a few years, the oldest member of the group. A tall and gangly man with a large hooked nose and fast receding ginger hairline, making him appear considerably older than someone only months away from his thirtieth birthday. Accompanied by an intelligent and sometimes haughty demeanour, he complemented his character with a penchant for tweed jackets and moleskin trousers, earning him the distinguished nickname of *'Professor'* or *'Prof'* from other members of the group. Eldest son of an extremely wealthy family, Neil had been given *'carte blanche'* to travel the world as a gift for his eighteenth birthday. The only proviso was that he returned to complete a university degree before his thirtieth; a promise he wisely kept. Now a graduate in advanced business studies, he was determined to go on one last trip before settling down to join the family clothing empire, *'Fermdale's'* or as he jokingly preferred to call, *'The Firm'*.

To make sure everything ran smoothly, Neil utilised the formidable skills of his best friend Adam Cartwright, a genial young man and by far the most intelligent member of the group. Fluent in several languages, brilliant computer programmer and excellent in logistical organisation, Adam was persuaded by Neil to negotiate with Reginald Black, the owner of the Yacht registered to Portsmouth marina. In addition, to organise everything else required with Kristy, Reginald's daughter and junior partner who acted as quartermaster for the voyage. Neil had even selfishly asked Adam to take charge of travel requirements for everyone, including passports, visas, insurance, and all necessary currencies. This masterstroke allowed him to take a step back, with the supreme satisfaction that Adam had assessed and catered for every eventuality that could possibly affect the group.

The two young men had become instant friends from day one, with a chance meeting during fresher's week when they both signed up for the debating society, over the next three years this grew ever stronger. The sight of this odd duo wandering in and around the university campus became commonplace, with Neil, standing well over six feet tall, walking alongside Adam who barely cleared five. There were even rumours that they were a couple, but even though Neil shared equal physical attraction for both men and women, their relationship was strictly platonic. Adam's short stature and puny physique made him a weak specimen of manhood; but lack of height and physical strength he more than compensated for with his warm and caring nature. He also possessed a willingness to utilise his incredible intelligence, assisting others with their studies whenever required.

For months, Neil had frequently promised to take everyone on his family yacht following the graduation ceremony. A claim that most of the group took for what they believed to be an idle boast on his part. He only proved their point when he announced three weeks before the graduation ceremony that the yacht had been caught in a tropical storm, hit a reef, and sunk off the coast of Barbados. Hurt by the sarcastic comments, Neil remained undeterred and true to his word. He chartered a second even bigger yacht at a favourable discount thanks to Adam's charms and the fact that Reginald Black was a good family friend and the yacht's owner. Knowing the limited maritime skills of the group in question, Reginald Black insisted on Kristy accompanying the holidaymakers as ship's captain, and to also to look after her father's very expensive craft in the hands of Neil and all of his friends. Being of a similar age and intelligence, Kristy quickly bonded with everyone, and as the weeks passed by, the job turned into more of a paid vacation.

Sailing south from Portsmouth across the English Channel and keeping within sight of the coasts of France and Portugal, she expertly navigated east into the Mediterranean and called at every requested port this European melting pot had to offer. The initial plan was to return along the north coast of Africa and then head for home, but as they reached Port Said on the eastern tip of the Nile Delta, Neil had an idea. He persuaded Kristy to sail down the Suez Canal so he to tick an item from his personal *'bucket list'* and go scuba diving in the Red Sea. As he was the one footing the bill for the entire trip, no one had any objections and the detour went ahead. This diversion had not been part of the itinerary and with the planned refuelling stop naively overlooked, it all ended with their current predicament. Without a breath of wind to ease the way, and a limited amount of marine diesel in the tanks, they regularly had to start the engines and avoid collisions with the massive tankers and cargo ships that passed constantly up and down this very busy stretch of sea.

Becalmed for nearly three days, the yacht now drifted aimlessly on the crystal-clear aquamarine tinted waters. This was a considerable annoyance for Adam who had been aware of the situation, but found out that Neil had selfishly lied regarding the level of fuel to allow for the diversion, making a mockery of all his planning. Luckily, there were no other problems, such as the supply of food or drinking water, that with careful use would last for another five days to a week. The only thing beyond Adam's control was the incessant daytime heat, contributing to bickering and short tempers amongst the group as the boredom wore on. It was impossible to stay for any length of time in the cloying air below deck, as Kristy had turned off the air conditioning to conserve fuel. For some, being out under the near equatorial sun burning high in the cloudless sky it was far worse. With this in mind, she managed to rig up a spare double-layered sail into the shape of a gazebo, providing welcome shade for all. It also allowed the gentlest of sea breezes to cool heat frazzled nerves.

One of the gang currently relaxing on deck was the group ringleader, a handsome twenty-two year old named Jason Cook. He was of average build and height, but with his slender features and shoulder length, straight, light-brown hair, he bore an uncanny resemblance to the popular western Christian depiction of Jesus Christ. Coincidentally bearing the same initials, his nickname of JC often became his address.

Accompanying Jason on this trip was his twin sister Amy. Similar in height and build to her brother, but visually appeared the more masculine of the two. Her short brown hair, a flat chest, reluctance to wear make-up, and penchant for men's clothing enhanced a tomboy persona, causing embarrassment on many occasions when she was often mistaken for a young man.

"How on earth can you wear anything as thick as that on a day like this? You'll boil; take it off for God's sake!" Jason chided Amy as she emerged from below decks in blue shorts and matching long sleeved sweatshirt.

"I don't have anything else to wear that doesn't need washing and I thought we were trying to conserve water. Anyway, I can't, I'm completely naked underneath." Amy replied, turning her head towards John Turner, hoping to solicit a reaction from her saucy comment. Unfortunately, the idea fell on stony ground, as all he could do was roll his eyes and talk through an exaggerated yawn,

"Nothing to look at anyway, I've seen ironing boards with better curves."

Amy blushed deeply, fuming at John's comment. He completely ignored her scowl and rolled over to stare longingly at the object of his own affections who politely sat away from the group near to the bow while drawing deeply on a cheroot and blowing smoke rings into the air. Amy had been in love with John from the first day they met and it was not surprising; handsome, tall, eloquent, with blond hair and blue eyes, there was nothing not to like. The classic cliché was that John was in love with another and barely gave Amy the time of day, but she never gave up hope for a change of heart, even after she found out John was gay and the subject of his affection happened to be Neil.

At that moment, Patrick Hardy, Amy and Jason's second cousin, (who had talked his way into coming on the trip), called for everyone's attention when he looked to the western horizon and spied a boat that appeared to be heading their way. Kristy immediately ran into the bridge, retrieved a pair of high magnification binoculars, and trained her sight on the approaching craft. Idle curiosity encouraged everyone to the rail, straining their eyes to the horizon to make their own personal assessment, while waiting for Kristy to give a report. Lowering the lenses from her emerald green eyes, it was plain to see that the colour had drained from her face, contrasting sharply with her long ebony hair hanging loosely around her shoulders and almost down to her waist. Without a word, Kristy turned and hastily forced the binoculars into the arms of Patrick, who happened to be standing the closest. To the confusion of all on board, she then ran to the bridge and started the engine, turning the yacht directly away from the approaching vessel. Ignoring the raft of questions fired at her, Kristy sent out an automated distress call for immediate assistance on the new Global-Sat 3000 worldwide positioning system that relays the exact location of the sender to the nearest emergency services and any other vessels in the area that could offer assistance. Neil flicked his cheroot into the sea and ran to the bridge along with the others who were anxiously crowded around the outer door. Kristy ignored all the questions as she frantically switched off all non-essential electrical equipment that she could think of, to glean every ounce of power from the engine. Only when satisfied that was all she could do, she finally addressed the group with an answer.

"Sudanese Pirates!" She exclaimed in all seriousness, but the reaction was not what she expected. Some laughed while others shook their heads or raised eyebrows in disgust at the poor joke. Kristy barged through the group, snatching the binoculars back from Patrick on route, and then stared again at the now larger blob closing in across the shimmering water. A sudden realisation dawned on the group that she was not joking, causing panic, resulting in even more frantic questions firing in from every angle. Kristy directed all her answers through Neil, explaining loudly so everyone could hear how Sudanese pirates hijacked all kinds of ships and often kidnapping passengers and crew for a ransom. Neil remained remarkably calm, listened carefully, then attempted to ask the questions that everybody else was thinking.

"You will find that we are many hundreds of miles from Somali waters so I doubt that very much. You'll probably find that it's just a harmless fishing boat."

John interrupted with his usual arrogant manner, shaking his head wearily at the others, like a pensioner dealing with a bunch of five year olds.

"I didn't say Somali pirates I said Sudanese. I know the world has heard of all the famous hijacks that have taken place over the years and they are always attributed to Somalia. What most people don't know is that the Sudan has also had its fair share and as we are less than seventy miles from the Sudanese coast, so I'm taking an educated guess. When they get here you can ask them yourself if you'd like!" Kristy snapped, the colour quickly returning to her face in anger at John's semantics during such a critical time. Neil ushered his friend out of the way to ease the situation and addressed Kristy with a more logical form of questioning.

"Have you informed the emergency services?"

"Yes an automated distress tracker signal is already operational." Kristy replied, still annoyed and staring hard at John following his crass question. Before long, she regained her concentration due to the seriousness of the situation.

"Can we outrun them?" Neil asked next, even though he knew the truth, he hoped that he was wrong.

"I doubt it with all the weight we are carrying and also the fuel is very low."

Terror spread across the faces of the remaining group as Adam interjected with his own opinions.

"The best we can do is to prepare for the worst. First, would it help if we threw any unwanted weight overboard to increase speed and preserve fuel?"

Kristy thought for a second, and then gave a negative answer before making a statement to the rest of the group.

"Right everyone listen up. The boats they use are fitted with high-powered engines designed for pursuit. We are still in the middle of nowhere and rescue is probably hours away. I suggest everyone get suitably dressed ready for a long hike, and when boarded, do exactly as you are told. The pirates will be armed with rifles and won't think twice about shooting someone who annoys them or disobeys. So don't be a hero and don't be stupid, I hope I've made myself clear!"

She returned her glare towards John, who avoided her gaze, choosing to remain silent as he waited for his turn to go below deck to his cabin and chose the most suitable clothes to wear. Kristy peered again through her binoculars and she could now see the outline of at least six African men armed with rifles standing on the deck of a shabby, considerably large, motorised fishing boat that was closing quickly on their position.

It was not long before the group began to re-emerge, all suitably dressed in walking boots, trousers and rain jackets, they climbed one by one up onto the deck. With everyone present, Kristy stepped away from the bridge to give some last minute advice.

"Listen up! I repeat, do as you are told and don't offer any information that isn't asked for or required, especially you Neil! If they find out your family is loaded the ransom will double. If they want to know how we can afford this yacht, tell them that we won a holiday competition. These pirates see this as a business and want to conclude it with the minimum of fuss. The ransom amount is not usually too excessive as they hope for a quick result and the longer they keep us prisoner, the more we cost to feed. Anyone got any further questions?"

One at a time, Kristy surveyed the terrified faces of the group, scowling once again at John as she reached him standing at the end. With no further reply, she too went below deck ready to change clothes. Amy shook visibly with fear and received a comforting brotherly arm around her shoulders from Jason while they watched the pirate boat draw ever closer.

When Kristy re-emerged, the two vessels were now less than fifty yards apart and everyone startled to the sound of automatic gunfire, watching in fear when spits of seawater flew high into the air as the bullets drew a straight line ten yards from the bow of their yacht. Kristy immediately walked back to the bridge, throttled back, and killed the power to the engines, bringing the yacht almost to a standstill. The pirate vessel drew up alongside and one of their crew threw a rope across the narrow divide and waited as Kristy obediently tied her end tightly to a mooring hitch.

Steadily the two vessels drew side by side as the terrified group stood silently staring down at their armed captors while Kristy also secured a cargo net to the rail of the yacht. From below deck, a small shifty looking member of the pirate crew emerged, carrying on his back what appeared to be a fat attaché case. He expertly climbed the net up onto the yacht and ignoring the group, headed directly into the bridge. Wondering what was happening, Kristy turned to follow him only to be pushed back violently as she reached the door. Returning to the group, she stared along with the others at the handful of very young black men training their rifles upon them while they waited for their leader to emerge from below.

The minutes ticked by agonisingly slowly and the group of friends sweated profusely in the intense heat, greatly increased by the fact that they now stood greatly overdressed in the hot weather. Neil drew breath, ready to ask questions, but at the last moment Kristy caught his eye, followed by a brief shake of her head, ending his speech before it even began. Eventually the pirate leader stepped out onto the deck and stared silently at the terrified group. He was a tall, well-built bald-headed man with skin so dark it shone with a purpurate hue in the bright sunlight. Unlike his filthy crew, he wore clean, three-quarter length, khaki cargo-pants and a pressed white-cotton, short-sleeved shirt, open to the waist revealing a muscular chest covered in a symmetric pattern of tribal scarring. The only part of his attire not freshly laundered, was an old sweat stained white and blue peaked captain's hat that had seen much better days. Eventually he addressed everyone in colloquial French mixed with a smattering of the local dialect, drawing nothing but confusion from most of the group. Luckily Adam understood the majority of the speech and he replied in the same language who they all were and asked why was this happening, before asking if the leader knew English. The man nodded briefly and continued to address everyone in a manner everyone could understand.

"Lady and gentlemen, my name is Captain Moses Ikambu, these are my soldiers and you are all my prisoners. If you do as you are told, my men will care for you accordingly. If you refuse or cause trouble, I assure you there will be severe consequences, do I make myself clear?"

The group nervously acknowledged the captain, allowing him to continue.

"You, this yacht and all contained within are now in my possession. You will be transferred to my boat for safekeeping and then transported back to land where you will remain until a suitable fee is paid. Is that also clear?"

Again, everyone nodded except Patrick, who stood slightly away from the others. He seemed quite agitated and appeared to be fiddling with something jammed in the back of his waistband. Captain Moses stared hard, waiting impatiently for Patrick's acknowledgement, when to everyone's shock the young man pulled out a flare pistol and aimed it directly at the captain's bare chest. "Leave us all alone and… and I won't shoot." He stammered, trying to sound calm and in control, but making a very poor show.

Surprisingly the captain made no attempt to hide, but he did raise a quizzical eyebrow and placed his hands on his hips as he watched Patrick's hands shaking violently in his attempt to maintain aim and make his demands.

"Put that down or you'll get us all killed!" Kristy hissed through gritted teeth. Trying not to make any sudden movements and risk being shot herself.

"I won't tell you again!" Patrick yelled, refusing to back down. The captain looked sorrowful, staring down at the deck and slowly shaking his head. Quickly his mood changed, lifting his gaze, he revealed a menacing grin of pearly white teeth, contrasting starkly against the colour of his black skin. He turned and nodded to the member of his crew who stood on top of the wheelhouse, placing him level with Patrick. He knew what to do and had been watching intently, waiting for a signal. Before Patrick had time to act upon his demands, a short rataplan of gunfire shattered the silence, catapulting the young man backwards as four bullets slammed into his torso. The flare gun flew high into the air, but somehow in the split second before he was shot, Patrick must also have pulled the trigger. The makeshift weapon released the charge in a flattened arc just a few feet over the captain's head. Fizzing loudly, its magnesium based contents reacted with the seawater and skimmed haphazardly across the top of the ocean before disappearing from view in a cloud of grey smoke. The pistol clattered loudly as it hit the deck and the world about the group suddenly appeared to slow down as Patrick's arms flew up and his body twitched violently as each bullet thudded into his chest. Narrow jets of blood ejaculated over six feet from the rear of the young man's torso, splattering onto the shiny hardwood deck as the velocity of each round tore almost unopposed through his soft flesh and eventually splashed into the seawater nearly fifty yards away. Unable to stop his momentum, a stunned faced Patrick staggered drunkenly back, stumbled into the low deck rail and swiftly upended as his thick-soled shoes slipped in his own blood. A second later, his body splashed heavily into the sea. Amy screamed as the horrified group, ignoring the fact that they too had guns trained on them, ran to the rail to see the gut wrenching sight of Patrick's body floating face down in the water. The extra layer of clothing that the young man had dressed for the journey had ballooned with partially trapped air, temporarily keeping him buoyant. Bloody puncture holes in the back of his jacket indicated the exit wounds to his body, including one that had clipped the left ventricle of his heart and it stopped beating seconds after he fell into the sea. Surprisingly quickly, dark crimson blood decanted from the wounds, clouding the clear azure water around his body to the colour of quality claret. Subsequently, this diluted into a pale rosé haze as Patrick's body drifted away.

"You bastards!" Adam screamed, turning around angrily to confront his captors only to find himself and nearly everyone else up-close and personal with the point of a rifle. While the group of friends all stared aghast at Patrick's body bobbing gently in the water, the pirates had already climbed up onto the yacht to seize their prize. With the echo of the rifle fire still ringing in their ears, the group remained stunned and silent as they were roughly searched for any communication devices, herded down the cargo net onto the pirate boat and forced one by one down a ladder into the stinking hold of the recently used fishing vessel. When everyone had reached the bottom, the ladder was hoisted quickly away and three-quarters of the available light disappeared as the two wooden hatch doors slammed back into place, leaving a checkerboard of sunlight shining down onto the grieving and terrified group. Panting for air in the rank smell of fish and sticky oppressive heat, their

eyes adjusted slowly to the darkness of the surroundings, as Neil was the first to speak.

"Is anyone hurt in any way?" He shouted over the growl of the idling engine reverberating from the next-door compartment, adding yet more heat into the hold. No one looked in his direction or bothered to answer the question; they were still dumbstruck over the situation and grieving for the loss of their friend. The silence ensued until Jason suddenly became aware of Oliver Smithson crumpled up on the floor, gasping for air in the dark. Oliver was a small and scrawny man with mousy hair and sallow complexion, whose weak nature seemed to inflict the poor man with a procession of different maladies and ailments since birth. Born very premature, due to his mother's drug addiction, Oliver spent the first six months of life in an incubator and given only a one in ten chance of survival. Beating the odds, he developed a dogged determination in everything he attempted in life, ignoring his regular bouts of illness and studying hard to replace his lack of freedom to run and play outdoors like his contemporaries. His efforts paid off when he graduated with a first in chemical engineering. The only thing that now held him back was his chronic asthma, and the cloying heat in the hold combined with emotional stress of the situation induced a massive attack. Jumping immediately into action, Oliver's best friend Jacob Morton grabbed him under the armpits and using his hugely muscled frame, effortlessly lifted Oliver to his feet where the air tasted a little sweeter.

"Don't panic buddy, use your inhaler, where is it?" Jacob asked as he frisked Oliver's body for the telltale bulge of the pressurised canister. Oliver shook his head and in-between gasps; he managed to whisper three words into Jacob's ear.

"In... my... cabin."

"You've got to be kidding me man; that should have been the first thing you picked up. Never mind buddy, I'll soon sort this out." Jacob replied as he almost threw Oliver into Jason's arms, straightened up to his full height, cupped his hands around his own mouth, and aiming at the hatch doors, shouted with all his might for help. When there was no response, Jacob grabbed hold of Neil as he was the tallest, crouched down, put his head between Neil's legs and stood up, hoisting the surprised man onto his massive shoulders directly under the hatch lid.

"Bang the lid with your fists and get some attention." Jacob instructed Neil, who proceeded to knock politely, akin to standing at someone's front door.

"For God's sake man nobody can hear that, bang it with your fist." Jacob ordered as he tried to maintain his balance in the semi-darkness and against the swell of the open sea. Neil did as ordered and banged his fist hard against the heavy wooden lid. To his surprise, it was not locked and jumped up as he hit it. There was nobody guarding the hatch, so Neil tentatively hinged one flap over, eased himself up, and peered around. The boat appeared deserted, so urged on by Jacob and holding tightly to the rim of the hatch, Neil was able to stand atop of the big man's shoulders and clamber out. Believing the prisoners to be safely ensconced in the hold, the captain had left only one man on the bridge of his own vessel while he and the rest of the gang, jumped across to assist in disabling the distress beacon and loot the captured yacht.

Inside the clean and shiny bridge, bedecked with chrome and varnished wood, Captain Moses had assigned the task of turning off the distress call to his second in command and also to find the correct code of the location beacon that maritime law insisted all sea going vessels must possess and keep enabled. Thus allowing all craft to be monitored, improving search and rescue times, also to keep a log of every individual journey, thus reducing smuggling and illegal immigrants. Moses' assistant had already placed the battered old attaché case onto the map desk and opened it to reveal a touch screen computer in the bottom half and a row of five thumb sized fishing floats nestled in the top, all were embedded in custom cut packing foam. Connected to the rear of the screen and folded up neatly to one side, lay a ribbon cable that was quickly attached by the free end to the input slot sited underneath the yacht beacon's housing. Immediately the computer screen flashed into life and began a sequence of preliminary diagnostics that completed just as Moses arrived. Satisfied all was well he ordered his aid to leave the bridge while he covertly tapped in the eight-digit password needed to access the main program. Moses trusted no one, with good reason, as there was always someone willing to take his place to receive a larger share of the ransom. By making himself irreplaceable, it would make any usurper think twice before challenging for control. The truth was that his aid already knew the password and was ready to kill Moses at the earliest opportunity as soon as he could identify the vital contact who dealt with the ransom demands. With the password accepted and the secondary program loaded, Moses allows his assistant back inside the bridge to complete the essential task that would eventually turn the red distress call back to idle green. The rest of the gang were given free run of the yacht and they had all descended below decks and into the cabins searching for anything of value that could be traded on the black market.

Moses glanced out of the window while he waited for the program to complete, and to his surprise, he could see one of the prisoners standing on the deck of his ship and creeping towards the bridge. Pushing his assistant out of the way, he ran out onto the deck, removed his pistol from his shoulder holster, aimed it a few inches above the escaped prisoner's head, and pulled the trigger. A shot rang out and splinters flew from the side panel of the bridge housing on the pirate vessel, bringing the half-asleep guard running out through the door to find Neil cowering on his knees with his head buried under trembling hands.

"Please don't shoot, I'm not trying to escape, it's just that my friend needs medical help." Neil pleaded with the guard who did not understand a word and had now placed the end of his rifle barrel directly onto the back of Neil's exposed neck. Pressing his forehead on the deck, Neil prayed silently to his god as he shook with fear and expecting to die any second, when he heard the familiar sound of the captain as he closed in on his position. The next thing Neil felt was the blinding pain of a swift kick in the ribs followed by the terrifying panic of trying to catch his breath when his lungs temporarily refused to function. Roughly dragged to his feet, Neil was pushed heavily back towards the hold when he finally found enough breath to talk.

"Please believe me, I wasn't trying to escape, only raise the alarm; one of my friends has chronic bronchial asthma and will die if he doesn't get his inhaler."

Moses listened carefully to Neil's plea, then stepped closer to the hold and peered into the darkness to see a small white man frantically gasping for breath while being cradled in a hugely muscled black man's arms. Not wanting to lose any more hostages, Moses shouted down, asking what the man needed and Jacob replied immediately.

"In the sleeping quarters there is a grey plastic holder with a canister attached to it, my friend needs this to help him breathe!"

Moses straightened up and barked an order over to one of his crew aboard the yacht who had all scurried onto the deck at the sound of gunfire. While everyone waited, Neil was forced to jump back down into the hold and even though his friends tried to break his fall, he still landed heavily, twisting his left ankle in the process. The seconds ticked slowly by and the group stared anxiously at Oliver's face as beads of sweat ran down his temples and he became weaker with every breath. Suddenly Moses reappeared above the hatch and in his hand, he held Oliver's inhaler. The huge ego Moses possessed gave him an idea, and holding the inhaler high for everyone to see, he told the group what he wanted.

"I am a reasonable man and I would like to give this to help your friend. The only thing is that I may drop it over the side, accidently you might say. What I need from you is your assurance that upon your release, you will tell the world how well how courteously Captain Moses Ikambu looked after you and that I am not a pirate, I am just a businessman trying to make his way through life the best way he can."

"You've just murdered my friend." Neil mumbled as he sat in the darkness, nursing his sore ankle.

"What did you just say?" Moses scowled, quickly losing his genial manner. He tightened his grip on the canister and leaned menacingly over the hatch trying to decide who had spoken in the darkness.

"We will praise you to the end." Adam shouted back. Thinking quickly was his forte and he hoped to have made it sound like Neil's outburst. With his ego boosted by the mock praise, Moses dropped the inhaler into the hold and watched curiously, as Jacob scooped it up and placed in Oliver's hand. One quick burst inhaled from the pressurised aluminium can and thirty long seconds later, Oliver relaxed his shoulders and finally breathed much easier thanks to the cromoglicic acid stabilising the inflamed cells in his lungs. The medicine was quite archaic compared to the many treatments available today, but none of the newer drugs seemed to work quite as well so Oliver stayed with whatever worked best. Bored with the show Moses slammed the hatch door closed, then turned to slam his fist into the left temple of the man whose job it was to guard the boat while the rest of the crew was aboard the yacht.

Eventually Moses finished berating the cowering crewman and his assistant returned with the attaché case. He had successfully deactivated the distress beacon and turned off the locator signal, but not before retuning another portable battery operated signal emitter to the same frequency as the yacht, placing it inside one of the fishing floats, and dropping it into the sea. Should the authorities begin a search for the vessel, they will be automatically drawn to the wrong location.

Still angry with his other crewman, Moses angrily snatched the attaché case and carried it below decks to be locked away for safekeeping. When he returned his smiling demeanour had resumed as he thought of the money coming his way as he ordered all but one of his men to return. With well-practised ease, his crewmen detached the two boats and as the fishing vessel manoeuvred in front of the yacht, a stout towing line was reattached and the craft set off in tandem for the long trip back to base.

CHAPTER TWO

Deep in the heart of what appeared to be the wild African savannah; three men stood on the edge of a small plateau watching the sun go down. The giant deep-orange ball began to sink behind a grove of massive baobab trees slowly filling with chattering birds come home to roost for the night. The small group watched the black finger-like shadows reach out towards them across the grassy plain and sadly realised it was nearly time to pack up and go home from what had been one of the most glorious days of their lives.

In the middle of the trio stood Oberon P Dodson, the incumbent sheriff of Holtsville police department, Triplerock County, Louisiana. Red faced and sweating profusely, this short, grossly overweight man stood with both hands shielding his eyes, as he appeared to be looking for something far on the horizon. Standing to his right, his brother in law, Clifford '*Duke*' Thornbuck, a tall, scrawny middle aged specimen of low moral rectitude who found all his courage inside a bottle of whisky. Standing on the sheriff's left was his second cousin, Tom '*Elvis*' Maybury, a mealy-mouthed young man with a naive manner who liked nothing better than to style his hair and appearance on '*The King*', as he often referred to his long dead idol. Both men were Holtsville police deputies and also hailed from Triplerock.

For many years, Sheriff Dodson or '*Boss*' as he preferred to be called had held a dream of big game hunting in Africa. A fantasy born on the endless plethora of ancient black and white adventure movies when as a child, he used to watch on the television while sitting at his grandfather's knee. Nearly every day after class, the old man begrudgingly picked him up from school in his worn out pickup truck and ferried young Oberon home, providing a babysitting service for the family while both his parents worked to make ends meet.

Nearly fifty years later and still obsessed with his childhood celluloid fantasy, Sheriff Dodson had been syphoning untraceable amounts from every department of the public purse into his own private fund, to provide him with enough money to fulfil his dream of big game hunting. The sport had been declared illegal worldwide for many years, but the advent of android technology and holographic reproduction techniques courtesy of the Hologram Dreams Corporation had realised his fantasy. Unable to afford the deluxe package supplying hundreds of robotic extras forming part of a baggage train that normally accompanied Victorian hunting parties, the sheriff still had what he wanted and that was the visceral thrill of the hunt and a wish to shoot a gun and kill something, anything.

He had intended to go alone a few years ago, until one night Duke and Elvis were on a routine patrol and chanced upon an old blue Cadillac parked near the north Shore of Chickasaw Lake. Closer investigation revealed two half-naked people having sex on the car's back seat. The highly embarrassed pair turned out to be Sheriff Dodson and his personal secretary Jolene Fanshaw. Duke was furious at the sheriff for cheating on his wife who also happened to be his oldest sister Mary. Only a promise from the sheriff that it would never happen again, plus the added bonus of joining him on the much talked about trip of a lifetime persuaded Duke and Elvis to keep their silence.

The day had fulfilled all of the sheriff's wildest dreams, hunting and shooting many big game trophies, Honey badger, Lion, White Rhino, and last, but not least, a gigantic bull elephant that terrified everyone when it appeared suddenly from a nearby thicket of trees. Flapping its massive ears wide as a barn door and bellowing loud enough to strike fear into any man, the huge pachyderm raised its trunk high in the air and almost charged everyone down, but it was stopped dead in its tracks by the sheriff's bravery and marksmanship. The entire scenario gave the trio a real belief of danger and excitement, but they could not be further from the truth. All the animatronic wild animals had built-in safety systems and had he missed or turned and fled, the elephant would just have charged harmlessly by and carried on into the distance.

Big game hunting is just one of the options available through franchises of the Hologram Dreams Corporation, contributing to a massive increase in revenue. All of this was helped considerably by the addition of hundreds of lifelike human and animal robotics, provided at knockdown prices from the parent company now that their own technology dispensed with three-quarters of its androids and similar robotic equipment.

"Well boys, didn't I tell ya' both that this would be the best day ever?" The sheriff announced grandly while raising his hat to mop his wet brow with a khaki neckerchief that matched the rest of his safari costume he insisted all three should wear to make the day appear more authentic. He believed that he looked every inch the great white hunter, but in reality, he was just an ordinary, short, fat, sweaty man in a costume.

"Cain't wait to see the playback of you bringing down that huge bastard elephant Boss. That mother was as big as a mountain." Duke exclaimed between gulps of whisky that he had poured into a water bottle and smuggled passed security. He offered it to Elvis and then to Boss who both refused politely, neither wanted to taste the nasty chewing tobacco that Duke favoured when off duty, as it had fouled the bottle's neck every time he took a swig. Elvis cleared his throat and waited until he had full attention, then made his own announcement.

"On behalf of me and the Duke here, we'd like to say a big thank ya' Boss for the most incredible experience. There sure ain't a sheriff as good as you who would go to such personal expense for their deputies, ain't that right Duke?"

Duke was not really listening, he was taking another drink, but he seemed to get the gist of the speech. Spitting out a wet, dark brown gobbet onto the dusty earth, he wiped his mouth with the back of his right hand and then grabbed hold of the sheriff's pudgy manus, shaking it a little too heartily due to his partially inebriated state. Snatching his hand away as quickly as possible, even though it seemed a little rude, the sheriff tried his best to ignore the tobacco fingerprints covering his skin, but in the end, he could not resist removing a moistened tissue from a packet he kept inside his breast pocket and thoroughly clean every inch of his soiled hand. Neither deputy passed any comment; they were used to his fastidious ways and behaved as if nothing had happened. Happy with the praise, Sheriff Dodson stepped back and made a speech of his own.

"Thank ya' kindly boys, but the pleasure was all mine. If I cannot treat my two favourite deputies to a day's hunting then there must be something wrong with this big ol' world. But before we go, I have one more treat left in store for ya' both. A little surprise you might say for keeping my ass out of the mire."

He then nodded to one of the rangers who had accompanied the trio for the day and the man radioed something just out of earshot to the control room. To help boost profits, some of the more unscrupulous franchise organisations offered services that were strictly outside current legislative guidelines of law or moral decency. This tricky and controversial subject had been argued all the way to the World Court. The plea was that if no harm were done to another living creature it would not be considered a crime. It was finally decided that if the intent to create an illegal scenario for personal satisfaction whether real or fake, they were both considered to be against the law. Philip Sanderson was well aware what went on behind the scenes and as long as he could not be directly implicated, he considered it unavoidable. If the smaller overseas operations were to succeed against the plethora of similar companies developing their own brands of personal entertainment, Sanderson was prepared to let them do whatever it takes.

Approximately one thousand yards away on a small hilltop, their attention was taken by a horse drawn canvass topped wagon as it emerged from behind dense scrub and halted in the middle of a clearing. The driver got down from his seat, walked to the rear of his vehicle and climbed inside. Ten seconds later, two young men, one black and the other half-caste, and one young black woman, all semi-naked, climbed awkwardly down from within the confines of the covered wagon, followed by the driver pointing a handgun at their backs. All three were chained by the ankles and cowered openly when he waved the weapon in their direction. The wagon driver stepped away from the group and then dipped his hand into a pouch attached to his belt resting on his left hip. The curious trio watched as the low sunlight glinted from a small bunch of keys that he ceremoniously detached from a metal ring and proceeded to throw each one separately to all points of the compass and deep into the bushes. He then climbed back up into the driver's seat of the wagon and drove away back down the far side of the hill. Elvis and Duke glanced at one another in puzzlement, then back at the sheriff who looked as if he was going to explode with excitement.

"This is a special treat for you boys. What you see over yonder is the grand finale, somethin' I've been looking forward to all day. But before we begin I have a little story to tell you both."

Elvis and Duke were none the wiser as to what he was talking about and knew only too well that the best thing to do was for them both to remain quiet and let him just get on with it. Almost unable to remove the grin from his face he finally calmed down and began his tale.

"Many years ago, before I was even a twinkle in my momma's eye, my great-great grand pappy's occupation was a slave catcher. All across Triplerock County he'd be called upon by the rich gentry to round up slaves who'd escaped from their cotton plantations, some of which were not a goose honk from our own hometown. The exciting stories that he told by the fireside have passed down through the generations all the way to me and I'll tell y'all they were the best hunting tales I'd ever heard. There is nothing more cunning, nothing more desperate nothing more devious than them coloureds, and today gentleman, we are going to pay tribute to this great man by chasing down three of those god forsaken heathen over there."

Unsure whether the sheriff was just playing the part or his speech really came from the heart, Elvis and Duke stared back at each other in astonishment, neither sure how to react. Their first instinct was excitement at the prospect, as they were both from dirt-poor families and their bigoted upbringing made them despise people from every different race, colour, and creed. This, coupled with their own lack of intelligence and credence, led them to believe that they were somehow better than everyone else on the planet was by the grace of the pale hue of their skin. The second reaction was that of caution, they both wondered if this was an elaborate trap, encouraging them to reveal their racist opinions openly on camera and the evidence held against them, levelling the playing field regarding the sheriff's infidelity. Feeling a little put out by their lack of reaction, he tried to tempt them again.

"Come on boys this is goin' to be the thrill of a lifetime. If them darkies put their heads together and use whatever limited intelligence they can muster, they will soon realise that one of the keys thrown into the bushes will fit the lock on their chains and allow them to escape. Pretty soon they will be scratting around for the right one and then they can make a run for it."

Relishing the prospect, the sheriff rubbed his chubby hands together and peered myopically at the frantic search that had already begun on the distant hilltop.

"Now I'm a sporting man, but I'm not gonna wait forever while they make a bid for freedom. I want the hunt to be as thrilling as possible, are you with me?"

As he ended the speech he stared intently at his men then took a drink of water from his own water bottle before heading off towards the first of three modern off-road buggies that had just arrived for the occasion. The correct method would have been to engage the hunt on horseback, but the sheriff was just too fat and physically weak for such an endeavour, leaving him no choice but to go with a much less authentic option. The two deputies were still not convinced so he turned and made one last plea.

"They ain't real humans boys, only robots made to look lifelike, just like the animals. No one's going to get hurt. Oh, and I nearly forgot, I'm told one of them is a fine young filly, the first to capture her will get the chance to do whatever they desire and I have been told that every part of her body is anatomically correct down to the smallest detail, so someone could get real lucky if you know what I mean!"

The sheriff gave a huge theatrical wink, and then chuckled to himself as he set down heavily in the passenger seat of the first buggy and began examining a replica 19th century, colt 45 pistol, rigged to shoot electrically charged paintball rounds instead of a real bullet. He had already been informed that the android *'slaves'* had been coated with a clear, receptive body gel that instantly absorbed the charge on impact, spreading a paralysing effect through the skin to all the inner synthetic muscles. This ceased motor function of the immediate area, and the more accurate the shot, the more damage it caused, in similar fashion to a real bullet.

Duke glanced at Elvis then shrugged his shoulders before turning away and headed towards the next vehicle. Elvis really did not like the idea at all, but did not have the backbone to stand his ground on the subject. Not wanting to be the one left out, he also followed suit. Inside a minute, the two deputies were equally armed and following the dust trail of buggy number one. At five-hundred yards from his prey and closing in fast, Sheriff Dodson still struggled to strap the lap belt under his ample stomach in an effort to stop his corpulent body rolling right out of the buggy as it bounced along a heavily rutted track. Luckily the driver realised this and slowed down, keeping the rocking motion to a minimum until the sheriff finally clicked the metal ring into the locking tab. This allowed him the freedom to set his sights on the cloud of dust rising from the small clump of bushes where the three escaped android slaves were desperately looking for the keys to gain release from their shackles. The two deputies were now safely ensconced in their own vehicles and radioing instructions to one another on what to do next.

"Elvis this is Duke, do ya' copy c'mon?"

There was a harsh static on the line as Duke released the trigger and waited for Elvis to reply.

"That's a big ol' ten-four Duke, I can hear you good buddy, but I cain't see you, there's too much dust thrown up by the sheriff's buggy to see anythin' at all."

"That's why I'm callin' you Elvis, cain't see anythin' either. Tell you what, I'll head out to the left and you move out to the right where the air is clear and we can form a pincer movement trapping them bad boys on top of the hill."

"Copy that Duke, I'm already on my way."

As the two rear buggies split formation, the sheriff cut in with encouraging words of his own.

"Hurry up boys it won't be long before they find the right key and be on the move!"

On the hilltop, a pretty, young woman screamed as she looked up from her search to see plumes of dust caused by three vehicles heading at great speed in their direction. It was blatantly obvious that in their current predicament that this was not going to be a rescue mission and the shriek of terror only added a greater urgency to everyone's search. Frantically all three delved into the thorny scrub, wincing occasionally, but not really caring as the needle-thin, barbed prickles pierced their skin through the thin fabric of cotton jerkins and pantaloons in the search for the discarded keys. The off-white material already filthy with dirt and sweat, quickly included spots of red from the blood of innumerable scratches from the razor-sharp points, while the shafts snagged like fish hooks into the skin's outer dermis.

Finally, she spied a key suspended on a split ring deep inside a mature bush, but this still posed a problem. The young woman soon found out it was impossible to reach in, as the gnarled old branches refused to bend under the pressure and the thorns anchored tightly to her cotton jerkin. Out of fear and frustration, she pulled the baggy shift, clean over her head, and left it hanging on a neighbouring bush. On any other day, the two other men would have enjoyed the impromptu strip that exposed her bobbing naked breasts, but they were lost in their own panic filled world. Turning sideways and pressing a left forearm across her chest to protect the sensitive tips from injury, she snaked out her left arm, gritting her teeth against the pain while reaching deep into the thorny interior. The plan worked, but the deeper she eased her naked upper torso through the bush, the mass of dark brown prickles raised innumerate welts, flecking blood trails across the skin. Eventually her fingertips hooked around the large metal split ring holding the key, placing it finally within her grasp. Bursting with relief, she began to retract her body from the bush, but this was the hardest part. The majority of the needle-thin thorns pointed downwards, allowing an easier entrance than exit and the tips jabbed at her naked flesh. One of the thorns stabbed into the soft cup of her left breast, sliding in easily and continuing its journey just under the surface. Closing her eyes and saying a silent prayer, she tugged even harder until the point emerged from the inside and her young elastic skin bulged into a tent-like point then began to tear. Crying aloud from the stinging pain and with tears rolling down her cheeks, she pulled violently, ripping open a thin flap of skin. Slowly deep-red blood oozed to the surface, creating a sticky paste as it mixed with the sweat and dirt caked around the injury. Thankfully free from any more of the hooked barbs, the blood stained, half-naked woman emerged, trembling out into the open. Ignoring the continuous burning pain of her flesh wounds, she dropped to the ground, and tested the key on her fettered ankles. The mechanism was gritty with dirt, but there was a soft click and the leg iron popped open.

"I've found the right one." She screamed to the two others who immediately hobbled as fast as they could to her side and took turns to undue their own shackles while she pulled frantically at her jerkin that the bush refused to release.

"Ye har, I can see her tiddies and they big ones boys!" The sheriff yelled loudly down his radio to his deputies as his buggy was much closer and he could see the drama unfolding before him, adding an erotic twist to the already thrilling chase. Casting a quick glance across to his driver and seeing that all his attention focused on the dirt road ahead, the sheriff slid a hand under his belly and tightly squeezed his already semi-erect penis sending a wave of pleasure through his body.

"Heard you loud and clear Boss. This day just gets better and better." Screamed Elvis over the noise of the engine as his buggy finally circled around a small ridge and he stared avidly through the dust in hope for a better view. The two male captives, now free of their fetters began to run away as fast as they could, only to stop when they realised the woman was not behind them. Turning back, they could see she was still at the drop site trying to free her jerkin from the bush before setting off. What she did not realise was that the bush was a cat claw mimosa. This native shrub, known locally as the wait a minute bush, held on tightly, courtesy of its stems covered in thousands of backward facing spines hooking deep into the fabric.

"Leave it, you can have mine." The elder of the two men shouted, he was desperate to leave but felt a compelling urgency to protect all in his group, especially a woman. Suddenly a shot rang out and she watched horrified as the jerkin jumped when a bullet, tore a hole clean through the fabric and splattered against the trunk of a nearby tree. Without the need for any more encouragement, she immediately let go of the stained clothing, turned on her heels and burst from standstill into a full-blown run like an Olympic sprinter. Her fellow escapee began to remove his top, ready to pass it over only to see her blaze straight passed the two of them without a word as yet another shot rang out, this time it from a separate direction. A quick glance from left to right, confirmed that there were two more buggies closing in fast.

"Split up, ***now***!" The youngest member gasped between breaths as he veered off to the left, away from the group and down a hill towards a shallow river hoping that his pursuers would be unable to follow. It seemed like a good plan, but in his haste, he committed a vital mistake. Expecting to run ankle deep through the cool shallows he completely misjudged the water's depth and plunged up to his knees. The violent halt to his forward momentum tipped the poor man his full length, making a huge splash as he landed, knocking the wind from his lungs in the process. For a few seconds his stunned body lay face down in the clear water and he began to float downstream until the need for a fresh intake of air brought him to his senses. Coughing violently and spluttering from his initial breath that seemed to contain more fluid than air, he quickly scrambled to his feet and wiped the stinging cold water from his eyes.

Slowly his vision began to clear and the first thing he managed to focus on, was the silhouette of a man standing in front of the setting sun less than eighty strides from his position. The next thing he was immediately made aware, was a searing pain as the stranger took aim and deliberately fired a shot into the water between his legs. Even though the shot missed, it acted as an electrical conductor, spreading a brief but violent charge up into the poor man's groin.

"Got ya' now boy; did that roast ya' stones? I sure hope so." Elvis yelled, beginning to revel in the excitement. Doubled over from the pain, the young man tenderly clutched his genitals as he backed out of the water and onto the bank. The muscles in his legs still cramped from the charge and were very reluctant to respond while the pain from his testicles nauseatingly spread across the whole of his lower torso. Tilting his head birdlike from one side to the other, Elvis stared curiously while his limited intelligence figured out what do next. Luckily, for his prey, this gave him time to recover and with his body almost back up to full strength, he suddenly turned and began a scramble up the far bank. Instinct kicked in and taking aim for a second time, Elvis fired another shot, his time much higher up the ridge. As he tried to climb, the impact of the bullet rained loose earth and stones all over his wet body. Ignoring the filthy shower, he wondered why his attacker did not fire for a third time and it was there he made his second mistake of the day. Turning his head to look back, he immediately lost his footing and slid on the loose shale all the way back down to the river's edge.

"Dance for me boy!" Elvis yelled as he fired one bullet after another as the young man got to his feet. Elvis was an excellent shot and he aimed each round very close, but at the soft earth, making the poor man jump and hop for fear of injury. Cackling loudly at the belittling performance, Elvis pulled the trigger for a seventh time today and to his surprise, there was only a click against the empty chamber. Unlike the almost unlimited firing capacity provided by the pulse guns of today, the replica pistol needed reloading after firing six times. Instead of taking the opportunity to run away, Elvis noticed that the android appeared fuelled with anger, and encouraged by the sudden evening up of the odds, stooped to grab a fist-sized rock then roared as he charged back into the shallows. Elvis madly tried to reload the gun's empty chambers hoping to avoid what he believed to be certain death. From the corner of his eye, he could see huge water droplets flying high into the air, glinting in the sunlight before splashing back down into the river as the robot man doggedly high stepped through the fast flowing water. Prey now became the hunter as he quickly reached the opposite river bank and frantically scrambled up to the ridge where his enemy hid. Fumbling in panic, Elvis had grabbed the box of live ammunition from his front jacket pocket and in his haste attempted to open the wrong end, spilling all the remaining rounds into the dirt. Now down on his knees, he pressed the chamber release lever, exposing the ring of six cylindrical compartments, quickly snatched up the nearest round, and slid it into one of the waiting chambers. At this point, he suddenly found himself in the shadow of a foe that had finally cleared the top of the ridge. Falling onto his back in a hurried defensive pose, Elvis snapped the pistol shut, held the gun tightly in both hands, closed his eyes, took a well-guessed aim, and fired. To his surprise, nothing happened and a surprised attacker closed in for the kill. Letting go with his left hand Elvis covered his face with a protective forearm while repeatedly pulling the trigger with his index finger of his right. Eventually the full chamber rotated towards the firing pin and just as he prepared to have his head caved in, the gun fired. The shot was point blank and it hit his attacker square in the chest. The charged bullet did not kill his assailant, but the force of the impact knocked him backwards, and as Elvis lowered his arm, he watched his adversary cartwheel clean off the edge of the ridge. Unable to raise his hands and block his fall due to the electrical charge causing a spasm of nearly every muscle in his body, the young man landed head first onto the rocks below. In a flash, his world turned black and he died instantly from a broken neck. The loud, sickening crack as his neck snapped when he crash-landed, was lost in the echo of the gunshot. Elvis clambered to his knees to peer over the ridge, and all he could see was the body floating face down once again, but this time bumping into the river boulders as it meandered down river and out of sight. Testing the shallow depths of his brain, Elvis found it hard to believe that it was not a real human, but as he wandered away from the river and back to the vehicle, he concluded that due to any visible evidence of blood it therefore must be a robot, and that closed the matter completely.

Back in the first buggy, the sheriff was having the time of his life making the driver slow down to prolong the chase as the young man ran desperately for his life.

"You can run, but you sure ain't gonna hide from me boy." He yelled over the roar of the engine while taking pot shots at the man's feet, making him jink from side to side in terror. The torture carried on for over ten minutes until luckily for the pursued, the track narrowed enough to halt the vehicles' progress, forcing the driver to skirt around the perimeter of a small copse, hoping to catch up when he emerged from the other side. What came next was unfortunate timing for both, as the man suddenly burst from cover directly in front of the speeding buggy. The driver tried to swerve and he stamped his foot on the brake pedal but it was already too late. The last thing they both saw was the shock registering on the man's face just before the front bumper smashed both his lower legs and the front grill imploded his chest. Next, the man's head bounced violently, snapping back as it impacted the bonnet, before the rest of his body cartwheeled high into the air directly over their heads and landed with a sickening crump, over thirty feet behind the skidding vehicle. When the buggy finally slewed to a stop, Sheriff Dodson looked back through the plume of rising dust to see a deformed muddle of torso and limbs coated in dirt. He had seen many victims of car accidents in his time and even though this was only a robot, he still felt nauseous at the sight and remained in his seat while the driver walked back to inspect the damage. He watched through the wing mirror as the driver crouched down, then bizarrely placed his fingers on the side of the victim's neck as if to feel for a pulse before he shook his head then radioed for collection of the body as he walked back.

"I think your hunting is over for the day, sir." The driver stated impassionedly, not waiting for an answer before restarting the engine and heading off towards base camp.

"Don't we need to pick it up and bring it back with us?" The sheriff asked as they drove away. The driver silently shook his head and offered no more information.

Duke could not believe his luck. Both Elvis and Boss had peeled off in pursuit of the two men leaving him to sate himself on the pleasures of hunting down the young woman. The fact that it was an android held no qualms to his raging alcohol fuelled lust and as long as that was satisfied, it was all that mattered.

"You should both see what I can see boys, them tiddies are bouncing all over the place!" He yelled down the radio mike as the buggy thundered along only yards behind the terrified young woman. His excitement increased even further as she turned her head to gauge how close her attackers were and screamed loudly.

"That's it bitch, squeal for the Duke." He whispered to himself while taking aim. Getting an accurate shot even at close range was almost impossible from a moving vehicle and as he squeezed the trigger, a front wheel hit a pothole, jolting his arm and the bullet missed her back, nicking the point of her right elbow sending a much smaller shock up the arm and into the shoulder. Clutching her pained limb with her free hand, the injured woman veered off course down into a small high-sided dry riverbed leaving Duke furious at losing his quarry. The driver stopped the vehicle and quickly informed his irate client that the gully had been formed by rainwater pouring over a steep-sided cliff about a quarter of a mile away and that she was running into a dead-end. All he had to do was follow the trail and she would be there waiting for him.

"This day is sure full of surprises ain't it? Tell you what, you wait here, and I'll follow on foot." Duke replied as he slapped the driver hard on his back. Drunkenly clambering out of his seat, he tried to run down the embankment but lost his footing and slid painfully on his backside down the to the gully floor. Embarrassed, Duke turned back to see that the driver had purposefully not observed the incident and was facing away as he radioed back to base.

"Time to get my reward." Duke spoke loudly to himself as he brushed himself down, reloaded his gun, and set off towards his goal.

The poor frightened woman soon reached the far end and fell to the ground sobbing when she realised there was no way out. It was not long before Duke caught up and licked his lips at the erotic sight of a semi-naked female cowering defencelessly in the dirt. Very slowly, he raised his gun, closed one eye, and took aim. The poor woman did not stand a chance as the powerful charge struck high in the chest, flipping her onto her back. The ensuing spasm now cramped nearly every muscle in her body into an unresponsive state.

"Bull's-eye, now it's time for my prize." Duke chuckled as he trotted over to her side. He did not pay much attention to the slurred pleas for him to resist, as all the poor wretch could do was mouth a few garbled words for clemency and this was not anywhere near enough. He gazed lustfully at her filthy exposed breasts while he undid his trouser belt buckle, and then lowered his zip exposing his excitement as he dropped to his knees. Unable to resist due to her cramping muscles, she lay almost motionless while Duke roughly grabbed hold of her pantaloons and jerked them down her legs, until she lay naked in the dirt. Without any hesitation, he easily forced her knees open, fell on top, and raped her where she lay. If there could be any relief for this poor woman from this bestial act, it was that the attack was over almost as soon as it began. Sated quickly, Duke drunkenly staggered to his feet and readjusted his dress. He wanted the other two to join the party so he unclipped the radio from his belt and called in.

"This is Duke, calling Elvis and the Boss man, do you copy?"

Both men had finished with their own hunt and responded immediately, using the signal from Duke's radio to home in and join the fun. Molly overheard the message and with some feeling returning to her legs, she tried to get to her feet and run away, but her muscles were still far too weak and she collapsed in a heap, once again sobbing into the dust. Duke stood silently watching while taking a swig of whisky from the bottle, and then sauntered over to where she lay to make his threat.

"Don't think you're going anywhere bitch, when the other two get here they're gonna each take turns, and by the time they've finished with you, I'll be ready to go again."

The terrified woman could do nothing in response, but stare painfully at Duke's baleful shape silhouetted by the setting sun at his back.

Inside a quarter of an hour Elvis eagerly marched up, then stopped abruptly, gawping, slack jawed at the sight of the naked woman curled up in the dirt, shyly trying to hide her private parts from his stare. Even though he knew that it was only a robot, the fear in her eyes and familiar behaviour seemed far too realistic for comfort. Glancing briefly at Duke who grinned sadistically, Elvis dropped his gaze to the ground in embarrassment, turned his back, and walked quickly away.

Five minutes later the sheriff arrived, breathless and sweating heavily from the forced march along the dry gully. Taking immediate stock of the situation he observed Duke emerge from behind acacia bush as he fastened up his urine stained trouser zipper and Elvis squatting some distance away in full glare of the sun. Too breathless to say anything straight away, he sat down on a low rock, took a long drink from his water bottle, and mopped the sweat from around his neckline.

"Well boys, didn't I tell you it was going to be a great day? I take it that you've both had a ride on the young filly over yonder. I hope there's some left for the Boss."

Duke laughed heartily and Elvis blushed heavily while he mumbled something about *'waiting his turn'*. Acute to the young man's embarrassment he decided not to press the matter any further as he stood up and walked across to where the young woman now sat up hugging her knees to her chest. Dropping heavily down on his own knees at her side and loosening the front his trousers, the sheriff first glanced at her face, and then stared lasciviously, focusing on much more interesting parts of her body. But something nagged at the back of his brain, drawing his gaze back to her face and he stared intently at her features. There was something familiar about the woman, but he could not for the life of him, quite figure out what it was. He was amazed at how realistic her body appeared, and as he continued his examination with a seasoned lawman's eye, he caught sight of the colour of her skin around the hairline, noticing how much paler it appeared compared to the rest of her body. With considerable effort, he got himself back up onto his feet, scratched the back of his head, and furrowed his brow until suddenly the truth hit him.

"Jesus on a jet-ski! If you ain't Molly Dawson, Cousin Edith's girl." He exclaimed realising that although he recognised her facial features his confusion lay in the hue of her skin. He could see now that the poor girl must have been stained a dark chocolate brown and that was why he did not recognise her first-hand. Tears welled up in the young woman's eyes at the mention of her name, it was the only thing she remembered after weeks of mind numbing drugs that had been forced down her throat following her abduction along with dozens of other women and men to be used as a cheaper substitute for the more expensive robots and androids. Feeling very embarrassed, the sheriff quickly refastened his trousers, then removed his own jacket that he put tenderly around her shoulders and tried to fasten the front to cover her nakedness. Molly angrily brushed his hand away, put the jacket on properly, and fastened the buttons herself. The effect of the charge was starting to wear off and her body now clumsily responded to her will. With a little help, Molly managed to stand up and stagger drunkenly into the shadow of the cliff face where they sat back down and slaked their thirst from the sheriff's water bottle.

Both deputies had purposely walked far enough away to be out of sight and sound of the forthcoming activities and were dozing in the shade of a small clump of scrub bushes further down the gully. Eventually the sheriff's voice carried on the breeze enough to distinguish him calling their names and they quickly ran to his aid.

"Where the hell have you been? I've been shouting for you dimwits 'till I'm hoarse."

Both men were as confused as each other, especially as nothing appeared to have happened, apart from the fact that the sheriff was wearing his trousers and a sweat-stained white vest, while the robot was wearing the sheriff's jacket that looked like a mini dress on her slender frame.

"Sorry Boss, we both thought we'd give you some privacy while you got yourself some action. If you've finished, I'm sure Elvis is rearing to have a ride."

Duke replied, panting like a dog, as he looked Molly up and down. The sheriff could see the lust in his eyes and put a stop to his thoughts immediately.

"Listen very carefully boys, before you both get over excited things ain't what they seem. The young lady here isn't a robot of any kind she's made of real flesh and blood just like you and me."

Elvis looked on curiously, wondering if the old man had a touch of sunstroke and was becoming delirious.

"Are you sure Boss; 'dem androids are very lifelike you know?"

The sheriff glared back at his deputy while rocking back and forth, to gain momentum and get his massive bulk back onto his feet.

"D'you think that I'm stupid or something? I've been a lawman since your pappy was knee-high to a June bug and I think that I know when I recognise someone. That young woman sitting there is Molly Dawson, Cousin Edith's girl. You know the one that went missing a few months back."

This did nothing to convince the pair as they looked at one another, then at the woman's chocolate brown skin and then back at the sheriff. Sighing heavily, he jabbed a chubby finger at Molly and tried again.

"Look closer, you numbskulls, her skin's been dyed dark brown to hide her identity, but whoever did it did a piss-poor job, you can plainly see paler skin inside her hairline. On top of that, she's obviously drugged or somthin' 'cos only thing she can recognise is her own name. "

The two men moved closer to inspect the woman who pulled the bulky jacket tightly around her frame and backed away fearfully along the sandstone bank as Duke approached. Seeing how terrified she reacted, the sheriff reined in his men.

"Back off you two, cain't you see, you're scaring the poor child. Come over here and take a look at this."

The sheriff dipped his hand into his breast pocket, then pulled out and unfolded a small, clear, hand-sized piece of malleable plastic. In response to his thumb print it suddenly turned opaque, then produced an image of today's date and the first colour photograph taken of the three of them this morning dressed in their clean safari outfits as they stood outside the briefing post before setting off. Holding the device closer to his lips, he spoke the words *'Jamie's christening'* and instantly the first image appeared of a family baptism taken late last year, a function that Molly Dawson attended. Scanning steadily through the series of photographs taken that day, he eventually found the one he was searching for that included Molly in a group shot. Repeatedly touching her image lightly with his fingertip the photograph zoomed in to the point required until her face filled the screen. Both deputies studied the image and then looked back at the frightened woman's face two or three times before they had to agree at the striking resemblance, even down to the small white fleck across the dark brown iris of her left eye, something Molly and the photographic image both shared. Moving his two deputies out of Molly's earshot, the sheriff explained the situation.

"Assuming that you both now believe me, the first thing we need to do is get young Molly and ourselves out of here and to safety. The fact that we are all lawmen won't mean a spit on a hot shovel to these people if this is what they are capable of. Our little extra-curricular activity today as you know is illegal and as I can assume that the both of you have had your jollies with the poor girl, we can only hope that she won't remember anything. Anyway, if she does, it will be her words against ours, d'you catch my drift?"

Duke nodded sagely as Elvis opened his mouth ready to protest his innocence regarding Molly, but he decided that now was not the right time following a glare and subtle shake of a head from Duke. Sitting back down in the shade, the sheriff closed his eyes and called for silence while he deliberated over a suitable plan.

CHAPTER THREE

Set deep in the heart of the English countryside, the largest film production studio ever created is currently in full swing, dealing with several hundred clients every day. The entire site covers over fifty-five square miles and has franchised offices in over two-hundred and ten countries around the globe. As one of the originators of the personal video concept, developed more than five years ago, the competition was almost non-existent and bookings flooded in, keeping the main enterprise at 93% operational capacity and an order book full for the next decade. Wise reinvestment of this newfound wealth into research and development, quickly led to a great leap forwards in holographic reproduction. Within a year of this new technology being announced to the world, the share value of the Hologram Dreams Corporation rocketed by over a hundred and fifty points, taking it immediately to pole position as the biggest company in the world. The majority of this success was obviously down to the brilliance of Philip Sanderson, but also a significant contribution in other areas, came via his best friend and second in command, Edward Langton.

Standing alone, and staring absentmindedly at the dreary, unmemorable landscape, spreading out from one horizon to the other, 'Ted' Langton, as he preferred to be called, took a deep breath and tried to remain focused on the job in hand. He was usually not so distracted when working on major projects, but his mind constantly flashed up images of his starring role in what he regarded as a very cheesy company advertisement, broadcast yesterday in nearly every cinema and on the majority of infotainment screens across the globe.

Two months ago, Ted's friends and co-workers had challenged him into doing this, claiming that in all the productions Hologram Dreams had made, he never once had the guts to stand in front of the camera. Dented male ego and too much alcohol on a rare night out far outweighed rational thought and swept away on a tide of friendly enthusiasm, he agreed to become the new face of the company.

Since the dawn of commercial television, product advertising had slowly developed from low budget one-camera *'buy now'* salesmen, into extremely sophisticated promotions. These featured some of the world's biggest stars in multimillion-dollar cinematic productions that for most of the advertisement did not reveal the product until the end. Today the concept had come full circle, parodying the low budget adverts of yesteryear that often starred the company owner, bed salesmen, or used car traders standing in front of the camera overacting as they excitedly shouted out their great deals. Cajoled into portraying this role, was much to Ted's chagrin.

Bringing his thoughts back to the present, he continued to stare at the featureless vista that lay before him. The complete lack of any visible projection equipment made the area the last place on earth that had the possibility of transformation into anything basic, let alone something sophisticated, like a lunar landscape or futuristic city featuring silver skyscrapers and flying cars. The secret to this breath taking illusion lay hidden out of sight, with the majority of the projection equipment housed under the earth. This included a massive square mile network containing over ten-million state of the art projectors, each one armed with a three by three square of nine pads arranged in grids buried just under the ground. Each grid contained the business end of over one-hundred thousand ultra-thin fibre optic cables producing the incredible projection.

"I think it's time to get this show on the road." Ted suddenly announced to apparently no one at all, but someone must have heard, as the terrain all around him began to morph. Akin to time lapse photography used to record ultra-slow moving images, the topsoil began to shiver as tiny shoots of self-cleaning ultra-soft transparent filaments emerged just a few millimetres above the ground. When the dust settled, the fibre optic cornfield revealed a massive floor plan of the three Great Pyramids contained within the Giza Necropolis in Egypt.

It never failed to amaze Ted as the units powered up and each one projected a perfect three-dimensional holographic image that seamlessly blended with its neighbour, as stone by stone the breathtaking monument rebuilt before his very eyes. However, this image, apart from its geometric shape bore little resemblance to the famous Pyramids visited by millions of curious travellers every year. The sides were not stepped but perfectly smooth as the sandstone blocks beneath were now covered in highly polished white limestone. A feature that adorned the Pyramids for nearly four thousand years until it all but disappeared following an earthquake in 1300 AD. The tremors shook away the outer casing, leaving the more familiar sandstone stepped feature seen today.

To preserve the aesthetics of the site, the piles of rubble were removed for use in what was deemed at the time, more important construction projects. Marking the importance of this amazing funeral tomb, the summit of the Great Pyramid of Cheops was at the time, adorned with a Benben capstone based on the solar temple of Heliopolis. The original polyhedron shaped summit was coated with a layer of gold, reflecting the light emitted by the burning desert sun, making the tomb visible from over fifty miles away. At the entrance to the incredible site, a much smaller grid powered up, recreating Horus-in-the-horizon, more commonly known from Greek mythology as the Sphinx. Originally carved from a single block of limestone, this massive sculpture stood 66 feet high and 240 feet long. The famous statue gaudily painted originally in red, blue and yellow, constituted the body of a couchant lion with a human head peacefully keeping guard over the Pyramids sited behind.

Using the most up to date information currently available, the reproduction added a temple in the foreground, used originally to chart the seasons. It even contained twenty-four stone pillars arranged in lines that precisely marked the time of day. Every feature currently known to historians lay in place, including a workers village, a manufacturing complex, and several cemeteries producing the most physically accurate reproduction of the site from around the time where the second incredible tomb neared completion around 2600 BC. Forming a perimeter to the production, and with a radius of nearly three miles, several thousand projectors raised up from the earth surrounding the entire project. Not only did they create the illusion of sand dunes on the distant horizon, but thanks to additional horizontally facing projectors, a vista containing much more verdant green fertile lands surrounded the sprawling ancient city of Cairo; a scene completely different to the desiccated environment known today.

Ted stared in wonder while all around him the remainder of the panorama, quickly neared its completion. Happy to turn away from the eye-pain inducing sunlight, reflected from the golden capstone, he blinked away the green dots floating before him to see that the newly project was truly incredible. It seemed impossible to believe that he was viewing something that only existed as a collection of ones and zeros stored inside a computer.

Fifty thousand hours of painstaking programming and research, had produced as much vibrancy and detail that was humanly possible, bringing to life the original city, just as it would have appeared well over twenty-five centuries ago. The list included farms, villages, bustling riverside markets, and city bazaars filled with hundreds of traders selling their chattels and goods.

At first glance, what looked like a giant length of shiny, deep-blue ribbon, cast with indolent abandon across the desert floor; was in fact the river Nile twinkling with reflected artificial sunshine as the life giving waters meandered lazily across the river valley. The illusion even included an assortment of fishing boats and trading dhow's transporting their wares from far away across the Mediterranean Sea.

Every conceivable detail had been included in the production, down to the decorative flags fluttering on the breeze, and if required, even the smell of this ten thousand year old metropolis, giving Ted great difficulty in believing that he was still standing deep in the heart of the English countryside.

Although he had only been at work for half an hour, Ted remained ill at ease as he plodded wearily down the hill towards the worker's village. He had managed to put the embarrassment of his acting debut to the back of his mind, but it had all come flooding back when the advertisement aired last night. Flashes of his wooden acting and the cheesy one-liners interfered with his concentration and he even involuntarily flushed with embarrassment over the entire episode. All of this had contributed to him consuming nearly half a bottle of single malt and now the thudding pain behind the eyes, caused by a massive hangover, did nothing to ease his mood. As usual, he refused to let everyone down, as the current development was the culmination of six months very hard work featuring the latest groundbreaking technology.

Dedicated to the end, a self-induced headache was not going to stop him as for the first time in history, a full working simulation produced entirely by computer was ready to test. Ted's personal pride in his work pressed him hard to make sure everything created was nothing short of perfect.

Previous visual concepts created by Hologram Dreams had always utilised specially constructed film sets, housing top of the range robotics, animatronics, and more often than not, human extras to complete the scene. Now everything visible in every direction was a state of the art hologram created by thousands of projectors, hidden deep inside their own self-generated image, created by the three-dimensional overlay mapping technology.

The original process had been around for quite a while, producing static objects such as a car or a building in such breathtaking detail that it could be viewed from any angle, inside and out. Now, thanks to the invention of the ice cube, light speed central processor, that could process information nearly a thousand times faster than its predecessor, any type of moving object could now also be added at will. This new development could simultaneously calculate all the three-dimensional vectors for the image, incorporate its velocity, and still create a projection of over a hundred trillion pixels per cubic centimetre per second.

The site that Ted now anxiously stood was completely devoid of anything physical at all, no real life actors, robotic machinery, film sets, or any type of lifelike android previously used to create and complete the scene. The beauty of the new generation ice-cube processing unit is that with the minimum of fuss, it is possible to connect thousands at a time to share the load, allowing infinite computing muscle to produce anything to the limit of your imagination. With this remarkable invention at his disposal, the man in charge of production, stopped and put his hands on his hips while he critically surveyed the incredible vista.

Even though he fitted the movie star critique, with his rugged good looks, broad shoulders and slim waist, Ted decided that his main role in this creation of dreams was from now on, going to be well behind the camera and not in front. His expertise lay in his skill of getting the best out whatever he is provided with, producing what is asked for, all of which should be under budget and on time.

"Ok Stan; let me see the camels." Ted announced to what appeared to be thin air, but a unidirectional microphone receiver sited far away on a hilltop, and completely invisible beyond the limit of the projection, picked up every word. It tracked Ted's every movement, enabling his good friend Stanley Gibson to respond immediately. Stan, the chief controller and technical wizard for the company, currently sat miles away in the central command room of the corporation's vast underground site. He was easily able to monitor the situation via video images relayed from hundreds of observation drones hovering in a perfect halo formation hundreds of feet above the production site. Using on-board cloaking technology developed by the military, the surveillance cameras were virtually invisible to the naked eye as the outer shell of each device was coated with chameleon synthetic skin that could mimic the colours and textures of its surrounding environment. This allowed the drone to remain undetectable while relaying video images from every conceivable aspect of the illusion. The live feeds were then displayed in dazzling quantum definition onto a series of malleable polycarbonate reactive spheres, suspended beneath a motorised grid, mounted across the ceiling of the command centre. This allowed complete unobstructed view from every conceivable angle of the ultra-realistic image displayed inside. These spheres could be inflated or deflated according to work requirements and if necessary, moulded into one super globe for a single video feed. It was not too long before the technicians who came to work within this unique environment to give it the nickname of *'The Bubble Hub'*. With precise computer-controlled alignment every sphere could be viewed by the majority of technicians at all times, allowing minor adjustments to be made to the projection while monitoring the impact from multiple sources at once.

Akin to mission control at a space program, dozens more highly trained employees hurried back and forth between wall-mounted monitoring stations keeping every aspect of this sophisticated project running smoothly.

The room itself is the most secure place in the underground city as it was formally the central intelligence and command bunker for the ex-military base. Cited in its centre a twenty-foot diameter circular table still existed where all the highest ranked military and heads of state used to sit and direct the cold war. It now supported a perfect high-definition three-dimensional miniaturised reproduction of the current project, allowing technicians a real time godlike view of the current proceedings, including an image of Ted, who resembled a tiny action figure as he walked around the set. A scenario that could be only dreamed about by the pre-graphene generation.

Currently happy with today's proceedings, Stan spun around in his seat to face his favoured battered old-fashioned computer keyboard connected to the terminal via a pale grey curly cord. With a flurry of finger taps to the faded square faced plastic keys, he initiated the next phase of the program.

Ted knew what to expect, but still stepped back in astonishment as two fully grown camels suddenly appeared from nowhere and began to walk across his line of sight less than twenty-five feet ahead. He quickly circled around the simulation, closely inspecting the detail, looking for any break up in quality, gaps in the projection, interference pixilation, fluidity of movement, and most of all realism. Ten silent minutes passed by while everyone in the command centre watched and waited as he studied the images from every conceivable angle. Ted finally decided that he was satisfied with the result and ordered the next stage.

"That's great Stan; for my personal preference increase the colour intensity a notch on the dust trail, then start adding the interactive residents."

The dust cloud kicked up by the walking motion of the camels immediately darkened a few shades, and then a few seconds later, groups of authentically dressed locals appeared to rise up through the ground until they stood firmly on top of the sandy earth. At the flick of a switch, they began their preprogramed tasks as market traders, slaves, and members of the general public.

Ted deliberately stood in one man's way and as the image stepped aside, it gesticulated and shouted at him for his rudeness. The sound appeared to come from the mouth of the projection, but it was actually produced by miniature auricular grommets. This amazing implant, already inserted into Ted's ear canals, had the capacity to confuse the brain into believing that the sound created from within these tiny amplifiers, actually came from somewhere else.

Ted continued to interfere with the new moving images and each time the result was different. Some even bumped into Ted and thanks to Philip's remarkable new invention of an image density profiler that appeared to create solid matter out of thin air; they even gave the sensory feeling of touch, just like a real person. For all intense and purpose, everything was real until Ted found out to his cost when he absentmindedly leaned against a wall and sank into the image like quicksand.

For the next two hours, Ted wandered in and out of meeting places and down filthy alleys as he continued with his real time analysis. His intention was to find a flaw or a glitch in the programming that would have to be resolved before he would allow it to be used to complete the classic ending from *'Pharaoh's Revenge'* a favourite film of the latest client who wished to take the starring role. This project was one of the biggest ever created by the organisation and had taken hundreds of the world's best animators over six months to reach this critical stage of combining over one million simultaneous moving images to seamlessly interact with every other moving or static part of the scene. Relaying information directly to Stan regarding adjustments that were required, Ted was on the whole, extremely impressed, and as he returned to the original marketplace, he ordered the finishing touches.

"Ok Stan lets activate the sensory systems; one at a time."

Stan was primed and ready for the instruction, and with a list displayed graphically before him on his computer screen he first chose olfaction and then zone one from a secondary drop down menu displaying a range of suitable smells. These ranged from pleasant to repulsive that had already been pre-programmed for this event. Sited under Ted's feet, well below the earth, a network of aluminium pipes similar to an irrigation system crisscrossed the vast landscape, making it possible to deliver any scent or aroma required to a precise location. Computer controlled electronic gate valves controlled remotely, released a regulated amount of alcohol-based liquids infused with any number of chemicals to create thousands of delicate or pungent smells. The concoction moistened the patch of earth directly under the chosen projection, allowing the odours to diffuse into the air and carry away on the breeze. Immediately Ted could smell the tantalising aroma of roasting meat carrying over from the corner of the market and then the reek of the camels standing nearby as the smaller of the two defecated where it stood, adding yet another assault to the senses.

As Ted wandered purposefully around the huge set, the smells waxed and waned according to the location. Sweaty unwashed bodies blended with the smoke wafting from hookah pipes, and when the wind suddenly changed, the stench of a communal latrine added far too much to the experience. Even though it was more than thirty-five yards away, Ted gagged from the assault to his sinuses and while shielding his nose in the crook of his arm he gave a muffled order.

"Turn down the shit smell Stan, it's making my eyes water."

From a vast grid referenced wall map of the entire city, Stan typed in the coordinates of the latrine and a list of programmable adjustments for the selected zone appeared. Choosing olfaction again, he lowered the emissions by changing the output from seventy-five to twenty-five, immediately reducing the stench by two-thirds. Tapping his earpiece with his index finger a curved microphone arm attached to his headset, dropped into place allowing Stan to relay his report.

"Poop smells decreased; see if that's more suitable boss."

Ted waited for a few seconds the lowered his arm and tentatively sniffed the air. Happy with the result, he gave Stan the thumbs up signal to continue with the trial run, but before they could proceed any further, Stan relayed another message.

"Sorry to stop you Ted, but Philip wants to see you right away, and before you ask, the answer is no, it can't wait, apparently it's urgent."

Ted took a deep breath while trying to calm his temper, and then wished he had not. A lung full of the acrid urine smell still hanging in the air, snatched at his throat inducing a long coughing fit. Stan waited patiently until Ted recovered before informing him that transport was already on its way. Ted knew that Philip needed his help, but why was he getting more and more dependent by insisting on his best friends' presence at all the big meetings. Philip must have hundreds of upper management aids on whom to call, but for some reason it was always Ted.

"Ok Stan shut down operations for now, I will be as quick as I can but if previous meetings are anything to go by, we will have to resume tomorrow."

Before Stan had time to respond, approximately fifty yards away a patch of earth suddenly began to shake and accompanied by the sound of hydraulic rams squealing into life, one end of a ramp big enough to house a large truck, hinged up out of the ground like a huge gaping mouth. Through a cloud of loose soil spilling over the sides of the raised earth, a white electric four-person buggy suddenly emerged. At the wheel, was a young woman wearing the regulation beige one-piece coveralls and matching baseball cap. Driving much too fast she drifted the buggy around in a large arc, spooking the camels as she weaved erratically around the market stalls much to the annoyance of several traders who amazingly jumped out of the way and responded by fist waving and verbal abuse. Expertly she skidded sideways bringing the buggy to a halt with the passenger side inches away from Ted's legs. With an exasperated look on his face, he shook his head and climbed in.

Like a rainbow on a cloudy day, the incredible projection began to fade then disappeared completely, leaving the buggy alone in the middle of a twelve-hundred acre patch of barren landscape. The fibre optics regressed back into the ground and the only reminder that anything had been there at all were the random pattern of damp patches staining the ground and the lingering smell of bodily waste still hanging in the air.

"Before you say anything, it wasn't me!" Ted exclaimed as he stared at the startled face of his driver and answered the unasked question. Of all the people to pick him up it had to be Gemma Cassidy, a longtime close friend with benefits, whom Ted wished would consent to it being on a more permanent basis. Unfortunately, for Ted, she had rejected his offer of marriage on more than one occasion, citing the lack of freedom, not to mention her bad first marriage that left physical as well as emotional scars. Gemma's face quickly turned a deep shade of pink as she screwed up her eyes and puffed out her cheeks while holding her breath long enough to drive the buggy back down the tunnel and wait for the metallic clang as the ramp closed behind them. Exhaling rapidly, followed by a few deep breaths, her colour quickly returned to normal, and as she regained her composure, the teasing began.

"I'm sorry to tell you Ted, but apparently you smell of poop. Have you had a little accident or something? It comes to us all as we get older you know. It's nothing to be ashamed of."

"Ho, ho, ho, very funny, you should be on the stage with material like that. You know full well it's not me, I told Stan to turn it down."

Ted replied sarcastically hoping that it would end the matter, but Gemma just chuckled softly as she prepared for her next round of teasing.

"You know Ted that you can get adult nappies nowadays, ordering can be done online, and you don't have to worry about the delivery guy knowing what's in the package; everything is enclosed in a plain brown wrapper. It's all very discrete."

Ted was used to Gemma's sarcastic humour and he realised it was impossible to defend himself against her well refined skill, so he did the only thing left in his arsenal and he fell into a sulk. Gemma tried a few more times, but unable to elicit any further response from her man she quickly grew tired of the joke and they both remained silent while listening to the soft whine coming from the electric motor of the buggy as they headed down the brightly lit subterranean curved walled highway towards the central hub.

From the outside, a casual observer would be completely unaware that an underground facility existed. They would also be unable to identify any discernible landmark across the former military air base and weapons testing ground, and now restricted area.

Fifteen years ago the Hologram Dreams Corporation bought the land at a knockdown price from the government, with the promise that it would clear the area of any dangerous unexploded hardware and to pay for the safe disposal of all radioactive deposits found on the site. With all legislative riders completed, Philip Sanderson Enterprises bankrolled the conversion and expansion of one of the biggest underground facilities known to man. Inside five years and a few billion pounds later, a subterranean city, big enough to house over ten thousand workers buzzed into life, producing fantasies and dreams on an almost unimaginable scale.

It was down highway nine-alpha that Ted and Gemma now headed. This was one of twelve underground access roads radiating outwards from a massive central hub that when viewed on a map resembled the spokes of a cartwheel. Each one of these numbered tunnels stretched out over five miles and contained dozens of off ramps easily linking the underground city with any part of production or operation. The alpha part of the tunnel address referred to the uppermost level of the facility, with twenty-three lower levels, each named after letters of the classical Greek alphabet. The lowest level, omega comprised of an entire floor of computer server units housed in a chilled temperature controlled environment.

Approaching the central hub where a perimeter buggy park housed over eighty electrically powered units, Gemma stopped the buggy directly over an inductive charging point and they both climbed out, heading for the world's first operational linear transportation shuttle. This unique system could convey up to four passengers vertically as well as horizontally, allowing access to any part of the central complex simply by two touches of a sensory screen mounted inside the pod. When the shuttle arrived, Ted turned to thank Gemma for the lift, but before he could say a word, she had pushed him backwards into the empty pod and closed the door. Wrapping her arms tightly around his neck, she kissed him passionately on the lips as the shuttle sped off into the darkness, prompted by a long list of destinations programmed by the fingers of Ted's hands as he pressed them onto the map while trying to maintain his balance. Before the seduction could progress any further, Gemma had to stop as the pod quickly slowed as it approached and then passed by a busy junction full of people waiting patiently for their next ride. Seizing the initiative, Ted quickly pushed Gemma down into her seat while he sat opposite and wiped *'Damson Blush'* lipstick from his own lips with the back of his hand.

"That was very naughty Gemma; Philip will give me the push if word gets out."

Gemma smiled, feeling highly aroused from Ted's embarrassed reaction.

"Philip would never give you the push, this place will fall apart without your guidance, and you know it. I know, meet me tonight at the 'Blue fairy' for a bite to eat and a few drinks, then later on I will show you how naughty I can be!"

Gemma purred as she slipped off her regulation light brown slip-on comfy shoe and ran a well-pedicured foot up the inside of Ted's left leg. She almost reached his crotch before he grabbed her calf tightly between his knees and then pushed her foot down with his free hand while casting a cursory worried glance at the security camera mounted in the top right-hand corner of the pod.

"Spoilsport, Gemma wants to play." Gemma scowled, acting like a chastised child while she slipped her foot back into her shoe. Pushing out her bottom lip as far as possible, she tightly folded her arms across her ample chest, lowered her eyebrows, and gave Ted her best brooding glare. Ted ignored the dramatic gesture, as he knew Gemma's station was fast approaching, so he closed his eyes, hoping to ease his headache that was flaring up again. Gemma smiled inwardly as an idea came to mind and by the time Ted eyes reopened, she was already on her feet and had deliberately turned around while bending over straight legged to pull up a sock that did not need any attention. This placed her backside inches from Ted's face and he could not help but stare at the tight material outlining the contours of her womanly shape and smell the sweet warm musky scent emanating from her young body. The display was just too much, and giving in to temptation Ted reached out to stroke his hand up the inside of Gemma's thigh when the pod quickly decelerated as it approached the platform. Immediately the door swished open and without another word Gemma straightened up, stepped outside, and disappeared into the crowd on the busy concourse. This allowed room for another to enter; leaving Ted staring open mouthed as a fresh passenger stepped in and sat down.

The middle management co-worker nodded in acknowledgement to his senior colleague, then looked puzzled as he stared at the long list of destinations Ted's fingers had randomly programmed. Too polite to question the validity of the list, he politely added his own at the bottom and sat down. Slightly flushed, embarrassed, and aroused, Ted shifted awkwardly in his seat and leaned forwards to delete all the unwanted zones he had accidentally chosen, then passed his left hand over an adjacent scanner giving him clearance to add Philip's office as the pod door closed and moved silently away. Three mute embarrassing minutes later, Ted arrived at his destination and with relief stepped out onto an empty platform. Any curiosity from his silent passenger as to what Ted might have been doing in the pod with Gemma was quickly dispelled by his wide-eyed fascination at actually stopping outside the front door to Philip Sanderson's quarters, a rare occurrence for almost every employee. The pod silently moved away, leaving Ted standing alone on what was a very austere brightly lit platform, that had only two exits; a fire escape at the far end and the secured doorway leading into Philip's quarters.

To gain access, Ted pressed the palm of his left hand onto a laser scanner sited on the wall next to the door and waited. It was a quirk of Philip's that the left hand be used, as he himself, although ambidextrous, favoured his left and was very proud of the fact that even though right handedness outnumbered the left by nearly tenfold, many of the most creative and successful people throughout history have been left handed. Philip liked the idea of belonging to such an exclusive clique.

The reaction time of the scanner was surprisingly slow and Ted wondered if Philip had purposely programmed a delay, so he could watch via the surveillance camera how visitors react while they wait for the door to open. As Ted waited his mind wandered, casting back to the many times at senior school he witnessed Philip antagonise everyone with his haughty attitude and condescending demeanour, which would often end in a beating, unless Ted was there to protect him. The trouble was that Philip could not really help it; diagnosed at a very early age with a rare brain condition made him socially inept, but at the same time gifted him with a genius intelligence that went completely off the chart. Philip Sanderson, the boy with only one friend was now the chairman of the world's largest corporation, and inventor of the 3-D overlay hologram-mapping program underlining the future for the entire organisation.

Finally, the scanner beeped as it identified Ted's handprint and with a near silent hiss, the steel security door slid open, allowing Ted to walk through. To the uninitiated, what lay behind was a bizarre an experience as you could imagine. The corridor leading from the entrance towards the inner door was a twenty-yard flat-bottomed reinforced glass pipe suspended fifteen feet above a coral strewn ocean bed. The transparent seven-foot diameter tube passed through the centre of a huge eight-million gallon seawater aquarium containing over one thousand species of rare and beautiful tropical fish. Even though technically underwater, the clear floor gave the illusion of walking on air as you made your way towards Philip's inner sanctum.

Having walked the corridor many times, Ted paid little attention to the incredible display, marched purposefully to the far end, and pushed open the heavy wooden ornately carved doors that once graced the entrance to a Nepalese monastery, but now guarded Philip's private quarters. Inside, a massive domed-roof cavern carved out of solid rock and adorned with priceless pieces of artwork, *'My office'* as Philip christened it, resembled a cross between a science fiction dream of the future and a cinematic vision of a super-villain's underground hideout. Philip heard the door open and turned his head sharply to greet his friend.

"Ah Ted, sorry to interrupt your trials, but I would like you to meet the client who's going to fund our most ambitious project to date. Ted this is music legend Jensen Boley, accompanied by his partner the award winning and very talented singer, Mary Lightfoot."

Ted smiled as he crossed the floor and politely shook hands with both parties before they all sat back down around the table. Philip looked relieved now that his friend had arrived, as social interaction on any level was extremely difficult and tedious. Ted was completely aware as to why his company was needed and slipped into his usual pleasant banter to entertain the mega-rich guests. Aided by Ted's charm, good looks, and friendly disposition, Philip was positive that he would persuade the celebrity couple into adding millions to the already overpriced deal.

CHAPTER FOUR

Elvis avoided eye contact with his partner at the sickening realisation of what Duke had done. Staring hard at the ground where the incident had taken place, his stomach churned at the thought that it could have also been himself. He tried not to think of it as rape in the literal sense of the word, but the intention was there and he was at a complete loss as what else it really could be. Duke also remained unusually mute as they waited patiently in the hot sun for the sheriff to come up with a plan. Spotting the discarded pantaloons, Duke picked them up and offered them back to Molly, who angrily snatched the garment from his shaking hands and hastily covered up her bare legs while shunning Dukes lame apology. For Sheriff Dodson, that was really a side issue and he closed his eyes, trying to blot out the image of Molly's naked body lying there in the dirt so he could figure a safe way out, while at the same time get Molly safely back to her family.

Duke pondered until an idea came to mind and he produced an interactive field map from his back pocket that every client is issued with before being allowed out onto the set. Although it was only a fraction thicker than the average sheet of paper, it acted similar to a satellite navigation device combined with a '*You are here*' map. This identified the recipient's current position, and also produced route to safety, should you get lost. Spreading the map out on the sandy earth, Duke pressed his thumb onto the wafer thin fingerprint scanner embedded in the corner of the sheet and it immediately indicated that they were less than five miles from the exit gate. He calculated that if they commandeered a buggy, everyone could be out of there in ten to fifteen minutes.

What clients are not told is that upon activation, the map is also a homing beacon and it informed the control booth of Duke's location to within a few yards and relayed his current direction. The sheriff studied the map carefully while scratching his chin before he straightened up and gave his orders.

"Right boys, I want the two of you to go on ahead and secure the transportation. I don't care how you do it, but we all need to be together in one buggy so we can make a run for it if need be."

Both deputies nodded, turned away, and began formulating a plan as they headed off back down the trail. The sheriff looked back at Molly and held out his hand.

"It's ok little missy, we're gonna get you out of here safe and sound. You have the word of Sheriff Oberon P Dodson. If you're wondering what the P stands for, it stands for polite, because my momma said that you should always be polite to a lady."

Molly resisted at first, but as she looked the sheriff in the eye, something deep down inside told her to trust him and she eventually placed her slender fingers inside the stranger's chubby fist.

"There you go, that wasn't so difficult was it?" The sheriff cooed as he clumsily tried to place a reassuring arm around Molly's shoulders, but his girth hampered the attempt so he settled with linking arms and for a slow walk back. By the time they reached the high bank that Duke had slid down in pursuit of his prize, both the deputies were standing waiting.

"What happened to the driver?" The sheriff asked as it appeared that the man was nowhere around.

"The two other vehicles had already returned to base as we were now all together and only one was required, and I sent the driver off on a wild goose chase. Told him that you had doubled back in the other direction, fallen down a steep bank, and twisted your ankle. He looked really worried that he had left you alone, ran off down that-away, and didn't look back."

Elvis grinned from ear to ear at the praise for his quick thinking, but the smile soon faded as both he and Duke struggled in the heat to push their overweight boss all the way up the steep bank to the waiting vehicle. Even Molly helped, for what reason she was not quite sure, but it felt the right thing to do at the time. Breathless and finally all aboard, they set off as quickly as possible for the nearest exit. Within minutes, they came upon a tall chain linked fence, spreading out from one horizon to the next, with no apparent exit gates in sight. All they could do for now was to continue to follow the perimeter and hope that the highway was not too far away.

Startling everyone from an un-enforced silence, the buggy's on-board radio burst into life with a call from the central office.

"Buggy nineteen, calling buggy nineteen, respond please."

Everyone remained silent and stared at the receiver with the gold 19 emblazoned on the back of the handset that hooked onto the dashboard.

"Repeat, buggy nineteen, buggy nineteen this is the control room please respond. Our tracking beacon reports that you and three guests have wandered from your designated area and are close to the edge of registered franchise territory; this is a breach of regulations, please respond."

The silence continued and as everyone looked to the sheriff for an answer, he idly scratched the five o'clock shadow on the side of his face while he thought rapidly what to do. The control room called for a third time and he hastily snatched up the microphone as an idea came to mind.

"This is buggy nineteen, I repeat buggy nineteen; sorry for the delay, we are just responding to an armed trespasser caught within the grounds. I am proceeding to the nearest exit station with our clients; that by good fortune happen to be police officers. They insist on immediate transportation of the detainee to the nearest sheriff's office, so if you could alert the guards of our imminent arrival and have the exit gate open this will avoid delay."

The radio clicked as he let go of the transmission trigger and everyone held their breath while they waited for an answer. Seconds felt like minutes and the longer the radio remained silent, the more the sheriff believed that the exit guards were already being warned and would have their rifles aimed. When the response finally came, it surprised everyone.

"Buggy nineteen this is the control room, your situation has been related to the security guards at the gate and will be opened ready for your exit. Please raise the alert if any more assistance is required."

The sheriff was ready and squeezed the transmission trigger immediately.

"Thank ya' kindly there good buddy, we sure will, but at the moment, everything is in hand, over and out!"

Breathing a heavy sigh of relief, he replaced the receiver and looked anxiously towards the fast approaching exit. Thanks to his quick thinking, they watched as the long yellow metal stop barrier slowly hinged up into a vertical position. Elvis slowed the jeep down to a fast walking pace, allowing the sheriff a quick cursory nod to the guard as he allowed them all to pass through and out onto the open road.

"As soon as we reach the nearest town we'll change vehicles at a car rental. The control room knew where we were and will easily be able to trace the buggy on the outside as well as in." The sheriff announced over the rush of the wind in the open sided vehicle as they headed down the highway trying to put as much distance as possible between themselves and the day full of dreams that ended in a nightmare.

An hour later Sheriff Dodson sat in front of a desk directly opposite a young woman working for the Ashtown car rental company; *'Your one stop shop for great car hire'*.

Embarrassed by the strange looks from curious staff members, he had to wait fifteen minutes before he signed the papers and received the keys for an aged nondescript hatchback, paid for with a scanned thumbprint and digital currency card. Because of Molly's attire that was even more bizarre than the safari outfits the men wore, she waited out of sight behind the neighbouring gas station, while Duke disposed of the buggy in the back corner of a supermarket parking lot. With the car fully fuelled the sheriff rounded everyone up and ordered Elvis back behind the wheel as they set off on the one-hundred and forty mile homeward journey, giving them plenty of time to discuss what to do next.

CHAPTER FIVE

Several hours passed and common in this part of the world, daytime quickly turned into night. Without any other light source, the prisoners sat in near darkness, exaggerating the endless drone of the diesel engine vibrating throughout the hold. Oliver's condition had thankfully calmed down and apart from a general thirst and mild hunger, the group were holding up well. Adam had explained to those who wished to hear that although Patrick had been shot dead, he was a fool for trying to be the hero and it was a wise reminder not to antagonise their captors and do exactly as ordered. There was the odd noncommittal grunt, but most remained silent on the subject even if they disagreed with what Adam had to say. He attempted to try to spread calm amongst his friends by stating that it was a very rare occurrence for anyone to be harmed during such an event as it would devalue the ransom and further demands would be negated. The effect was probably negligible, but in the current situation, his good heart gave the best it could offer.

A sudden decrease in the throb of the engine accompanied by a smoother ride indicated, according to Kristy, that they now probably heading inland along a river estuary. For the best part of the next hour, the aged craft chugged along until the engines slowed sharply, clunked into reverse and with a loud thud, the hull bumped against a rickety wooden jetty. Amid barked orders and frantic movement up above, the hatch lid swung open and crashed heavily back onto the deck, allowing the light of a nearly full moon to penetrate into the hold. Two rifle barrels poked over the opening and one of the crew lowered a ladder down to the group.

"Get out, get out, get out!" Ordered an unfamiliar voice, as one by one the terrified prisoners climbed the ladder onto the deck. Stretching cramped muscles and adjusting their eyes to their new surroundings, they all looked around, staring at the endless dense jungle encroaching right up to the narrow river's edge. At the far end of a jetty, a small clearing contained twenty to thirty poorly constructed rough wooden huts with rusty corrugated tin roofs. The yacht was no longer behind the boat; it had been released from its tow line over an hour ago, topped up with fuel and sailed fifty miles up the coast to a remote hidden inlet. This was standard practice for the kidnappers should the authorities trace any signals from mobile phones or hidden distress beacons that had not been disarmed and could act as a locator for a rescue attempt.

Immediately the last of the group set foot on deck, they were all hastily frogmarched down the jetty towards the encampment and made to sit grouped close together on the dry earth and under armed guard while Captain Moses issued some last minute orders. He eventually joined them on the riverbank and stood with his hands on his hips while putting on a broad, toothy smile. He then addressed the terrified friends with the calmness of a holiday rep en route to a hotel.

"Lady and gentlemen, I trust that the journey was not too arduous and you are probably ready for something to eat. Very soon the women of our group will bring you each a bowl of most delicious stew and bottles of water to sustain you for the journey ahead. Should anyone have the need to relieve themselves you will find a latrine at the far end of the village. You will be on trust to visit it one at a time only and should anyone try to escape my men will execute two others in punishment. Do I make myself clear?"

The grin quickly disappeared as he glared at the group. To encourage the correct response, he overtly ran the tips of his fingers across his holstered pistol and smile again when everyone nodded silently. Bizarrely satisfied that he had acted as a genial '*mein host*', Moses turned and walked calmly away. Within minutes, two of the camp women carried over a large cast iron cooking pot full of stew, a pile of dried, hardened calabash-gourd bowls, and an assortment of hand carved wooden spoons. One by one, the lead woman ladled out a healthy portion of stew and passed it to every member of the group. They all tucked in gratefully apart from Oliver, who had no appetite and stared vacantly at the steaming mass.

"Eat it up, you don't know when we'll eat again, you'll need all your strength with your condition." Jacob ordered his friend as he placed a spoon into Oliver's hand; gripped it tightly within his own massive fist and forced it into the broth. Oliver reluctantly obeyed and begrudgingly welcomed the nourishing warm feeling as he steadily emptied his bowl.

Fifteen minutes later Moses returned, and in basic Arabic, Adam graciously thanked him for the food. He purposely chose a language so his friends could not understand as some might take offence by his obsequious manner and think he was trying to curry favour with the captain. The simple truth was that Adam was playing up to the captain's narcissistic nature, hoping for as little grief as possible until the ransom is paid and they can be freed from their forced internment. Moses actually raised his head, puffed out his chest at the compliment, and turning around; he repeated the edict to everyone within earshot of how gracious he was as a host. Reverting back to English, he once again addressed the group.

"It has been a very long, trying day for everyone and I am sure you are all tired, but we must make our rendezvous by morning so everyone on your feet."

The confused group wearily stood up and waited while one of the captain's crew arrived in an ancient Red Cross ambulance bus, driven in from around the back of the camp. Leaving the engine running, he left the cab, ran around to the back of the vehicle, and unlocked the rear double doors. Moses then ordered two guards to shepherd the group into single file and climb in. When everyone had taken a seat, the two armed men split up and sat one at the front, and one at the back of the bus. Moses instructed the driver to close and lock the rear doors, and then he too climbed aboard, settling himself into the spare front passenger seat. With his orders completed, the driver climbed back behind the wheel, revved the engine, pumped his foot several times on the clutch pedal, and began fighting two handed with the reluctant gear stick. Finally winning the battle with the aged gearbox, the driver finally found a forward gear, lowered the handbrake and bus pulled noisily away. The transport, although dilapidated and filthy, was a considerable improvement on the stinking hold of the old fishing boat. Inside its dark interior the seats were old but comfortable and vision was slightly improved by two small courtesy lights embedded in the ceiling. Every window had been painted black to hide occupants from the prying eyes of the local population, but many scratches from the branches of bushes and overhanging trees allowed glimpses of light coming from the surrounding villages as they bounced along the heavily rutted track.

Dawn was well behind them on a new day when the bus finally arrived at one end of a very poorly maintained cracked cement airstrip. Waiting on the runway was an aged Cessna 680 passenger aircraft. Its twin engines were idling and the passenger door lay open, ready to receive its human cargo. The paint on the fuselage was all but worn away and it even bore the scars of being strafed by gunfire across the cockpit. The starboard side-window had also received damage and repaired with a piece of plywood and a strong polymer adhesive. The plane did not seem to be in a much better condition than the ancient Red Cross bus, but this was not an international airport with a choice of airlines. It was a surprising sight, but a much welcomed ride home. For the hostages, right now anything would do.

Moses climbed down from the bus and out of earshot conversed briefly with the pilot while his men ushered the tired group from the back of the bus and handed them over to two other uniformed guards, who had just stepped down from inside the aircraft. Confused looks were exchanged between the friends, but opinions were kept mute in case any of the guards overheard and saw it as a sign of trouble. Finally, Moses gave the pilot a broad grin, shook his hand, returned to the hostages, and began shouting over the noise of the engines as he made his final speech.

"Lady and gentlemen, it is my pleasure to announce that a fee has already been paid for your release from my custody, and so I bid you my goodbyes. If you would now all get on the plane, it will take you back to England."

Hugs, tears, and huge sighs of relief quickly spread through the group, with the exception of Adam, who appeared very troubled and looked as though he suddenly carried the weight of the world on his shoulders. Not really noticing his mood, his friends hurriedly climbed aboard their third different mode of transport in the last twenty-four hours. Following brief pre-flight check that consisted of testing the wing flaps and tapping a few dials with his index finger, the pilot fastened his seatbelt and increased engine thrust. Very quickly, the small passenger aeroplane taxied down the bumpy runway, soared up over the dense jungle and headed for home. Adam purposely chose a seat next to Neil and after take-off; he began to voice his concerns.

"I don't want to rain on everybody's parade but my gut tells me there is something wrong."

Neil's smiling face dropped to one of serious concern, as he knew Adam was rarely wrong. Looking around, he leaned in closer encouraging his friend to share his thoughts in a low voice, in case they were overheard by the others.

"I know this may sound stupid, but I can't believe that the ransom has been paid as quickly as that. The usual format is for the authorities to make any kidnappers wait a few days so they aren't encouraged to ask for more."

Neil pondered over the suggestion for a moment and then nodded in agreement. Before he could make his own comment, Adam continued.

"I have never heard of kidnappers flying their hostages back home, they are always picked up by the authorities or a go between. Also, I know this sounds really paranoid, but Moses mentioned a fee paid, not a ransom. I think we have been sold and are going to be transferred to another group of kidnappers, possibly terrorists."

Neil's face blanched at the statement as he struggled to absorb all the facts. He quickly regained composure and the next half an hour they discussed at length all the possible political activists, religious factions and even another pirate group who may have paid Moses immediately, and were prepared to play the long game for a larger ransom.

Using the sun as a guide to their direction and an educated guess at air speed, possible organisations and factions were removed one by one from a mental list, as countries were flown over and then left behind. Fortunately for everyone, the aircraft maintained its north-west heading. Inside the next hour they could see the watery expanse of the Mediterranean Sea glittering thousands of feet below, providing an incredible relief as it proved that they were heading away from all the middle-eastern countries, most of whom still held a hatred for the west. Adam was beginning to wonder to himself if all of this was the result of stress and an overactive imagination, a thought shared by Neil but he was too polite to voice his opinions out loud. Neil guessed that all this could be Adam's tired brain reaching all the wrong conclusions, but still troubled by the strength of his friend's conviction; he stared blankly through the cabin window and prayed silently that this was the case.

Early in the afternoon the engine speed decreased, reducing air speed and the plane began a helical descent over a small remote island that Kristy estimated was somewhere between Cyprus and Greece. The pilot exchanged a few indecipherable words via a two-way radio with someone on the ground, and quickly landed the plane on a small airstrip overlooking the sea. The entire facility consisted of one aircraft hangar, adjacent to two storage barns, and a very small control booth with the requisite communication aerials mounted on its roof. The only other way off the island appeared to be via a small motor boat moored to a wooden jetty, a little less than fifty yards from the edge of the runway. Both Adam and Neil had decided it was best not to alarm the rest of the group in case Adam's fears were wrong, but the sight of armed and uniformed men guarding the facility did nothing to allay their fears. Adam had kept another idea to himself, of the possibility that everyone could be split up and sold to the highest bidder, but to his relief it looked like the only thing required for now was for the plane to refuel. At Neil's request, the guards allowed the group out for a comfort break. Even though his friends were reluctant to step out into the blistering heat on the cement runway, he encouraged everyone to walk briskly up and down to alleviate the dangers of thrombosis due to their dehydrated state. This bizarre ritual amused their captors, easing tensions slightly, but inside ten minutes everyone climbed back on board, and the human cargo continued its northwesterly heading, then hopefully home.

As the hours ticked slowly by, the sight of cloudier northern skies lifted Adam and Neil's spirits, especially when Kristy leaned forwards to whisper they were now crossing the English Channel. Quite unexpectedly the guards opened a chest at the rear of the aircraft and issued everyone with a litre bottle of water. This was all eagerly accepted and quickly drained, as it was their only type of sustenance since breakfast. Although relieved somewhat from the pains of dehydration, the group were still tired and very hungry.

Within half an hour they touched down somewhere in what they hoped was England, but dense, low cloud and heavy rain made it impossible to make an accurate guess. The airstrip was again, very bumpy and overgrown in places, also the entire area seemed devoid of any sign of human habitation. Unable to determine anything else with his limited vision through the filthy cabin windows, Neil leaned close to Adam and whispered.

"I don't like this at all, where the hell are we?"

Trying to make the best of what he considered was a worsening situation; Adam shrugged his shoulders and smiled weakly. Neil tightened his grip on Adam's forearm, fixed him with a serious stare, and tried again.

"What aren't you telling me Adam? In all the years I've known you you've never been without an explanation for anything and everything, so now is not the best time to start!"

Adam grimaced at the pain, then glanced around to make sure that none of the guards were listening as he waited for Neil to let go.

"The fact that we are hopefully back home is a big plus and if a ransom has been paid I expected to land at some sort of private or military airfield where we will all be debriefed and made to sign the official secrets act to keep this information out of the press. As you know the first rule is never give in to threats, but there are still some things that don't add up. The first is that an intermediary should have flown in with the pilot when he picked us all up and we should have been taken to the nearest country that had a treaty with the United Kingdom. That brings us to the fact that why on earth would they allow this rust bucket to fly across Europe with two armed guards on board? This could be a flying bomb or carrying a deadly airborne nerve gas. Also, once we have all been released there is nothing to stop the authorities from grounding the plane and arresting them all."

"Perhaps Moses in his greed didn't think it through properly." Neil interrupted believing that Adam's paranoia was way off the charts and hoped to find a logical answer to the bizarre situation, but Adam immediately shook his head and continued.

"Not a chance, Moses is a veteran in hostage taking so you can rule that out completely. Now we are on the ground, the lack of any type of military vehicle, or sign of life at a government air base makes me very nervous."

Adam slumped back in his seat and Neil looked desperately through the window to see if he could prove Adam wrong, but all he could see was the shape of an aircraft hangar half-hidden by the rain. To his surprise, the pilot taxied the aircraft directly towards the building and as they approached, huge shuttered doors began to roll up to reveal a massive vehicle ramp descending into the earth, akin to the entrance of an underground car park. Without check, the pilot steered the aircraft down into the ground and the shuttered doors rolled back down automatically behind them.

Finally snapping under the strain, Neil jumped to his feet and demanded to know what was going on, only to find himself staring directly down the barrel of an old AK-47, that the guard at the rear of the aircraft was only too eager to use. Neil raised both hands in surrender and watched wide-eyed in horror as his captor moved closer. Everyone else stared, unable to breathe, fearful that they were about to witness their friend's last moments. Neil began to tremble and flop sweat poured down his ashen face as the guard lowered his aim and pressed the muzzle painfully into the centre of his victim's chest, pinning the poor man against the seat in front.

Adam turned to look at the other guard, hoping that he would do something to stop Neil's murder, but he made no effort to intercede and eagerly licked his lips in anticipation of the event.

"You die now!" The guard growled, pushing the barrel even harder into Neil's chest. Adam could wait no more and took a deep breath, trying to overcome his terror and stand up ready to plead for Neil's life, when everyone startled at what happened next.

"**BANG**!" The guard yelled, and then roared with laughter as Neil screamed, his legs gave way, and he collapsed between the seats in fright. Everyone else cowering in fear for their lives quickly followed suit. Within minutes of sheer terror, everyone in the group suddenly shared a joint feeling of calm, settling back in their seats as the long descent continued until they were over four-hundred feet below ground and the tunnel opened up into a cavernous floodlit interior. In the near distance, a man dressed in a green boiler suit and wearing a yellow regulation hard hat used two glowing white batons to direct the pilot to a halt adjacent to two other similar aircraft. Everyone stared silently through the windows at their new surroundings, fearful of making a sound in case the guard happened to change his mind; Patrick's death was still fresh in the memory and the wrong move might just be a bullet to the head.

The engines finally fell silent as three men carrying rifles approached their plane and following a brief conversation with the pilot they signalled for the doors to be opened. Warm air, tainted with exhaust fumes, flooded into the cabin, mixing quickly with that of the stale recycled mix that everyone had been breathing for most of the day. To the amazement of all on board, Neil got to his feet yet again with a series of questions that he hoped would not cost him his life, but for the last five minutes he had been trying very hard to remember what they were. Putting it all down to stress and lack of food, he managed to maintain some of his composure, but as he filed out and his feet touched the concrete floor, all about him began to lack focus. Looking around at his friends, they also appeared to be in a similar condition as though under the influence of alcohol or illicit drugs. Suddenly Jason belched loudly, breaking the enforced silence, the act of which he found extremely funny, clutching both hands tightly to his stomach he doubled over in hysterical laughter. This infected the rest of the group and they all found the situation hilarious. The guards apparently did not find this at all strange and smiled along with their prisoners, as they snapped a shiny tubular, numbered metal collar, no thicker than a man's little finger, around every prisoner's neck. The friends were then ushered towards a waiting small electric land train that had silently emerged from one of a series of tunnels radiating horizontally outwards from within the cavern, that were just big enough for the custom built vehicle to pass through. The near silent engine towed a dozen flatbed carriages, each one housed what can only be described as a giant, black, pet-carrier, complete with a two inch square galvanised and hinged wire grid across the front to confine whatever was placed within. Each pod unlocked using a magnetic swipe card carried on a lanyard around the neck of the head guard who ordered his men to place one prisoner in each unit. The drugged group offered no resistance and as Kristy was the first inside, she turned around and sat cross legged facing the exit while pretending to clean her face by licking the side of her hand and rubbing it over her imaginary pointed ears. The LSD dissolved in the water bottles handed out before landing gave the prisoners no cause for concern and they all willingly entered each unit with the minimum of fuss.

With everyone safely loaded on board, the head guard joined the driver at the front of the train, as it set off in a wide circle around the standing aircraft then disappeared worm-like down another similar curved wall tunnel.

CHAPTER SIX

"You've been quiet for quite a while now Boss, have you come up with a plan?"

Elvis broke the silence as he blurted out his question through a mouthful of cheeseburger as they all sat in the parking lot of a drive-through, fast-food franchise just off highway twenty-nine en route to Holtsville. Sheriff Dodson ignored the question and continued feeding a fistful of fries into his mouth followed by a noisy slurp of diet cola, a source of constant amusement for his deputies. With his appetite partially sated, the sheriff cleaned his hands, delicately wiped his mouth with a moist tissue, held the thumb side of his lightly clenched fist against his lips, and belched softly before deigning to give an answer.

"You should know by now young Elvis that I always have a plan and this is no exception. First thing we do is get young Molly here to Doc Booth for an examination and then inform Cousin Edith that her only daughter is safe and well. When we get back to the station I will inform the FBI and they can take it from there."

"Is that it Boss, are you just gonna sit back and do nothin'?" Elvis replied, amazed at the sheriff's apparent lukewarm grasp of the situation, but the reply came in an instant.

"All matters have to be addressed according to state law and by informing the FBI we can be sure to follow the correct procedure."

The sheriffs' tone of voice and narrow stare over the rims of his horn-rimmed spectacles was enough to close the matter, leaving Elvis confused and silent. Luckily Molly paid little attention to the conversation as she wolfed down her first meal in two days and her starving stomach growled noisily in welcome at the repast. When everyone had finished, Duke reached over from his front seat to take Molly's rubbish from her lap only for her to lash out and knock his hand away. She then curled up into a protective ball in the corner at the back of the car, next to the sheriff.

"What on earth do you think you're doing scaring the poor child like that? Didn't your momma teach you any manners?" The sheriff chided Duke, and then anxiously looked around hoping that she had not drawn any attention from members of the public. Shushing softly to stop Molly crying, the sheriff reached into his pocket and produced another moist tissue for her to wipe her hands, and then a dry one for her tears. Using a genteel manner he carefully removed the empty meal wrappers sitting scrunched up on her lap and passed them over to Elvis allowing him to take everything over to the trash bin. Her reaction was slow but positive and by the time Elvis had returned, the sheriff ordered him to start the engine and leave as quickly as possible.

"I need to pee!" Molly suddenly blurted out, startling everyone in the car as it was the first time she had spoken since what the sheriff had labelled as *'The unfortunate event'*.

"Cain't it wait? There's a lot of people about and you ain't exactly dressed to be seen in public." Duke snapped as Elvis stopped the car abruptly, making him spill what was left of his whisky down his chest.

"I need to pee ***now***!" Molly yelled and tried to open her door, but the child locks had been activated and she failed in the attempt.

"What the hell do you think you're playing at, why am I locked in? Let me out now or I'm going to scream."

Molly began to kick violently at the door and lashed out at the sheriff when he tried to grab her legs.

"Now calm down little missy, Elvis will let you out if you want to, but please don't make a scene for all our sakes."

The sheriff nodded to Elvis who was already getting out of the car and he opened Molly's door. Immediately she fell silent and jumped out, purposely barging into the deputy before marching across the parking lot straight into the restaurant.

"D'you want me to follow her Boss? She might decide to run away." Elvis asked, but Dodson just shook his head.

"It's gonna look a mite suspicious to see a man dressed in a safari suit standing guard outside the ladies powder room. Give her a little space to gather herself; the poor thing's had a very traumatic experience. Anyway, where's she gonna run to? She knows that we're on our way home and unless she's thinkin' about walking the rest of the way I'm sure she'll soon be back."

Elvis returned to his seat and sat quietly waiting for Molly's return. Duke mumbled something that sounded like '*stupid bitch*' to himself a he dabbed at his wet shirt with a cloth from the glove box, but Elvis was not listening. His brain was awash with questions, but he guessed that now was not a good time to ask and it would have to wait for later. Luckily it was not too long before a much calmer Molly returned and silently sat back in the car. The rest of the journey, although quiet and uneventful, remained tense, but the sheriff was happy to see a small smile on Molly's face as he offered her a chocolate bar from his private stash that was rarely from his side.

Within two hours Duke and Elvis sat waiting in the car outside Doctor Morton Booth's private residence, clinic, and surgery in their small rural town of Holtsville. Luckily the doctor was home and while the sheriff waited in the hallway, the doctor took Molly into the surgery and gave her a thorough physical examination.

The oppressive heat in the airless room and the accompanying monotony of the heavy tock resonating like a slow heartbeat from the grandfather clock, soon had the sheriff sound asleep. He awoke with a jolt to find the doctor standing before him and lightly shaking his shoulder. Before a word could be said, the doctor raised his index finger to his lips for silence and ushered him into the front parlour. Once inside, the doctor quietly slid the rosewood double doors together and turned to offer his guest a seat. Choosing a high wing-backed worn down leather chair, the sheriff waited while the doctor eased his old bones down to perch on the edge of an identical chair facing either side of a small coffee table sited in front of the fireplace. The doctor was full of questions, but keeping his voice low, he first reported on Molly's condition.

"The poor child is very undernourished, dehydrated, and covered from head to toe in minor cuts and bruises, but apart from that she appears to be in good health. There are also signs of recent sexual intercourse, but it is hard to tell whether coitus was consensual or forced. Due to her delicate condition I have not questioned her on the subject. I have given her a sedative to calm her nerves and she fell asleep almost immediately. When Molly awakes I see no reason why she shouldn't be allowed straight home. Have you informed Edith?"

Sheriff Dodson's jowls quivered as he shook his head before giving his response.

"First thing I needed to know was that Molly's ok before I can consider calling her mother. Before the old buzzard arrives and starts bombarding me with hundreds of questions I have a few of my own."

Doctor Booth looked puzzled at the attitude towards a distraught mother, but he decided not to complicate matters and sat back in his chair. With his elbows on the armrests and fingers forming a steeple under his chin, he waited for the sheriff to begin.

"Does she have any memory of what happened today or where she has been for the last few weeks?"

It was now the doctors turn to shake his head before trying to clarify the matter.

"That was the first thing I asked the poor child, but she appears to have an emotional blockage of some form or another. The only thing she recognises is her name and where she's from that's it. I did not press the matter any further as she began to show signs of distress. Give her a few days to convalesce and I'm sure her memory will return. I was hoping that you would endeavour to fill in a few blanks for me."

The sheriff blushed and squirmed in his seat as he recalled what his deputies had done and what he himself had also intended to do to the young woman, but it was not the first time he had had to conjure up a believable story. Projecting an air of confidence that he himself did not feel, he sat up as straight as his bulk would allow and began.

"Strictly off the record you understand, me and the boys were enjoying a day out at that hologram theme park pretending to be big game hunters and I recognised one of the dark natives as young Molly. Being on the wrong side of the state line and fearful for our own safety, we decided that it was best if we snuck her out of the place and brought her straight here before informing the state police and the FBI. She seemed very confused and rambled on about being chased across the plain but I've no idea what she's talking about."

"That explains her skin colour and the rest is probably a delirium brought about by heatstroke and dehydration as I have just mentioned." The doctor replied, still feeling that the sheriff was not telling him the whole truth, but before he could ask any more questions the big man stood up and thanked the medic for his time, satisfied that he had planted a seed of doubt in the doctor's mind.

"The official statement will be that we found her on the side of the road as we made our way home so don't go repeating anything that I just told you. I don't think it's safe that the public know the whole truth until me and the boys have done some investigating of our own. Now if you could be so kind as to inform Edith that her daughter is safe and well, we can be out of the way when she arrives. If there is anything else needed, you know where to find me."

Without waiting to be questioned any more, the sheriff walked quickly away, leaving the doctor still wondering whether how much of what he had just been told was the truth.

"Back to my house boys, we've got some investigating to do." The sheriff ordered as he dropped heavily into the back seat of the car.

"Don't you mean the station Boss?" Elvis replied, who was anxious to see, how the FBI conducted the investigation.

"If I wanted the station I would have said the station. Now do as I say, take me to my house and stop asking dumb questions."

Both deputies glanced at each other at the curt reply, but declined to question the matter any further as they took the short journey to Sheriff Dodson's home. Fortunately, his wife Mary was out of town for a few days for a school reunion, so no questions would be asked as to why they were all back so soon. With all the doors and windows having been locked tight, the study in the house was too hot and stuffy for comfort, so they all sat on the rear veranda drinking an ice cold beer from the fridge. Elvis suddenly realised that they were still wearing their safari costumes.

"Hey Boss are we gonna have to drive all the way back to get our stuff or d'you think they will send it to us?"

The sheriff lowered his bottle in disbelief and stared hard at his deputy.

"Did your momma drop you on your head as a baby or somethin'?"

Elvis looked puzzled as the rant continued.

"Let me explain everything in simple words that I hope even you will be able to understand. First, I have paid money for an illegal slave hunt, something that that even with robots and holograms is banned in all fifty-one states, now that you now have to include that commie Cuban island. Second, I have just discovered a cousin of mine who had disappeared over two months ago, disguised as a slave, and covered in chocolate coloured dye. This happens after you, me, and the Duke here have all violated the poor girl in some form or another, in the belief that she was some kind of a machine that we can have sex with. Thirdly, and this is a guess, but a damn good one, is that her two other companions were also human and that you and me hunted them across several miles of scrubland and killed the poor bastards."

The sheriff closed his eyes and took a long drink as he allowed the evidence to hit home. He watched the sudden realisation register with Dukes semi-inebriated state, and then back at Elvis, whose colour had blanched and he looked like if he was going to vomit.

"What are we going to do Boss?" Duke blurted as he finally found his voice. Elvis still had his hand clamped over his mouth and trying to concentrate on keeping his lunch where it belonged.

"I'll tell you what we are not going to do and that's to involve the FBI, and if we are lucky, young Molly won't remember anything that happened today. What we need to do at the moment is just bide our time. I'm sure there will be a lot of local media interest in her story and we will have questions to answer, but as long as we stick to our story, we cain't be implicated in anything. Now, you two go home, get changed, and get rid of the rental. Oh, and while you're doin' all that, keep your ears open and eyes peeled for any suspicious behaviour. The company knows where we live and if they are prepared to deal in slavery, I am sure they will want to tie up any loose ends, do you get my drift?"

Duke nodded before he chugged down the rest of his beer, then he watched impassively at the sight of Elvis, gargling his last mouthful before spitting out the contents over the veranda fence into the azaleas. Putting the empty bottles on the table, they ignored the sheriff's disgusted glare and quickly nodded their goodbyes, leaving him alone to analyse every possible outcome.

CHAPTER SEVEN

Somewhere deep underground the English countryside, the journey along the curved walled access tunnel lasted less than ten minutes, as the curious land train carrying its latest contingent of prisoners stopped inside a similar but smaller rock hewn cavern. The entire facility had been a hidden cold war American underground military airbase that was completely unknown to all but a privileged few. The lack of any military activity, apart from the occasional sight of aircraft flying to and from the camp did not raise anything more than idle curiosity as locals had been informed that it was a weather research base. The real truth was that it previously housed over two thousand military personnel who were kept on site at all times to protect and maintain fifty, long and medium range nuclear missiles; also a collection of nearly eighty aircraft ranging from surveillance planes to B-52 bombers. Cleared of American military hardware and defunct of its original purpose, it was now owned via a bogus company set up through P. Sanders holdings to keep it completely separate from anything to do with the Hologram Dreams name. Over the last eighteen months Philip had diverted millions from his own private offshore accounts, turning over half of the base into a preparation facility, capable of preparing hundreds of inmates at a time, purchased from slave traders based all over the world.

The cost of producing an endless supply of androids, only for them to be completely destroyed by rich clients on a daily basis, wreaked havoc with the company finances so the preparation of drugged or brainwashed *'missing persons'* provided a much more viable alternative, as modern technology made it increasingly more difficult to distinguish androids from a real human. Over three-quarters of the franchise bases across the world were prepared in turn to accept this alternative heavily discounted deal offered by the parent company, thus enabling them to stay afloat. It had reached such a lucrative sideline of the operation, that apart from sophisticated, remote controlled units, or robots possessing super-human capabilities, nearly four out of five disposable extras were now abducted and carefully processed humans.

This refurbished three level underground barracks section of the facility previously housed over five-hundred military personnel. It had been converted into two floors of living accommodation for prison staff, and the bottom fifty billets that used to house up to eight soldiers at a time were now prison cells.

The land train carrying its latest consignment of prisoners stopped suddenly as it passed over a computer controlled parking sensor, allowing an automated laser guided fork lift truck to remove the laden pods and place them side by side onto a slow moving conveyer belt. With the task complete, the forklift reloaded a batch of waiting empty pods back onto the land train ready to return and collect the next set of arrivals.

Still heavily sedated, the sorry group of friends sat dreamily watching the concrete walls drifting slowly by as they traversed down a short tunnel, then stop abruptly inside a large, bright, white tiled room, accompanied with the cloying smell of disinfectant hanging in the air. Simultaneously, all the cage doors popped open and akin to a family of curious meerkats, everyone in the group cautiously peered out at their new surroundings; but there really was not much to see. Apart from the pods and a conveyer belt, the place was void of any other furniture or equipment. The only contrast to the thousands of shiny white ceramic wall and floor tiles adorning the room, were two aluminium doors sited at either end, and a hinged flap covering a rubbish chute embedded in the far wall. Within seconds, the right-hand door slid open and eight people, wearing white lab coats, and carrying sensor touch clipboards filed in. This caused the entire group to shrink back into the relative safety of their pod as the technicians approached. Although still highly fearful, they were still under the persuasive influence of the heavy sedation, and when ordered, they all obediently climbed down carefully to face their assigned handler. A short silence ensued until Neil (who still had not learned to remain quiet!) was the first to break the unwritten rule and attempted to speak. The result was for him suffering the pain of an electric shock coming from his neck collar when his handler typed in Neil's assigned number, then pressed an activation button mounted on a wrist mounted controller. The burst only lasted for a fraction of a second, but it was enough to spasm every muscle in Neil's body, putting him in excruciating pain. As he doubled over, gasping for breath, Neil and his friends quickly understood what the numbered collars were for.

"All prisoners will now remove their clothes." Boomed a male voice from a ceiling mounted tannoy system; startling the group even further. They all looked aghast at one another, wondering if the order given applied to them or perhaps someone else. The answer was clear and painful when this time they all suffered the same punishment as Neil, who within a few seconds, received a second shock while he was still panting heavily from the first. Shyly they disrobed down to their underwear, increasing their feelings of embarrassment and vulnerability. Everyone now nervously wondered what was coming next, with the horror of human experimentation or being harvested for their organs riding near the top of a long mental list.

"Prisoners will remove all of your clothes." The faceless voice boomed out again. Extremely embarrassed, but fearful of yet further punishment, the heavily drugged group reluctantly stripped away every last scrap of clothing and blushing heavily, used their hands and arms to shield private parts while staring straight ahead, hoping that every other companion was doing the same. The handlers, void of any visible signs of emotion, collected every pile of clothing, and deposited it all through the opened rubbish chute door. With the task complete, the next procedure was a close inspection every inch of their captives' naked bodies, making note of any unusual skin defects or characteristics. Everything the prisoners owned was confiscated for incineration, including any personal items, jewellery, and removable body decorations of all kinds. Naked as a new born child, each group member was then taken one at a time through the far door and into the next room.

Similar in design to the first, this room contained a rather outdated full body medical scanner, but for what was required it proved fit for purpose.

"Climb onto there, lie flat on your back, and don't move until ordered to do so." John Turner's handler ordered briskly as he pointed to the ergonomically human shaped powered gurney designed to pass the patient slowly through the hollow core of the scanning equipment. Apart from diagnosing any major health problems, the primary use of the machine is to locate any foreign objects or medical implants that could identify the recipient pending an investigation. John trembled violently while trying to block out the rising claustrophobic panic and clamped his bloodshot eyes tightly closed as the gurney slid almost silently into the confines of the scanners' donut body.

"Prisoner must remain completely still." The handler ordered from within the confines of the glass walled control booth. John tried his best to stay calm, but the longer he remained inside listening to the rhythmic throb of the revolving scanner, the greater the panic set in.

"Remain completely still." The barked order was issued for a second time as the aged machine repeatedly failed to take an accurate scan. Suddenly it all became too much and John frantically attempted to squirm his way out. At that precise moment the test completed and John re-emerged into the brightly lit room. Before his guard had time to leave his booth, John rolled off the gurney onto the floor and made a dash for the exit, crashing through the door and into the next room.

"What the hell are you going to do to me?" John yelled in panic at the sight of what now appeared to be a fully equipped operating theatre. At the far end, yet another door gave hope for release and he burst into a full blown run, but his escape was short lived. The futile attempt lasted less than three seconds when he burst through into a corridor and his legs failed him. John's second shock of the day locked almost every muscle in his body and his naked skin slapped loudly onto the floor tiles. Unable to block any of the kicks and blows that followed, John desperately attempted to protect himself by curling up into a foetal position but it was of little use as his reluctant muscles trembled violently from the effects of the electrical charge. Roughly grabbing the stricken man by his hair, the handler yanked John to his feet, manhandled him back into the theatre, and forced him onto the operating table. Blinded by the brightness of the circular overhead light John gritted his teeth and turned his head away as he braced for whatever lay ahead.

"Hold out your left arm." His technician ordered gruffly. John looked back and tentatively offered out his hand, wondering what torture was to follow, only to find his arm being twisted around to expose the inside of his wrist that bore the tattoo of a snake climbing up his forearm. His panic quickly subsided as he watched his handler carefully paint the tattoo with an ultra violet pen and while it dried, a small incubator sized Perspex container with a circular aperture in the side was wheeled over to his side. Under instruction, John inserted his hand through the hole until it reached his elbow and then watched it clamp air tight onto his skin. With everything secure, the technician inserted a small canister into the top of the machine then switched it on. John watched as the box filled with a fine violet anaesthetic mist, soaking into his exposed skin and completely numbing his arm within the box. With the first process complete, the canister was replaced with another containing an acidic substance that only reacted to the solution applied to the tattoo. John was terrified, but surprised at the lack of pain as his skin bubbled and blistered dissolving the image completely into a glue-like stain. A third and final canister was inserted and artificial skin particles rained down onto the exposed arm, bonding only with the sticky portion of John's forearm, obliterating the wound without a trace. Within five minutes, the process had dried and John was allowed to his feet before being ushered into a small telephone box sized booth to be given a complete all-over body colour mapping similar to a cosmetic spray tan. With legs apart and arms held aloft, John followed orders to stand for five minutes under heat lamps and feel the blast of a huge overhead fan circulating the warm air to dry his skin. The end result was perfect uniform tone identical to that of the android units that the prisoners were all being prepared to replace. With bodily examination complete, modesty was eventually reinstated with the provision of basic cotton underwear, slip-on training shoes, a set of grey flannel baggy trousers, and matching smock top.

When everyone in the group had received their own treatment, they were reunited and led away down another long corridor, leading to an area the size of a basketball court. Around its perimeter were several key-card operated sliding steel doors fronting eight-person prison cells converted from army billets. Each room was a basic square design, with automated lighting supplied via the latest light emitting ceiling paint that glowed when connected to an electrical source. Inside each cell the grey painted walls contained four sets of angled-steel and wire-sprung two tier bunk beds, each furnished with a thin foam mattress, one single duvet, and a pillow. A swing door to the rear of the room led into a separate smaller washroom facility with two hand basins, single shower, and lavatory. Soap, towels, and teeth cleaning equipment were provided, but nothing else. As the last one of the group entered the room the steel door slid silently home and a high pitched beep signalled that it was securely locked.

Exhausted and starving from the events of the day, everyone instinctively chose a bed and within minutes they were all asleep. The only member not to travel with the group was Jacob who had shattered his leg five years ago playing rugby and had had it repaired using new liquid bone that was poured into a preformed cast sited around his damaged fibula. This wonder liquid bonded seamlessly to any osseous tissue, adopting the properties and function of the original. When fully set it was actually stronger than the bone it replaced. The added bonus was that it mimicked the genetic characteristics of the skeletal structure to which it was attached, replicating it to such a degree that it grew like real bone when placed into a growing child. The problem for Jacob was that every bone operated upon legally had to carry a digital reference tag that provided the name of the manufacturer and held all the patients' information necessary should they require medical assistance. This tag had to be removed or Jacob could be easily identified, so he was immediately prepped for surgery.

Three hours later he arrived at the cell, still unconscious and strapped to a gurney. His arrival woke everyone up and as some wearily got to their feet, they watched as the straps holding him down were unfastened and he was unceremoniously rolled off onto an empty lower bunk. His two orderlies turned away and pushed the empty gurney back out into the corridor without saying a word. The cell door once again slid silently closed and for the first time in days the gang were together and properly alone. Following the operation, Jacob had been dressed like the others and his baggy trouser leg had been pulled up to his knee exposing a white bandage on his lower right shin. Slowly the young man's eyes opened and he began to moan. Kristy kneeled at his side, placed a hand on his forehead to assess his temperature, and then checked the rapidity of his pulse. Neither seemed unduly worrisome, so she assumed it must be the effects of the anaesthetic wearing off. At a loss of anything else to do, the group returned to their beds.

Early the next morning Adam was the first to wake and apart from a sensation of sunburn to his shoulder where yesterday he had had a port wine stain removed, he was relieved to find that the cocktail of drugs had finally cleared his system, allowing clarity of thought to resume. Food was now high on his list and in an effort to ignore severe hunger pangs in his belly Adam set his brilliant mind to work assessing the dire situation. First, he meticulously surveyed his new surroundings, looking for video observation equipment. The task did not take very long and he soon established the positions of five micro cameras in total. Four in the main living quarters positioned facing downward from the top corners of the cell, and one in the ceiling of the bathroom, although mercifully angled away from the toilet. All the cameras had multi-directional microphones attached and each camera lens was positioned behind a clear toughened Perspex bubble to protect it from damage. It seemed like there was no place to hide or fail to be heard. Hoping not to be punished for the spreading of his findings, Adam informed the rest of the group, minus Jacob, (who was still asleep!) where all the cameras were positioned and braced himself for the inevitable shock, but luckily nothing came and with a sigh of relief he began to talk. As long as their chatter was regarded as inane or trivial they were all allowed to converse. But as soon as observers recognised talk regarding escape or details of the last few days, an observer triggered a shock to the guilty person's collar.

After breakfast, consisting of porridge and a glass of water collected by Kristy via a hatch in the bottom of the cell door, orders were issued on the tannoy for all to take a hot shower and wash away any residue from yesterday's spray tan.

"I think that we are being kept in good condition so we fetch a good price at auction." John stage whispered while Neil took his shower and he made use of one of a collection of rechargeable shavers left for purpose. Neil nodded his agreement and mused how long they would all be held prisoner before the sale began.

"There might be a monthly auction like a cattle market." He replied darkly, trying to ignore the tightening knot in his stomach at the thought, but bravely tried to show little fear.

* * *

As the days passed, they quickly found out that the running shower head or similar sound drowned out a person's voice, and provided you turned your back to the camera, whoever manned the observation room could not listen clearly to anything said. This happened accidentally when Amy forgot the rules and spoke of escape to Kristy as she rinsed her hair. Realising the subject of her comments, she braced herself for the inevitable punishment but nothing happened. Whispered word soon spread and a secret way of communication began.

Being underground, distinguishing the hour of the day was virtually impossible and the only way anyone could mark the passage of time was the regular arrival of meals, something that if the rules were obeyed were remarkably good. This regular feeding pattern and the overhead lights being turned off at the same time every day helped maintain the synchronicity of a prisoner's body clock. Apart from the issue of regular sustenance, everyone was supplied with a tracksuit and allowed out of the cell every day for two hours of vigorous exercise in a basically equipped gymnasium. Again a faceless voice issued the orders and this format was to copy a cartoon figure displayed on a video screen performing a yoga warm up followed by high-impact aerobic workout. Attendance was compulsory for all able bodied prisoners, that for the moment excluded Jacob, who was still convalescing from his operation. This was the only time the small group had the chance to see any of the other inmates who they guessed lived behind the other doors on their level. During the exercise routine, Adam painfully found out that there was to be no chatter between groups when he passed comment on how alike everyone looked to the young woman standing next to him. This punishment also resulted in the whole group receiving shock treatment, adding an extra incentive to remain mute.

During the next few weeks, a curious regimen introduced to the group was an individual mental agility test that began with the basic pre-school level of sorting coloured plastic shapes into a preformed grid. Success within a predetermined time frame moved the test subject incrementally upwards to more difficult tasks until three failures on one level concluded that the prisoner could progress no further. As university graduates, including Kristy who had a degree in marine biology; they all moved swiftly up the rankings to a high level. The exception was Adam who with his genius level IQ succeeded in easily completing every task put his way. This gave him great cause to wonder why on earth his captors were doing this and what was to come next.

CHAPTER EIGHT

Philip Sanderson was finding some difficulty in the simple job out of driving a four man buggy up an access ramp and out into the open countryside. His intention was to give his latest clients a live demonstration of a fantasy set recently completed for yet another very wealthy customer. It had been a few weeks without Philip needing his help, but to Ted's annoyance; his presence had been required yet again. This latest couple were Paul Johnston, twice world footballer of the year who was infamous for his string of affairs with models and actresses that brought an end to his first marriage, also his alleged connections with South American drug cartels. Accompanying him was his second wife Astelle, a world famous catwalk model. This was a not too surprising choice for Paul, as her beautiful features have been lauded with the title *'Face of the millennium'*. Together they have been rated as the richest celebrity couple in the world.

Ted sat at the back on the bench seat with Astelle, who was sitting uncomfortably close, gripping tightly to his arm as the vehicle bounced over the rough ground. For the last two and a half hours, Philip and Ted had endured the tedium of giving the couple a guided tour. The major part of which, included a visit to Stan's control room, where Astelle wandered around the facility flirting openly with several male computer terminal operators and then with Stan himself, who behaved like a love sick teenager in her presence.

From there, it was on to the animation department, where an opportunity arose to show how the facility maps an exact three-dimensional duplicate of a client's face and physique so it could be reproduced in minute detail. This was standard procedure if the scene to be filmed is deemed too dangerous for the actor and required an animatronic body-double. Astelle was only too willing to be the volunteer and held no qualms at stripping off down to a very revealing set of cream silk underwear that covered very little of her slender figure. It was obvious that someone whose semi-naked body had adorned billboards and graced fashion magazines across the globe, how they must be very proud of their form to display it in such a way

"I can take everything off if you want me to." Astelle purred to the programmers, but as she spoke it was clear that she was looking directly at Ted, who blushed as he caught her gaze and realised that she was not kidding. Looking down, he suddenly found his fingernails very interesting. Astelle revelled at his reaction and giggled coquettishly in front of the eager crew as she pouted and posed while waiting for the digital mapping program to load. In contrast, Paul seemed oblivious that his wife was willing to reveal nearly all to a handful of very excitable engineers; he was more interested in the technical side of the enterprise and continued to ask Philip an endless stream of inane questions driving his famously short patience to the very limit. Ted managed to interject as often as was humanly possible, but maintaining Astelle's unwelcome attention was currently his full time job.

It was soon common knowledge across the complex regarding the world famous arrival, and as usual in such matters, a reminder had been issued to all staff to maintain a polite distance from clients. But in this case, Paul and Astelle's worldwide popularity was irresistible. Wherever on the globe they happened to be, crowds appeared, with an endless stream of people taking video images or asking for photographs with their idols. With some relief, Ted could now distance himself from the couple while they greeted their fans. For such an egotistical couple he watched with increasing approval how they treated every single fan with the same level of grace and courtesy from both partners, no matter how bizarre their request.

Finally free from their adoring public, they stood side by side, out in the field, waiting patiently while Ted relayed instructions to Stan in the control booth to get the demonstration underway. Within seconds, six-hundred acres of apparent barren landscape miraculously turned a verdant green, thanks to several hundred thousand mats of tiny fibre optics buried just under the surface of the earth. Using a technique to criss-cross the projection tens of millions of times over, ultra-realistic images of grass and mosses appeared to cover the soil's surface. It was now even possible to feel the sensation of whatever was projected underfoot via electronic pulses confusing receptors in the skin into sending signals to the brain, corresponding with the projected image observed by the visual cortex. This electronic dermal stimuli woven into soil-coated, fibrous mesh, laid down at the same time as the projectors, induced a safe, minute electrical charge absorbed through the skin on the soles of the feet, or any other part the body that comes into contact with the earth. The current even passed through shoe leather or thick clothing. This combination of the two sets of visual and dermal stimuli convinced the recipient that they were actually walking along a hot sandy beach, crumping fresh snow underfoot, or maybe wading through near freezing water.

Far away into the distance, a huge snow topped mountain range rose up majestically from the earth, framing the incredible scene, while in the middle and foreground, the outlines of giant cycads, conifers, trees, and flowering angiosperms began as a basic outline shape, then rapidly filled with colour, shade, and texture. Hovering high in the air above, a halo formation of camouflaged drones added their part to the illusion by turning the sky from the dirty grey world of today into an unpolluted clear pale blue, last seen hundreds of millions of years ago. Utilising the current prevailing westerly breeze, the imitation flora and fauna wafted to and fro, matching the wind speed in perfect symmetry. This remarkable effect, accentuated even more authenticity as shadows fell across the ground in relation to the fiery orange sun.

Not every drone flying high above was employed to produce visual images, some housed low-frequency microwave emitters trained directly upon the humans below. The water molecules held under the skin were easily excited by the low grade radiation, causing heat, which in turn warmed the body. This, coupled with the skin stimulators buried in the ground, confused the brain into thinking that it was the real sun and not just a projection generating the heat. This type of microwave technology had been invented in the last century, but it took nearly eighty years before it could be proved beyond all reasonable doubt that it was safe. Now it was commonplace worldwide, and even in outer space, controlling body temperature without the need to heat entire buildings, putting an end to global warming.

With this idyll almost complete, the finishing touches were added, as flocks of tiny birds took to the air, flashing the fake sunlight from iridescent plumage as they swooped and soared high into the sky. The sight of this type of avian creature was historically incorrect for the ancient time period, but it was a special request from the client and whoever is paying the bill gets exactly what they desire. The requested list included butterflies as big as dustbin lids, flapping lazily in the heat as they nestled in the trees and on top of scented flowering shrubs. This sweet aroma mixed with the faint odour of hot sulphur thrown skywards from a distant volcano and carried towards the group on the steady breeze.

Stan sat upright at the main control desk working his magic like a virtuoso. Surveying everything with an experienced eye and making subtle changes that to the untrained eye went completely unnoticed. Out in the field, his combination of tweaks and adjustments produced an environment that was virtually perfect. With everything running smoothly, Stan stared at his monitor, waiting patiently for the subtle thumbs up from Ted to initiate the next phase. On cue, after a quick prompting by Ted to Astelle, Stan remotely controlled a beautiful song bird to flutter down from an Araucaria tree, circle the group, and then land on Astelle's outstretched hand. Philip as usual showed little emotion, but nodded his head appreciatively to Ted after he saw the joy and amazement on Astelle's face accompanied by the broad smile from Paul. He knew that once again, Ted and Stan had pulled it off; the deal was sealed.

Walking on through the Eden-like wilderness, Paul and Astelle held hands while marvelling at the realism of it all, even down to the scent of an exotic purple bloom that to Paul's amazement he was able to pick from a tree and place in Astelle's hair.

Everyone stopped to admire a narrow waterfall cascading hundreds of feet down a sheer cliff face, veiling everyone in a cooling mist as it plunged into an apparently bottomless pool of crystal-clear water, teaming with a myriad of brightly coloured fish darting in and out of the reeds. The tranquil scene was perfect for the next phase and Ted smiled as he was well aware what was about to happen.

With an embarrassing attempt at a hand flourish, Philip grandly announced, "And now it is time for the pièce de résistance." The initial confusion on Paul and Astelle's faces, quickly changed to one of horror, when on cue, a blood curdling roar resonated from the depths of the forest. This was precisely the response hoped for, but what Ted did not expect was Astelle's further reaction. Screaming loudly, she ran and sought comfort, but instead of seeking protection from Paul, Astelle grabbed Ted's arm, wrapping it tightly around the front of her slim body, and pressing his open palm flat against her left breast. Luckily Paul did not notice the flagrant display, as his own initial fear turned to excitement and he was already marching away with Philip, looking through the trees for the source of the incredible noise. Mortified at who might have seen the brief episode, especially Gemma, Ted snatched his trapped hand away, and without a backward glance strode purposely away to seek safety with the others. Furious with Ted's snub, Astelle dropped into a sulk and followed behind at a deliberately slow pace hoping to regain everyone's attention.

Stan allowed Paul time to continue with his search while he introduced brooding rain clouds from the western horizon. Passing them quickly across the image of the baking hot sun. This menacing contrast dulled the aspect, and with the addition of a chilling breeze whipping through the thick forest canopy, the resident birds also ceased their chatter. The eerie effect was perfect; hairs stood up on the back of Paul's neck and in the hush that followed, his pulse began to race. For nearly a minute all that could be heard was the thudding footsteps of something menacing circling their position, and then nothing. Stan lowered the temperature even further, while increasing the breeze from a whisper up to a strong bluster. The tree branches rocked wildly to and fro for nearly a minute until he killed the wind entirely. Pulses raced in anticipation of the event when suddenly the silence shattered, this time with a nerve jangling roar. It appeared much closer than before, then closer still as the creature bellowed yet again. Stan tinkered with even more controls, randomly varying the icy cold wind to swirl and gust, whipping up the dirt and dry forest undergrowth into a frantic dance within man-made dust devils. Darkening the thick clouds into a stormy grey, added just enough to heighten the tension. He then lowered the overall colour saturation and waited just a few moments more before implementing the main part. Even Ted's face looked fearful as the ground began to tremble to the thud of something very heavy heading their way.

"Jesus Christ." Paul gasped as he finally caught sight of a fully grown Tyrannosaurus Rex crashing through a dense thicket. Ignoring whatever lay in its way, tree branches snapped and fell, sending a confetti cloud of flora cascading to the forest floor. Suddenly, the creature turned and headed directly for the small group. Even Ted found it hard not to run from the blood chilling sight of the giant carnivorous lizard, and he gasped as the creature stopped, looked up, and then roared again, this time at a low flying Pterodactyl circling lazily overhead. The fright continued as the Tyrannosaurus turned frantically around, whipping its thick, leathery tail to within inches of the small group as it snapped its jaw hopelessly towards his airborne tormentor. This allowed everyone on the ground time to see inside its massive open mouth, revealing more than sixty slightly conical razor sharp incisors, some nearly as long as a man's hand. All of the teeth were arranged on opposing ranks around the upper and lower jaw and suitably ordered together as to interlock and tear away huge chunks of flesh as the powerful lower mandible snapped shut.

Supporting the body upright as it angrily spun around while looking at the sky, were a pair of massive grey, scaly-skinned rear legs as thick as tree trunks pounding its three toed feet into the earth. This threw clouds of dust into the air, some of which adhered to its leathery hide, still wet with blood from its last kill. Eventually the Pterodactyl glided away from view and the massive lizard dropped its gaze, fixing the quartet of humans in its sights. Pausing as it's limited brain decided what action to take, the giant lizard snorted heavily, blowing mucus from huge nostrils, then lunged forwards, dropping its head down low, to bellow directly at the group. With a roar as loud as a jet engine, combined with a blast of hot exhaled breath, this carried the stench of rotting flesh to the small group. The horrific display intensified even more by the sight of blood stained drool oozing out from between its teeth, whipped up into long sticky strands as it thrashed its head side to side in front of the stunned crowd. Even Philip seemed impressed at the attention to detail and made a mental note to congratulate the animation department for such a realistic creation.

Paul stood rooted to the spot, completely mesmerised by the incredible sight, but unfortunately his enthusiasm was not matched by Astelle, who, slightly adrift from the group was nearest to the great beast. Her brash, confident image paled as she stared, wide-eyed and transfixed in terror, shaking visibly as tears rolled down her immaculately made-up face.

"I don't like this I want to go home." Astelle cried to Paul, who seeing his wife's distress immediately ran to her aid, hugging her tight.

"It's not real baby, it's only an illusion." He whispered soothingly during a brief silence, hoping to ease her distress. If Astelle heard anything Paul said she did not show it and screamed in terror as the giant lizard closed in. Paul lost all his fascination for the show and turned angrily towards Philip.

"Turn this damned thing off right now!" He bellowed, trying to make himself heard over the continuing din. Philip paid little attention to the demand as he was still marvelling at the quality of the creation, only increasing Paul's anger.

"Are you listening to me, I said NOW!"

Ted immediately took charge, responding by slicing the flat of his hand across his throat, hoping Stan would cut the frightening display. Well aware of the situation and always one step ahead of the game, Stan decided not to follow the order directly. Instead, he adjusted the parameters of the projection along with the volume of the roar. Back in the field, the small group stood and watched with fascination how the deafening bellow softened in relative to the lizard's size, as it shrank rapidly before their eyes until it became similar in stature to that of a large cat; with a matching growl. Astelle's tears quickly ceased and she even managed to laugh at the new miniature version of the Tyrant lizard as it stumbled clumsily through the long grass. Thanks to Stan, the multimillion-dollar deal was back on track and as the incredible projections powered down, the quartet wandered back across the now featureless landscape. Luckily for Ted, Astelle was too excited about the project and paid him scant attention, as the celebrity couple exchanged ideas about the fantasy they wished to create.

"I want to be Helen of Troy, the most beautiful woman in the world, and you can be Menelaus, the man who launched a thousand ships to come to my rescue." Astelle cooed excitedly, although her enthusiasm was not shared by her husband. Happy to indulge his wife, he listened to her ideas, but his fantasy leaned more towards saving the earth from alien invasion.

Their exuberance kept Astelle and Paul talking all the way to the main atrium, giving Philip welcome relief from Paul's questions, and giving Ted time to plan the perfect opportunity to put some distance between him and this outrageous woman. As the buggy slowed to a halt, Ted Jumped straight out of the vehicle, using the excuse that he had a lot of evening work to complete, but Philip would have none of it.

"Cancel your plans for tonight. Paul and Astelle have expressed an interest to see the social side of my little enterprise so I have told them that you will take them to dinner at the Blue Fairy."

Ted scowled angrily at Philip and had to resist the urge to wipe the smug smile off his smooth face, when Philip added,

"Also, it will have to be without me I'm afraid, as I have a prior engagement that cannot be cancelled. That shouldn't be a problem for someone like you Ted should it?"

Ted knew that Philip had put him in an impossible position, and through gritted teeth he politely accepted. To regain some pride, Ted managed to drop his own bombshell.

"In that case I am going to have to bid my excuses right now to give me chance to rearrange my diary and to organise a table for tonight. I'm sure you will be able to continue the tour without me Philip, won't you?"

The horror on Philip's face was just reward for Ted's annoyance. Nodding his goodbyes to the clients while trying to hide a grin spreading across his handsome face, it took all his willpower not to break into a run as he walked hurriedly away.

CHAPTER NINE

Mentally fatigued from the effort of entertaining his latest clients, Philip Sanderson sat down behind his desk when the ring of a telephone shattered his solace. The sound apparently originated from under the desk's reflective upper surface. Cursing under his breath, he sat up and verbally accepted the considered rude interference.

"Receive call, Philip Sanderson speaking." He spoke loudly to the empty room. Immediately an eighteen inch high holographic image of a young man wearing a white boiler suit rose up from the apparently clear glass desktop. The representation was so visually perfect it looked just like a miniature person actually stood on top of the shiny work surface, akin to an illusion from a Vegas magic show.

"Sorry to disturb you, Mr Sanderson sir, but I have some information that you insisted to be delivered immediately the situation arose."

The employee trembled visibly as he spoke then stood silently waiting for his employer to reply.

"Well, spit it out man!" Philip snapped loudly. The poor man gasped and his mind went completely blank as to the reason for his intrusion. Frantically scanning his touch screen clipboard he silently prayed that something would jog his memory and produce an answer.

Irritated by the employee's incompetency Philip started drumming his fingers on his desk, causing the image to judder. Eventually someone off-screen came to the man's aid and passed over a hand written note; with relief in his voice he hastily read it out.

"I have a report from the facility that one of the inmates has beaten the highest ever level of the mental aptitude test and he also recorded several wins against your personalised computer chess program."

The terrified employee suddenly had Philip's complete attention and he demanded to know which terminal the subject was working on. With all the given information,

Philip ended the transmission without another word. He double tapped the left hand front corner of the desk and immediately the image of a computer keyboard appeared in the glass. After typing in the access code, another holographic image of a computer screen rose into view. Philip raised his left hand, waving it over the table to activate the built-in tracking system, replicating his movement with a small arrowhead pointer gliding across the display. Highlighting a file in the top left corner, Philip clicked his fingers and the file opened. Once inside the program he logged onto the surveillance cameras built into every computer terminal within the facility and instantly recognised the image of Adam Cartwright, the world's youngest ever chess Grandmaster.

For over an hour Philip sat back in his chair and watched Adam's incredible skill. His oblique perception and tactical nous for the game had only last year turned the traditional chess world upside down.

For Adam, this latest examination posed only a moderate problem as he had held a passion for the game for most of his life. Having the incredible memory skills of a savant, without the autistic characteristics that usually accompany this gift, Adam was able to mentally compute every game variation possible, giving him the advantage over other grandmasters with a lifetime of experience. He could instantly recognise the operational parameters of the computer program being used and always managed to keep one step ahead to win the game. Within another hour, Adam had recorded his fifth straight win and sat waiting patiently for the next game, but Philip could not resist temptation and changed the settings, placing himself as the new opposition.

Unable to identify the sudden change of algorithms currently applied, several trains of thought began to cross Adam's mind. The first was that the program could be trying a random thought modification mode to make it appear more lifelike, or that he was actually playing another person of equal ability and intellect. Several drawn and well analysed games later, Adam came to the decision that the opposition technique offered too many subtle variables for a computer program. Utilising his encyclopedic knowledge of the game and a mental list of all the world's current grandmasters able to match his ability, he began to analyse who on earth could be connected to the horror of his Orwellian nightmare.

CHAPTER TEN

Clouds of water vapour billowed out from inside the hot shower cubicle and rolled across the ceiling as Ted Langton clicked open the glass door and carefully stepped out into his well-appointed bathroom. The multiple jets of water that he had programmed to maximum pressure, aimed at massaging the kinks out of his tired and stressed muscles, ceased immediately the door opened and an extractor fan automatically engaged to clear the steam from the room. Normally the extractor would have activated as soon as the water began to flow, but Ted had altered the settings, as he liked plenty of steam while taking a shower. Crossing the heated tile floor, he ignored the warm air, drying fans, opting to dry naturally. With a soft white towel wrapped around his waist, he stopped in front of the sink, reached out his hand to wipe away the condensation fogging up the mirror sited on the wall behind and leaned slightly forward from the waist to study his watery reflection revealed within.

Critically surveying his chiselled features he noticed the dark shadows dulling the skin under his tired eyes adding greater longing that he was well overdue for a holiday. The problem was the long list of mega-rich clientele never seemed to reduce, and for the incredible amount of money paid to the corporation they demanded the best, so the chance for break seemed a long way away. Sighing audibly, he surveyed the amount of grey hair peppering the dark brown locks. Dipping his chin, Ted traced his fingers either side of his greying widow's peak that over the last six months looked more pronounced, due to his receding hairline.

Prodding and pulling at random parts of his body and checking for more signs of aging, he remained completely oblivious as the front door of his apartment slid silently open and a solitary figure stepped in. Stealthily the intruder crept down the hallway into the living room of his luxury accommodation at the far end of highway twelve, the exclusive part of this subterranean city. The humming of the extractor fan masked the sound of footsteps as his uninvited guest wandered around examining Ted's collection of vintage sporting memorabilia. The room also included a collection of antique military swords, displayed mainly in down-lit glass cabinets.

Lifting a razor sharp Japanese Katana from its holder on the wall, the interloper grasped the handle with both hands and gracefully pirouetted around the furniture while slashing the blade through the air in a short series of very professional co-ordinated manoeuvres. The only witness to this impressive display was a huge tank of tropical fish swimming happily in a huge five foot wide hollow transparent cylinder that reached from the floor to the ceiling, dominating the décor in the centre of the living room. Bored with the exercise, the trespasser carefully returned the priceless antique to its holder and looked around for something else to play with. Finding nothing of interest she finally closed in on Ted, who was still giving his features a critical review. Smiling to herself, she could not believe that still Ted had no idea that anyone was there.

"Don't worry about that, it gives you an air of authority." Gemma Cassidy finally mocked in a deep voice as she leaned her left shoulder against the bathroom door frame.

"What the hell," Ted yelled as he swung violently around to confront the intruder, Ted's towel immediately came undone and as it unwrapped from around his lean torso, he just managed to grab one end and hold it against his groin while the remainder of the damp material hung limply between his legs. Gemma opened her mouth and eyes wide in surprise, and then she collapsed in a fit of giggles at the sight.

"I, I only came for a visit; you didn't have to put on a floor show!" She gasped, trying to talk between fits of laughter and theatrically wiping away a tear that rolled down her cheek. Ted's face and neck turned purple in a mixture of embarrassment and anger at how easily someone could invade his privacy. Hurriedly re-wrapping the towel around his waist, he stormed out of the bathroom, marching straight passed Gemma only for her to make a grab and successfully relieve him of his only vestige of clothing. The lasting image Gemma had of Ted was the sight of his very white backside as he ran into the bedroom and slammed the door.

"Come on out Ted, how many times do I have to say that I'm sorry. It was only a bit of fun."

Gemma tapped repeatedly against the locked door, then leaned back against it and slid down onto her haunches while she waited for an answer. Ten long minutes had passed until the door finally unlocked and as Gemma hurriedly jumped to her feet Ted stepped out fully dressed in his best black suit, white shirt, and tie.

"Are you still taking me to the Blue Fairy?" Gemma asked coyly as he retrieved his shoes from a small wall closet and sat on the sofa to put them on.

"I'm not taking you anywhere. If you had checked your messages, you would have seen that I now have to entertain Paul Johnston and his wife Astelle."

"You're ditching me for some overrated footballer and that skinny tramp. It's all over the base how she flashes everything she's got, and flirts with anything in trousers. Not to mention the clip of you grabbing her breast in full view of everyone. That is if you can call it that; it looks more like a fried egg than anything else. Even so, you left it there a little too long for my liking. There's no way I'm going to leave you in touching distance of that little slut, I'm coming too!"

Ted opened his mouth ready to explain, but realised that Gemma had obviously seen the footage and was waiting for the right time to reveal the fact. Ted knew that what happened was nothing like she said, so he used it to lure her directly into his trap. Knowing that if he had invited Gemma directly, he was positive she would object, not wanting to appear as Ted's plaything. By telling her she was not invited he knew she would be unable to resist. His intention was for Gemma's presence to keep Astelle's advances at bay and make the odious task pass quickly.

"You can come along only if you promise to behave yourself." Ted ordered as he looked sternly into Gemma's face. Raising her eyebrows, she thought for a second, and while crossing her fingers behind her back, she nodded silently before blowing Ted a kiss and making a run back down the hallway.

"Where are you going now? I'm already late as it is." He shouted as she reached the front door.

"I've got to get myself ready; you don't expect me to go looking like this do you? I'll see you there."

That was her last word as she darted through the now open door. Ted shook his head as he gathered up his things and followed Gemma's sweet perfume scent as he walked from his apartment.

The Blue Fairy bar and restaurant based in the centre of the recreational zone was the most popular place in the facility even though it was also the most expensive. If you wanted to impress a date or ingratiate yourself with your work colleagues this was the place to go. Titled after the mystical fairy who grants children's wishes, this was a particularly apt name where for the right price any dream could be made into reality.

Ted had reserved a table for four, hidden as far away from the public gaze as possible in hope for a quiet night, but it seemed too much to ask for, as the entire promenade quickly filled up when word spread about the arrival of the world famous guests. The concourse was full of fans and onlookers all holding up the latest cameras and video recorders that consisted of a micro-thin lens and recording device embedded in the palm of a glove. The information recorded relayed directly to a clear credit sized card display and storage device that could be easily viewed in the opposite hand. This concept was the latest alternative to the previously very popular, but now illegal sight of miniaturised drones providing a video feed to a paired personal recorder and remote controller. The invention was originally a military surveillance device that found its way via professional filmmakers into the public domain. The concept was soon branded a hazard due to the sheer volume of numbers filling the skies like swarms of insects blocking views at public events. Following numerous high profile court cases, they were declared an immoral disregard for public decency. The tipping point occurred soon after topless images of the American President appeared on the web. Almost overnight the product disappeared from shelves, leaving eager fans reduced to standing with their hands aloft and trained towards their chosen celebrity like an over eager school child trying to attract their teacher's attention.

Ted smiled briefly at the bizarre sight until he spotted the eagerly awaited linear transport shuttle slow to a halt allowing Paul and Astelle to get out. The reaction that followed was incredible as people cheered the arrival, surging forwards to get closer to their idols, only to be held back by security guards acting as a living barrier to the celebrity couple. For Paul and Astelle this was a daily occurrence, they fell quickly into a familiar routine, posing graciously for photographs with fans and autographing all matter of merchandise as they slowly inched their way along the atrium towards the restaurant's ornately decorated entrance.

Looking intently through the rapidly swelling crowd, Ted began to worry if Gemma had changed her mind, as she was still nowhere to be seen. Standing to one side of the doorway and dressed in his best black suit, looking very much like a security guard instead of a dinner guest, he shifted more body weight onto his right leg to ease the pain he suffered constantly with his left.

The origin of his distress was caused several years ago at university, when he saved Philip from being mugged outside a student bar. Before the incident, Ted had looked forward to a promising career in association football, but a bullet from the assailant's gun shattered his kneecap ending his career before it began. Even using the latest medical technology on the planet, surgeons were unable to facilitate a suitable repair, leaving Ted with a limited running gait. In gratitude for his heroism Philip promised to take care of his new and only friend; this was not an empty gesture even though Philip already employed several other computer literate students in the genesis of the Hologram Dreams Corporation.

Not being technically adroit regarding computer programming as his student contemporaries, Ted utilised his natural charm and winning ways to organise finance and also to persuade the right people to join the company. Over time, Ted's vivid imagination and keen eye for detail saw him move into the production side of proceedings where he now resided at the top of the tree, second only to Philip. Ted's knee joint had been replaced several times with the latest liquid bone, but the outcome still remained the same leaving him with a persistent nagging ache that had plagued him for nearly fifteen years. One thing Ted had noticed during this time was that he could use the intensity of the pain as a barometer to measure his levels of stress and tonight the volume was increasing rapidly, warning him of a very tense night ahead.

To kill time, he peered into the nearly full to capacity restaurant to see the theme for tonight and was impressed at the quality and detail of the holographic production that had metamorphosed the entire room into a medieval banqueting hall. Cold grey flagstone replaced the white tiled floor and heavy embroidery tapestries hung from lime-washed walls akin to a thousand year old European castle. High overhead, hand sawn oak support beams, blackened with soot, cast eerie shadows from the flickering illumination of two-hundred tallow candles perched like roosting birds around a wooden three-tier chandelier swinging gently to and fro on a chain attached to the vaulted ceiling. The pass into the open kitchen was now a huge roaring fireplace full of crackling logs, and even had the addition of two Irish wolfhound hunting dogs eagerly gnawing away at cast off bones as they lay in front of the fire. To complete the illusion, the high-tech metal tables and chairs had been covered in fake fur pelts and rough jute cloth. To the right-hand side of the restaurant there was a small stage adjoining the dance floor, upon which a small robotic group of musicians dressed in period costume mimed to a mixture of Renaissance and early baroque compositions on lutes, bladder pipes, and fife. Even the Perspex holographic projection screens laminated into every dining table top had new backgrounds that looked like heavily grained wood. To complete the façade, every member of staff wore clothing customary to the period. The only exception to this incredible illusion was the restaurant manager. He flatly refused to wear any of the costumes provided and insisted on adhering to his traditional black suit and tie.

"I am a professional and I need to be identifiable at a glance to all employees, therefore I refuse to dress up like a performing monkey for people to gawp at!"

Was his plea to Philip, who surprisingly relented, sending speculation across all facility staff as to how he could possibly manage to change Philip's mind, a mystery that had still to be solved. The irony to the refusal was that in almost every situation he rarely blended into the restaurant's ever changing environment, bringing him even more attention than before.

Every week with the aid of the latest technology on the planet, a new theme was introduced, ranging from the stone-age right through to futuristic space settings and every manner of fantasy in-between. Requested ideas for special events were often accepted as this often went some way towards fulfilling the dreams most members of staff held but often were completely unable to afford.

Three-quarters of an hour had passed and there was still no sign of Gemma, making Ted even more anxious and his knee throbbed like never before. Paul and Astelle had finally smiled and signed their way through all of their fans to reach Ted's side and relieved at the chance to sit down, he summoned the maître d' to escort everyone to their table. Unfortunately, this also took a further ten minutes before Ted could rest his aching leg as everyone inside wanted to meet their celebrity diners. Finally the waiter offered Astelle a chair on the opposite side to Ted's but she quickly refused and tried to take a seat by his side when Gemma appeared from nowhere and sat hastily down in the chosen seat.

"Hi Ted, sorry I'm late."

Gemma flashed a smug and satisfied smile at Astelle as she spoke, launching Paul into action as he saw the scowl on his wife's face and he hurriedly pulled out a chair on Ted's opposite side, hoping to sit her down quickly before she could explode with one of her well documented temper tantrums. The men hastily sat down and a frosty silence ensued until the head waiter wheeled over a chilled bottle of the finest champagne.

"Mr Sanderson is extremely sorry for not being with you tonight and as way of an apology, he offers you the chance to sample a rare Dom Pérignon Oenothèque 1966. This is one of three bottles left in the whole world and he hopes you will enjoy its remarkable bouquet. Paul nodded his acceptance while Ted thanked the waiter and waved him away, hoping for a little privacy while he took command of the bottle. Holding the cork tightly in his right hand, he popped it with the minimum of fuss and poured everyone a drink. In his fluster Ted failed to introduce Gemma and instead proposed a toast, hoping to break the ice. Glasses clinked and as Paul and Astelle savoured the rare vintage they browsed floating images of starters displayed in holographic form on their side of the table, Ted leaned in close and managed a brief exchange of words with Gemma as he pretended to kiss her cheek.

"I don't know what you were playing at back then, but whatever it is I want you to stop it *now*!" He hissed in her ear, Gemma remained tight lipped and smiled coyly, choosing silently to ignore the instruction as she began to fidget about in her seat. To Ted's amazement Gemma proceeded to remove her pure white silk shawl draped around her shoulders and place it neatly upon her lap. The reaction around the table was stunned silence, when Gemma revealed a very low cut strapless dress displaying a more than ample amount of décolletage on her shapely frame. This marked a stark contrast to the flat-chested, pencil thin figure of Astelle who sat opposite. Conscious of her intent Astelle glared menacingly at Gemma, who matched her narrow eyed stare. Paul's wide-eyed reaction to Gemma's flagrant display did nothing to ease the situation and he received a swift kick in the ankle under the table from Astelle as he stared lasciviously at Gemma's breasts. Ted looked skywards wishing that he was anywhere else but here right now, and pondered the ramifications of setting off the fire alarm.

Slightly easing the tension of the situation, the waiter approached to take the first order, giving Ted an opportunity to break the silence and introduce a topic for conversation. By now even Paul sensed the female hostility and responded quickly to Ted's questions while both women glared one another down.

Suddenly Astelle changed her tack and opened with her first salvo.

"I don't think we have been properly introduced my dear, my name is Astelle and this is my husband Paul, I'm guessing you must be Ted's mother."

Both men halted their conversation and stared first at Astelle, and then over to Gemma as they anticipated the reaction. Luckily Gemma laughed it off, as she stood up and leaned over the table to offer her hand to Paul offering an even closer view of her gravity deifying cleavage, and then sat down slowly, giving her a few extra seconds of thinking time before retaliating with equal venom.

"I'm afraid you are mistaken Asterix; if that's your real name. Perhaps your eyes are failing, which to me is quite a surprise, considering how many carrots you must eat. But I do know all about you and your reputation. My name is Gemma by the way and I am Ted's friend and lover."

Gemma overtly reached her hand across and squeezed the upper part of Ted's thigh as she spoke, causing him to choke on his bread stick as he listened and openly cringed at the reply. In the embarrassing pause that followed, he cleared his throat with a sip of water and glared hard at Gemma but it had little effect. Paul, on the other-hand was actually enjoying the verbal cat fight and settled back in his chair to watch the show. He had been in this situation on many occasions and looking back at his wife, he could see the familiar patterned relief of veins standing out on the back of her skinny hands, as she tightly gripped the armrests of her chair and conjured up her own acidic retort.

"So sorry dearie, my mistake, it's just women of your ample proportions always look a lot older, don't you think so?"

Gemma's face flushed, but she still remained calm and even managed a smile.

"I've always had a healthy appetite Astrid, as you well know the bigger size you are, the better you are in bed. Isn't that so Ted?"

Ted pretended not to hear the remark and attempted to resume his discussion with Paul, who had no idea what Ted was talking about; he was more interested in listening to the conversation between their respective partners', and he waited avidly for Astelle's response.

"Tell me Gemma I'm a haute couture model, and to save you looking it up in a dictionary after the meal, I'll tell you now that it is French for high fashion. What is it that you do here exactly? I assume it involves the use of a dishcloth, mop, or broom; maybe a combination of all three?"

"Don't try and patronise me Stella, money doesn't by class and you drop your 'aitches same as everyone else at this table. But one thing's for sure and that my job is considerably more complicated than managing to place one foot in front of the other and not falling base over apex when trying to pout for a camera. I would have said arse over tit but it's obvious that you've got neither so it doesn't apply. I've seen more fat on a greasy chip!"

Astelle gasped at Gemma's insults, but she was ready, the simplicity of her occupation had been rubbed in her face for years and the return was swift.

"You know Gemma that it is always the jealous, coarse, overweight women of this world who have little understanding of beauty, poise, and grace attributed to the world of glamour, who always ask that type of question. So it comes with little surprise that you should ask me now."

"Each to their own Asti, but I'm sure Paul would prefer something more to get hold of in bed than just a bag of bones, He hasn't taken his eyes off my knockers since we sat down."

Astelle glared hard at Paul, who blushed and opened his mouth to protest but nothing came out. Looking back towards Gemma, who was thoroughly enjoying herself, Astelle played her trump card.

"That is a very pretty dress you're almost wearing there dearie, tell me are you paying for it weekly out of the catalogue or have you kept the receipt and intend to take it back to the department store tomorrow? They probably won't give you a refund when they see the sweat stains."

Gemma's eye twitched slightly as she glanced mischievously at Ted then eased out of her chair to reach for an appetiser. He guessed that it was a delaying tactic to think of another bitchy reply, but now it was her turn to change tack. Breathing in deeply to enhance her assets even further, (much to Paul's delight!), Gemma *'accidently'* knocked over a glass of champagne, spilling all of its contents down Astelle's front and puddling into her lap. Swearing loudly, Astelle jumped to her feet and pushed her chair with the back of her knees hard across the stone floor. If her loud profanity failed to alert most of the other diners in the restaurant, the teeth-jarring squeal of metal chair legs on the polished tile finished the deal, and the whole restaurant stopped to stare at her distress. From behind, it looked as if she had lost control of her bladder as the rare amber vintage poured from the hem of the silk designer dress, splashed over her high heeled feet and dripped onto the floor.

"Oops, silly me, it must be my coarse fat fingers!" Gemma exclaimed as she returned to her seat while theatrically holding up a hand in front of her mouth, making a poor attempt to hide a smile spreading across her face.

"You little bitch." Astelle hissed and angrily batted away Pauls hand as he tried to dab her dress with a napkin, succeeding only in plastering the wet material to her bony frame.

"Don't you mean big, sweaty bitch; that's a bit rich when I look at the state of you. I don't know what you're doing in a place like this, they don't serve cotton wool balls here you know. Perhaps you should try the pharmacy down the road, if you run you'll catch them before they close for the night."

Gemma replied as she smugly leaned back in her chair, ignoring the horrified look on Ted's face.

"We're leaving, *now!*" Astelle snapped at Paul as she turned and stormed away through the tables of stunned onlookers, only for her stiletto heels to loose grip on the wet floor, causing her to stumble into the lap of a fellow diner and treat everyone yet again with her fruity choice of words. Paul quickly jumped to his feet, threw the wet napkin onto the table, and mumbled an incoherent excuse before dashing off to catch up with his wife. Ignoring the looks from all the other diners as Astelle disappeared through the door, Gemma finally turned to talk to Ted who sat dumbstruck at the event.

"You needn't worry, I've already heard from a clerical friend of mine that Paul has already signed the contract, they can't back out now."

Ted closed his eyes tight to gather his thoughts, then finally made his reply.

"I hope for both our sakes you're right or we will be out of a job by morning. I think now is a good time to leave."

Gemma looked hurt at the idea and regaining some modesty by replacing her shawl she purposely settled back in her chair.

"I haven't spent the last two hours getting ready just for that! This is still a date and I expect you to buy me dinner, we're staying."

* * *

Having managed to avoid the meal, Philip was hoping for a relaxing time, but his evening became a much more cerebral affair than normal. Concentrating hard, his smooth brow furrowed only slightly as he struggled to maintain a grip with the ongoing chess battle against Adam

Cartwright. The honours had so far advanced evenly with both players winning several games each, but as the latest one progressed, it looked as if Adam had been testing his unknown opponent when the tactics turned considerably more aggressive and failed to follow any formal or documented classic approach. Adam had been biding his time and by using a raft of different manoeuvres, methodically whittling down his list of every possible opponent until he finally knew the one that he was sure fitted the bill. The only other viable option was that of another player at grandmaster level who was completely unknown to his world of chess. The logical solution was to stick with what he did know and after using a few more exploratory channels he was convinced it was fellow chess Grandmaster and billionaire Philip Sanderson. The next problem was to figure out how one of the world's richest men could possibly be involved in the slave trade.

As a well-known figure, it was common knowledge to anyone with an interest in Sanderson, that they also knew of his quirky personality, including his obsessive nature. Adam realised that the only way to keep him interested was to keep winning just enough to pique Philip's annoyance, making him continue and hope to succeed. Philip knew that Adam was getting the upper hand of a very difficult game, when he received a report of an incident regarding Paul Johnston, Astelle and one of his employees. Using this as an excuse to abort the game he was probably going to lose, Philip arrogantly terminated his connection to the program, leaving Adam staring at a blank terminal screen as he sat in the underground prison, many miles away.

CHAPTER ELEVEN

Adam's guards were busily talking in their observation booth at the far end of the room and paid scant attention as he stared at a flashing cursor in the upper left hand corner of the screen and waited for an input. Thinking quickly, he used his amazing technical ability to access the computer mainframe and before long he was committing every item of data he could find to his memory, long before the guards realised the chess game was over.

Nearly an hour had passed when they realised that the chess match had ended and Adam was taken back to his cell. Bursting with excitement at his gleaned knowledge he was already formulating a plan of escape. To gain further access, Adam had already written a small line of code into the programming, allowing him to shrink the chess graphic into a smaller window the next time he played. This gave him time to explore the vast computer network and finalise his plans. Should any of the guards walk behind him, a quick tap of the escape key would explode the graphic to fill the screen hiding what lay beneath. He calculated that within three days he would have all the information necessary for a successful escape. Arriving back at the prison cell he was ready to tell everyone, only to find consternation amongst his fellow inmates.

"They're splitting us all up into different sections according to ability." Kristy announced out loud, bracing herself for another violent shock from her collar, and then breathed a sigh of relief when nothing happened. Adam performed a visual roll-call of the room and immediately stopped at the pitiful sight of Oliver. He was sitting on his lower bunk with his knees pulled tightly to his chest, his head was down, and he rocked slowly back and forth.

"Where's Jacob?" Adam asked.

"Now his leg has mended, they've taken him away for training or something." Oliver mumbled into the narrow gap between his kneecaps. He was feeling very vulnerable and alone without his best friend and self-appointed bodyguard. Amy sensed his pain and sat by his side with her arm around his shoulders, trying to bring some comfort to her dear friend but it had little effect. Adam's excitement disappeared in a flash as all his plans to escape died on the vine before he even had a chance to tell anyone.

The group meal that followed was a fairly sombre affair with as most of the friends staring vacantly at their plate or idly pushing their food around having very little appetite. Jacob's absence felt more like a death and the sight of his empty chair at the end of the table just added to the mood. With the meal thankfully over, Adam retired to his own bunk and lay down with his eyes closed and trawled through his mental memory palace, opening cupboards and drawers hoping to figure out where Jacob's new cell could be and how he could factor in this new variable and still facilitate everyone's escape. Until Adam could come up with a plan that included Jacob, he decided to keep his discovery to himself until a positive report could be made. Even though the thought of possible escape would ease the mood, Adam realised that for the time being, the less everyone knew of his plans the safer they all would be.

Jacob's recovery from his operation had been remarkable. The bandage had been removed by a pretty, young nurse in the infirmary and to his amazement the wound had completely healed. The only evidence of trauma was a narrow pink scar running vertically along the front of his shin. Jacob tried to get up ready to leave the surgery only to find the nurse pushing him firmly back down onto the bed.

"I'm not finished with you yet young man. There is still the matter of skin matching to deal with."

Jacob was stunned, with the exception of his friends this was the first person to talk properly to him since he arrived at the place.

"What happens now?" He asked; dropping into polite conversation like it was just an ordinary check-up at the doctor's surgery. The nurse ignored the question and shook her head subtly, then glanced fearfully at the security camera. Jacob suddenly realised that she too could also be a prisoner here and not have any part in this evil operation.

"I understand." He whispered under his breath, as she turned her back to switch on the equipment sited at the end of the bed. She paused slightly, looking ready to say something else, but instead took a deep breath and continued with the task in hand, by placing the end of a skin tone scanner onto a patch of healthy skin adjacent to the scar tissue. Within seconds the exact colour match was transposed into a four digit numeric code that was registered on a small display screen mounted on the back of the probe. With this information to hand the nurse crossed the room and retrieved from a wall cupboard a miniature paint sprayer and a tiny nail varnish shaped bottle containing a dark brown liquid that bore the same number still displayed on the scanner device. Jacob watched silently as the nurse dripped precisely five drops of the liquid into the mixing jar of an empty miniature paint bottle, and then added a clear solution from an unmarked dispenser screwed to the wall. She clipped the new bottle of mixture onto the small paint sprayer housing and shook the solution for about thirty seconds. While the bubbles dispersed, she wiped down the scar with a swab dipped in surgical spirit, allowed it to dry, then proceeded to spray a thin coating of skin dye perfectly matching the colour of the skin on Jacob's skin. Several coats later and a brief stint under a warm air dryer; Jacob's leg looked as good as new and bore no evidence of scaring of any kind.

With the pretty face of the nurse on his mind, Jacob sat daydreaming on the land train as it headed back towards the cells. What he failed to notice was the change in direction and was completely surprised when the cell door opened and he walked in to find five strangers in a room sited on a completely different block.

"There must be some sort of mistake this isn't my cell."

Jacob turned around to explain to the guards only to be completely ignored and the cell door close in his face. He immediately began to bang his fists against the cold steel panel and demand and explanation, but his reward was a prolonged shock to his collar that dropped him to his knees leaving him unable to breathe. Thirty long seconds later, Jacob staggered to his feet and stared angrily upon the faces of five male inmates who failed to come to his aid and silently returned his gaze. Suddenly fearful for what may be happening to the rest of his friends, including Oliver, who looked to him for support, Jacob found his voice and began to demand answers.

"Does anyone have any idea what the hell's going on here?"

Four of the men looked directly at one older inmate sitting quietly behind the table. Sighing heavily and with a deep sadness in his eyes the silently appointed leader of the group used his foot to push out the chair nearest to Jacob and gestured for him to sit down.

"My name is Ivan Stefanovich and these are my friends Joseph Conrad, Stephen Bowen, Michael Smith, and Andre Costa. What is yours?"

Ivan looked at each friend in turn who nodded in reply to the mention of his name.

"My name is Jacob Tilson and I demand to know what I'm doing here?"

Jacob rarely lost his temper, but the stress of the situation, coupled with the complacent manner Ivan introduced everyone, pushed him clean over the edge. Jumping to his feet, he stared down at Ivan hoping to intimidate him into giving an answer to his question, but he did not expect what happened next. Ivan smiled and stood up to match, but when he reached Jacob's 5′ 10″ he just seemed to keep going until he finally stopped nearly 11 inches taller with muscles to match. What Jacob had failed to notice in his confusion was that all the men were as heavily muscled as him and that should have been a clue.

"Hold your temper, sit down and I will explain."

Some of the men chuckled as Jacob had little option but to do as ordered and waited while Ivan did the same.

"I assume that you used to reside in another part of the prison, am I correct?"

Jacob nodded silently in reply. He did not wish to explain his situation in detail in hope to speed up Ivan's explanation.

"As you plainly see, everyone in this cell is a much larger specimen than the average adult male including yourself, and that is the main reason. For the last few weeks our captors seem obsessed with gathering as many suitable candidates, and bulking everyone out with high protein meals and muscle building powders accompanied with weight training sessions to improve our strength, but that's not all; we've also been trained in the use of swords, nets, and spears, like a Roman gladiatorial school."

Jacob stared open mouthed as he tried to absorb the information, and for the next hour the rest of the group joined in, taking turns to inform Jacob with all the special training they have been given. The list also included use of modern assault rifles and small arms, rock climbing, and practice with a bow and arrow.

"Do any of you have any idea what this is all about?" Jacob asked when the tales finally ceased. None of the men had a concise explanation, but Ivan's answer seemed to be the most probable.

"When I was a small boy I used to sit by the fire with my family on the long winter nights and often my grandfather would regale me with amazing tales of monsters and magic. The tales that I found most fascinating were the ones of the great travelling circuses with their amazing performers and freak shows. He once told me that one of the ways that these shows made money, was to challenge their resident strongman to a contest against all comers, with a promise to double or sometimes triple the return that people cared to bet. There were many powerful men from my region, some of them giants in comparison to the rest of us. But these were just simple men who had been raised on farms and in the mountain villages and had little idea how professionals fight. In his great many years he never saw anyone defeat the circus strongman. Brute strength was just not enough and this man was a trained professional. He knew all the major techniques and was an expert in every underhand trick in the book. Hundreds of bets would be placed on the outcome by the partisan crowds in support of their local hero and hundreds of bets would then be lost. It is my belief that we are going to be trained up as professional fighters, pitted against other similar trained men in illegal arenas and bet upon, like dogs or fighting cocks."

The men talked long into the evening and continued long after lights out. Jacob could not remember exactly when he fell asleep as his dream state continued asking questions to giants while trying to analyse their bizarre answers for the rest of the night.

Early the next morning and still feeling tired from a poor night's sleep, Jacob was taken alone from his cell to journey on the land train into an extensive gymnasium at the far end of the complex. The large facility contained an impressive array of exercise equipment dotted around a large circular roped off area sited in the very centre. White coated lab technicians directed Jacob to a treadmill in the far corner, ordered him to remove his shirt and then attached a series of wireless sensor pads at strategic pulse points to his chest and arms, before issuing orders to commence walking on the powered conveyer. Facing into the gymnasium as his exercise began, Jacob had plenty of time to observe his surroundings and found it plain to see that his new cell mates appeared to be telling the truth. In a separate annex that was now visible from his current vantage point he could see some men having weapons training with an assortment of wooden short swords, spears, shields and rope nets. While elsewhere equipment used for high intensity workouts similar to a boxing gymnasium were dotted around the floor. Sited on the far side, a man climbed a rotating rock face, until completely exhausted he fell to the floor.

Amid the smell of liniment and sweat, Jacob continued his run as the technician steadily incremented the speed and angle of the treadmill until he was sprinting up an incline as fast as he had ever run in his life. With his heart thudding in his chest and lungs screaming for air, sweat poured down Jacob's muscular frame while supervisors continued to analyse his vital signs on their touch screen clipboards. Being a heavily muscled man allowed Jacob great bursts of energy or strength, but he was not built for endurance. He quickly began to tire from the length of the run and leg cramps set in. Grabbing desperately for the support rails sited either side of his runway hoping to steady his balance, Jacob felt relieved to feel the angle of the conveyer decline, while slowing rapidly almost to a halt as he fell to his knees, gasping for breath. Moving steadily backwards until he fell from the black rubberised canvas belt and onto the floor, Jacob lay on his side waiting for the punishment to follow, but when he opened his eyes the technicians seemed more interested in comparing gathered data than in his current condition. Eventually his breathing recovered and he sat up to receive a welcome vitamin drink, that he was allowed to finish while sitting on a chair by the wall of the gym. As the minutes passed by, he watched the place slowly fill with more inmates ready for training, and to his surprise this included Ivan, walking alongside another man of equal size and stature. Together, they headed directly for the central roped off arena. Both men were stripped down to a pair of shorts and each carried a short fighting sword and small circular metal shield. Jacob stared closely at the other man and could not quite put his finger on it, but there seemed to be something odd about his gait and awkward response to changes in the surroundings. Ivan on the other-hand had his eyes wide open and already breathed heavily as his body surged with adrenaline preparing for the fight to come. All the current exercise regimes ground quickly to a halt and like moths to a flame the entire contingent in the gymnasium was allowed to congregate at ringside to watch.

Ivan caught Jacob's eye and nodded to acknowledge his presence as he practised a few thrusts and parries to loosen up his impressive physique, while his opponent stood stock still and watched silently. Curiously, there did not appear to be an adjudicator or a referee present to control procedures, and at the sound of the klaxon, the opposition did not dance around to get a measure of Ivan's ability, he just threw himself directly into the fight. Time and time again the unnamed man launched his attack, and every time, Ivan professionally blocked the blow or sidestepped to avoid the thrust of the deadly short sword. Jacob could not believe his eyes at the ferocity of the attacks, although Ivan appeared relaxed, and for now, prepared just to dodge and block.

"The prisoner will fight back." A voice blasted out from the overhead tannoy system, obviously annoyed at the apparent lack of Ivan's aggression. Ivan ignored the order and continued with his defensive tactics. Two more minutes passed and it was obvious that Ivan had no intention of following the order. The voice from the tannoy blasted out again.

"This is your final warning, attack your opponent immediately or you will be punished."

Ivan behaved as if nothing had changed and quickly paid the price. The assembled group gasped when a massive shock ripped through Ivan's collar, paralysing his muscles, leaving him gripping tightly to his sword as he crashed to the floor like a freshly felled tree. Jacob held his breath expecting the worst as the other fighter raised his sword arm ready to strike, but he suddenly stopped dead in the middle of the manoeuvre and remained completely inert. Murmurs and puzzled looks passed between some of the other prisoners as they stared at the bizarre scene. The unnamed man stood rigid as a statue, while Ivan lay on the ground, unable to move to his own will although visibly trembling in fear and pain. Eventually the shock from the collar ceased, releasing Ivan from his restraint, and with incredible speed for a man of his size, he rolled to one side, sprang to his haunches, jumped up and circled around his stationary foe. In an instant the fighter sprang back into life, and with incredible force, slashed his sword through the air, cleaving the now empty space with such force, that the tip of his sword split the canvas and cleaved a large splinter from the heavily varnished floor. Encouraged by this advantage and fearful of further punishment, Ivan thrust the tip of his own sword into the back of the man's thigh, hoping to inflict a minor flesh wound, declare himself the victor, spare his opponent's life, and bring an end to the barbaric contest. What he did not expect was for the man to spin around as if nothing had happened and with a backward slash, cut open a perfectly straight, shallow incision across Ivan's chest from the right shoulder to his left nipple. A thin bright red line appeared almost immediately from the wound and tears of fresh blood caressed the fleshy contours, mixing with the sweat running down Ivan's muscular chest. Fortunately, Ivan was still able to continue unheeded, but now his attitude had changed. The scarlet battle veil masked his clear blue eyes and he launched a counterattack like a man possessed. The fight was now well and truly on, as loud clangs echoed across the vast hall. Every thrust and jab executed was expertly matched in defence of the ferocious attack, but unfortunately, whatever Ivan attempted it was blocked with equal measure. Before long he began to tire, although his opponent was not even breathing heavily, in fact, he appeared to be getting faster and Ivan's aching limbs were now struggling to parry every counter move thus receiving numerous flesh wounds adding to his woes.

Curiously the injury borne by the other fighter had torn a hanging triangular shaped piece of skin away from his thigh. It bled as much as any other wound, but it was what lay beneath that fascinated Jacob. Instead of revealing the subdermal layer, muscle, or even thigh bone underneath the skin, there was a semi-transparent latex sheet that was thin enough to reveal micro-thin ribbon cable feeding power to cogs and servo motors buried deep within the motorised leg.

Ivan was now down on his knees manfully blocking another attack and as his energy faded fast and the cheers from fellow inmates hushed into murmurs and groans of concern. A swift diagonally upward thrust from the relentless attack missed Ivan's his face by a whisker, but quickly found a second target as its momentum cleaved a thick metal splinter from the edge of Ivan's sword, tearing the weapon free from his aching fingers. In an almost slow motion display, the shiny metal blade cartwheeled high through the heavy dust-mote filled air, flashing through the spotlight beams trained down onto the arena floor. On its descent, some of the spectators had to dive out of the way as it landed with a loud clatter and well out of reach.

Completely defenceless and at the mercy of his foe, Ivan dropped his shoulders and calmly looked his opponent in the eye as he awaited his fate. The crowd held their breath for what seemed an age as the victorious fighter held his sword's hilt in both hands and raised the blade slowly over his head ready for the downward chop that would easily cleave Ivan's head in two. Jacob looked around waiting for someone to intervene, or for the bodiless voice to call and end to the fight, but neither happened. At a complete loss to understand why everyone was ready to watch an innocent man die, Jacob was suddenly on his feet, through the ropes and running across the ring to stop the execution; hoping rescue his new friend. Before he even managed to get half way across, a massive shock ripped through his collar, paralysing his limbs, and he fell, face first onto the floor. Unable to reach out his hands and protect his head, it thudded heavily onto the canvas. The last thing he saw before blacking out completely was the android fighter lowering his sword, turn around, and walk calmly away.

A few hours later, Jacob awoke with a pounding headache, the taste of blood in his mouth and painful swelling around the socket of his left eye. Someone had placed a cold, damp flannel over his wound to help reduce the swelling but it was having little effect. Slowly his wits began to return and as he turned his head, he was relieved to see that he was back in his bunk with Ivan sitting around the table with the rest of his cell mates eating a hot meal. Ivan looked up as soon as Jacob moved.

"You awake at last young Jacob; we had taken bets whether you were going to sleep through dinner as well as lunch. Come and eat while it's still hot."

Although his head throbbed with every movement, hunger gave him great determination and he gingerly pushed his body up onto one elbow before rolling out of bed. As he straightened to his full height everything in his peripheral vision began to darken and what remained of the room began to spin. Grasping blindly for the top rail of the bunk he waited while taking a few deep breaths until his sight cleared and the room ground to a halt once more. Stephen pulled a chair out for Jacob from under the table, allowing him to transfer his grip to the seat-back, take two unsteady steps and gingerly sit down. Ivan had remained quiet during the meal, but as soon as he had finished he began to talk.

"That was a very foolish thing to do my friend; you put yourself in great danger."

Jacob stopped chewing, swallowed what remained of his last mouthful, and stared back.

"I was trying to save your life, perhaps I shouldn't have bothered." Jacob snapped, feeling hurt at the comment. Ivan failed to reply and offered no further explanation as he got up from his chair and crossed over to his bunk for a lie down facing the wall. Andre shook his head to silence Jacob as he prepared to say something else, instead he waited patiently until the sounds of Ivan's snoring broke the silence. Andre beckoned Jacob to follow him into the bathroom and in hushed tones behind a closed door he began to explain.

"Ivan has been here for many months and always managed to avoid fighting the robot fighter until today. Very soon after facing this automaton, the inmate is taken through the red door at the far end of the gym, never to return. By showing your aggression for the fight, you may accelerate your progression to the red exit. All Ivan is trying to do is protect you from this fate."

Jacob pondered for a while before deciding it was best to let the matter drop and nodding his thanks for the explanation he returned into the main room to finish off his mug of tea.

The night passed slowly by as the pain from his injured head kept him awake, accompanied with his imagination running riot in the half-light of what new horrors lay behind the now infamous red door.

When the morning came Jacob was still sore with Ivan and after breakfast, he sat grumpily in his bunk refusing to join in with the conversation. His spirit soon lifted when the guards arrived and he was taken for a check-up with the same pretty nurse who previously applied the camouflage stain to the scar on his leg. This time it was Jacob's turn to be blanked as he tried several times to start a conversation with this young woman who repeatedly shook her head amid nervous glances to the security camera positioned overhead. The silent rebuttal continued to every question Jacob proffered, until he was just about to leave when she pressed a small folded piece of notepaper into his hand that he guardedly slipped into his pocket as he walked away.

Back in his prison cell Jacob faced away from the security camera in the bathroom and opened the handwritten note. It contained a four digit number. He could only assume that it was the security code for an exit door, but he had no idea which one. It would probably be a while before another check-up was due, so until then he would have to wait.

CHAPTER TWELVE

"Where on earth have you been? There has been a breach in protocol and somehow the press have been allowed onto the base. They were swarming all over the place since last night, asking all sorts of inane questions and as you know, if we forcefully eject anyone, it looks like we have something to hide. On top of all that just when I need your help, you are nowhere to be found." Philip Sanderson yelled at Ted Langton, who had purposely made himself scarce following the incident at the restaurant. Now he had finally emerged to face the music, he stood sheepishly like an errant schoolboy in front of Philip's desk.

"Now you're finally here I want you to tell me honestly what caused the fracas at the Blue Fairy."

"It was a storm in a teacup, an overblown incident caused by a minor accident, nothing more, nothing less." Ted replied, trying to remain calm, but still furious with Gemma for getting him into so much trouble. Against his better judgment he had remained at the table to suffer the gossip and sly looks from the other diners while Gemma, revelling in the attention, polished off two lobster tails all to herself.

"It looks nothing like an accident to me, let's take a look." Philip replied as he tapped a finger on a red triangular *'play'* icon, displayed on the surface of his sensor-glass desk, where a preloaded video already filled the desktop. Placing his index finger onto the centre of the display, Philip traced a small circle on the glass and the video image inverted, allowing Ted to watch last night's embarrassing scene in all of its high-definition glory from the comfort of his side of the desk. It clearly showed Gemma deliberately reach out to knock the full glass over, spilling the contents into Astelle's lap and revelling in the aftermath that followed. Ted scratched the back of his head as he stared at the video repeating for a second time on a loop. Before he could reach out and put a stop to the clip, Philip had already loaded another, and the scene was shown again from a different angle recorded via different camera.

"Still think it was an accident?" Philip questioned, raising the pitch of his voice as he vented his anger at Ted's denial of the obvious truth.

"Do you know how many different clips there are of this episode?"

Ted remained silent and defiantly stared his boss directly in the eye. Philip paused for a second and hearing no answer, he answered the question for him.

"I've counted twenty-one so far, including our surveillance camera footage that somehow has been leaked onto the internet. The whole thing has gone viral; this one alone has been viewed nearly eighteen million times. The national news even added it to their breakfast bulletin. What I want to know is what are you going to do about it?"

Ted closed his eyes and silently counted to ten before he gave his answer. He wanted to make sure that he was calm enough to choose his words carefully and not say what he really thought. Philip began to strum his fingers loudly on the top of his desk annoying Ted even further, but he refused to be rushed into the wrong decision. Finally, he took a deep breath and Philip stopped drumming in anticipation.

"I shall do nothing at all." Ted replied, reaching out and tapping the desktop to stop the latest video from looping for a third time. Philip looked ready to explode as he jumped to his feet, placing his knuckles onto his desk hard enough to make the skin turn white but curiously for some reason the colour remained the same. Before he had any time to ponder why, Philip's tirade continued.

"You will hold a press conference and make sure that Cassidy woman publicly apologises and then fire her on the spot. Then you will make a personal statement stating that this public demonstration relates to the extremely high value we place on every client and that will put an end to the matter. Hopefully this will go some way to recovering the embarrassment the little bitch has caused this company; overnight we dropped fifty points."

It was now Teds turn to vent his spleen and at risk of bearding the lion in his own den, he too leaned his fists onto the desk, placing his own reddening face inches away from Philips' surprisingly smooth skin.

"I will do no such thing." He growled, doing his best not to reach out to grab Philip's scrawny neck and throttle him where he stood. Philip reacted meekly to the act of aggression, coupled with the fact that he also hated anyone invading his personal space. So he cravenly sat back down in his chair, submissive to the act of the dominant male. All his billions in the bank and head of the world's largest company granted him incredible power, but it all paled to nothing when faced with a masculine one on one situation. Ted stepped back feeling a little embarrassed by his aggressive attitude to his best friend, but his affections for Gemma released a fierce protective instinct.

"I repeat, nothing at all." Ted softened his tone a little but continued to stare Philip directly in the eye. For the first time he noticed that there was something different about his friend, He could not put his finger on it, but there seemed to be a kind of spark missing from the man who through his genius became the richest man in the world. At a loss for an answer and cross with himself for letting his mind wander from the subject in hand, Ted cleared the thought from his head and began to rattle off a series of short, well-rehearsed, numbered statements.

"One; I regard real people above any fluctuation in points on some stupid share index. Two; today's news is tomorrow's fish and chip paper and people will soon move on to the next celebrity gossip. Three; wise investors will always purchase shares in a successful company, so the index points will soon bounce back. Four; Paul Johnston and Astelle have already signed the contract, as you well know, and I am sure you have made the deal water tight. And finally, if you want that Cassidy woman, as you seem to have labelled her, fired, you can do it yourself. But I will let you know right now that you will have to include me as well because I will not play any part in such a drastic over reaction. I know that you can't predict the future, but you must have seen Astelle's behaviour around me and then you go and invite the three of us out to dinner, while you yourself chicken out. I decided to invite Gemma to join us, that is her first name by the way. I wanted it to look platonic in front of the world's press, but the plan backfired. Astelle was jealous of the way Gemma flaunted her shapely figure provoking tit for tat reactions; this I admit Gemma took a little too far and will not go unpunished. She will be assigned to cleanup detail for the next two weeks, ordered to pay for Astelle's dry cleaning bill and docked one week's salary to be publicly donated to famine relief as an act of contrition for her behaviour in a restaurant. But until Astelle has said sorry to Gemma for the rudeness on her part, something I highly doubt, neither will Gemma have to apologise, and I will not be moved on this."

Philip listened calmly to his friend's speech and analysed the facts at his usual incredible speed. He was well aware that Ted's bloody minded attitude might just go so far as to lose him his second in command, and that could spell disaster for him and the company. Ted was excellent at his job and his natural ability in dealing with people was second to none. Everything else seemed logical and acceptable, but in his own mind, he still wanted Gemma removed, as she was a distraction. The best thing to do for now was to accept Ted's offer and figure out another plan to get rid of this thorn in his side permanently.

"I accept your proposal and leave all the matters to be dealt with by you personally. Now I think it's time we both got back to work."

Philip stood up and offered his left hand out to Ted. A quirk he had used since childhood. His pride at having a dominant left hand made him refuse to kowtow to the arrogance of the right handed world. In defiance, he made his own stubborn attempt not to assimilate with the norm. Ted raised his eyebrows at the rapid acceptance of the agreement, but had to accept that he will never come to grips with the speed his genius friend could compute information and determine the correct solution in the blink of an eye. Awkwardly, he offered his own left hand in return, but at the point of contact, Philip closed his hand and bizarrely offered a fist bump instead. Ted duly obliged, but it did nothing but add to the concern that there was something different about Philip and it would not go away. For now, Ted deemed that there were more important issues to deal with and he turned to leave. Before he had walked half way back down the glass tunnel, Philip was sitting back behind his desk already accessing Gemma Cassidy's file, making plans to transfer her to a place from where she would never return.

CHAPTER THIRTEEN

Late in the evening, Philip returned from his daily rounds to the comfort and solace of his office. Happy to be alone, he sat down behind his expansive chrome and glass desk. For the past few days his main concern was the disturbing report of a female prisoner who had escaped from a franchise somewhere in the southern backwoods of the United States of America. In addition to this problem, it appeared that a county sheriff helped facilitate her escape and this only further increased his anxiety. In response Philip had ordered two of his personal investigators to make inquiries regarding the matter, and allowing for the difference in time zones, to make a full report at 9:00 pm GMT.

It was already quarter past the hour and he did not like to be kept waiting. Five minutes later a small holographic image of an old fashioned rotary dial telephone with a red flashing light on the display, rose up from the surface of the desk. Accompanying the image, a jangling bell-tone rang out. Philip voice activated the incoming call.

"Your tardy behaviour will not be tolerated a second time Simpkins, do I make myself clear?" Philip snapped, assuming it was Lyle Simpkins, his senior investigator on the other end of the line.

"I'm very sorry for the delay Mr Sanderson sir, but this is Nathan Howton, Simpkins' partner. Simpkins is still monitoring the situation and has given me the task of checking in. I have found it almost impossible to get a decent mobile phone signal out here in Hicksville and I have had to drive almost to the top of a mountain before it is strong enough to get through."

Philip drummed his fingers on the armrest of his chair and took a deep breath while he listened to what he deemed as a lame excuse.

"Never mind all that, what have you found out?"

"The escaped prisoner has already been reunited with her family and it has caused a great deal of excitement with the local press and population, especially regarding her skin colour, but since then nothing more. The sheriff appears to have returned to work with his two deputies and his official report states that he spotted the poor woman wandering barefoot down the edge of local highway as the three of them returned home from a fishing holiday. He added that he was shocked to realise that it was his niece, a Miss Molly Dawson."

"Has the woman said anything about where she has been for the past few months?"

"No sir, she says that she has no recollection from the day she disappeared, right up to the time she was picked up by the sheriff. Shall we return to base?"

"No, not yet, stay in town for a few more days and make some more enquiries. If anyone asks who you are, tell them you are both freelance reporters and intend to tout the story worldwide. I fail to understand why the sheriff has lied about where he was, unless he too has something to hide. I want all the information available regarding his personal fantasy day and also speak with the franchise owner to see if any extras were paid for under the table. But the main thing is to keep very close tabs on the Dawson woman. If she shows any signs of lying, or begins to reveal any incriminating details she will need to have an accident, do you understand?"

"Yes sir, crystal-clear we'll get on it right away."

Before the field operative could add anything else, Philip terminated the call and idly watched the image of the telephone sink gracefully back into the desk. Nathan Howton returned to his hire car, but before he began the scenic journey back down the mountain, he gazed wearily at the view of Holtsville in the valley below as he massaged away the painful knots in the muscles of his neck. The orders from Philip Sanderson troubled him greatly and he wondered that in nearly half a century on this planet how he had managed to end up in such a dire situation. The possibility of having to take another person's life and was almost too much to consider, but the threat of blackmail from the corporation made it impossible to disobey orders.

It all started less than two years ago when desperate for work, Nathan took the job as a trouble shooter for the company. He had recently moved to the area, to avoid upwards of ten years in jail for embezzling funds from a charity organisation, where he used to be the treasurer. It only started as a few dollars here and there to cover his expenses, but his penchant for gambling quickly spiralled out of control. Foolishly covering his debts with money from a loan shark only made matters worse and the only answer was to *'borrow'* even more from the charity fund's coffers to save his knee caps. It seemed all too easy and with a bit of creative accounting the money would not be easily missed. He had every intention of returning the cash someday and came up with the foolhardy idea of placing even bigger bets hoping to replace all of the missing funds with the winnings; but before he knew it the account was dry. Being a coward, Nathan abandoned his wife and teenage son, fleeing the state to start again under an assumed name. Without the correct social security number, work became hard to find until he managed to get a cash job, as a bartender in a city centre club. It was there he met Lyle Simpkins, who happened to be in town on business. One thing led to another and before the night was over Lyle promised Nathan he could get him a job with the company. Nathan confessed that he did not have the correct documents for professional employment, but Lyle convinced him that it would not be a problem. Thinking it was just an idle, drunken boast Nathan thought nothing more of the conversation until Lyle returned a few days later with a firm offer. What Nathan did not know was that with the resources of the richest company in the world, it had little difficulty in finding his true identity. Philip Sanderson took a personal interest and placed Nathan on the investigation team with Lyle. This made the perfect pair to do his dirty work, under threat of being turned over to the authorities.

Back in the present and with an idea to ease his conscience, Nathan returned to his car and carefully made his way down the long winding mountain road back towards Holtsville. His decision was to tell his partner, who was also at the mercy of Sanderson, that he had been chosen to dispose of young Molly should the need arise. He knew that Simpkins would not dare check this order directly and if he ever did find out it would be too late.

CHAPTER FOURTEEN

Sheriff Dodson was still a very anxious man, but luckily for him and his deputies, Molly Dawson still had no recollection of recent events. However the knot in the pit of his stomach made him feel like he was sitting on a time bomb; counting down the seconds until all hell broke loose. The local TV, county newspapers and even a few nationals had run the curious and heartwarming story, but it soon became yesterday's news and everything had returned to normal in the sleepy backwater town. The residual problem was that there were still two strangers in the district. They claimed to be reporters and showed no intention of leaving anytime soon, putting the sheriff on high alert. He had run their names through the police computer and reached a dead-end on both counts, that to him spelled trouble, so he decided a more detailed investigation was due. A few phone calls to the major hotel chains soon revealed that they both shared a room at the Forest Lodge on the outskirts of town. With both Duke and Elvis keeping watch on their whereabouts, the sheriff changed into civilian clothes and set off in his private car over to the hotel for a closer investigation.

The desk clerk Howard Matheson, whom the sheriff reminded that he owed him a big favour, *'absentmindedly'* left a backup copy of the room key-card out on the counter top of the reception desk while he turned his back to attend to the mail. This intentional oversight was payback for receiving only a verbal caution last July, instead of the sheriff issuing the young man a speeding ticket. Another traffic violation would have cost Howard his driving licence, and as he required one for his job at the hotel, he would have lost that as well. The sheriff knew that Howard's wife had a baby on the way and feeling the pang of being unable to father a child himself, he relented to Howard's plea for leniency.

Promising that he would only be a few minutes, the sheriff looked down at the number on the card and felt his heart sink. The room in question was on the fourth floor and this posed a problem.

Many years ago when he was a boy, young Oberon often whiled away the summer vacation playing with school friends in the woodlands behind his home. One morning they chanced upon an old domestic refrigerator that someone had dumped off a highway bridge. As part of a dare the young Oberon climbed inside only for his friends to slam the door and lock it behind him. In spite of his screams and cries, the other boys carried on playing together and failed to release him for over fifteen minutes. This did not sound too long, but they did not realise that the door sealed off any fresh air and when they finally let him out he was close to suffocation. Ever since that day, Oberon held a fear of enclosed spaces, with elevators high on the list. This left him no choice but to take to the stairs up to the room. Being severely overweight and in poor physical condition, the sheriff was gasping for breath by the time he reached the fourth floor. There then followed a long walk down the corridor, leaving the poor man exhausted and on the verge of collapse before the search even began.

Panting heavily, the sheriff slipped the freshly acquired key-card into the slot of room 415 then struggled to don a pair of latex gloves onto his chubby sweaty hands before trying the handle and stepping quietly inside. Both deputies had already informed him that the two suspects were miles away and he had little risk of being caught. Nevertheless, his heart continued to pound wildly and sweat ran down his temples as he sat on the edge of a chair trying to regain his breath. Reaching for his nitroglycerine spray he used to relieve angina pain he cursed loudly upon realising that in his hurry, he had accidently picked up the old empty bottle from the pocket of his uniform jacket, leaving the new full one behind. The only thing left for him to do now, was to close his eyes and focus on relaxing in hope that the pain would go away. Minutes passed and using the steady breathing technique taught to him by Doctor Morton, the tightness eased enough to allow him to continue.

"Come to papa, I know there's something in here somewhere." He whispered to himself as he looked in every drawer and cupboard in the room. The air conditioning was out of action and the stifling heat forced him to take frequent rest stops. Breathing deeply once more, while using his handkerchief to wipe away the sweat from his forehead and loose-jowled chin, he pondered where to search next. There was really very little else, apart from a small selection of toiletries in the bathroom and a couple of suits hanging in the closet, so he decided on a brief dip into each suit pocket and then get out.

Something that the sheriff did not factor into his plan was that Elvis could be stupid enough to somehow lose track of Lyle Simpkins' hire car on the only busy street in town and end up tailing a similar vehicle of the same colour going in the complete opposite direction. Lyle Simpkins was now heading back to the lodge and he was only minutes away from his room. Oblivious to this fact, Dodson continued with his search. Fumbling around in the pockets of each suit he was just on the verge of giving up when his chubby fingers grasped a crumpled sheet of notepaper. There was nothing of importance written down, but it was the printed heading that gave it away.

"Hologram Dreams Corporation, I dang well knew it!" He voiced breathlessly, trying to remain calm in an attempt to stop his hand shaking so he could place the loose paper back inside the jacket pocket. It was not concrete evidence, but just too much of a coincidence for it not to be operatives from the company sent to investigate the situation. On this conclusion he quickly checked the room to make sure everything was in order before heading for the exit. Reaching for the door handle the sheriff stopped dead in his tracks and his heart lurched at the sight of the handgrip moving up and down rapidly on its own as someone operated the lever from the other side.

Suddenly feeling very short of breath for a second time, a wave of panic washed over him, he turned and looked frantically for somewhere to hide. His sheer size made it impossible to slide under the bed or position his massive frame behind the curtains, so with no other choice he ran into the bathroom and held the door almost closed so he could spy through the crack on whoever entered the room. Again and again the handle wagged up and down, but still the door remained closed. The sheriff had always had a keen brain that had kept him out of trouble on many occasions and every possible scenario flashed through his mind.

'If Simpkins was just outside the door why did he not just walk straight in? Perhaps his pass key was malfunctioning, or maybe it was housekeeping and they too were struggling to get the key-card to work. More likely it's some dumbass incapable of reading a three digit door number and was trying to enter the wrong room.'

One by one all the different scenarios flashed through his overactive psyche, but what he did not consider was that outside the door and across the other side of the hallway, a young couple paid scant attention to their four year old son who was bored with waiting and repeatedly tugged on the door handle of the opposite room. His parents continued to search through every pocket and bag for the pass card to their own room, only for the sheepish husband to find it in the breast pocket of his shirt, where he had placed for safekeeping. While all of this was happening, the sheriff watched breathlessly from inside the bathroom as the exit door handle continued to waggle up and down. The more the lever moved, the more anxious he became. This combined with puzzlement as to why whoever it was failed to enter the room just exacerbated his stress. Suddenly the handle stopped and everything fell silent, but the situation had become nearly too much for his enlarged heart to endure. His laboured breathing increased rapidly, followed by spreading chest pains that had every indication of a heart attack. Promising silently to the Lord above to go on a diet and eat more healthily he tried to ignore the signs, crept slowly from his hiding place, and pressed his ear against the fake wood door panel to listen for any noise. On hearing nothing unusual and not seeing anyone standing outside through the security viewer he peeled his sweaty face away from the cool wood veneer, opened the door, and cautiously peeped out. To his relief the corridor was void of people and he quickly made his way to the elevator.

The relief at not being caught eased, but not enough to warrant a descent of the stairs, so he pressed the call button and waited.

"Come on Oberon you can do this." He muttered to himself and received curious looks from a travelling salesman who had just left his own room and stood previously unnoticed by the sheriff's side. As soon as the elevator arrived and the double doors swished open, the salesman rudely walked straight in and turned around waiting for the fat man to follow. But no matter how hard he tried his legs refused to move.

"Are you coming?" The stranger asked as he stood impatiently waiting for the big man to remove his hand from holding open the sliding door. The colour rapidly drained from the sheriff's face as he ignored the question and stared silently into the gaudily decorated music box suspended on a thin cable above what he knew was a bottomless pit. Swallowing hard, trying to allay his fears, he took a small step forwards, but suddenly the elevator appeared to shrink before his eyes. The stranger's frame remained unchanged and he now filled all the available space as the metal sides morphed into the old abandoned fridge returning from his childhood to haunt him.

"I'm...I'm a…I'm a gonna wait for the next one." He finally blurted out and snatched his hand away, allowing the doors to close. Flushed with fear and embarrassment he just managed to stare the stranger in the eye and waited until he believed the elevator had gone, and then he turned sharply, heading for the stairwell. Out of curiosity the salesman pressed the door release button from the inside, and it reopened allowing him to poke his head back out into the corridor just in time to see the weird fat man disappear around the corner and out of sight.

Even though his world was spinning around him, all that the sheriff now wanted to do was get out of the place and into the fresh air. In panic, he hurried non-stop down the several flights of stairs, and by the time he reached the ground floor, he realised that this was a bad mistake, as he and was now feeling decidedly unwell. Unbeknownst to him, Lyle Simpkins had already reached the front door next to the reception desk, but he had stopped and returned to his car to retrieve a briefcase. This bought just enough time for the sheriff to hand the duplicate back to Howard, stagger into the air conditioned lounge, and breathlessly sit down. Noticing the big man's distress and hoping to remain in his good books, Howard purchased a cool soda from the vending machine and placed it in the sheriff's hand.

"Thankya' kindly son." He wheezed while wiping down his face with a moist tissue before placing the ice cold bottle to his temple and sliding it down the side of his flabby neck. Any other time he would sit and drink the cooling soda immediately, but before the opportunity arose, he caught the blurry sight of Lyle Simpkins, complete with briefcase, through the frosted foyer window, and he was already walking up the steps to the front door. With nowhere to hide he slumped down in his seat behind a large imitation parlour palm and prayed that Lyle would not notice his imposing frame. Watching curiously, and intrigued by the sheriff's reaction, Howard quickly read the situation and ran back behind his counter while calling for Lyle Simpkins to come over.

"Excuse me, Mr Simpkins, sir; I wonder if you could give me any indication as to when you will be leaving us. You see there is a convention in town and the phone never stops ringing to inquire if we have any vacancies?"

Lyle looked puzzled at Howard's request, because from what he had seen, the hotel appeared half empty. But he was just too tired to question further and politely gave his response.

"Probably another week or two, unless that will cause a problem." He replied, wishing that he was going home tomorrow and could turn his back on this whole sorry mess. The conversation at the reception desk continued with Howard asking Lyle Simpkins a series of inane questions keeping him facing away from the lounge area. Realising what Howard was doing, the grateful sheriff eased unsteadily to his feet, nodded his gratitude over Lyle's shoulder and hurried towards the exit. The added stress and exertion to his already over worked cardiovascular system, now developed into a crushing pain and the poor man believed that his heart was going to explode from his chest as he staggered drunkenly through the door to the rear parking lot.

Fortunately, his car was close by, and as the exhausted sheriff slumped into the driver's seat, he hoped that a cold drink would dull the pain. Removing the screw cap he upended the bottle and downed nearly all of the fizzy liquid in one go. Panting heavily, he even managed a smile as the coolness of the beverage offered a little relief to his pounding heart.

"Lord have mercy upon this poor tortured soul!" He wheezed as the pains eased once again. Feeling much better, he reached for his seatbelt, preparing to leave when the torment violently returned. Like an elephant sitting upon his chest, he found it completely impossible to breathe and the agony intensified beyond belief. Clenching his sweaty fists, crushing the empty plastic bottle with ease, the sheriff closed his eyes, and waited for death to come. Promises to go to church every Sunday and to donate some of his wealth to charity were just some of the resolutions he swore silently at the conviction that he could see a growing white light at the end of a long dark tunnel. Hoping that it would be angels and not the devil coming to take his hand, the sheriff cried softly as the pains grew even more severe and he hugged his arm tightly to his chest. It reached the point when he could not believe that a body could consciously endure such pain and not pass out, as the suffering was so intense he really did not care if death was the answer. To his surprise, the source of the pain began to work its way upwards, creeping higher up his chest until it reached the back of his throat. Believing he was going to vomit, he shifted in his seat and reached for the door handle. To his surprise what followed was the violent release of the loudest and longest belch of his life, accompanied by the sour taste of a three bean breakfast burrito now burning the back of his throat. In disbelief, a mother with her young child, stopped and stared, tut-tutting loudly as she headed for her car. The sheriff at this point really did not care, the chest pains quickly subsided and now with tears of relief in his eyes, an extremely happy man forgot all of his vows, started the car and hastily drove away.

* * *

Over the next few days the Sheriff was a very worried soul. The frequent flashbacks of what he believed to be a near death experience played upon his mind, leaving him too weak to deal with the situation himself. Throughout his life he had always managed to manage with trials and tribulations purely on his own, however, this time he was certain that additional help was required and he hoped this would come in the form of a woman named Gemma Cassidy.

They first met last year when she was on holiday and happened to be driving through the county after a raucous night in a bar on the outskirts of town. Forgetting completely on which side of the road she was supposed to drive, Gemma almost crashed head-on into the sheriff's patrol car as he rounded the corner, coming in from the opposite direction. Luckily for her, the proceeding breath test showed her only slightly over the limit, leaving the sheriff to decide whether she deserved to spend the night at the station. Luckily for Gemma, the sheriff was fascinated with her British accent and began a casual interrogation regarding her background. When he found that she worked for the Hologram Dreams Corporation in England, the conversation took on a different twist.

Twenty minutes later, the sheriff was in receipt of Gemma's employee discount code and personal telephone number should he have any problems using it. The reduction in the overall cost would bring his adventure forward nearly six months. In return the young lady was allowed to drive away scot free.

For quite a while the sheriff stared at the numbers on a scrap of paper in his right hand and hoped he was making the right decision, but at a loss of what to do next he picked up the phone.

CHAPTER FIFTEEN

Time passed fairly quickly as Jacob and his cell mates were trained hard in the gymnasium. Ivan took personal interest in Jacob's training with sword and shield, passing on all his knowledge to his new friend, hoping that someday it would save his life. Finally the day of his check-up arrived and as Jacob waited eagerly in the surgery his heart sank at the sight of the pretty nurse as she walked in accompanied by one of the guards. Her top lip had been recently split and her face bore the bruises of a severe beating. It was obvious that she had been found out and now the guards wanted to know which prisoner had been given the note. Jacob opened his mouth to speak, but a glare and subtle shake of her head stopped him before he began.

"Is this the one?" The guard demanded, pointing to Jacob, but she remained silent and shook her head.

"I said is this the one? Answer me!"

The nurse cowered as the guard screamed and raised his hand, ready to strike, only for Jacob to jump from his chair and push him away. In an instant, he lay twitching on the floor as his shock collar activated while the guard grabbed the nurse roughly by her arm and with the back of his hand, slapped her violently across her face demanding an answer. With defiance in her eyes, she whispered through her freshly bleeding mouth that Jacob was not the one. That was all the guard needed and quickly the nurse was bundled back through the door. A swift kick in the ribs added to Jacob's punishment and while he was still in chronic pain the guard frogmarched him down to the gym.

When he arrived, he found that all the other inmates had been lined up against the wall and a new, unknown figure walked up and down the ranks assessing each inmate. The nervous reverence of the men who accompanied this stranger made it obvious of his importance as they walked timidly behind, but not too far away. Standing at the end of the row, nursing his sore ribs Jacob realised that there was something very familiar regarding the man's gangly frame and geeky facial features, added to that it looked like he had never seen the sun or taken any exercise in his life. It seemed completely foreign that such a poor physical specimen aided only by a touch screen clipboard appeared to be the one selecting men from the line-up. He had already instructed a few men to step forwards from the line when he eventually stopped in front of Ivan. For what seemed like an age he switched his gaze several times from his clipboard to Ivan's face before finally making his decision. A brief nod to an assistant and the big man was pulled out from the line-up and told to stand next to the three others.

"What are you going to do with them?" Jacob shouted without realising what he was doing. Still angry over the injuries to the nurse, rational thought had completely disappeared. Everyone stopped and stared at the man who dared speak. Immediately his collar produced yet another shock and he fell like a rag doll to the floor.

"Turn it off." Commanded the thin man in charge, as he strode over to where Jacob lay. The collar was immediately deactivated and panting heavily, Jacob managed to get back up onto his knees. He thought it wise to remain in this position for fear of repeat treatment, but dared to stare arrogantly into the face of the stranger. The first words that came to mind was geek or nerd as he examined the man's sallow complexion and heavy dark whorls under his eyes from what Jacob assumed was from hours sitting in front of a computer.

"What is your name?" The strange man asked as he returned Jacob's detailed visual examination with one of his own. Jacob remained silent, fearful of more punishment.

"You won't receive any more shocks as long as you answer my questions. What is your name?" He repeated,

Jacob mumbled something incoherent in reply and then braced himself for another jolt, but mercifully nothing came.

"I want to know where you are taking my friend." Jacob finally asked, feeling a little more confident with the stranger's promise so he decided to get to his feet. The man stepped back slightly when faced by Jacob's huge frame, but still held his gaze while he gave a reply.

"These men, including you, all belong to me and what I do with them is no concern of yours. What you appear to be though is a little brighter than the rest of these grunts. I think I will have to find something special for you dear boy. As you show such a curiosity for their fate you can join the rest of your friends and find out."

Jacob had no option but to do as he was told and followed the rest of the small group headed by Ivan, across the floor and out through the red door.

To Jacob's surprise, himself and the small group were led down a long, narrow corridor behind the door and onto a waiting land train, similar to the one used when he and his friends first arrived at the hidden underground base. This one however had bench seats instead of the giant pet carriers that everyone found so amusing in their drug induced state. Including himself, Jacob counted eight prisoners who sat in pairs in the middle of the train with four guards in total split between the front and the rear. With everyone safely aboard there was a slight jolt as the electric motor took the strain as the carriages moved silently away. Jacob turned and tried to catch Ivan's gaze where he sat at the back, but the big man never raised his head, he just stared sullenly down at his knees. Still feeling the after effects of the latest shock punishment, Jacob thought it wise to keep his mouth shut for the time being and turned back to face the front.

In five minutes they emerged into the underground hangar containing heavy machinery and assorted light aircraft. One was away from its parking bay and with engines idling it sat at the foot of the ramp leading up to the surface. Jacob's heart lurched when he spotted the familiar row of giant mesh fronted carriers lined up on the tarmac near the open drop ramp of the plane. His expression matched the similar horror registering on the faces of his fellow inmates. Unable to refuse, they were all given a bottle of water to drink that everyone knew was drugged, and as they stood and waited for the effects to kick in they watched all the preparation being made for the flight. Jacob was now starting to see blurred images and brightly coloured vapour trails lagging behind any rapid movement, leaving him giggling just like a child at the visual effects he could produce with his hands as he waved them in front of his face. All the other inmates appeared to be affected the same, and the guards passed among them unlocking and removing the shock collars knowing that there was little chance of insurrection from the prisoners in their current state. One by one they were all ensconced into the giant carriers, manhandled onto a low wheeled trolley, pushed up the ramp and fastened securely into the cargo bay. Two of the guards followed on board and settled themselves in two of the few seats sited near the front of the aircraft. With everything in place, the tailgate began to rise and Jacob looked idly through the mesh corner of his cage as the giant metal lip hinged up from the concrete floor and slowly clunked into position, blocking his view of the last time he would see any part of his home country again.

The twin-engine propeller-driven plane roared deafeningly in the confines of the cavern as it taxied carefully up the exit ramp and out into the open. For the first time in weeks, even in the half-light of the hold, Jacob felt the warmth of the sun's rays briefly caressing his face as the aircraft turned and headed along the runway. Almost touching the grass verge at the far end, the plane circled back around and immediately began to accelerate. The bumpy ride seemed to last for ages until stomachs lurched as the small transporter swiftly became airborne, banked sharply around and headed in a southerly direction. The drugs and the low throb of the powerful engines made Jacob sleepy and before the plane reached its cruising altitude, he and most of the other prisoners were sound asleep.

Several hours later, Jacob awoke to the harsh rataplan of someone dragging the end of a military baton across the metal grid of his cage. To his surprise the plane had already landed and baking hot sun poured into the hold. The two guards that had travelled with them now took a back seat to the proceedings and chatted quietly as four men dressed in a different uniform organised the removal of the live cargo. Even though their sharp military looking dress smacked of efficiency, the organisation was pathetic and all they had to remove the giant carriers were four more swarthy looking men dressed like peasants, who literally each grabbed a corner and carried the cages out like a sedan chair, placing each one in turn, haphazardly onto the hot dusty runway. No sooner had the last cage been unloaded, documents were signed, exchanged, and the idling plane revved up. Jacob watched the tail gate rise once again, and within minutes the outline of the aircraft faded to a dot as it flew over the horizon. There appeared to be not a building in sight and from his vantage point Jacob could see one single-track road winding up into the mountains and also the back corner of a green army truck that he assumed had transported the uniformed men and manual workers.

Several hours passed, and as the fierce Mediterranean sun rose to its zenith, the small contingent of prisoners suffered badly in the intense heat. They had not had a drink since before take-off, added to this, the sedative dissolved in the water created a powerful thirst. The guards had all retreated into the shadow created by the back of the covered wagon, paying little heed to the state of the men in the hot sun.

"Water, I need water!" A dry voice croaked from inside of one of the cages. In an instant the talking behind the wagon ceased and the man with the baton walked out around from the back.

"Mother I'm thirsty, I need water." The poor man cried, obviously delirious from a combination of dehydration and the intense heat. The head guard retrieved a full bottle of water from the cab and walked over to where the crying man sat with his forehead pressed against the hot steel bars, while tightly hooking the ends of his massive fingers like bird's claws through the lower part of the grid.

"So you need a drink?" The guard mocked in English, wrapped in a heavy Castilian accent. He then proceeded to slowly unscrew the bottle top and take a long cool drink to slake his thirst as the poor man licked his own cracked lips and watched the cruel show. Half of the bottle empty, the guard reached out and poured the remainder of the water down the front of the cage. He laughed haughtily, encouraging the others who had come out from behind the truck to watch the performance. The poor wretch pressed his face as hard as possible against the steel grid and licked desperately at any available drop that ran down the hot metal. Any remaining liquid that made it to the floor, hissed and evaporated quickly as soon as it puddled onto the baking hot concrete. Sycophantically the group laughed heartily at their commander's degrading routine, but silenced just as quickly as he swiftly slipped the baton from under his arm and thrashed it down across the prisoner's finger ends that still protruded through the steel mesh. The effect was hideous, it ripped away the skin from the knuckles down to his fingertips exposing the bone beneath and tore away two of his fingernails from the force of the strike. Everyone winced as they listened to almost inaudible squeal that was all the terrified man could produce from his dry throat, as he snatched back his damaged digits, clutching them tightly to his chest and praying silently for the mind numbing pain to cease. Jacob retched at the sight of the blood splash already beginning to darken as it congealed on the hot surface, and one large finger nail, still wet on the underside with fresh germinal liquid skin, glinting in the sunlight as it lay in front of the injured man's cage. The other one still remained loosely attached to the fingertip although it was split down the middle and opened wide like the carapace of a beetle ready to take to the air. Rocking on his haunches for comfort and keeping his fingers vertical, the distraught prisoner squeezed tightly with his good hand as close to the damage as possible to ease the painful throb and stem the flow of shiny red blood that had already begun to pour from the visually repellent wounds.

"Does anyone else need water?" The commander yelled as he spun around and marched from one carrier to another, kicking the sides of the mini prisons and glaring angrily at the men cowering within. Everyone found the floor very interesting, even the soldiers and workers who knew of the commander's foul temper tried desperately not to catch his eye.

"Right answer." He bellowed, revelling in his self-importance as he continued to march up and down, whacking carriers at random to feast on the reaction inside. The excitement quickly died down and the soldiers retreated back into the shade of the truck leaving Jacob and his fellow captives yet another hour in the sun, listening to the pitiful moans coming from their injured colleague.

Just when Jacob thought he could take no more, relief came with the sight of a dust trail appearing at the top of the canyon as the long awaited transporter wound its way down the desert road and onto the airstrip.

One by one the carriers, complete with their human cargo, were roughly manhandled onto the back of a dilapidated low sided flatbed truck with the pod's mesh access doors facing inwards to avoid nosy locals being able to see what was inside. The two truck convoy then set off back up the winding dry road with the troop carrier taking the lead and the flatbed following on behind. The only relief from the journey was the cooling breeze, but it was poor compensation as the leading truck generated clouds of dust that enveloped the transporter and cloyed the already parched throats of the prisoners as they continued to swelter under the burning desert sun. Jacob luckily faced Ivan and he tried to pass the time hoping to engage the big man in discussion of possible means of escape. But he sat silent in defeat with his head down and ready to accept his fate.

"I thought Russian men never gave in, they fought to the bitter end?" Jacob shouted over the rush of the wind and the droning engine. Ivan finally lifted his head to reply.

"I am Ukraine not Russian, and yes, it is true we never give in, but this is hopeless, so we may as well accept our fate and wait to see what lies on the other side."

As he finished his sentence, he once again lowered his head and stared at the floor.

"You are a coward!" Jacob yelled back. Ivan flinched, but did not react.

"Did you hear me; you are a big yellow bellied coward who brings shame upon his family."

Jacob hoped to reignite his friend's fighting spirit to give him a chance with whatever lay in store, but the reaction was much more than he had bargained for. With the speed of a Cheetah, Ivan launched himself across the small confines of his one-man prison, throwing all his weight behind his shoulder, thudded heavily against the steel mesh door, sliding man and cage across the truck until it crashed directly into Jacob's tiny prison. Snarling like a wild beast he jabbed his fingers through both sets of mesh in a vain attempt to reach his friend who fell back in fear.

"Nobody calls me a coward and lives to tell the tale." Ivan screamed; ripping away thin slices of blood-smeared skin from in-between his fingers as he foolishly and repeatedly thrust his hands against the thin metal grill. Jacob tried to reason with him, but Ivan released all of his pent-up rage and the attack continued. His next idea was to tightly grip both doors and use his strength to rip both of them away from their housing. But even his immense muscles were no match for the mild-steel heavy duty hinges. Eventually he began to tire and as the angry scarlet veil lifted, Ivan slumped back quietly and suckled childlike at the blood oozing from his damaged skin.

"I think I can help you escape." Jacob yelled, but all he received was a cold hearted stare followed by a shake of the head.

"Listen. You've just given me an idea. If you repeatedly throw yourself back and forth and slide your pod against the sides of the truck, I'll bet the flimsy bit of rusty wire that holds the wooden side-skirt in place, will give way and you'll be able to slip right off the back."

Ivan showed little reaction at first, but a few seconds later he narrowed his eyes and looked up as he contemplated the idea. In an instant his face changed from one with a depressive acceptance into another filled with hope and without another word he began to test it out. Time and time again, the big man threw his considerable weight from one end of his tiny prison to the other. Aided by the truck's smooth worn, dusty wooden surface, he alternated from crashing forwards into Jacob's cage with thudding backwards into the low wooden skirting that formed part of the shallow hinged sides of the truck. Sweat poured down his bearded face from the extreme exertion, but continued his effort encouraged by reports from Jacob of how much the wire appeared to weaken. Eventually, and to

Jacob's surprise, it was not an impact from Ivan's battering, but a deep pothole in the road jarring the entire rear end of the truck. The bounce snapped the now over-stretched wire loop that held up the wooden side, and three feet of skirting hinged from vertical to horizontal at the end of a small length of chain akin to a miniature drawbridge.

"Jesus Christ, it's down! Go for it, go, go!" Jacob screamed over the noise of the engine and the rushing wind. Ivan did not need to be told twice and once again he threw his impressive bulk to the back of the cage. Agonisingly slowly he slid across the dusty surface, inching towards his goal, but the road had begun to incline and to make matters even more difficult the pod was hampered by repeatedly sliding into the wooden flap enclosing the back of the truck. Just when Jacob believed that it was impossible, fate intervened when the truck driver drove quickly around a tight bend and every cage shifted to one side. With one last Herculean effort, Ivan added his own momentum and Jacob watched with tears in his eyes as his friend tipped silently over the side. Sorely tempted to try the same thing for himself, Jacob copied what Ivan had been doing, but then decided that Ivan had a greater chance of going solo. So as not to instigate mass panic, he selflessly managed to shuffle his own pod halfway across the back of the truck to stop any of the others from sliding further back and alerting the guards. Content with his own sacrifice he prayed desperately that his friend would survive the fall.

Without a grass verge or a dry stone wall to stop the cage, its momentum carried it directly over the steep escarpment running parallel to the side of the road. Over and over it skidded, flipped, and bounced down the sharp incline almost knocking the life out of its single occupant bouncing about terrified on the inside. Mercifully, it came to a cushioned halt against a clump of old scrub-brush clinging doggedly to the mountainside. Thinking that his descent was over, Ivan gathered his wits and began to kick violently against the steel mesh door of the pod. What he could not see was that below his current perch was a sheer drop to the bottom of a small ravine with a deep river raging below. Repeatedly he lashed out his powerful legs bouncing his pod violently up and down, further loosening the roots of the bushes beneath him. Again and again he kicked the entrance to his cage and the door began to buckle from the onslaught, giving him hope of freedom. Suddenly the old brushwood finally gave way and in a shower of branches, leaves and dry soil he found himself weightless as man and cage plummeted silently through the air. All he had time to do was to tuck his head into his chest, brace his limbs against the inside of the pod and wait for death. After what seemed like an age, his tiny prison reached the bottom of the gorge and plunged deep into the clear river below. Luckily the plastic compound of the pod's structure saved it from sinking too far and even with Ivan's weight it bobbed like a cork back up to the surface, but ice cold mountain water gushed in filling it rapidly while the heavy current carried him quickly downstream. Still unable to escape, Ivan snatched fleeting gulps of air in the swirling water as he bounced like a pinball from one river boulder to another. Light became dark and dark became light as he rolled end over end, praying for the torture to stop. Once again he became weightless as he tipped over a small waterfall but this time his world turned black when the pod crashed heavily into a huge flat topped rock lying below. Rendered unconscious, but mercifully above the level of water inside, Ivan and the semi-submerged pod drifted aimlessly down the mountain side. Once again, fate intervened and he finally came to rest in the shallows of a sharp river bend.

Several minutes passed until he finally came around and his vision cleared. Ivan's heart leapt at the sight of a jagged crack letting in a shaft of sunlight through the high density moulded plastic lining. First, he checked his body for serious injury, but apart from superficial damage, that included a huge lump over his right eye, he somehow appeared to be in one piece. Summing up the energy, the giant Ukrainian braced his shoulders against one side of the pod and simultaneously lashed out with both feet. The weakened state of the structure was no match for desperation and as the entire side split open Ivan emerged like a chick hatching from a giant egg to taste freedom for the first time in over three months. Ignoring the pain from cuts and bruises, he stretched out the kinks in his cramped muscles, then pushed the pod out into the faster current, watching impassively as it floated away and out of sight. In the distance the cloud of dust created by the two truck convoy climbed higher and higher into the mountains and he knew that for the moment at least that he had escaped undetected. The first thing on the new agenda was to put as much distance between him and the route as possible. With water not an immediate problem Ivan drank his fill and realised that a high vantage point was necessary to survey the area for signs of human habitation. With this in mind, he took a deep breath and loped off into the distance.

CHAPTER SIXTEEN

"What the hell do you mean a week's wages? This had better be some form of sick joke. I don't have huge savings like you, you know. If there's nothing left for food I'll starve."

Ted Langton stood cautiously by the door of Gemma Cassidy's one bedroom apartment in the accommodation zone at the end of highway five. He was primed and ready for anything as he revealed the punishment regarding her involvement in the restaurant incident. The level of Gemma's sanctions had already been thrashed out between him and Philip Sanderson and Ted believed that if he waited long enough it would all blow over. That was until Paul Johnston and Astelle refused to pay their deposit until they had proof of Gemma's punishment, leaving Ted with no choice.

Gemma was usually averse to remaining calm during arguments or stressful situations, resulting in many an ornament or any other small object that came to hand, flying at great velocity in Ted's general direction. Unable to interject with his offer of financial help for her problems he lacked the courage to deliver the rest of the bad news regarding her temporary demotion and payment for Astelle's dry cleaning.

"Do you have any idea how hard it is for a single woman to make her way in this world? I have to work twice as hard as all the other men on my level just to get noticed and they are the ones who get the promotion, it's just not fair."

Gemma flopped down on her sofa and burst into tears. Ted guessed that the dominant emotion would either be violence or breakdown; thankfully it was the latter. He sat down by her side and offered a comforting arm around her shoulders. She quickly rolled into his embrace and sobbed quietly while she let it all out of her system. Ted needed to be miles away to continue field testing the latest holographic program, but his anger towards Philip cancelled any guilty feeling he had about work. The only thing that mattered now was Gemma and he was determined to show support. Ten minutes later, she still lay peacefully in Ted's arms when her wrist watch that doubled as a mobile phone, burst into life, flashing the name Jen in red light emitting diodes on the jet-black clock face. Before Ted had a chance to ask her to block the call, Gemma had already voice activated the device to answer.

"Hi Jen what can I do for you?" Gemma asked without having to move, the receiver had already been programmed to respond only to her voice pattern and could pick up her unique inflections and intonations from as far away as ten feet and still transmit coherent sound.

"Just heard the news that you've been docked a week's pay; that's a real bummer!" Jen replied. The unit on Gemma's wrist constantly monitored the surrounding area and compensated for resonance and weather such as a windy conditions, automatically adjusting the volume and pitch so as to be heard perfectly every time.

"Wow news sure travels fast around here, Ted's only just told me. It'll take all of my savings to last until next payday but I'm sure I'll manage."

She could feel Ted tensing up and lifted her head to see what the matter was as Jen continued to talk.

"How d'you feel about having to pay that bitch Astelle's dry cleaning bill?"

"What dry cleaning bill?" Gemma snapped as she glared menacingly through her tear reddened eyes at Ted, who was already shuffling across the sofa to get out of reach and silently praying for Jen to shut up. Ted mouthed that he was just about to tell Gemma this information when the phone rang, and he continued to look shell shocked as Jen dug him an even deeper hole.

"Hasn't Ted told you yet, I hope that I haven't put my foot in it but thought he would have told you by now. You probably don't know about having to join the base cleanup duty for the next fortnight either!"

At this point Ted was already on his feet and backing up to the door; Gemma was angrily looking around for something to throw, as Jen continued.

"I've heard that this week, it's cess pit maintenance, I don't envy you much at all Gemma."

Gemma's face had turned a rich shade of puce and Ted could see the vein on her forehead pulse with the increasing beat of her heart. Even though he feared for his safety, he had the annoying habit of laughing at the most inopportune moments and the sight of Gemma looking ready to explode with anger, this happened to be such a moment.

"So now you think it's funny as well do you?" Gemma yelled. Jen heard her voice and worried for her friend's safety.

"Gemma, are you alright, you sound very tense. Are you there Gemma?"

"We'll talk later, end call." Was all that Gemma had to say, and as the communication ended, she picked up a large pottery vase from a side table and hurled it at Ted. Luckily, his reactions honed from previous battles were razor sharp and he easily dodged the vase that shattered on the door behind him. Deciding that the cemetery was full of dead heroes, he repeatedly pressed the button mounted on the wall behind, desperately trying to get the front door open. As is the usual case, technology refuses to obey in times when speed is paramount and the door stayed tightly closed. Gemma was now warming to her task and eagerly looked around for another suitable projectile. Hearing a grinding sound, Ted looked down to see a piece of broken pottery jammed between the door and the frame, stopping the mechanism from sliding the door open. Dropping down onto his good knee to free the shard was a fortuitous manoeuvre as another larger vase smashed into the wall exactly where his head had just been placed. Free of the obstruction, the door squealed along gritty runners just far enough for Ted to crawl through and limp away as another unidentified object landed with a dull thud against the back of the half-open door. He was hoping to soften the blow to Gemma's ego by offering to pay for the dry cleaning and replace her missing weeks' wages with his own money but it would now have to wait until she had calmed down and he could use it as a peace offering.

"You low-down, miserable, scum sucking, son of a bitch! Come back and face me you coward!" Gemma screamed to the empty room, but all she heard were Ted's limping footsteps fade as he hastily made his way down the corridor to the exit.

For the next fifteen minutes, Gemma prowled around her apartment trying unsuccessfully to calm her temper, when her attention was diverted as a second telephone call flashed onto the face of her wristwatch. The display identified the caller as an unknown number. Guessing that it was someone trying to sell her life insurance or asking to be part of a survey she almost ignored it, but relishing the idea of venting her anger on someone else, decided to answer.

* * *

Over four and a half thousand miles away, Sheriff Dodson closed his eyes and gently massaged his throbbing temples, trying to relax before he made the international call. It had only been a few days since he found out who the investigators worked for and they seemed to have no intention of leaving any time soon. This increased his anxiety to levels previously unknown, which in turn had a detrimental effect on his already poor health. Unable to find a more effective solution to the ongoing problem, he decided it was time to enlist some extra help.

With the dog-eared piece of paper containing Gemma's number in his hand, he stared at it for nearly a minute, took a deep breath, and finally made the call. There was a slight delay due to the distance involved but a vaguely familiar voice answered the call.

"Howdy Miss Cassidy, this is Sheriff Oberon P Dodson from Triplerock County police department, Louisiana. I'm not sure if you will remember me, but you arranged a discount for me and my deputies to go big game hunting at the Alabama Hologram Dreams franchise."

Gemma remained silent; unsure what to say next as she wondered if this was a set up by Philip Sanderson in his attempt to get rid of her once and for all. She quickly analysed everything she could remember about the situation and was confident to be well within the rules regarding the special discount she had given away.

"Err, yes, I do remember you, if there was a problem with the trip you will have to complain to customer services at the head office. I have the number somewhere if you would hold on a minute."

Gemma was already searching through her digital phone book when the sheriff replied.

"Yes, it is about the trip, but it is not something I can discuss on an open line. If you would be so kind as to continue via the secure channel I will accept all charges from both sender and recipient for the call."

The request for the secure channel left Gemma stunned and completely intrigued. As an average single low income worker, she considered her private conversations were not worth the extortionate cost of a secure line. This relatively new service was introduced following the years of repeated media phone hacking scandals, mainly snooping on the rich and famous. It must be something very important if a sheriff was worried about being overheard with what he was about to say.

"I guess so, it's your dime."

The line went dead and she wondered if it was a prank call when her wrist receiver lit up with ***'secure line'*** flashing repeatedly across the watch face.

"This is a secure line call, all charges have been accepted by the sender. Do you wish to continue?" A pre-recorded voice announced. Gemma verbally accepted and sat down as she waited for the sheriff to begin.

"Miss Cassidy, I trust that you have no other connection with the Hologram Dreams Corporation other than as an employee of the company?"

Even though he asked the question and hoped that Gemma would tell the truth. He was already having serious doubts whether this was the best course of action and perhaps he should notify the FBI directly and deny any involvement in the extra-curricular activities.

"If you mean working for that weasel Philip Sanderson then your assumption is correct." Gemma replied. Her negative tone reassured the sheriff greatly and gave him the lift he needed to continue.

"As you are well aware Miss Cassidy, in return for not spending the night in jail, you allowed myself and two of my deputies to use your staff discount code for a day out big game hunting."

Gemma recalled the offence and wondered if she was about to be blackmailed for something else.

"Yes officer, I do recall and am not at liberty to offer any more favours, as far as I am concerned the slate is clean and I don't owe you anything."

Gemma was about to end the call before any threats could begin, but the sheriff promised that he was not asking for anything else and begged her indulgence.

"I wish to inform you of an incident that occurred at the end of the experience. It is something that I am embarrassed to reveal, but my conscience insists that I do."

This peaked Gemma's curiosity and she remained silent, hoping that the old man would stop his procrastinating and come to the point.

"The fact is this Miss Cassidy. I paid a little extra for a recreation of a man hunt as a treat for the boys. Before you say anything I know it is against the rules but as you realise sometimes rules can be overlooked occasionally."

Gemma was slowly becoming annoyed at his reference to her DUI and it was common knowledge to most of the employees about all the extras that clients paid for. This usually took the form of one kind of depravity or another and was dependant on the scruples of the franchise involved. The general consensus was that only androids and holographic projections were involved and even though requests were morally offensive and illegal in the outside world, nobody came to any harm.

"I have already heard of such extras as you like to put it, but if your conscience has got the better of you I am sorry, also why do you need to tell me about it?"

The sheriff realised that he was still skirting around the point and blurted out the tag line.

"The slaves we hunted weren't robots, they were real humans!"

"I'm sorry sheriff I don't understand."

"There were three slaves released for us to chase, whom we thought to be robots, but they were actually made of flesh and blood just like you and me. Two of them were men who were killed during the hunt, and the third was a young woman who we captured. Now I know that these robots are very realistic an all and you think that I am just confused, but when I managed to get a close-up of the young woman I recognised her as the recently missing daughter of a cousin of mine. She had been sprayed chocolate brown and drugged so as she couldn't even remember her own name."

Gemma sat opened mouthed and silent at the revelation, prompting the sheriff to continue.

"We managed to smuggle the poor child out and reunite her with her family. But due to the sensitivity of my involvement I am unable to proceed any further with a public investigation, that's where you come in. I thought you would like to do some digging for yourself. My hands are also further tied as I have good reason to believe that I am being followed by two investigators from your organisation."

Gemma's mind reeled from the full and frank disclosure. For the present moment in time all she could agree to do was call him back if she managed to glean any information.

"If anything regarding my involvement is leaked to the press I will deny any knowledge, but I will remember your little misdemeanour, which will also include a few of my own extras if you know what I mean. So make sure you call on a secure line, we don't want anyone else listening in do we?"

Protecting all of his involvement in the proceedings, the sheriff had made his point very clear and he ended the call leaving Gemma staring into space wondering what to do next.

CHAPTER SEVENTEEN

"I think I've found a way to escape!" Adam exclaimed while he took a shower and Neil stood in front of the sink brushing his teeth. The fast running water masked the sound of his voice and fogged up the surveillance camera lens as the room filled with condensed steam. Neil tried to remain nonchalant at the news, but the shock caused him to inhale a gobbet of toothpaste, leaving him with tear streamed eyes from the menthol taste, burning the back of his nasal passages as he repeatedly coughed over the sink. When he had sufficiently recovered, he slowly and methodically continued with his ablutions while Adam explained how he had managed to hack into the computer mainframe and accessed everything needed without triggering any security alarms. One thing he had found were a set of building plans of the prison, including a blueprint for the ventilation ducts which he calculated were big enough for a person to crawl through all the way from the gymnasium up to the surface. The only problem was that as soon as anyone was discovered missing, they would receive an electric shock and it may be possible that every collar contained a locator beacon pinpointing exactly where they were. Neil's initial elation quickly faded and he hung his head over the sink, as he knew it was impossible to remove the shock collars. Even Jacob's great strength was not enough to pull them apart.

"I'm not finished yet!" Adam mouthed in a stage whisper when he saw his friend's crestfallen face.

"If there are plans for the building, perhaps I can hack into the controller for the collars. I didn't want to give you false hope but I thought any positive information no matter how small would boost morale."

Neil smiled back and nodded, eager to pass on the information to the others, especially Oliver, who had sunk into a depression following Jacob's departure. He prayed nightly that Jacob would soon return and whatever lay in store for the group, they would all face together. What Neil did not know was that Adam had not told him everything he had discovered and that he knew some of the terrifying truth of what lay in store for him and his friends. Also the second and more sickening news was that Jacob had already been transferred out of the prison and if he were not already dead, he soon would be.

CHAPTER EIGHTEEN

Sheriff Dodson took a sip of hot black coffee to calm his nerves before he made his daily telephone call to Doctor Booth. He was sure it would be a repeat of the same answer that the doctor had given since he initially examined Molly Dawson nearly two weeks ago. He knew that the doctor would say that there was still no change in her memory loss and that in his professional opinion he doubted that it would ever return. But the chance that a change in her condition was still possible constantly gnawed away at his insides necessitating a daily confirmation. Sooner or later he was positive that Molly would remember something that happened on that fateful day, and although on his part, no real crime had been committed, the intent was still there. He knew that the public outrage would force him to hand in his resignation, lose his pension and the disgrace would probably drive him from the district altogether; this recurring thought was breaking his heart. The sheriff was an eighth generation Holtsvillian and very proud of that fact. He had purchased the oldest home in the district that used to belong to Jedadiah Holt, the first settler in Triplerock Valley and of whom the town was named after. It was in this house he intended to see out the rest of his days. The daily reminder of the investigators from the Hologram Dreams Corporation watching his every move was taking a terrible toll on his already poor health and the comfort eating made him pile on the pounds at an alarming rate.

As usual the doctor took an age to pick up the receiver, giving the sheriff plenty of time to think. He had still heard nothing back from Gemma Cassidy and he now wished that he had never told her in the first place. It only added another person to the list who knew at least some of the truth. Staring absentmindedly out through the open door of his office and into the reception area, he saw his two deputies wander into the station ready to clock on for another shift, when a sudden clarity came to mind and he terminated the call.

"Elvis, Duke get your sorry asses in here, we need to talk."

Cursory puzzled glances between both men silently confirmed that neither knew the reason why they were being called into the office.

"Shut the door and sit down."

Elvis clicked the door closed, much to the annoyance of Jolene who was hoping to eavesdrop on the conversation held within. She knew that the three men shared a secret and was ready to burst with curiosity, but it was impossible to hear anything now the door was closed.

"Boys, I have been in law enforcement since the day I left school, and through hard work and endeavour I rose through the ranks until I became sheriff of this fair town for more than twenty-two years now."

Both men remained silent, curious as to the content of the statement, but wondering if they would have to endure another long winded trip down the Boss man's memory lane. Feeling a little choked up, Sheriff Dodson cleared his throat, and then blew his nose on one of many polka dot hankies that he always carried about his person. To add a dramatic effect, he decided to stand up, turn to the window, and partially pull down a slat of the recently installed white venetian blinds so he could wistfully stare through the gap just as he had seen many times in his favourite detective shows. Duke rolled his eyes and tilted his head sarcastically towards Elvis as the sheriff finally gathered his thoughts. Heavily clearing his throat for the second time he managed to continue.

"There comes a time in every man's life when he has to stand back and take stock of what he has achieved, what's also important for the future. I have given the best years of my life to this job and I hope to have made a difference to this fair town of ours."

At this point he paused, waiting to receive positive affirmation to the statement, but the silence that ensued only reasserted his bitterness at the lack of appreciation his job now held. Both deputies were really not paying attention as they had become accustomed to the old man waxing lyrical about every matter of interest, but they both pricked up their ears when he finally came to the point.

"Men, I have thought long and hard about this problem and have come to a momentous decision. We got to get them two nosey parkers from Hologram Dreams out of the picture and when that is achieved, I'm going to take an early retirement."

Inhaling deeply through his nose to stop getting over emotional, he wondered why his deputies had nothing to say and turned around to see both men sitting open mouthed and dumbstruck. They knew that everyone had to retire someday, but both of them had assumed that due to his obesity and poor state of health he would probably die from a heart attack or a stroke way before then and they were more than happy to see him feed his face at every opportunity. Each deputy held a secret desire that when the inevitable happened, they would be the one to take up the vacant post. The sheriff on the other-hand took it as a sign of affection and he cordially thanked his men for their support.

"Anyway, enough of all that. What I want is for either one of you to come up with a plan that will get rid of these men once and for all. I don't care how you do it; just get on with it. This is my town and I'm not goin' down without a fight. The one who succeeds in this task will receive my full gratitude, if you know what I mean!"

The sheriff tapped the side of his nose with his index finger and glanced down at his empty chair, then looked back at two men trying very hard to conceal their excitement.

Encouraging the two deputies to stand up ready to leave the office, he added a few more choice words.

"That'll be all for now, so go out and do your duty and not a word to anyone!"

Jolene only just made it to her seat as Elvis opened the office door. She had tried to listen at the keyhole, but there was too much background noise coming from within the reception area to make any sense of the private conversation held within. Her frustration was only exacerbated when en route to their desks Elvis mumbled,

"Do ya' think he really means it Duke?"

Both deputies dearly wanted the sheriff's job and remained deep in thought as they sat behind their desks, straining what limited intelligence they possessed to come up with a scheme to win the soon vacant post. Elvis decided that he would bombard the two investigators with repeated parking tickets and traffic violation penalties, followed by the threat of jail time until they finally upped sticks and returned home. Duke on the other-hand, believed that a more permanent solution was required.

In a much more settled state of mind, the sheriff picked up the telephone and redialled Doctor Booth. In the inevitable delay before the aged medic answered, he opened the lowest drawer on the right-hand side of the office desk to reveal it overflowing with assorted bars of caramel and chocolate. Caressing the shiny wrappers with his chubby fingertips, he finally settled on a current favourite packet of double thick chocolate coated peanuts, ready to celebrate his latest plan.

Inside Doctor Booth's surgery, the medic repeated the same answers to the same questions that the sheriff had asked since the day he brought Molly home. He then ended the call by replacing the aged plastic telephone receiver back onto its cradle, picked up a small black personal voice recorder from the top of a stack of patient files perched precariously on the corner of his desk, and leaned forwards ready to continue. He generally used the device for storing plot ideas for short story crime thrillers that he often wrote for men's adult magazines. A pastime for which he used a pen name for obvious reasons, but the regular stipend helped supplement his limited income. Waiting silently as she sat across the other side of the desk, a much paler looking Molly Dawson smiled smugly as she listened in to the conversation. As soon as he was ready, the doctor tapped the red button on the voice recorder and nodded, allowing Molly to continue. Her revelations began with her abduction and subsequent sale, to a group of men that the doctor informed her, through a few enquiries of his own was a franchise of the Hologram Dreams Corporation. Embellishing every sordid detail, she continued her sorry tale of imprisonment, forced drug abuse, dying of her skin and hair, through to her pursuit and rape by Deputy Clifford Thornbuck and the intent of rape by the sheriff until the very last second when he recognised her features and subsequently helped her to escape. She told the doctor the truth about almost everything, apart from her whereabouts between leaving Holtsville and the time of her kidnap. She claimed to have been on a shopping trip when she was snatched from the side of the road while waiting for the bus. What Molly did not want revealed was that she had been working as a prostitute more than a hundred miles away and that she had run away from home to earn some easy money. It was from within the brothel where she lived, following a heated argument with the madam regarding commission money, she was abducted from her room in the dead of the night and sold to slave traders.

Doctor Booth could hardly contain his excitement and insisted that the story would be auctioned to the highest bidder, be it to a newspaper, magazine, news channel, or even Hologram Dreams directly to buy their silence. The last one on the list he decided not to reveal to Molly as it carried considerable risk, and if the company was capable of abduction and murder, they might just decide to silence both of them permanently. For now all he wanted her to do was give him every little detail and he would do the rest, positive that he would have the networks clambering over one another for the rights to the story. The majority of Molly's memory had returned long before she had even reached the doctor's surgery door, but still fearful of Duke, she continued with her charade. She also knew that the doctor was a writer of sorts and as he was also a man of reputation she confided in him from the start, suggesting that he could write and sell her story for a share of the proceeds. Molly was the only other person who knew of the doctor's talent, a fact he had to reveal over a year ago when she was employed as a house cleaner and she chanced upon a stash of adult magazines in an unlocked cupboard in his bedroom. To avoid being labelled a dirty old man, the doctor embarrassedly explained the reason they were in his possession and showed Molly typed copies of his stories printed within, while insisting he only kept them as records of his writing success. Unfortunately, this was not enough and only the promise of a wage rise, dental care, and holiday pay would buy Molly's silence.

"All you have to do, young lady, is to say nothing and act dumb until I can sell the story. Don't tell anyone, not even your momma. Do you understand me?"

Molly shifted awkwardly in her seat and avoided eye contact as she silently nodded her acceptance. She did not have the courage to tell him that her mother already knew everything and it was her who encouraged Molly to sell her story. She too swore to remain silent about what had happened to her daughter, but her heavy drinking sometimes loosened her tongue and on more than one occasion Molly had to cover up her tales of *' Molly's great adventure'* as her mother like to call it. Luckily no one paid much attention to the old woman's drunken ramblings, but Molly feared that very soon someone just might.

With every detail of the latest chapter of the story dictated to the doctor, Molly picked up her coat and headed out of the surgery front door. She had agreed with the old man to split all the proceeds fifty-fifty, but the truth was that she had no intention of letting him have one cent of the money and was going to blackmail him with accusations of sexually molesting her when she visited his surgery as a young teenager. Deep in thought with her own nasty ideas, Molly reached the end of the surgery driveway, turned right through the high walled gateway and almost bumped into Lyle Simpkins who was waiting outside next to his hire car.

"Excuse me Miss Dawson, could I have a word?"

"How you know my name and waddya' want?" She snapped without breaking stride, making him run alongside her long legged gait, as he was considerably shorter than Molly's near six foot frame.

"Everyone knows your name in these parts Miss Dawson. You caused quite a stir in the local press when the sheriff brought you back into town. Is it true that you have been missing for two months? What happened during that time, where on earth have you been?"

Molly maintained her long stride, ignored his questions, and went on the offensive by asking some of her own.

"Who are you, are you a reporter or somethin'?"

Lyle hastily produced a business card from his top pocket and passed it to Molly. As soon as she spotted the Hologram Dreams logo sticking out from under his thumb her blood ran cold. Stopping dead in her tracks she stared hard down at Lyle's face.

"Whatcha' call this? The Hologram Dreams Corporation, are you trying to sell me time shares or do you belong to a cult?" Molly continued the verbal attack, trying to play for time while she regained her composure.

"Not at all Miss Dawson, Hologram Dreams is a fantasy film production corporation and I am an investigator for the company. It just so happens that on the day the sheriff found you at the side of the highway he had just exited one of our sites in rather a hurry and we wanted to know if you saw anything suspicious regarding the situation."

Molly knew immediately that Lyle Simpkins knew the whole truth and was hoping to find out how much she did too.

"If you had read all the newspaper reports about my return you would realise that I can't remember anything between leaving Holtsville and the time the kindly sheriff picked me up in a buggy at the side of the highway as you have so rightly reminded me. You could have saved yourself the trouble of coming out here and wasting my time."

Molly's hoped her attitude and story sounded convincing, and was relieved that Lyle apologised and stepped out of the way. Before she left, Molly tried to hand back Lyle's business card, but he insisted she keep it.

"Just in case you happen to remember anything, anything at all Miss Dawson, you can reach me at the Forest Lodge near the interstate on the outskirts of town."

Molly obliged by keeping the card and walked away, wondering the same as the doctor if her life was still in danger, or now that she was out, how much money Hologram Dreams would pay for her silence.

With a heavy heart Lyle Simpkins returned to his car, sadly knowing that Molly's bluster proved she was lying and the fact that an off-road buggy had never been mentioned by anyone was proof she was hiding something, as they arrived back into town in a hire car. If word were ever released through Molly about the Philip Sanderson's connection with the slave trade, he would pay with his own life. It was now down to him to silence her permanently, and what he needed now was to figure out just how to do it.

CHAPTER NINETEEN

The fierce Spanish sun continued to beat relentlessly down onto the tops of the transportation pods rattling about on the back of the aged truck, but thankfully the heat generated was relieved by the markedly cooler air current pouring down from the mountainous peaks. This small crumb of comfort did little to ease the torture of severely potholed roads and the constant nerve-wracking crunches of yet another badly meshed gear change as the driver constantly moved up and down through the truck's crawler gears to reach the summit of yet another steep incline. Overheating from the constant strain on the aged engine, steam began to billow from the radiator and out from under the centrally hinged bonnet, forcing the driver to pull over into a passing place and cut the power.

Fifty yards ahead, the driver of the troop carrier glanced in his wing mirror, saw what happened and stopped immediately. Dropping the gearbox into neutral and using only the footbrake, he used gravity to reverse slowly down the incline towards the broken down wagon, before backing expertly into the narrow space directly behind the stricken truck. Stepping down from the cab, the officer in charge who was riding in the front with the driver, immediately spotted the side-skirt hanging down from the side of the flatbed truck and the glaring gap at the back where Ivan's pod used to be.

Furiously he beat the side of the truck with his cane, and screamed for everyone to get out as he quickly counted the remaining prisoners to make sure that it was not just the way the cages had settled in transit. Jacob did not need to understand the language as the officer swore loudly several times in his Castilian tongue, then grabbed the bemused driver by the lapels of his jacket, shaking him violently to demand what had happened. Realising that he was wasting his time, he threw him back against the cab door and ordered two men to guard the vehicle while it cooled down, as he marched towards the troop carrier to set off back down the valley hoping to find the missing man. Passing the rear of the truck, the irate officer suddenly stopped and glared directly at Jacob, who immediately looked down hoping not to catch his eye.

"When did the cage fall from the truck?" He demanded in heavily accented English. Jacob ignored the question and kept his gaze fixed to the floor.

"I asked you a question boy, answer me!" The officer yelled, thrashing his cane on the side of Jacob's cage, leaving the terrified man curled up in a ball and shaking with fear and dehydration. Again and again the officer used his cane, taking out his frustrations against the toughened side panels, leaving brown scuff marks with every blow. Eventually having to stop out of exhaustion in the thin mountain air, he removed his pistol from his shoulder holster and aimed it directly at Jacob.

"How long ago did the cage fall from the truck?"

As he spoke the officer used his thumb to click the hammer back at the rear of the barrel of the aged weapon. Jacob was prepared to sacrifice his own life for that of his friend so he remained tight lipped, lowered his head, and waited for death. Seconds ticked by and in the tense silence that followed, Jacob continued to stare down at the shadow of the gun cast upon the deck of the truck. Like the time shadow cast upon a sundial, the angle of the gun slowly appeared to alter and the pistol fired. Dozens of birds nesting on the shady branches of nearby trees suddenly took flight and as Jacob's body flinched violently, he realised that he was still very much alive and could not feel the searing pain of being shot. Looking up it was obvious that the officer had deliberately fired the pistol into the air. Jacob believed that now the standoff was over, a broad search would be conducted, but the officer was still furious at being out manoeuvred. Smiling menacingly, he did the next best thing and pointed his gun at the prisoner in the next pod. It happened to be the same man whose finger the commander had whacked with his cane and at the sight of the gun aimed at his face, he began to squeal and thrash about in the confines of his tiny cell. Jacob watched in disbelief as the officer pulled the hammer back for a second time and repeated the question.

"If you don't value your own pitiful existence, perhaps the life of another would change your mind. I repeat, how long ago did the cage fall from the truck?"

Jacob knew that he was beaten; his horrified face was enough to tell the grinning officer that he would not be held responsible for another man's life, leaving him no choice but give the best answer he had, hoping that it would be enough.

"Five to ten minutes ago." Jacob whispered hoarsely through cracked lips and parched throat.

"What did you say?"

"I said about five to ten minutes ago." Jacob raised his voice as much as he was able. Thankfully, it was just enough.

"You had better not lie to me pig." The officer snarled, looking almost disappointed at being denied the chance to kill. Easing the hammer back into its safe position, he re-holstered his pistol and crossed over to retake his place in the front passenger seat of the troop carrier that had already turned around for the descent. Jacob held his breath and listened to the sound of the engine as it faded into the distance, then he relaxed, knowing that they were looking in the completely wrong place.

Far down the mountains as he tracked hastily along the riverbank, Ivan stopped and looked up when he heard the sound of a single gunshot echo down the valley. Alerted by the report, he doubled his pace; knowing that his free time was up and the search had begun.

Jacob guessed that it had been at least half an hour since he watched the cage disappear off the side of the truck, putting several miles between Ivan and the guards. From what he could see through the steel mesh that formed the door to his cage, he had been lucky enough to choose a steep terrain covered in a thick scrub. Knowing that it would be almost impossible for them to find his friend, he prayed silently that he had survived the fall and managed to break free from his tiny cell.

Lowering his gaze Jacob closed his eyes and breathed deeply, trying to blot out this living hell, only to flinch at the welcome cooling sensation of water pouring over his head via an observation hole sited in the roof of his pod. Looking up, he saw the face of the kindly soldier left in charge who had taken it upon himself to offer succour to the poor prisoners by offering them all a drink of water from his own personal supply. There was not much to go round, but what was given was gratefully accepted and Jacob immediately cupped his hands to catch the life giving liquid, gulping it down as fast as he could, ignoring the cramping sensation as the cool water reached his shrunken stomach. All too soon, the bottle emptied as the soldier moved on from one prisoner to the next, but the gesture reinstated some belief that they might just survive this nightmare.

Within the hour the truck had cooled down, and with everyone, including the engine's radiator topped up with fresh water, the sorry looking cargo braced their cramped bodies for the rest of the uncomfortable journey. The troop carrier had not yet returned, but being the faster vehicle it would soon catch up. In the meantime, any personnel left behind who could not fit into the cab had to ride in the back, sitting in the space left behind by Ivan's missing pod.

Night time comes swiftly in the mountains and the truck, still without its extra military presence, rolled into a guarded secure farmstead en route to their destination. Dragged bodily from their tiny cages, the prisoners were kicked and prodded across the farmyard while still barely able to walk from the pain of cramping muscles, only to be herded into a filthy stinking hut that looked to Jacob like it had been previously been used as an animal shelter. Extra bars had been fitted across any open windows and the main construction of corrugated sheeting, had been sufficiently patched up to make escape impossible. There were no hi-tech shock collars or surveillance cameras this time, only two armed men standing guard outside the door. Slowly and with considerable pain, the men were able to finally straighten up from their enforced confinement and limp around the shack in an attempt to stretch out the kinks in their weary frames.

The stretching regime continued until suddenly everyone stopped and looked to the door as it reopened. A young woman dressed in peasant clothing, walked in carrying in a small pot of bubbling hot stew for the starving men. Following her close behind was a nervous looking child of not more than ten years of age who bore such a striking resemblance to the woman that Jacob guessed she must be her younger sister. She carried a stack of small wooden soup bowls and spoons, that she carefully placed beside the stew pot, all the time staring wide-eyed at the motley crew. Jacob smiled when he caught her eye, but in the half-light his wide mouthed toothy grin contrasting against the black hue of his skin had a negative effect and fearfully the child backed away, clinging tightly to the older woman's skirts as she left the shack. The more able bodied of the group began to ladle out healthy servings of the much needed food into the wooden bowls, passing one to each member before helping themselves. It was piping hot and tasted very salty, but Jacob did not care and wolfed his down, feeling the satisfying warmth easing the knots to his belly. To his surprise there was enough for second helpings and this time he tried to chew more slowly, trying to ignore the advent of nausea coming from the salty rich overload. Replete from the meal and now feeling much more alive,

Jacob crawled around to whisper in turn to everyone if they had any idea on how to escape, but the response was not what he expected. The majority seemed resigned to their fate and were ready to accept whatever came their way. Some even turned their backs as they stretched out on the dirt floor to sleep off the meal. Only two men showed an interest and moved closer to Jacob forming a tight huddle. Although they were both eastern European, they understood English very well and listened intently to Jacob's ideas.

"I think it's best if we try immediately, while over half of the guards are out looking for Ivan. The corrugated sheets are only loosely fastened to the wood frame and I am sure we could force one out at the back and slip away behind the rest of the out buildings."

Both men looked around and studied the far corner that Jacob spoke of and nodded their agreement.

"What do we do after that?" Asked the smaller of the two. He was of similar age to Jacob, but as yet he did not know his name. Shrugging his shoulders Jacob thought for a moment and then added,

"Beyond that I have only a vague idea, I suggest that we head for the wooded area that we drove through on the way here, that will provide enough cover, then it's just run and hope for the best."

With a full belly and fuelled with adrenaline, they positioned themselves in the back corner of the hut and began to push carefully against the boards hoping to force out the nails holding them in, but it was harder than it looked. As soon as they managed to get any purchase, the rusty nails embedded into the old knotty wood creaked deafeningly in the twilight hush, causing alarm among their fellow prisoners who begged them to stop for fear of punishment. Changing tactics, they began to claw away the soft earthen floor in hope of tunnelling their way underneath, but less than a foot down; the earth petered out leaving a base of solid rock. Undeterred, they began to claw away tiny chunks of planking, but fingernails were no competition for mountain hardened timber and before long the three men collapsed tired and bloodied onto the floor.

No sooner had they replaced the soil and smoothed over the surface, shafts of light from truck headlights traversed across the room as the truck containing the officer in charge and the rest of the troops, drove into the farmyard. Jacob ran to the front of the hut, pressed his face to the side of an open knothole, and watched with his heart thumping wildly in his chest for any signs of Ivan. The officer's face said it all as he jumped down and yelled something unintelligible to his men before marching away into the small homestead. Realising that his friend was still at large, Jacob's heart leapt with excitement in hope that he was on his way to freedom. Buoyed up with hope, Jacob settled down, rested his head against and upright wooden beam; before he knew it he had fallen asleep.

Within a few hours, Jacob and the rest of his group all awoke to the sound of a commotion in the farmyard and they all scrabbled around in the darkness to find any available crack in the wood planking or a gap in the corrugated sheeting to see if Ivan had been captured and returned to the fold. What they did not expect to see was the dishevelled figure of the truck driver held tightly by his upper arms and supported between two uniformed men as they dragged his semiconscious body into the half-light cast by the farmhouse windows. For the next five minutes they waited patiently, ignoring the voice of the driver whose head hung down while he spoke incoherently to the ground with what Jacob presumed was pleading in vain for his freedom. It was obvious that everyone related to this part of the enterprise had been ordered into the courtyard and they all stood silently dreading the upcoming event. Jacob even spotted the young girl who carried the dinner bowls earlier that evening, as she held tightly to an old teddy bear and stood sleepily in her nightshirt alongside the rest of the group. Eventually the farmhouse door opened and to the horror of the assembled peasants, the officer in charge stood posing on the porch. Pausing for full effect he eventually sauntered out and stood an arm's length away from the quaking driver who had seen the familiar shadow approach. Over the top of the frail old man's head, the officer began to address everyone loudly in his native Spanish. Jacob could only understand the odd word he remembered from his boyhood language classes, and he struggled to make sense of the situation. Suddenly, from out of the darkness one of the other prisoners whom Jacob had never spoken with, stage whispered an on the fly translation for the benefit of everyone else in the shack.

"Today an unforgiveable event occurred, resulting in the loss of a valuable asset. This will have an effect on me financially and will in turn affect all of you. I set my standards very highly and do not tolerate such pitiful failure. Therefore, you are all here to witness what happens when someone lets me down."

Walking around behind the terrified driver, the officer roughly grabbed a handful of what remained of the old man's greying hair and painfully yanked his head back. The reluctant crowd gasped when light from the farmhouse kitchen illuminated his battered and swollen face. Greatly enjoying the horrified reaction of the assembled group, the officer allowed everyone a continued look at the damage, before releasing his grip and the poor driver's head flopped down, with his chin thudding heavily upon his chest. Looking disgusted with the deposit of cheap hair oil coating his fingers, the officer then proceeded to wipe his hand clean on the already blood stained shirt tail of his prisoner. In the prolonged silence that followed, the only sound that could be heard was the gentle mountain breeze rustling the leaves in the trees until the officer continued with his judgemental summation.

"I like to think that we are part of one big happy family here, and if one member lets himself down he lets us all down. Therefore, I must provide you all with a permanent visual reminder of what happens when standards fall."

At this point the officer had already walked back around to face the terrified man then proceeded to unbutton the leather holster containing the pistol carried above his hip. The farm workers began to move forwards in the man's defence only to stop abruptly as the remaining soldiers trained their rifles on the stricken group. Suddenly aware he was in mortal danger, the old man looked up to stare through swollen eye lids down the barrel of a gun positioned less than six inches from his face. Jacob screamed and desperately banged his fists against the insides of the shack, but the officer just smiled at the added attention. In a repeat of events earlier in the day, he slowly cocked back the hammer on the vintage pistol and then pressed the end of the barrel to the centre of the man's forehead. Jacob held his breath and the tension seemed to last forever, punctuated only by the pitiful pleading of the driver as he attempted to alter his fate. The young girl, realising what was about to happen, turned and buried her face in the skirts of her older sister who wrapped a protective arm around the child's shoulder.

Suddenly, the officer burst into laughter and to the relief of everyone he lowered the gun. Panting heavily, Jacob closed his eyes and dropped wearily to his knees on the dirt floor, only to scramble back up to his spy hole at the crack of a single gunshot followed immediately by a woman's scream. To his horror, the officer was still laughing, but this time at the sight of the old man who had been dropped by his guards, allowing him to roll around on the ground, clutching his bloodied naked left foot, that was minus one or maybe two of its toes. The woman who had brought the prisoners their food, ignored the guard's threats, pushed the rifles out of her way and ran over to offer comfort to the wounded man as the officer's jovial demeanour disappeared and in a loud angry tones concluded his speech.

"Let this be a lesson of what happens when I am let down. The sight of this man as he hobbles about for the rest of his days will be a visual reminder to you all."

Without another word he re-holstered his pistol and walked swiftly back into the farmhouse. The soldiers quickly dispersed allowing the injured man to be picked up and cradled gently in the arms of one of the other farmhands as he carried the patient into a separate outbuilding. They were followed by most of the group, leaving Jacob and the rest of his friends sitting in the darkness trying to comprehend the barbarity they had just witnessed.

The night passed swiftly, and next morning, everyone awoke to the sound of a wooden stick being dragged across the corrugated waves of the tin fronted walls of the shack. The guards had all also been given a severe dressing down for the escaped prisoner and they desperately ran around trying to complete tasks in record time hoping to keep out of further trouble. Bleary eyed and tired, the prisoners were led out into the chilly morning sunlight and forced to line shoulder to shoulder in front of the shack. The guards already had their rifles locked, loaded, and aimed; they were not going to take any chances in losing another. Fifteen minutes passed by until the officer in charge appeared, freshly washed and clean shaven, with his arm around the waist of the young woman who had brought last night's food. For the benefit of his men and much to her disgust, he roughly kissed her on the mouth before smacking her behind as she turned to get away. Smugly he sauntered across the yard, heading straight for Jacob, who immediately stared directly at the ground. The point of the officer's baton, placed under his chin and violently forced upwards, painfully raised Jacob's gaze and the two men stared each other in the eye.

"You lied to me yesterday and if it was left to me, I would kill you where you stand, but I also have a job to do and you are currently worth more to me alive than dead." He growled through gritted teeth while dragging the end of the baton down Jacob's chest. The courtyard remained silent and Jacob bravely maintained his gaze. In a flash, the officer drew his arm back and rammed the end of the leather covered swagger stick into Jacob's belly. Doubling over and fighting for breath, Jacob then suffered the acute pain of a swiftly raised knee smashing into his face, leaving the poor man collapsed on the ground. Turning away as if nothing had happened, the officer gave another order. Bursting into life, the guards forced the prisoners back into the cramped cages and four of the peasant men manhandled the pods onto the back of the truck. Within minutes, with the task completed, the bizarre consignment was back on its way for the final leg of the journey.

Wiping away the stream of warm blood running from his nose, Jacob closed his eyes and rubbed gently at his sore stomach. Trying to take his mind off the throbbing pain, he took succour that the level of the officer's anger proved that Ivan was still at large, a small price to pay for his friend's freedom. Opening his eyes to memorise as much of the journey as possible he found to his disappointment that he had very little vision of the surrounding countryside due to his cage being placed very close to the door of another, leaving only one tiny air hole at the back with which to see the terrain. What he did feel however, was that they were now descending into the next valley as the temperature steadily began to rise.

Inside four hours, the truck convoy drove through a high gated compound and directly into a large warehouse sized structure, with large metal doors that clanged shut behind them. Inside there were dozens of people milling about who excitedly helped to unload the prisoners and shepherd them into a large single cage that looked more suitable for a wild animal than a human. Before they had the chance to stretch out tired limbs, they all startled to the fanfare of roman cornum horns being blown somewhere not very far from where they all stood. It sounded to Jacob like the announcement of royalty at a major event and he wondered if they were going to be involved in some type of parade.

Suddenly an outer door burst open and three men walked in carrying an assorted wardrobe of gladiatorial costumes fitting for the period of ancient Rome. At gunpoint, the prisoners were forced to strip and pass their old clothes through the bars in exchange for the strange dress. Under the protection of an armed guard, an assistant was allowed in with the men and he helped each man to don the correct attire.

Surprisingly, they were then assigned swords, or nets and tridents according to a list on a clipboard held by a young woman, who appeared to be in charge of organising the event. Jacob observed that they all wore costumes designed for use with the weapon provided, but most outfits consisted of sandaled feet, held in place by thin leather thongs that crisscrossed up to the knee, a white linen loin cloth for modesty, and an 8″ wide thick leather cingulum belt that fastened around the waistline, offering the gladiator extra protection. Jacob was left bare-chested but allowed the addition of a shaped metal shoulder guard, held in place by a leather strap secured across the chest and around his sword arm. A simple crested tin helmet with a neck skirt and nose guard completed his particular fighter's deadly ensemble. He was then handed a circular shield and his short broadsword identical to the ones used in training, except that this time they were hardened metal and not the wooden weapons used in practice.

With his heart thumping heavily in his chest and imagination running riot, he looked around at all of his comrades to see matching fear on every face. With rifles trained on their every move now that they had weapons of their own, the men were ushered from the cage, along a stone tunnel that echoed to thousands of cheers growing louder with every step. When they reached the far end, the dark passageway suddenly exploded with sunlight as two men opened wide a set of double doors to reveal a lowered portcullis. Every prisoner stopped and stared in amazement at the site of a sand-covered, gladiatorial arena.

The amazing construction, based on a similar design to the Coliseum in Rome, began with a twelve foot high perimeter wall, with tiered bench seating around the top. Above this there were four or five floors sited directly above the last, with the uppermost decorated at the rear with stone arches, topped with a canvas canopy to shelter the audience from the baking hot sun. The entire amphitheatre was filled to the brim with thousands of spectators dressed in ancient roman attire, who at the sound of a second fanfare, stood up as one, to cheer the emperor as he stepped out onto the balcony of his imperial box. Regally dressed in a purple toga and wearing a golden laurel wreath around his shiny bald head, this short, fat man playing the Roman leader, revelled in the adulation. He turned to face all sides, offering a self-satisfied wave with the back of his hand to everyone before eventually taking his seat on a gilded white marble curule chair, signalling for the games to begin.

The entire spectacle had been organised under the directorship of Philip Sanderson and was the culmination of several clandestine meetings beginning nearly two years ago with the man taking the part of the emperor. This resulted in a one-hundred and fifty million dollar transfer into Philip's Swiss bank account from the richest drug smuggler in Europe, setting the ball rolling for today's illegal event. Jacob tried to turn and run, but a secondary gate had already closed behind, and several rifle barrels poked through the bars. All he could do now was to turn back, face the front, and watch events unfold.

The circus began in a light-hearted fashion as dancers and acrobats ran whooping into the arena. The performance consisted of some very daring and entertaining routines, but Jacob took scant notice of the spectacle, it was the people in the audience that he found much more fascinating. His eye was drawn to one particular young couple sitting on the front row of tier two. The closer he studied their movements, the more bizarre everything appeared to be. At the end of periods approaching five minutes long, he noticed that the couple twitched slightly and then repeated the same previous set of movements over and over again. Picking out other spectators at random he found that the result was also the same, drawing him to the conclusion that they were preprogramed androids or some type of a very clever projection. His prediction was soon confirmed when due to a fluctuation in power output an entire section of the audience suddenly disappeared, leaving several rows of empty seats before reappearing less than ten seconds later. At one point the entire top row began to pixilate, revealing the distant mountains, easily visible through the faded projection. The only physical piece of architecture was the arena floor itself and the first tier of seating perched on top of the arena wall. This lower level included all the human spectators ready to watch the spectacle, but they amounted to no more than a fifth of the crowd overall.

With the opening performance complete, the serious matter of the main events began. Across on the far side of the now empty arena a heavy wooden door opened and several terrified looking men were forcibly ushered into the ring. As they stood huddled together looking wide-eyed in terror, everyone's attention was taken by a smaller fanfare, when high in the stands an announcer dressed in a floor length white linen toga, stepped up onto a podium next to the imperial box. To an accompaniment of mocking jeers and boos coming from the crowd, he gave an unctuous smile and waved as if the crowd were actually cheering his presence. Eventually the noise abated and following a short speech in Spanish he read out the name of each man standing below, followed by a list of their crimes committed, pausing for maximum effect from the crowd between each one. Jacob looked intently at the face of the man dressed as the emperor as he sat on his dais and observed the disgusting smug satisfaction written across his face as he stared intently at the semi-naked men huddling together less than fifty feet away. It was obvious to even the casual observer that their emaciated bodies displayed all the signs of recent torture and even though Jacob did not fully understand the words spoken about them it was easy to assume that they must have somehow crossed a line or broken this man's rules to have ended up in this terrible predicament.

With the platitudes finally over, the announcer stepped down and took his seat, as three men on horseback galloped into the arena. Each rider was dressed in roman military-hardened leather body armour and carried an eight foot long wooden spear, tipped with a forge-hardened metal point. Without pause they headed straight for the huddled men who scattered in all directions like a shoal of fish fleeing from a large predator. Jumping to their feet in excitement the crowd cheered and roared at the spectacle as the hunted tried their damndest to stay alive, repeatedly dodging from each deadly assault. Time and time again the riders attacked and incredibly the men were quick enough to survive, but they were no match for the strength and vigour of a horse, as fatigue began to take its toll, meaning death would not be too far away. The bloodlust grew as one of the hunted men lost his balance when he narrowly evaded the point of a spear, but unluckily he ran into the path of another rider as he rode by. Thudding into the horse's hind quarters, he bounced violently away, knocking the wind from his lungs and fell heavily onto the sand. Seizing the opportunity, his attacker cross reined his horse, circled tightly around, and lined up his mount for a fresh attack. This time instead of launching his spear from the shoulder in the classic hunting strike, the rider lowered his arm and changed to an underhand grip. Leaning forwards in the saddle, he spurred his mount into a full charge as he held the weapon horizontally and out to the right-hand side, roughly chest height from the ground as he closed in swiftly for the kill. Half blinded by the sand in his eyes, the poor man staggered to his feet, turned away, and tried to run. But this time he had no chance as a clinical strike pierced him directly between the shoulder blades, narrowly missing the spinal column and passed clean through his rib cage until eighteen inches of wet spearhead protruded from the front of his chest. There was so much blood that the spatter from arterial spray even reached as far as Jacob and the others as they watched horrified, but astounded at the same time that somehow the man still remained on his feet. Jacob stared wide-eyed and disgusted with himself, but the visceral fascination of the gruesome event made it impossible to look away. The surprise on the victim's face at the sight of the bloodied spear jutting forth from his upper torso added to his confusion as he tried to push it back, but only succeeded in worrying the mortal wound, making the blood flow even faster. Still clutching the tip of the spear he staggered drunkenly around in a circle with blood spilling from his gaping mouth. Seconds later his body surrendered and once again he fell down face first onto the ground. This almost pushed the spear out through the back of his chest, but it still left enough to pin him to the earth, bearing semblance to a giant insect exhibited in a natural history display.

The crowd cheered repeatedly, wild with blood lust, as one by one each man buckled under to the repeated onslaught until they all lay dead or dying. The horrifying spectacle finally ended after each horseman retrieved his bloodied spear and then galloped away through a freshly opened gateway. All that remained were the slaughtered men who were lassoed around the ankles and unceremoniously dragged away, leaving glistening, wet, blood-trails converging into one as the bodies left the crimson stained arena.

The next event saw the introduction of three half-starved and very mangy lions. Excited by the smell of fresh blood, they rubbed their faces into the wet sand and padded menacingly around the arena, snarling and pawing the air as they tried to reach the baying mob. They even roared at Jacob and his friends, jabbing their paws through the gaps in the bars, but mercifully falling short as the men shrank back in terror at the fearsome sight. The animals may have been starving and in very poor condition, but they were still lethal killers and with five inch razor sharp claws they could easily eviscerate a man with one swipe.

Trumpets sounded as yet three more men were forced through another side gate into the arena. All three bore the same swarthy complexion similar to the occupants of the surrounding villages, and Jacob watched as the self-appointed emperor leaned forwards eagerly in his seat at their recognition. It was obvious that all the unfortunates were probably from rival gangs or maybe even members of his own clan who had somehow caused displeasure. The man in charge wanted to give a clear broadcast to everyone what happens when he is crossed. For the next five minutes the lions surprisingly ignored their lunch as the men huddled terrified in the centre. They seemed more interested in the movement of the crowd and the poor souls like Jacob, trapped behind the bars around the arena's edge. To hurry things along, adding torment to the captives, the gate that they had just come through, swung open offering escape. Seizing his chance, one of the trio made a bid for freedom, and like a cat, enticed by a mouse, the sudden movement triggered a natural instinct as all three lions burst into life. Charging swiftly across the bloodstained sand, one of the lions quickly reached the poor soul, who had barely made it halfway before five-hundred pounds of claws, teeth and muscle thudded into his back, pinning him to the ground. Kicking and screaming, he somehow managed to roll over as he tried to free himself, but the effort was futile. Easily holding him down with one enormous paw, the lion opened his mouth wide and clamped it around the man's neck and head. Surprisingly, this action did not snap his victim's neck and for the next minute continued to thrash his arms and legs violently around until he died from suffocation. A similar hideous fate quickly befell the two other two men, and as Jacob tore his eyes away from the sight of human flesh being ripped away from warm bodies; his own blood ran even colder at the sight of complete rapture on the face of the emperor as he gazed enthralled by the gruesome spectacle. The crowd and the projection predictably went wild, clapping hands and cheering at the horror that had already loosened the bowels of the man to Jacob's right, adding the smell of excreta to the horrors before them. As the ghoulish spectacle continued, Jacob wondered how soon he would have to enter the arena.

CHAPTER TWENTY

Elvis and Duke both dearly wanted the soon to be vacant sheriff's post and over a coffee down at the local diner, they decided it best to keep well apart and let the best man win. After a short discussion, they each agreed to target their individual efforts upon one field agent each, thus making the outcome easier to decide. Duke took a nickel from his trouser pocket and tossed it high into the air.

"This one's for you Elvis, heads you get Howton and tails Simpkins." Duke announced to what seemed like the entire diner as he slammed his palm loudly down over the still spinning coin when it landed on the table top. Dramatically, he rolled his hand away from the varnished wood surface to reveal heads.

Over the next few days Sherriff Dodson received frequent reports of how Elvis hounded his chosen target with a series of tickets for minor misdemeanours that the harassed man promptly paid at the station. But to the young deputy's frustration, he still doggedly refused to leave. Philip Sanderson had such an iron grip over both of the investigators that a few traffic tickets from a Hicksville cop would not deter them from the case. Duke on the other-hand surprised the sheriff by apparently doing nothing at all. What he did not know was that Duke's inactivity concealed a much bigger plan that he was convinced would soon result in victory, leaving Clifford 'Duke' Thornbuck sitting in the coveted big chair.

"If you want to be sure of getting rid of Howton, I can show you how to do it." Duke casually mentioned to Elvis while they both looked up from their oppositely facing office desks to watch Nathan Howton leave the station, following the paying off yet another trumped up traffic violation on Elvis's part. The naive deputy furrowed his brow and curiously looked back at his cousin, wondering why on earth he would help him win the contest. He was at a loss at what to do next so he decided that there was nothing to lose and leaned in closer so he could listen carefully to the idea. Duke smiled inwardly at the ease he made Elvis rise to the bait, and tried hard not to laugh out loud as he carefully explained what needed to be done.

"Every day Howton drives all the way up to the top of Jenkins Bluff to give a daily report back to his boss man. As you well know, that's the place where the phone signal is strongest."

Duke watched as Elvis nodded sagely, trying to prove that he knew where the conversation was going. He knew the location, so he figured he could follow Howton up the mountain road but after that he still did not have a clue.

"And then what?" Elvis replied, tapping the ends of his fingers rapidly on his office desk and growing impatient at Duke's frequent habit of leaving long pauses between statements, thus turning a short story into a very annoying long one.

"I'm a comin' to that, stop getting your breeches in a twist." Duke tormented, knowing how much it irritated his cousin. Enjoying a long, slow drink of coffee, he then proceeded to wipe his mouth with the back of his hand, take a deep breath and continued.

"It's very simple Elvis, so pay attention while I spell it out. In the evidence locker there are still several dozen small measured out packets of cocaine relating to the big Tucker brothers bust last fall. Now I'm sure two or three will not be missed and you can use them to plant evidence in Howton's jacket pocket, when you give him a pat down."

"Why would I be patting him down?" Elvis replied, looking very confused. Duke sighed, sat up straight in his chair, and scratched the back of his head, wondering how on earth Elvis passed the test to become a police officer. His best guess was that the sheriff must have rigged the result to keep family members close at hand in case he needed help. It then occurred to him that the sheriff might have done the same when he took the test and he was not a smart as he first thought. But it did not matter now, before long he would soon be in charge and part of that plan was getting rid of the competition. Trying to remain calm, he leaned in closer, encouraging his cousin to do likewise while he explained step by step what Elvis had to do.

"Follow Howton to the top of the bluff, make up some story that he was seen carrying a concealed weapon. Give him a pat down and suddenly find the bags of cocaine in Howton's jacket pocket. There will be no witnesses to back up his claim that he was framed and you can offer him a deal to leave the county and never come back."

Even with Duke's step by step guide it was still a few seconds before Elvis managed to comprehend the gist of the plan, but as soon as it all clicked into place he jumped to his feet with a huge grin spreading across his face. Unusually for such a well-mannered and polite young man he failed to thank Duke apart from a cursory pat on his shoulder as he dashed eagerly towards the evidence locker, leaving the rest of the office staring blankly at each other and wondering what was going on. Even as he retrieved the tiny packets of white powder, it never occurred to him why his opponent for the job of sheriff would so gallantly step aside and let him win, and that error in judgement would serve to be his downfall.

CHAPTER TWENTY-ONE

Jacob swallowed hard to settle the wave of nausea passing through him when the portcullis suddenly rose, and along with the others in his group, he was forcibly herded out into the arena. On the opposite side, the same number of similarly attired strangers trotted out into the centre, lined up like soldiers facing the emperor, and raised their swords saluting the crowd, while Jacob's group looked on absolutely terrified what was coming next. Once again the trumpets blared and another man dressed in a fine white and gold trimmed toga stepped onto a plinth and made his announcement in Spanish then surprisingly in English akin to an event at an international theme park.

"The emperor now invites you to witness the main part of today's event. Standing in the arena below is a collection of some of the finest gladiators the Roman Empire has to offer. Opponents will select each other at random and every fight will be to the death. To the victors, if the fight pleases the emperor, there will be the chance of living to fight another day; for one lucky fighter he will be given his freedom."

Cheers and whistles rang out from the capacity crowd as they steadily modulated into a slow handclap encouraging the gladiators to begin. Jacob found it hard to believe that anyone who had borne witness to this carnage would ever be released to tell his tale, but it was obvious that the opposition believed the proclamation as they began to advance. Instinctively swords and shields were raised and Jacob's group stood back to back, forming a tightly huddled defence. This mattered very little to the advancing fighters who circled like wolves around the terrified pack and selected an individual for combat. Jacob now understood how one of his group lost control of his bowels as he himself struggled to control his bodily functions as he came face to face with a tall similarly built white man carrying a trident and net. There appeared to be no fear at all in his opponent's eyes and his dilated pupils made Jacob wonder if the other group had been drugged to make them aggressive and spoil for a fight, because it was obvious that none of his friends had the desire to kill or even hurt someone else.

Like the heartbeat of a massive leviathan, the crowd slapped their hands together and stamped their feet in a slow methodical rhythm. They grew tired of waiting for the anticipated fight and wanted to see more blood. Time and time again the opposing fighters tried to goad Jacob's group into attack, relentlessly attempting to split apart the tight porcupine based strategy that seemed impossible to penetrate. Eventually, it was Jacob who was the first reluctant fighter to break ranks, as his adversary swung his net around his head and cast it forwards. Instinctively Jacob raised his shield to protect himself, but the rough hemp mesh snagged tightly around the shield's rim. Using his superior strength, the fighter stepped back, yanking violently on his end of the net, pulling Jacob out from his safe enclosure to sprawl helpless at the man's feet. Like a tribal hunter spearing a fish, the gladiator raised his trident and thrust down hard towards Jacob's chest. Fear of death gave him the edge, and with lightning reflexes Jacob used his sword to parry the thrust and the three razor sharp prongs glanced across his shoulder armour and stabbed harmlessly into the sandy earth. Not waiting to see what his attacker would do next, Jacob hastily rolled away and sprang cat-like to his feet, luckily unravelling the attackers net from his arm in the process. The breach in his group's defence quickly opened wide and steadily his comrades spread out across the arena in pockets of one on one combat, raising the volume of the crowd, as the anticipated spectacle finally got underway.

Cheers and groans alternated with the clanging sounds of metal striking metal as each man fought valiantly for his life. All the training that Jacob had received back in

England held him in good stead with the constant attacking moves from the unnamed foe, who lacked greatly in refined technique but presented incredible tenacity and determination. Over and over the gladiator advanced, probing and jabbing with his trident which Jacob repeatedly blocked with his shield.

The secondary problem for everyone on the arena floor was the possibility of getting tangled up in someone else's fight, risking a blow from the back-swing of a club or being bowled over completely from a mistimed thrust. With the fear of this in mind, Jacob spied a clear zone near the wall directly under the view of the emperor, and reversed steadily towards it.

"Foit back ya' coward." The announcer screamed as he eased off his seat and leaned over the rounded coping stones running along the top of the arena's perimeter wall. The sudden burst of English was not that out of the ordinary, but his clipped vocals had slipped into a broad West Country accent where Jacob was born and raised. For a fraction of a second, he thought about his home town, taking the edge off his concentration. Seizing his advantage, the attacker once again hurled his net directly over Jacob's head, tugged him violently to the ground, and lunged for the kill. Yet again, Jacob's reflexes saved him from instant death, but he was not as fortunate as before. The longer middle spike of the trident squealed loudly as it struck the metal of Jacob's shield, gouging a shiny rut from the centre-boss out towards the edge. It halted briefly on the slightly raised rim, but the attacker steadily increased the pressure forcing a tilt in the angle of the shield until the prong slipped off. In a flash, the downward pressure pierced Jacob's bicep muscle, glanced across the humerus bone, and re-emerged through the skin on the other side, pinning his arm to the earth. Jacob remained silent, stunned at first, but suddenly screamed in agony, not as the trident struck, but when his adversary stamped his sandaled foot on his lower arm and worried the barbed point back out through the wound ready to give the execution blow. The human extras dotted within the crowd, watching on that side of the arena gasped and cheered wildly, feverishly anticipating the next gruesome act. Hot blood poured out from the freshly torn skin, drenching Jacob's arm and staining the porous earth below.

Through tear stained eyes all he could do for now was stare painfully at the sun darkened silhouette of his brutal adversary and wait for death. To Jacob's surprise, instead of issuing the killer blow, the attacker stopped and looked up towards the emperor, waiting for his approval. This brief pause was all Jacob needed, and ignoring the immense pain from his wounded arm, he bashed the edge of his shield into the anklebone of his would-be executioner buckling the foot beneath, then kicked violently against the back of his opponent's remaining standing leg, bringing the gladiator down heavily onto his backside. With all the strength he could muster, Jacob jumped up and thrust the point of his sword firmly into the gladiator's throat. The flat blade sliced easily through the soft flesh, clean through to the spinal column and protruded out through the back of the man's neck, causing instant death. To Jacob's amazement, the spray of blood at the withdrawal of his sword was accompanied with a teeth-jarring squeal of metal grinding against metal as the lifelike robotic man twitched and fell flat to the ground, immediately followed by cheers of adulation from the ecstatic crowd. Unable to do anything for his wounded arm, Jacob forced the shield's mounting straps up beyond his elbow and jammed his fist and lower half of his forearm through the centre of the two leather straps crisscrossing his chest. The idea was to protect his torso as much as possible and also support his injured limb from further damage.

The thought of taking another man's life would normally fill him with revulsion and the fact that it was only an android did not alter the original intent, as at the time he believed his foe to be human. The scarlet veil of battle had descended and now it was a case of kill or be killed. Luckily the trident had not severed any arteries and surprisingly the bleeding slowed to a steady trickle thanks to a plug of arena sand and dirt.

Clanging sounds of sword against sword echoed alongside guttural yells and cheers from the crowd as predictably half fell to a stronger or smarter foe. Both camps lost an equal amount of men, but as soon as the victors from the enemy camp won their battle, they immediately sought another opponent and fight again.

With his skin coated in a grotesque batter of blood-caked sand, Jacob resembled a creature of nightmare as he staggered wearily around and scanned the arena, witnessing the carnage around him. Some of his friends had already succumbed to a grisly fate, and the few remaining were fighting valiantly, but reaching the end of their strength. Feeling light headed from the heavy bleeding, exhaustion, and the baking heat of the late afternoon sun, Jacob returned for shade and rest, under the overhang of the emperor's balcony.

Fresh from his latest kill, an android gladiator looked around and spied Jacob trying to catch his breath. Playing to the crowd, he yelled something unintelligible and charged straight into the fight. Suddenly recharged in panic, all Jacob had time to do was dodge the initial thrust and run back out under the burning sun. Parrying and blocking as best he could from the relentless onslaught, chunks of hot metal flew from the clash of opposing blades until the two came face to face in a test of strength. Jacob's courage quelled as he caught his own face reflected in the cold, soulless stare of his opponent's eyes, giving him cause to wonder whether it was another android or perhaps a real human being who had been pumped full of amphetamines.

Spinning away from one another with the fight delicately poised, Jacob failed to anticipate a quickly executed reverse swing, as the tip of his opponent's sword flashed through the sunlight, slicing upwards across the side of Jacob's neck, chipping his jawbone as it sliced through the flesh of his left cheek all the way to the hairline. A woman screamed, cutting sharply through the roar of the crowd as Jacob's head snapped back at a sickening angle and he fell heavily to the ground. Dizzy from the pain of the blow, and blinded by the glare of the sun, Jacob rolled over, struggled to his knees and there he stayed.

Planting the tip of his sword vertically into the sand, he shakily held the hilt inside his battle scarred fists and painfully lowered his forehead onto the makeshift support. Fresh warm blood continued to pour from his wounded face, through trembling fingers, and down the battle scarred blade, adding another cherry-red puddle to the arena floor. For a few seconds, all this was just a nightmare and Jacob was transported back with his friends onto the deck of the yacht, as they cruised around the warm Mediterranean Sea. But the sound of waves lapping gently against the yacht's hull slowly morphed into the slap of decorative pennants flapping lazily in the breeze as the crowd hushed in anticipation of the emperor's judgement. With Jason's weakening heartbeat thudding wildly inside his head, the image of his family, standing on the front door step as they waved him off to university nearly four years ago appeared in the forefront of his mind. He smiled lovingly back, but sadly this was Jacob's final memory as the emperor gave a nod and the tip of forge-hardened steel sword plunged deep into the back of his ribcage, forcing Jacob's tired body to the ground. In a triumphant pose, the victor placed one foot heavily upon Jacob's spine, forcing out a final groaning breath that was completely lost in the bloodthirsty roar of the crowd.

CHAPTER TWENTY-TWO

Armed with two small clear polythene pouches of high grade cocaine that he had managed to steal from the evidence locker, Elvis tried to resume his normal daily duties, but every time he thought about the drugs in his shirt pocket, it weighed heavily on his conscience. Eventually the time came and at a distance he trailed Nathan Howton's hire car down the turnpike off-ramp leading up through the forest to the Chickasaw lake camping ground. It was here he was reminded not that long ago how it all began, when both he and Duke were bribed with the safari trip after they found Boss in the back seat of his car having sex with his secretary Jolene. He wished now that he had given in to the migraine that he could feel building up when he awoke that morning, and taken a sick day. His dedication to the job put him in the wrong place at the wrong time and now he was heading out to frame an innocent man to save his own skin.

Leaving the far side of the camp site and skirting around the lake, the trail climbed steadily higher along the narrow mountain road, through the forest and up to the high bluff overlooking the entire valley. He knew the road well, but had rarely had the chance to drive it nowadays, especially during daylight hours. The site is a well-known make-out place for the younger population, but even though he was barely into his twenties he somehow felt that those days were long gone.

The stomach churning sight of nearly a thousand foot vertical drop down to the river gorge below was considerably more nerve-wracking than driving in the dark with a pretty girl by your side. Time and time again, the bumper of the squad car seemed to hang right over the abyss as he carefully navigated the tight hairpin bends slowly zigzagging the way to the top. The difficulty of the route did nothing to ease his troubled state of mind as he followed the dust trail thrown up by Howton's car along the snaking dirt-track road all the way to the flat topped summit.

The mid-afternoon was already heading for a spectacular sunset as his patrol car finally cleared the tree line. The road levelled off and with the sun almost blinding his vision, he circled around and saw the familiar sight of Howton's pale blue sedan parked at the end of a short run of three other cars whose occupants took one look at the police decals emblazoned on the bodywork of his vehicle and quickly vacated the scene. With his car window fully wound down, Elvis could hear that Nathan Howton was deep in conversation with a loud male voice who Elvis correctly presumed was from head office, and he blatantly eavesdropped on the end of the conversation.

"I'm very sorry Mr Sanderson sir, but I have no idea where Simpkins is at the moment. The last time I saw him was yesterday during lunch. He told me that he had an important lead out of town, and he would tell me all about it today, but he still hasn't come back and he isn't answering his phone. Yes sir, I will keep looking and as soon as I see him, I will tell him that you need him immediately; Yes sir, no sir, I won't forget sir, as soon as possible sir."

The call ended abruptly and Nathan slipped his phone back into his inside jacket pocket, then opened his car door ready to stretch his legs, only to see the familiar sight of Officer Maybury walking towards him. Sighing heavily, Nathan could not believe his run of bad luck and dropped his head in frustration. Trying to get yet another trumped up ticket over with as quickly as possible, Nathan foolishly got out of his seat ready to receive his penalty.

"Good day Officer Maybury, what type of citation are you charging me with this time, jaywalking perhaps?" He challenged sarcastically. Just at that moment his ancient mobile phone vibrated silently with another incoming call. Praying that it was Simpkins on the other end, Nathan paid little heed to the consequence of his actions and slipped his hand swiftly inside his jacket to retrieve the device. Elvis reacted immediately by drawing his gun as he shuffled into a wide legged pose kicking up a plume of dust that carried on the swirling wind right into Nathan's face.

"Hold it right there mister, what the hell do you think you're doing." Elvis ordered, Nathan automatically clamped his eyes shut and turned his face away until the dust settled. When his vision cleared, he stared wide-eyed down the barrel of a standard issue police revolver held by a very agitated officer.

"Whatever's in there boy you'd better let it go, real slow like. Move your hands where I can see 'em and then assume the position against the car."

Mortified, Nathan realised what it looked like, dropped the phone back into his breast pocket and removed his empty hand. Slowly easing his arms into the air, he turned around and gingerly lowered his palms onto a very hot car roof. Elvis stepped up and placed his spare hand squarely in the middle of Nathan's back, kicked the inside of the worried man's left foot to widen his stance and then proceeded to pat him down.

"I was just trying to answer a call I'm not armed if that's what you think." Nathan tried to explain, but Elvis was not interested. His primary concern was in palming the two packets of cocaine into Nathan's jacket.

"There's something in there, carefully empty out your pocket." Elvis commanded, waiting for Nathan to obey. Angrily losing his patience, Nathan jabbed his own hand into the same pocket and lifted out the recently placed evidence.

"My, my, look what we have here; it seems that whatever company you work for pays you far too much money." Elvis added feeling extremely pleased with his sleight of hand. Nathan stared dumbstruck at the two tiny half-filled plastic bags pinched lightly in his fingers, then over his shoulder at the officer who was already reaching for the handcuffs. He guessed immediately what the powdery substance was from the countless detective shows he had seen on television, and quickly realised how easily he had been set up.

"You are in an awful lot of trouble Mr Howton. Possession of this class of drug carries a mandatory five years minimum, but I'm sure a good looking man like you will become very popular inside and that will help to pass the time."

Nathan's coordination lost control and as his world shifted on its axis, he spun around and dropped to his knees in terror. With tear filled eyes and both hands clamping the drugs between them, he began to plead.

"I'm begging you please don't do this, if I promise to leave town and never come back will you let me go?"

Elvis could not believe how easy it had been and he found it hard not to punch the air in celebration. Instead, he calmly holstered his gun and he held out his empty hand for the two packets of drugs that Nathan eagerly handed back.

"Get up, get in the car, and get out of this county immediately before I change my mind. If I ever see your face again, you know what will happen!" Elvis growled, sounding a lot more menacing than he actually felt. Nathan did not need telling twice and jumping to his feet, he bolted into his car, started the engine, and in a cloud of wheel spun dust drove hastily away. Suddenly feeling short of breath, Elvis leaned forwards, placing his hands on his knees as a wave of euphoria washed over him caused by the sudden adrenaline rush to his system. He watched the car disappear around the first bend and feeling elated at his cunning, he stupidly decided to force the issue and chase Nathan down the mountain, all the way to the interstate.

With a better knowledge of the road, Elvis quickly caught up with Nathan's blue sedan. Ignoring rational thought, he positioned his front bumper inches away from the rear of the hire car as they careered at an ever more dangerous rate down the steep mountainside.

"Yee-har I'm right behind you boy. I'll show you what happens when you mess with the King of Rock 'n' Roll."

He could see Nathan repeatedly glancing anxiously in his rear view mirror and that only added to the excitement of the chase. Confused at what Maybury was up to now, and fearful that he had changed his mind, Nathan foolishly increased his speed to something well beyond his comfortable limit. Elvis easily maintained his close proximity to the rear of the blue sedan and was so confident of his driving ability, he even had time to daydream about how he would run the office when the sheriff retired; in particular how he would soon be able to give orders to lowly officer Clifford 'Duke' Thornbuck. If he had given even a little thought as to why his cousin was helping him out of a tricky situation, he might have realised that there had to be a hefty price to pay for such a good deed. Elvis stupidly believed that Duke appeared to have lost all interest in competing for the promotion and had not been doing much at all. In fact the complete opposite was taking place and Duke had already started his master plan to rid himself of anything and everything standing in-between him, and the desired position.

* * *

A little over twenty-four hours ago, Duke had already begun his campaign by leaving an anonymous note, written in pencil on a plain piece of paper and placed under the windscreen wiper of Lyle Simpkins' car. The short statement written in block capitals claimed to have important information regarding his investigation. The message insisted that the meeting had to be well away from Holtsville and gave the location of the old closed down gas station on the quarry hill road, just off highway nine at seven o'clock. Lyle at first believed the note was a prank, but he desperately needed something positive to report to Philip Sanderson, so against his better judgement he decided to give it a go.

It was already dark when he eventually found the correct location. His satellite navigation system had already updated its software and the gas station had been deleted from memory. As is the case with most rural locations, there were very few road signs to assure him he was on the right track.

The site itself was no more than just a shell, as the fuel pumps had long since been removed and everything of value stripped from inside the convenience store and home of the Tatt family. Attached to the left hand side of the house a two bay repair garage had rolled its shutters down for the last time over two years ago when the they were declared bankrupt. This sad atypical image was the face of rural America, with thousands of small enterprises being forced into submission by the faceless multi-billion dollar conglomerates. In this particular case, less than two miles away and just a few years ago, a massive forty pump station, service bay, and mini mart had been installed at the side of the new interstate by one of the big oil companies. The meagre turnover of this small family run business halved overnight and within a year they were forced to close down.

Duke had been waiting patiently inside for nearly an hour, but he really did not care, it just gave him more time to sit and drink. He had brought along a small battery operated camping light that he placed on the corner of the store counter, so when Simkins pulled up in his car he would know where to come.

Lyle drove slowly onto the forecourt, spotted the amber glow through the half bordered-up window, stopped his car, and tentatively got out. Even though it had been closed awhile, the heavy taste of old engine oil and used tyres still hung in the air, doing nothing to help the nagging unease stirring in his gut. Clearing his throat loudly as if to announce his arrival, Lyle opened the door and stepped inside. The old coil spring mounted bell screwed to the top of the frame still jingled as the door opened and Lyle immediately spotted Duke staring back from his position behind the counter. It did not come as much of a surprise as he had heard regular reports from Nathan about police harassment and he wondered when it was going to be his turn. What was peculiar, and to an investigator such as himself, he should have paid more attention to, was the white one-piece semi-transparent coverall that Duke wore over his police uniform.

"So, can I assume that you are my mystery informer, are you going to come clean and tell me everything?" Lyle asked sarcastically, ready to turn and head straight back to his car. Duke remained silent and seemed more preoccupied with something placed under the counter top. Lyle was tired and stressed, so he instantly grew angry as to why the police officer failed to speak, so he decided to stand his ground and demand an answer.

"What are you going to do now? Give me a few tickets like the other dumbass cop and hope that I'll go away, or are you going to make a more serious threat?"

Duke smiled, ignoring the accusation as he slipped his finger inside the trigger guard of the shotgun that he had wedged under the counter.

"Just as I thought, you're just another one of them moonshine, hillbilly, rednecks who thinks the south will rise again!"

Those were the last words Lyle Simkins would utter as Duke cold heartedly tightened his grip and pulled the trigger. The poor man was already dead before he could feel the pain of the shotgun blast bursting his ear drums in the confines of the small building. The antimony coated lead pellets ripped through the front of the highly varnished counter, tearing away great chunks of wood and filling the air with debris. The high velocity blast hit Lyle squarely in the centre of his chest and as he was only six feet from the end of the barrel, the impact tore a double-fist sized hole, clean through his body cavity. Rib bone and shattered vertebrae, accompanied by near liquefied heart and lung tissue, spray painted the boarded up window behind him before the body fell to the floor. Duke remained motionless as the dust settled and the echo of gunfire faded from the room.

"Sorry I didn't catch what you said." He mumbled to himself as he removed a pair of foam ear plugs, walked casually around the counter, and stared unemotionally at Lyle's bloodied face. His entire upper torso bristled with wooden splinters and Lyle somehow still managed to look surprised as his bloodshot eyes stared up at the ceiling. Checking outside for signs of any passers-by, Duke propped open the spring loaded front door, and by rolling the body onto an old dust sheet that he had found in the back room, he dragged Lyle's still warm corpse out onto the forecourt. Using a crowbar that he had placed next to the rusting anchor bolts that previously were used to secure the old petrol pumps, he levered up and hinged open the cast iron lid to the main underground fuel storage tank.

Unceremoniously he lifted one end of the dust sheet, rolled the body over the hole, and with a dull thud it dropped inside. The dust sheet was next, followed by the heavy clang of the lid as he dropped it back into place. Checking all was well, Duke re-entered the empty shop to collect his belongings, checked around for a second time, and then crossed over to Lyle's car parked outside. Dropping wearily into the driver's seat he placed the shotgun and the lamp on the passenger seat, and fumbled behind the steering wheel for the car keys.

Suddenly his heart lurched, all he could feel was the cold metal of the ignition ring, triggering a sharp mental flashback. He remembered watching carefully through the grime coated window, as Lyle got out of his car and instinctively dropped the keys into his pocket as he walked towards the building. They now resided twenty feet below the ground, still in the dead man's jacket.

"Sonofabitch!" Duke yelled as he slammed his opened fists repeatedly against the steering wheel sending shooting pains up both arms to the shoulder. Trying to ignore the self-inflicted punishment, he angrily got out of the car and marched back towards the forecourt. His initial thought was to find a way to retrieve the keys, but realising how deep the fuel pit was, and that he had no means of climbing down, he quickly put it out of his mind. Reaching inside his white coveralls for his hip flask, Duke took a long swig of bourbon to dull the ache and wandered around hoping for inspiration. The sight of the rusty old revolving tyre sale sign, still squeaking as it turned lazily in the breeze seemed to attract his attention and as he turned to face it, his foot kicked the crowbar still lying on the ground. Instantly an idea came to mind and snatching up the heavy metal rod, he returned to the car.

As a young tearaway, Duke used to hot wire cars of all shapes and sizes, joyriding with his friends and then abandoning the vehicle when it ran out of fuel. Today's modern cars were all but impossible to start without a key of some kind, but no one had allowed for vandalising the lock and pushing the car away.

Smashing away the cheap black plastic cowling covering the mechanism attached to the steering column, he easily jimmied away the aluminium casing holding the lock in place. It was then that his heart sank for a second time when he realised that Lyle would have placed the automatic gear lever in 'park' position, making it impossible to disengage without the ignition key, even if the steering lock had been forcibly removed from the car. Holding his breath, he reached tentatively around behind the steering wheel and let out an audible sigh of relief to find it still set to neutral. Lucky for him, Lyle had been having trouble with the parking gear of the old worn out vehicle and had opted to use the hand brake instead.

Taking the strain on the outdated lever, Duke depressed the release button and lowered the handle to release the brake. He then positioned himself outside and behind the opened driver's side door, braced himself against the top of the front door pillar and began to push the mercifully lightweight car out onto the dusty back road. What followed, was a fifty yard lung busting steady incline, but as he breathlessly pushed the car to the top of the rise, Duke was able to jump in and managed to freewheel the rest of the way. Without the engine operating the power steering and braking system, it was very hard to guide the car down the single-track road, but he managed the gentle descent and also to skirt around the edge of a disused quarry. The dead-end road was the only access to the open cast mine that had previously been exhausted of its gravel deposits and had now been flooded to turn it into a nature reserve. Forcibly turning the wheel, Duke steered the car onto the grey dust covered grass verge and stopped the vehicle a few yards short of an eighty foot high man-made cliff. Reaching over, he collected his belongings from the passenger seat and climbed out. Another swig of bourbon later, Duke raised his forearm to protect his face and used the crowbar in his other-hand to smash in all the car's side windows, before finally walking round to the rear. With a gentle push on the back bumper with his left foot, he allowed gravity to take the vehicle silently away over the high grassy lip. A few short seconds later, an almighty splash signalled that the car had landed onto the surface of the deep muddy water below. Inching cautiously to the edge, Duke looked down into the pit to see the upended vehicle quickly fill with water and in a minute it was gone, with only a few bubbles rising to the oily surface, signalling that there had been anything there at all. Turning away satisfied, he collected his things and walked halfway back up the road to where he had hidden his patrol car behind a small copse of silver birch trees. Carefully securing the shotgun in the lock box in the trunk, he got back in and drove back to the same spot where not so long ago Lyle parked his own car and never returned. With the engine idling, Duke got out and stepped back inside the shop ready to add the finishing touch. Gathering up a few old rags and faded tourist leaflets, he made a neat pile in front of the counter, and with the aid of an old disposable cigarette lighter he set the dusty collection alight. Quickly removing his paper based coveralls and throwing them onto the rapidly growing pyre, he watched smugly as the material contracted from the intense heat then suddenly burst into flame.

As if to seal the deal, Duke stepped back and spat out a large dark brown plug of well chewed tobacco that hissed like a snake as it landed in the heat of the burgeoning fire. Satisfied with a job well done, Duke wiped his brown stained lips with the back of his hand, casually walked from the building, climbed into the patrol car, and drove away.

Fifty years of farmhands, truck drivers, motor mechanics had created a filthy black swarf-stained footpath between the door to the counter, and now bright yellow flames danced quickly across the oil impregnated floorboards all the way to the window pane. Within seconds, fiery tongues licked silently up the surrounding wall, boiling the abstract blood spatter that was already congealing on the sun warmed shiplap. By the time Duke had driven back to the highway, he looked in his mirrors and could see the entire building was well alight, by the seething orange glow darkening the surrounding sky. Smiling to himself, he knew that by the time the fire service were alerted and had arrived on the scene, there would be nothing more than a pile of smoking embers, eradicating any possible evidence that a murder had taken place within.

* * *

Less than twenty-four hours later, Duke hid in the bushes three-quarters the way up the same mountain road that Elvis and Nathan Howton were hurtling down at a dangerous pace. He knew that Elvis would never harm an innocent man, so he proposed that he run Howton out of town under a serious threat of arrest.

This second part of the evil plan was falling perfectly into place. The sound of combustion engines grew louder and watching from his hiding place Duke's heart raced when both cars suddenly came into view. The setting was perfect, the most difficult bend in the road overlooking the sheer ravine that bottomed out a stomach churning eleven-hundred feet down onto the rock strewn base of Chickasaw Falls. Duke gasped, he could not believe his luck as this two part section looked like it could be executed in one go as both cars appeared to be so close together that they could almost be attached. Scrambling quickly out from the cover of the bushes, he stood up at the roadside and with practised timing threw out one end of a standard police issue rapid tyre deflation device, commonly known as *'The stinger'*. The scissor action of the loosely attached crisscrossed thin metal base plates, extended the device across the entire width of the narrow mountain road. This gave Howton no chance at all to avoid the dozens of vertically mounted thumb sized hollow spikes from piercing the rubber compound of his tyres, releasing all the pressurised air in a fraction of a second, making driving the vehicle almost impossible. This also included trying to stop the car as he slammed his foot on the brakes and the steel edges of the front pair of the now exposed wheel rims gouged into the already sun softened, badly maintained, tarmac and dust. Instead of hugging the inside of the narrow mountain road, the car hurtled like a freight-train in a perfect straight line until it flew clean over the edge of the ravine. A fraction of a second later, Elvis, following closely in his patrol car, had no time to see the stinger and did not even have time to brake before he too suffered the exact same fate.

Almost synchronised in descent, the high revving of both engines muffled the screams of their two occupants, who in a futile attempt at control, held tightly to the steering wheel and stomped hopelessly on the brake pedal. Duke watched in fascination as the two pairs of brake lights streamed concentric glowing arcs of ruby-red through the waterfall moistened woodland air, as the heavy weight of both the front mounted car engines, pulled their descent into a balletic forward roll. The brief performance ended with a deafening crash and a heavy boom when the fuel tanks exploded as both cars crashed upside down onto the jagged rocks below. A gigantic double fireball engulfed the scene, and even from eleven-hundred feet away, the heat from ignited fuel rushing up the cliff side, hit Duke full in the face as he peered with ghoulish fascination down into the bottom of the gorge. The blast also startled hundreds of birds nesting in the surrounding trees, to take to the skies an attempt to escape from the rising flames below. He knew from experience that the fire would wipe out any evidence of tyre damage and the investigation that he himself would probably lead, would conclude that an unfortunate tyre blow out in the rear car resulted in it pushing the one in front over the edge. Retracting the stinger he scuffed away any remaining evidence left in the dirt, took a final look around, and then treated himself to a congratulatory swig of bourbon as he carried the heavy device back down the mountain footpath. By the time he reached the patrol car, the hipflask was empty and due to his inebriated state, he threw everything loose into the trunk and quickly drove away.

CHAPTER TWENTY-THREE

"Ok Stan where were we?"

Ted Langton had finally returned to the site of his latest project. Nearly twenty-four hours had passed since he ran from Gemma's apartment and he decided that it was best to let everything cool down; they had not had any contact since then. For the present moment in time everything was calm, leaving Ted to get back to the job in hand, and do what he did best.

"I'll set it up exactly how we left off." Stan announced into Ted's earpiece, jerking Ted from his daydreams when he suddenly found himself between the gigantic front paws of the Sphinx. Over the next few seconds he watched the Pyramids, Cairo, and a cast of thousands appear from nowhere, instantly transforming the deserted English moor into a bustling ancient Egyptian land.

"You know what Stan? There's hardly a breath of wind out here and it's a sunny day, so why don't we try out the sand storm?"

"Ok by me boss, I'll check the forecast."

As Stan answered the request, he remained in his chair and pushed himself away from his desk. Aided by the nylon castors gliding him silently across the surface of the polished floor, he spun around through a hundred and eighty degrees and stopped precisely at the weather control desk.

Even in his Shangri-La of computer technology, any outdoor project was still at the mercy of the elements and he checked the reports from surrounding purpose built weather stations. The prevailing wind was less than half a metre per second and had been for over an hour. This passed all safety protocols allowing the artificial storm to begin.

Nearly half a mile away and hidden by the projection of an enormous sand dune, a phalanx of fifty high power fans that would normally have a home in a wind tunnel, rose slowly up out of the ground and noisily whirred into life. Using finger touch slider controls displayed on his computer screen, Stan carefully raised the wind speed up to a healthy fifty knots, and then on a separate touch screen, he tapped in a numerical value to open valves sited above mammoth silos of sand buried deep underground in front of the turbines. Powered corkscrew feeders slowly turned and raised a controlled amount of sand up to the surface, releasing a fine sprinkle of the golden dust into the fast flowing air. Ted waited patiently, shielding his eyes with sunglasses as the first grains whipped across the open desert and began to irritate his face.

Returning to his main control desk, Stan added a high level projection, akin to light brown smoke drifting across the sky transforming the blue hue into a dirty brown. It never ceased to amaze Ted how the projections of the animals and people sited about him, interacted with the conditions, turning their backs to the stinging wind, and closing shutters on the windows of the buildings facing into the storm. Turning his own back to avoid a mouthful of sand, Ted reported in.

"That's great Stan but can you crank it up any higher, the client demanded the feel of a real storm reaching biblical proportions."

The response was almost immediate as Stan increased output by fifty per cent and almost obliterated the morning sun with the intensity of the projection. It was days like this when Ted wondered where he would now be had he turned another corner, missing Philip with his attacker, and avoiding a lifetime of pain for his heroics. He also admitted to himself that his antagonism towards Paul Johnston was only borne out of jealousy and Paul's blatant disregard for his own footballing talent. For Mr Johnston it was all about money and fame.

By now, Ted had no option but to turn up his collar and try to shield any exposed skin from the painful stinging as the tiny sand grains flew horizontally across the terrain. Without the protection of modern day equipment like sunglasses or visors he realised that this was far too dangerous for the client and decided that a rethink was in order with a lot less sand and a lot more holographic projections.

"That's enough Stan, turn it off." Ted yelled, but the immense wind noise obliterated the sound of his voice and the storm continued. Stan should have been constantly monitoring the situation but his attention was for the moment taken by the arrival of a fresh cup of tea and a chocolate biscuit. Added to this, the short skirt of the woman who brought his drink, raised its hem just high enough to reveal a thrilling flash of thigh above her stocking tops, every time she reached for something from the lowest shelf of her trolley. When she eventually walked out of sight, Stan returned to his surveillance screen to see Ted crouched down on his knees doing his utmost to protect his face and hands from the desiccating blast of the storm. Dropping his tea, Stan skittered hurriedly across the floor to force an emergency shutdown of the turbines, and as soon as the wind dropped, he tried to communicate with Ted.

"Ted… Ted, can you hear me? Talk to me buddy, are you ok?"

Ted slowly eased himself out of the embankment of sand that had built up around his prostrate body and staggered clumsily to his feet. Shaking like a wet dog he enveloped himself in a cloud of sand particles that drifted slowly away on the latent breeze as he finally managed to speak.

"Well, I'm still breathing, just. Face and hands are a bit red and sore, but apart from that I'm ok. What the hell happened?"

Stan was relieved that Ted could not see his face because he always blushed if he told a lie making it almost impossible to keep a secret.

"Oh, erm, sorry about that, the err, control program froze and I had to reboot the system. Are you sure you're alright?"

Stan gasped as Ted turned his face towards the camera. The sand had blasted a milky white sheen across his sunglasses, and what Stan could see of the rest of the exposed face, was an angry red hue looking like a nasty all-over graze, or severe case of sunburn. Ted removed his sunglasses to reveal two white circles around his eyes, a thin white line over the bridge of his nose and matching horizontal bars across his temples to the top of his ears. The protected skin beneath contrasted greatly with the rest of his face and looked like he was wearing a white eye-mask.

"Your face looks really burnt mate; I think you should see a doctor immediately." Stan advised, hoping that it was not as bad as it looked. Ted agreed as he surveyed the damage to the backs of his hands while he waited for Stan to shut down the program and raise the exit ramp.

* * *

Within the hour, Ted visited the on-site doctor and was back in his apartment. His face was coated in a soothing salve and he was trying to take an uncomfortable nap when there was a knock at the door. Swearing under his breath, he voice activated the intercom and instantly recognised Gemma's surprisingly deep but feminine tone.

"I heard that my baby has been hurt today, so I've brought my nurse's uniform and have come to give you a bed bath."

Ted knew that Gemma was in good spirits and was relieved that it appeared she had forgiven him for her punishment following the incident at the restaurant.

Ted verbally ordered the door to open. There was a soft click, followed by the swish, as the door slid to one side allowing Gemma to come in.

"Oh my poor baby, what on earth happened?" Gemma exclaimed when she saw the glowing red sore skin on Ted's face and hands.

"Nothing much, I just had a disagreement with a man-made sandstorm and a faulty off switch. D'you fancy a cup of tea?" Ted replied as he awkwardly tried to get to his feet without using his hands and head for the kitchen.

"Sit back down mister, I'm here now, and I'll take care of you. Can I fix you anything to eat?"

Gemma pushed Ted back down onto the sofa and proceeded to make tea and sandwiches for both while he rested. By the time she had returned from the kitchen, he was already asleep and she sat facing, quietly eating her own lunch while his drink turned cold.

* * *

"Good morning sleepyhead." Gemma purred, blowing Ted a kiss when he finally awoke early the next day. She had thoughtfully covered him with a blanket and stayed the night, sleeping on the sofa opposite to be on hand in case Ted needed her care. To pass the time she had been watching the wall-mounted infotainment system. It contained the latest unidirectional speaker system allowing Gemma to watch at any volume she liked as the sound was funnelled only to those sat directly in front of the screen. Anyone sited outside of this narrow band found it impossible to hear anything. Scanning randomly through the thousands of channels, she chanced upon a news bulletin that immediately grabbed her attention.

'Here is the latest news around the world from Global 555. There is still no information regarding the disappearance of a group of university graduates who were last seen several weeks ago on board a yacht passing through the Suez Canal on route for the Red Sea. Authorities and all neighbouring countries have conducted an extensive search of the area and have failed to find any wreckage, leading them to assume a kidnap, possibly by Sudanese pirates to have taken place. This is still subject to

speculation, as they are yet to receive any type of ransom demand. Unconfirmed reports from other media groups suggest that this may be the latest in a long line of bizarre disappearances that have occurred in the last three years, of major academics from the field of science and technology as one of the missing graduates, Adam Cartwright, is classed as a genius in computer programming. There is no evidence to substantiate this claim, but until any evidence is found, it cannot be ruled out.'

Gemma wondered if there was any connection between the sheriff's story and the missing people and she watched intently as photographs of every member who had gone missing were flashed up on a looped slideshow behind the news reader as she made her report. Gemma had already investigated Molly Dawson and found the story substantiated by various news reports following their return to Holtsville. But any chance of making a connection was lost, as it appeared that Miss Dawson had no recollection of where she had been following her disappearance nearly six months ago.

At that point Ted awoke with a snort and her attention focused directly upon him.

"Let's have a good look at you and see how your handsome face is doing." She announced while jumping up and opening the curtains to reveal a wall projection of an English cottage rose garden, complete with rolling green hills in the background. This feature was one of the numerous landscapes available, and came as a prerequisite in all modern subterranean accommodation, helping to regulate the body clock and reduce depression from a visual lack of outdoor life. To complete the illusion, the projection also bathed the room in warm, ultraviolet-free, morning sunshine through fake leaded windows.

Ted winced as his eyes adjusted to the brightness, but his focus cleared quickly, allowing him to study his hands and take note of any improvement. Kneeling at his side, Gemma carefully studied Ted's features before gently brushing away a few stray hairs that had stuck onto the gooey salve.

"I think that it's looking better already, there's certainly a lot less wrinkles and you now have a healthy glow. D'you know that there are women all over the world who'd pay thousands for what you've just had. Perhaps you should market the treatment." Gemma teased, there was some improvement, but the skin was still angry and it would be a few days before it was ready for the next step.

"Give it another day or so and then you'll be able to go down to the clinic and get a replacement spray-on skin while yours continues to heal underneath. Anyway, you must be hungry, how about I make us both a good old fashioned fry-up?" Gemma added, not waiting for an answer as she jumped up and walked into the open plan kitchen to prepare breakfast. Ted gave a noncommittal grunt over her appraisal of his recovery, reserving judgement for himself as he stood up and headed for the bathroom.

The stark lighting offered within, reflected by the shiny porcelain tiles, exaggerated his skin's reddish appearance, but it still looked like sunburn and it was very sore. He carefully applied a fresh coat of aloe based healing gel and when he emerged, Gemma had a pot of tea mashing on the breakfast bar. He sat down and watched wistfully as she finished cooking double egg, bacon, sausage and fried bread as a treat for her man.

Not wishing to spoil his meal, Gemma waited until they were sitting back in the lounge before she began with her other reason for the visit, but it was Ted that spoke first.

"Shouldn't you be at work?" He asked; giving her his serious face, but it did not show very well though his glowing features.

"I've called in sick to come and nurse you, is that alright?"

Gemma tried to take offence, but Ted knew it was any excuse to avoid the punishment detail that she had recently been assigned. He decided not to press the matter any further and sat back in his chair to listen to her news. Not sure how to best to begin, Gemma decided to start with how she first met Sheriff Dodson.

"Last year while on my sightseeing trip across America, I passed through a small hick town in one of the southern states and was pulled over for erratic driving. The sheriff attending insisted I take a sobriety test, where he found me apparently over the limit. I still believe he was lying, but in these situations it doesn't pay to argue. As a matter of course he wanted to know where I was from and where I worked, becoming very interested in the fact I work here. One thing led to another and he let me off a night in jail and a visit to the judge in the morning for my promise of staff discount at the nearest franchise to his town."

Ted frowned at the admission. It was against the rules to pass on discounts to anyone other than family, but nearly all who worked for the company did, so he remained silent allowing Gemma to continue.

"The thing is, you know how there are a lot of dodgy extras that weirdo's out there like to pay extra for, well he confessed to me yesterday how he had paid under the table for the thrill of an escaped black slave hunt."

Ted closed his eyes and drew a deep breath in his disgust at the revelation, but still managed to remain calm allowing Gemma to finish her tale.

"He claims that instead of hunting three lifelike androids, the sheriff and his deputies believe that they have actually killed two men and almost killed his own cousin who a few months ago had gone missing. She was captured while running for her life. Her skin had been dyed dark brown and she had been drugged to the point that she barely recognised her own name. Somehow he smuggled her out of the area claiming that they happened to find the poor girl on the route home wandering down the hard shoulder of the old interstate. To cut a long story short, she was happily reunited with her family back in Holtsville where they all live."

Ted was still holding his tea cup and had stopped half way to his mouth as Gemma revealed the gruesome details of her story. He replaced the cup on its saucer and tried to revert to his habit of scratching his chin when faced with a dilemma or serious information. But denied the pleasure of that soother, he stood up and began to pace the room, trying to comprehend the information.

"Are you sure it's not a prank call? Do you think Astelle might be setting you up? I wonder if Philip knows about this."

Ignoring Ted's musings, Gemma added the last nugget to her statement.

"Oh, I nearly forgot; he is also worried about two men who claim to be reporters who are still hanging around, even though every other news organisation has packed up and left town."

Ted tried to absorb the latest information, but his mind was reeling at the possibility of kidnap, murder, and the slave trade. Stories had always circulated and often dismissed regarding this type of crime, but now faced with the problem head-on, he did not really know what to do. His main hope was that everything was blown out of all proportion and this was just an unfortunate mistake. Gemma knew Ted's usual reaction to difficult problems, so she calmly let him burn himself out until he retook his seat allowing her to resume.

"First thing is that I haven't told anyone else about my deal with the sheriff, so it's almost impossible to be a stitch up or a prank. Unless the man has lost his faculties, I can't think of anything he could gain by using the expense of a secure line to ring me from the other side of the world so I have to believe what he has told me is the truth until I can prove otherwi…"

Ted jumped straight in, cutting Gemma off before she could finish her sentence.

"You're not going to prove anything missy, I don't want you to breathe a word to anyone until I've made my own enquiries. The best we can hope for is that this one hell of a misunderstanding. But if all this turns out to be true, then we are facing a major criminal organisation that wouldn't think twice about both of us having a serious accident so they can remain in business. You haven't told anyone else about this, have you?"

Gemma shook her head as Ted's thoughts now turned to Philip. It filled him with disgust to contemplate the possible involvement of his best friend in such a heinous crime. The logical answer was to proclaim him innocent until proven guilty, but even so, Philip's obsession with profit bordered on maniacal and Ted wondered what lengths his friend would sink to in order to make even more money. This nagging doubt made him decide not to inform Philip regarding the information before he had done some in-depth investigating of his own.

CHAPTER TWENTY-FOUR

By the time Duke had slept off the effects of the cheap bourbon and found his way back to the police station, the place was a hive of activity. Reports had already come in regarding the two car accident at Chickasaw Falls and word soon spread that one of them was a police vehicle. Unable to verify whose vehicle it was, owing to the difficulty of reaching the crash site. The sheriff frantically issued a roll call and everyone was accounted for except Elvis and Duke. He had deliberately turned off his mobile phone and police band radio to avoid any interruptions to his celebrations. When he finally sauntered into the station, Jolene quickly ended one of her many telephone calls trying to locate both men, and jumped to her feet, standing directly in Duke's way.

"Where the hell you been Duke? Your disappearance has got the sheriff madder than an old wet hen! Why in hell you not answering your radio? Ain't you heard 'bout the accident?"

Ignoring her raft of questions Duke stared back through throbbing bloodshot eyes, took Jolene firmly by the shoulders, and moved her gently to one side. He then walked straight into Sheriff Dodson's office, bracing himself for a tirade. Shocked and embarrassed, Duke instead received a manly embrace from the sheriff who looked distraught and relieved at the same time.

"Glad to see you boy, why didn't you answer my calls?"

Duke took a seat while mumbling something about a flat battery and blown fuse, then denied any knowledge of events, allowing the sheriff to explain all.

"I'm sorry to say that now you are here that leaves only one officer unaccounted for and that's Elvis."

Duke put on a confused face, but he knew exactly what the sheriff was talking about and only half listened to the story. The sheriff explained everything and Duke nodded every time there was a pause, but all he could think about was sitting at the opposite side of the desk. His attention was finally piqued when the sheriff reached the crucial part to the story.

"I'm sorry to tell you son that Elvis is dead."

Finding it hard to keep a straight face at the absurdity of the comment, Duke clasped a hand to his mouth in feigned shock. The sheriff, taking it as a sign of distress, placed a comforting hand on Duke's shoulder and continued with his tale.

"We're not rightly sure what happened, but it looks like Elvis was chasing a suspect down from the lookout point over Chickasaw lake and lost control of the vehicle on a hairpin bend. His patrol car must have clipped the rear bumper of the car in front, spinning them both off the road and they plunged into the gorge."

"Who was the other guy?" The sheriff looked puzzled at Duke's question, but put it down to grief.

"Forest rangers positioned at the top of the gorge using high powered binoculars have managed to read part of the number plate of the other vehicle and the tech guys have narrowed it down to a hire car rented by one Nathan Howton."

"Ain't that the guy from that Hologram Dreams Corporation who Elvis was trying to run outta town?" Duke asked, trying to look like he too was piecing bits of the puzzle together.

"Damn right it is and now it's cost him his life. I'll never forgive myself for asking you two to do a job that I should 'a' done myself."

The sheriff sighed as he finished the statement, walked back round his desk and dropped heavily into his high-backed reinforced office chair. His instinct was to reach for yet another chocolate bar, but as he opened his goodie drawer a sudden bout of guilt regarding Elvis made him slam it shut.

"Do you want me to inform the family Boss?" Duke asked, trying to break the sheriffs' morose silence.

"Thanks for the offer Duke, but this is my sad duty and I ain't about to shirk it now. You stay here and man the fort and I'll be back as soon as I can."

The sheriff choked his last word as he withdrew one of his many polka dot handkerchiefs and soundly blew his nose to cover his emotion. Duke continued to watch silently as the obese man tried to stand, but it was not until the second attempt that he rocked his considerable bulk out of the chair and strode wearily from the room. Duke stood up and walked over to the window, watching silently through the dusty slats of the venetian blind as the sheriff reached his reserved parking bay adjacent the station main door. With considerable effort, the sheriff wedged himself into the driver's seat of his patrol car, started the engine and drove away. Turning around, Duke quickly settled himself down in the still warm chair, leaned back and smugly placed both feet up on the corner of the desk.

"Jolene, can I get a coffee in here?" Was his first order of the day, the fact that he was supposed to be in mourning for the loss of his partner never crossed his mind, and as the sheriff's secretary duly obliged, she could not help to notice Duke's surprisingly cheerful demeanour.

"Very sorry to hear about Elvis, just wanted you to know that we all feel terrible about it." Jolene commented softly as she placed the steaming hot mug on the corner of the desk.

"We all got to go sometime Jolene." Duke replied, then shielded his closed eyes with the pulled down the brim of his hat. Confused by his attitude and the cold reply, Jolene paused, waiting for Duke to continue but he just waved her away.

"Close the door on your way out."

* * *

It was almost midnight when Sheriff Dodson returned to the station. To his surprise, the place appeared deserted when he walked in, but he guessed that everyone had gone home to be closer to their families during such a tragic event. Looking drained and red-eyed from the emotional turmoil of coming to terms with death, and spending the day with grieving family members, he sought the solace of his office and the memories contained within. Opening the door, he scowled deeply at the sight of his deputy, sound asleep in his chair while still clutching one of what the sheriff believed to be hidden bottles of Kentucky whisky. As if that was not enough, Duke was still wearing his muddy snakeskin boots and had his feet up on the corner of the desk, taking the sheriff close to his limit. He then caught sight of the spurs that used to belong to Elvis, were still attached to the grubby heels. The star shaped rowels that plainly showed the name '*Elvis*' engraved around the inner rim, had left a random pattern of indentations damaging the desk's wooden surface, and that took the sheriff clean over the edge. They had been a very personal and expensive gift that he gave to Elvis on his twenty-first birthday and the young man proudly wore them at every excuse. The sight of his deputy showing them off to almost everyone was a source of extreme pride for Oberon who looked upon him like a son. For nearly three months Duke endured this daily reminder, steadily increasing his animosity until he managed to win the prized possession from Elvis, in a rigged and very drunken poker game. The fact that Duke refused to return or sell the spurs back as a friendly gesture, or even give the young man the chance to win them in any game of Duke's choice, annoyed the sheriff greatly. With Elvis so soon departed it was just too much.

"I thought I told you I didn't want to be disturbed Jolene." Duke growled angrily from under the brim of his hat, thinking that it was the secretary who had disturbed his sleep. Immediately red faced, the sheriff exploded in rage.

"What the hell d'you think you're playing at? This is my office and you should be in mourning for your partner. Show a little respect you no good son of a bitch!"

The sheriff reacted vehemently, spraying spittle into the air from his outburst as he slapped Dukes feet off the desk and onto the floor. Violently woken from his dreamlike state and without even thinking, Duke jumped up and grabbed the sheriff roughly by the throat, easily slamming the immense bulk back hard against the filing cabinet. Snarling and angry, Duke pressed his own body against the sheriff and glared menacingly into his attacker's eyes. In the pause that followed, a decorative fern caringly placed on top of the cabinet by Jolene, toppled onto its side then proceeded to roll slowly off the edge, shattering its terracotta flowerpot as it hit the floor. Broken pottery and compost, decorated an assortment of well-thumbed *'Fly Fisherman Quarterly'* magazines that had also slipped from the top of the same cabinet as both men stared each other down.

With no obvious sign that Duke was willing to let go, the sheriff took matters into his own hands and violently raised his right knee into the deputy's testicles, the impact lifting the younger officer clean off his feet. Inside a second Duke had released his grip, dropped to the floor, and lay curled up squealing in pain with both his hands tenderly cupping his groin as he prayed for the sickening ache to go away.

"Do that again and I'll have your badge you drunken bastard. You're nothing more than a jumped up hayseed who only got where you are today because of me! If you want my opinion, the wrong deputy died today; the best part of you ran down your mother's leg."

The sheriff growled as he stepped over Duke and sat down heavily into his chair. With his pulse still racing and in need of a sugar fix he pulled open his desk drawer, revealing his private candy store and selected a long caramel log, unwrapped it and began to suckle the chocolate from its outer coating.

Gingerly getting to his feet as the debilitating pain in his genitals faded, Duke turned to leave when he remembered the whisky bottle that still remained intact on the office floor. Painfully easing himself down to retrieve his prize, the sheriff pushed him one step too far.

"You can leave that just where it is, seein' as it's mine in the first place. Oh, just to let you know, I've decided not to retire now following the accident. Anyway, it was only Elvis that I had in mind for the job seein' as you like the bottle a bit too much; the smell of whisky-sweat in here only goes to confirm my assumptions."

Duke straightened up immediately and stared in disbelief at the face of the sheriff who smugly leaned back in his chair, smiled at Duke's horrified reaction, then returned to sucking loudly on his candy treat. Being called an alcoholic was one thing, but after three murders, to realise that the post was never his to win was just too much. The pain in his groin suddenly disappeared and Duke dashed around behind the desk lunging for the sheriff yet again. This time instead of trying to strangle the poor man, Duke used the flat of his hand to ram the enormous caramel bar hard down the fat man's throat, instantly clogging his airway. Moving quickly around behind the chair, he wrapped both arms in a bear hug across the front of the Dodson's face and held the sweet candy firmly in place as the sheriff chocked and convulsed, fighting desperately to breathe. Every time he tried to inhale, the sugary sickly substance mixed with his saliva and oozed down the back of his throat, stinging the inside of his windpipe as he fought for air. Panic induced perspiration, poured down his chubby face and mingled with chocolate coated snot as it bubbled from his flaring nostrils, coating Duke's interlocking fingers, making it impossible to get any purchase as his own chubby digits clawed desperately for release. Unable to raise himself out of the chair, the sheriff twitched and turned trying to slide down, but Duke swivelled the seat, rammed the old man's knees against the desk drawers, and held on tight. An excited wave of euphoria surged through Duke's muscles, intensifying his strength as he felt the increasing rhythm of his own heartbeat pounding louder and louder inside his head from the visceral thrill of holding another man's fate in his hands. For the sheriff, the excessive strain on his over worked heart quickly began to take its toll, as chest pains radiated up his neck and black spots formed before his eyes. To compound the torture, Duke leaned in closer and growled into the old man's left ear.

"Listen carefully, you fat freak, I killed both a' them field agents to get this post, and by the way, I killed your precious boy Elvis too. I laughed real hard when I heard him scream all the way down to the bottom of Chickasaw Falls, then ***boom,*** Elvis has left the building."

The sheriff's eyes bulged at the revelation and it was just too much for his grossly enlarged heart to take. Incapable of any further strain, his body stiffened almost lifting his imposing bulk clean out of the chair as a violent spasm tore through his muscles. His heart thumped for one final time, and he slumped back down, dead. In his rage, Duke held on tight for another minute just to make sure he was not bluffing. Finally satisfied that the task was complete he loosened his grip and pushed the dead body face down onto the desktop, firmly wedging the candy bar into the dead man's throat. Following a quick cleanup in the washroom, Duke returned to the office and did not even glance in the late sheriff's direction as he retrieved the bottle of whisky then headed for the door.

CHAPTER TWENTY-FIVE

For Ted it had been a frustrating few days. Philip had insisted on only the best medical care for his friend, and the Harley Street dermatologist provided, had advised that Ted should spend time in hospital and make use of an oxygen tent to speed up the healing process.

Unwilling to leave the base at all, Ted promised to stay at home to avoid contamination, increase the levels of oxygen to the apartment, and maximise output to the air filters. All of this left him unable to investigate the disturbing report from Sheriff Dodson, until today.

Ted was prepared to let his face heal naturally, but Gemma and Philip had recommended facial treatment so as not to scare away any prospective clients, as the sight of the damage to his face could cause upset. Ted reluctantly agreed, but the main reason he conceded to the request, was the necessary excuse to poke around and ask a few questions regarding the cousin of Sheriff Dodson. Who as a Caucasian female, appeared to have been dyed to match the skin tone of a native African.

Ted tried to relax as he reclined in a chair not too dissimilar to one used by a dentist. The first layer of liquid polymer skin had been painstakingly matched to his own, sprayed onto his damaged face and was drying under the heat lamps in the dermatologist's surgery. He had been assured that his skin underneath, would continue to heal unhindered, but should infection set in, the top layer could be removed as easily as peeling a ripe banana.

"Tell me err, Sally; How many times have you changed someone's skin colour from white to black?" Ted began as he opened one eye and read the dermatologists name badge. Her puzzled reaction was what he had hoped for and she proceeded to explain that apart from the androids that her department spray painted to order, she had never changed the colour of anyone.

"The only humans I treat are people like you who need blemishes covered up like scar tissue or birth marks. Why d'you ask?"

Ted was ready for the question and he quickly concocted a story about a client who wanted to portray Jesus who he believed was actually black and wanted to be as accurate as possible.

"So, how much of this stuff do you get through in a year then?" Ted asked, nodding to the row of waist high liquid skin polymer canisters lining the far wall, waiting to be mixed with the appropriate skin tone before application.

"Probably fifty to sixty gallons a year, although not as much as the other place in Salisbury."

Ted pricked up his ears at Sally's answer. Not about how much product used, but the fact that she mentioned another site that Ted had never even heard of.

"What place did you say again?" Ted probed, trying to sound curious but not totally in the dark as to where Sally referred.

"You know the Salisbury plant where the old American air base used to be. The orders were mixed up once and the delivery driver tried to make me accept a consignment of over a thousand gallons. They must be taking baths in the stuff to get through that much, I ask you!"

Ted agreed readily and smiled at the joke, only to be reprimanded for creasing the new skin before it had fully bonded to his face. He quipped about being overworked and stressed to have temporarily forgotten about the Salisbury part of the operation, before quickly changing the subject as Sally applied the final touches. At this point Ted became very anxious to get out and investigate this hidden side of the corporation that less than five minutes ago he did not know even existed. The next ten minutes seemed to last forever as Ted had to lay back and keep his face as still as possible while the last coat had time to adhere with the layer beneath. When Sally finally gave him the all clear and let him look in a mirror, he was amazed at the results.

"I look ten years younger, how long will it last?"

"I'm afraid that the results are only temporary. The polymer skin will slowly wash away over the next few weeks and by then your new skin will be healed and gradually show through."

Ted thanked Sally for the treatment and dashed off back to his apartment to access the company records and see if he could find any information regarding the Salisbury unit. He was still very conscious of his new look, feeling very insecure as people returned nods of acknowledgement as he made his way back home and was thankful that his blushes were hidden by his brand new face. He had not been inside his apartment for more than five minutes when Gemma arrived to see the results.

"It's unbelievable, you look young again, people will think I've gone and got myself a toy boy. Can they do the rest of your body as well?"

Ted chose to ignore the sarcasm and proceeded to recap his conversation with the skin care expert, before asking Gemma to use his computer and search through company records for anything to do with Salisbury, while he grabbed a sandwich. It did not take long and within minutes she looked up and shook her head.

"Sorry Ted the computer search doesn't reveal anything. What do we do now?"

Ted thought for a moment, then realised that it needed a higher clearance level to access private accounts.

"Move over Gem let me have a go."

Ted typed in Gemma-Langton into the computer and she smiled warmly at his choice of password. Ted verified the request with a voice recognition program that gave him clearance equal to Philip, allowing him to access any file available, or so he thought. Once again Gemma was allowed to take over, and she searched for the Salisbury unit, only to be blocked and asked for a secondary password that Ted did not know.

"That proves Philip is definitely hiding something." Gemma concluded, leaning back on the sofa while Ted tried every other password he could think of but the result was just the same. He remained staring at the screen, while deep in thought, typed in a few more searches and found that there were payments for items that never arrived at the main site, including aviation fuel and aircraft spare parts.

"Now what do we do?" Gemma asked, still trying to stay focused, but still remained fascinated by Ted's new face.

"*We* do nothing, *you* are going to stay here and monitor the situation while *I* take a road trip. If there is anything to be revealed I'm sure it's Salisbury where the answers will be."

Gemma pouted at being excluded, but she knew that when Ted set his mind to something it was impossible to change. While he was away she had every intention of doing a little investigating of her own.

CHAPTER TWENTY-SIX

It was just before six-thirty the following morning when the cleaning staff arrived at the station. They found the sheriff where Duke left him, but by now his head had lolled to one side and the caramel bar hung part way out of his mouth. As soon as they recovered from the gruesome sight, they raised the alarm informing all personnel connected with the local police department, who immediately made their way back to the station. The only exception was Duke who arrived hours later looking dishevelled and reeking strongly of alcohol. He had celebrated his success in a seedy bar on the outskirts of town and had passed out in the back seat of his patrol car, totally oblivious to the police radio announcing the sheriff's demise. In spite of his appearance, Duke insisted on taking command of the situation, assuming the role of Acting Sheriff, much to the disgust of the other officers. A few strong cups of coffee, hot shower, and a fresh uniform soon saw him sobered up to play the role of heartbroken friend and work colleague who was doing his utmost to support a police station in mourning over two recent deaths.

Within twenty-four hours a preliminary coroner's report documented that Sheriff Oberon P Dodson had probably died from a heart attack caused by excessive choking on badly ingested food. A later report suggested that the he possibly blacked out and fell face down on his desk, with the lack of oxygen caused by the blockage bringing on the fatal heart attack. All of this was confirmed following a post mortem examination. The only fly in the ointment was the floor strewn with fishing magazines and the broken terracotta plant pot. Duke's suggestion that the sheriff must have had a diabetic dizzy spell, then bumped into the filing cabinet before sitting down in his chair seemed a reasonable explanation as there was no other evidence of foul play. A few days later, as expected, a verdict of accidental death was confirmed. At a loss for any other suitable experienced replacement, senior police officials took note of the way the station had been kept running since the tragic accident and they offered Duke the role of sheriff for a six month probationary period, drawing a satisfactory conclusion to Duke's Machiavellian plan.

For the time being, everything was happening exactly as he had hoped, until late one evening, a familiar face walked in. Duke was alone in the station savouring the taste of a much better quality of whisky now he had a senior salary, when he heard the floorboards creak outside his office. To avoid wagging tongues all the station staff had been dismissed for the night, allowing him to drink in private, so unless someone had returned, there was a stranger snooping around outside. His immediate reaction was to carefully unlatch the holster to the gun on his hip and remain still until he knew it was safe to move. Unable to identify who it was through the frosted glass mounted in the door, Duke used his thumb to ease off the gun's safety catch as the office door creaked slowly open. His finger was already poised on the trigger, when to his surprise Molly Dawson stepped in from the hallway. Maintaining his grip, Duke remained silent as he assessed the danger.

Dressed very soberly in a royal-blue jacket and matching knee-length pencil skirt, Molly looked every inch the latest junior assistant to Triplerock County's incumbent Mayor Thaddeus Wilson. He had noted the level of her popularity and offered Molly a job, hoping to gain approval from the local population, as he was falling behind in the polls and elections were less than a month away.

Duke narrowed his eyes and grinned, but it looked more like a leer as he looked her slowly up and down, revisiting the memory of her naked body hidden beneath the officious outfit.

"Now what can I do for you little missy?" Duke asked as he released his grip, restored the safety catch, and dropped his feet to the floor. Molly's flesh crawled at Duke's lascivious gaze and tried hard to focus on her reason for the visit.

"Heard 'bout the sheriff, and have come to pay my respec', that's all. If it weren't for him I'd still be a prisoner for that Dreams Company or worse still, dead."

Duke dismissed the statement, as he knew that it had nothing to do with Molly's visit tonight. Sitting up straight, he yawned loudly before giving his reply.

"That's very good of you to say so, Miss Dawson but Dodson's been gone for a while, and you leave it 'til now to offer your condolences. My guess is that you have something else on your mind, so out with it."

Molly was quite surprised at Dukes insight, but she did not show it. She had him down as a brain addled drunk, but the new sheriff was smart, clean, and on the face of it sober.

"It's quite simple '*Acting Sheriff*' Thornbuck."

Molly drew invisible speech quotes in the air to emphasise his current probationary role, but the snide had little effect.

"Over the last few weeks I have been fortunate to discover that my memory has completely returned. I now recall with perfect clarity how you hunted me down and raped me out there on the desert floor. I figured that your friend the deputy who died in that car crash and the late sheriff would bear witness to your defence and say that I imagined the whole event. But dead men tell no tales, so now my recompense falls squarely with you. I ain't gonna axk for no stupid amount that you cain't possibly afford, so I've decided on a figure agreeable to both of us."

Molly paused, waiting for a reaction, but Duke stared back, narrow eyed, and silent. This unnerving reaction caused her to stumble slightly with her well-rehearsed speech.

"I... I want compensation of five thousand dollars to be transferred into a numbered bank account. I know that even on your salary that amount of money is out of the question, but I'm sure a man of your dubious nature can become creative enough with the police department accounts to pay my fee. By the way, this arrangement is to continue on the first of every month while ever you hold the position of chief lawman for this fair town of ours."

Duke chuckled to himself as he stood up, and then in a gorilla-like aggressive pose his face dropped into a scowl. With straightened arms, he leaned forwards, resting the knuckles of his clenched fists on the pile of files sitting on top of his desk. Arrogantly, Molly had already rested one cheek of her behind on the far side of the desktop while supporting herself with her trailing leg, and she trembled visibly at his close proximity but refused to back down. Duke hunched his shoulders and moved closer, invading her personal space until he was only inches away. Waiting silently for Molly's reaction, but receiving none, he menacingly growled his reply.

"If you think for just one second that you can just walk in here and attempt to threaten the Duke, then think again. It's still your word against mine and who d'you think everyone round here is going to believe, The sheriff of this noble county or some filthy good for nothing po' cracker who ran away from her sick momma to work as a whore at the cat house in Jackson Valley?"

Molly flinched at the realisation that Duke knew all about her sordid past and she swallowed hard when he leaned in even closer to whisper into her ear.

"Now get out!"

The sensation of his hot breath on her skin made her flesh creep and Molly finally moved away. Although this was born out of fear, she stood up and waved a hand repeatedly across her nose, making sarcastic comments regarding his chronic halitosis. Regaining some of her bravado, Molly stopped in the doorway and turned around to play her final hand.

"I'm sorry you feel that way, but if you try to take me down I'm going to take you with me."

Duke was already sitting back down in his chair and he raised a curious eyebrow as to what evidence Molly had that could cause him any harm; but he did not have to wait very long.

"I'm sure you remember the day the three of you found me and brought me home do you not?"

Duke nodded slowly, biding his time and waiting for Molly to place all her cards on the table before he made his reply.

"Well, Doctor Booth gave me a thorough examination and his written report states that I was subject to a violent rape. He also has samples of pubic hair and semen taken from my person and you know damn well who it belongs to. Now if you fail to agree to my terms I will go public, it's as simple as that."

This time it was Duke's turn for a shock as his body visibly stiffened in his chair. Looking down and breathing heavily, he frantically tried to think of a suitable answer. Molly placed both hands on her hips and stared hard, hoping that Duke could not see her quaking with fear as she waited for his response. Luckily, his attention was lost in his own thoughts, and after a very lengthy pause, he raised his head to give his reply.

"Looks like I got no choice in the matter don't it Miss Dawson. Give me a few days to make some arrangements and I will get back to you as quick as I can."

Duke's sudden obsequious manner fooled Molly into believing that she had played the game winning hand, and found it hard to maintain a calm exterior as she made to leave.

"I'll give you forty-eight hours, no more."

She called from the outer office, luckily for her Duke could not see how much her legs trembled as she walked unsteadily towards the exit at the rear of the building.

Duke barely even heard the fading click of her stiletto heels on the polished wooden floor as he closed his eyes and formulated a plan to destroy the evidence and if necessary Molly, in that order.

* * *

Before the night was over, Duke was hiding in the bushes under the ground-floor, side-window of Doctor Booth's home, located in the oldest part of the town. It was around midnight and for some unknown reason the blind was still raised, with the internal light shining brightly, illuminating a large part of the heavily planted front garden and boundary wall. Duke tentatively checked the perimeter, then slowly rose up from his crouched position and peered in. The doctor had been avidly writing up Molly's dictated story and had absentmindedly forgotten to turn off the desk light before going to bed more than half an hour ago. Taking a risk at being silhouetted by the lamplight, Duke reached up, slid a flat blade between the upper and lower frames of the overlapping sash window, then forced back the small brass thumb lever used to lock the two halves in place. Checking around for one last time, he carefully eased the lower window up and climbed inside. Fearful of being seen from the roadside, Duke quickly eased the window back down and lowered the blind, thus hiding him from anyone who happened to be passing by. What he wanted now was to find Molly's medical records and any physical evidence that the doctor possessed. It was obvious that the doctor was in league with Molly regarding the blackmail, or he would already have been arrested. So the assumption was that all of the evidence must still be somewhere in the doctor's house.

"Right Doc, where would you hide it?" Duke mumbled under his breath as he searched through the old wooden filing cabinets looking for Molly Dawson's name. In his haste he had forgotten to bring a torch with him so he reached out for the doctor's brass and green glass shaded bankers lamp, perched on the corner of the desk. As Duke's concentration was taken up by the job in hand, he turned too quickly, catching the top of the lampshade with his left elbow. The lamp shifted and tilted sharply, teetering on the bevelled desk edge. Realising what he had just done, Duke quickly twisted his body around and tried to cup his free hand around the lamp stem, but all he succeeded in doing was knocking it further, resulting in a resounding crash, shattering the glass as it hit the floor. The room was now in total darkness and Duke froze, looking up at the ceiling as he held his breath, listening for the sounds of any activity coming from upstairs. At first there was nothing, and all he could hear was the heavy tock of the grandfather clock standing in the hallway. Its regular resounding thud echoing like a drum beat inside his head. Suddenly a creaking sound of an old sprung metal bedstead came from the first floor, followed by shuffling footsteps along the upper landing, signalling that the doctor had been disturbed and was heading for the stairs.

"Who... who's down there? I don't keep drugs on the premises and the prescription pads are coded. I've also got a shooter in my hand and I'm not afraid to use it, so get out *now!*" The doctor called tentatively over the gallery landing. He was lying about possession of a gun, as he abhorred firearms of all kinds and refused to have one in his house, but at this moment in time he was having a change of heart. In his younger days he would have stormed down the stairs and confronted whoever had broken in, but old age and health issues had taken the fire from his belly.

Duke remained silent and as his eyes adjusted to the darkness he crept into the hall and waited under the rise of the open plan staircase as the old man fearfully walked down. The broken desk lamp had tripped the breakers in the fuse box, leaving the doctor also fumbling blindly in the dark. As he neared half way, he never saw Duke's hand reach through the balusters, grip tightly around his ankle and pull. Completely startled, the doctor swore loudly as he tried to free his leg, but due to his advancing years he quickly lost his balance and started to fall. He had already let go of the banister and flailed his arms like a madman for some other support but found none. Within seconds, his entire body length crashed face down onto the lower half of the stair run, bounced up and continued with its forward momentum before thudding heavily onto the quarter space turn at the bottom. The first impact cracked two ribs and the second snapped his right clavicle bone clean in two, poking one end out through his aged skin as his shoulder bore the brunt of the second part of the fall.

Passing out for a few seconds, the doctor awoke to the sound of a familiar voice.

"Where's Molly's evidence?" Duke growled. He had climbed the first three stairs and knelt down beside the doctor, demanding an answer. Semi-concussed and wheezing heavily, the doctor was unable to talk properly, due to a badly punctured lung. Suddenly recognising the sound of Duke's voice he began to whisper his thanks, but he could not understand how the police had managed to arrive on the scene so quickly and yet not find the intruder.

"There's a man in the house Duke, did you get him?"

The old doctor tasted blood in the back of his throat and choked on his words, but Duke did not care.

"I won't ask you again old man, tell me!"

The doctor lost consciousness and Duke's anger increased from the lack of response. With the small amount of moonlight filtering down through the frosted glass panes surrounding the front door, Duke could see blood seeping from the wound around the fractured collarbone beginning to soak into the fabric of the doctors pale blue night shirt. Shuffling forward a little, he pressed his right knee onto the broken bone, painfully waking the doctor up in his attempt to force out the answer.

"This is your last chance doc before I get real nasty, where is it?"

Confused and in agony, the doctor squealed weakly as the two ends of the collarbone were forced back against one another until the parchment dry skin tore even further. Gasping at the pain from the additional infliction, the doctor began to cry and pleaded for release.

"Please stop, I'm begging you. Take what you want, but please stop!"

Duke's patience had already passed its limit and he was just about to slap the old man across the face, when another idea crossed his mind. Wary of the aged doctor telling the authorities that he had seen Duke inside his house and the fact that he was still no closer to finding where the evidence was hidden, he decided to solve both problems in one go.

Carefully retracing his steps in the darkness, he re-entered the office and raised the window blind, offering enough light from the three-quarter moon for him to proceed with his plan. Striding back into the hallway, he grabbed Doctor Booth roughly by the heels and ignoring the further screams of pain, he began to drag him from the landing onto the hall floor, banging the back of the old man's head down every remaining step in the process. In the half-light, shuffling backwards towards the surgery, Duke misjudged the width of the opening and jammed his left boot spur into the wooden doorframe, twisting his ankle and falling heavily onto his backside. Cursing the world loudly for his own misfortune, Duke yanked his boot free, jumped back to his feet, and brushed pieces of broken lamp glass from the seat of his trousers before returning to pull the doctor into the surgery. The fear of death carries an inner strength of its own and in a feeble attempt to stop Duke dragging him to what he knew was going to be his demise, the semiconscious doctor grabbed at anything lying around. This included the hat stand and then same door frame that had felled his attacker.

Feeling the pain of a sore ankle did nothing to improve Duke's patience, and an extremely painful kick under the doctor's broken ribs instantly loosened the old man's grip. Heaving for breath and well beyond his limit, the doctor clenched both fists to his chest as Duke positioned him adjacent to the broken desk lamp on the floor.

Similar to his murder of Lyle Simpkins, Duke decided to use fire to eradicate evidence, only this time it had to look like an accident. The investigative authorities would assume that the doctor had clumsily knocked the lamp from the desk, breaking the bulb and tripping the power to the house. In the darkness he had probably lost his balance and fallen heavily over the desk, knocking himself out. The second part of the plan was fairly simple. In spite of being a medical man, it was well known that the doctor loved the taste of a Cuban cigar, even more so now that they were considerably cheaper as Cuba was a newly elected part of the union.

Retrieving a small pre-cut stogie from the humidor on a shelf at the back of the office and stealing some of the best smokes for himself. Duke ignored the doctor's plaintive moans as he carefully lit one end, and placed the glowing tobacco tube by the side of an upturned ash tray carefully placed on top of some loose papers on the floor. Within seconds the paper set alight, causing the doctor to wheeze and cough painfully from the increasing smoke. Duke knew that the fire would destroy any evidence the doctor possessed and with a smug grin spreading across his face, he slipped back through the open window, pulled it down tightly behind him, and disappeared into the night.

The old timber framed building was well alight by the time the alarm had been raised and firefighters arrived on the scene. All they could do was to contain the blaze from spreading to other nearby properties and allow it to burn itself out. Luckily for Duke he had parked his patrol car only a few streets away and after a quick change of clothes, he created the perfect alibi by being the first police officer on the scene. Quickly organising a police cordon around the area, Duke's watched avidly at the inferno lighting up the clear night sky.

Later that morning, fire investigators entered what remained of the smoking building and it was not long before they carried out the charred remains of Doctor Morton Booth. One of the many curious bystanders was Molly Dawson, and as she watched the rear door of the coroner's wagon slam shut, sad realisation dawned upon her that it was her bluff that had sealed the doctor's fate. The irony was that there originally was evidence that Molly had described, but the incompetent doctor had accidentally sent it for incineration along with a consignment of other medical waste from the practice, leaving her blackmail attempt without any substance. Her sadness turned to fury when she caught Duke's eye as he headed back towards his police car. With a slight exaggeration, he touched the rim of his hat between thumb and index finger, nodding his head in what looked like a polite southern gesture. But it was a sign that the game was over and she knew it.

CHAPTER TWENTY-SEVEN

Ted Langton's very expensive solar powered, white, two-seater sports car, rolled almost silently up to the heavily padlocked double gates marking the main entrance to the now abandoned Salisbury military installation.

He had already driven as close as possible around the entire perimeter of the massive base and apart from a few holes torn by vandals in the miles of chain link fencing that marked the boundary to the site, he could see no practicable way in. Every other serviceable entrance had been blocked by massive concrete blocks to stop unauthorised vehicles getting onto the site. The empty buildings in the distance at the side of a weed infested runway looked to have been abandoned for many years and a detailed view through the high powered thermal imaging, zoom camera mounted in the grill under the bonnet of his car showed no human signs of life. The only option now was to find and investigate the nearest distribution warehouse and hope to get lucky. Switching the camera back to its original use of a landscape recognition system, it allowed the driverless vehicle to guide itself to any destination in the country. Using this technology, it was not long before Ted found the depot entrance and he parked across the road so he could comfortably watch the endless parade of trucks and vans come and go.

Every driverless arrival was the same, the wagon stopped directly over a sensor embedded in the tarmac at the depot gate, leaving the cab level with a mechanised code reader sited a few feet away. Depending on the vehicle's size and shape, a small hand-torch sized sensor pod mounted on a vertical screw threaded column, wound up to the necessary height and then slid silently forwards on an extendable rail to stop less than a hand's width away from the tinted cab window. Prompted by a coded signal from the pod aimed into the cab, all the information required, appeared in green computer code displayed in the reactive side-window glass. A soft red light from a laser scanner flickered across the proffered documentation, relaying the information to the main computer. Providing that supplied data was correct, the warehouse shutter rolled up and allowed the vehicle inside.

For nearly a year there had been protests around the globe against the new automated delivery warehouse depots as hundreds of thousands of jobs had been axed and Ted was surprised not to see anyone picketing the gate today. Even though he sympathised with the cause, he was well aware that it was almost impossible to stop the juggernaut of technology changing the world. Since the Luddites smashed up the new labour saving machines in the nineteenth century there always have and always will be objections to progress.

All Ted now had to do was settle down and wait for the right consignment to be collected, and then follow to see where it goes. Hours passed and darkness fell, luckily Ted did not feel the autumnal chill, as England and the majority of northern countries now enjoyed balmier and much more regulated seasons, thanks to the geostationary array of weather control satellites that now orbited the earth, a boon to every industry whose production is influenced by the unpredictability of the weather.

He was just deciding whether to call it a day, find somewhere to eat and a room for the night, when an empty flatbed wagon entered the warehouse. A few minutes later, the same wagon departed, full of crates with the recognisable logo of the liquid polymer skin manufacturer emblazoned in one foot high bright yellow stickers on every side. Unsure whether the truck contained any security cameras Ted slid down in his seat, waited for the wagon to pass by and reach the end of the street, before he started his car and began the chase. Luckily the surrounding roads were fairly deserted, so keeping a healthy distance behind, Ted relied on the car's thermal imaging camera to keep track. To his surprise, the wagon headed directly towards the abandoned military base and passed unopposed through a now open set of previously locked security gates. Stopping on the perimeter, Ted watched from inside his car, as a wagon shaped thermal image maintained a direct course for the empty buildings before it disappeared completely from the dashboard display. Luckily the gates still remained open so Ted quickly drove onto the site, heading for the last place the wagon was seen before it vanished. Switching his headlights to full beam, illuminated a vast expanse of the runway, and Ted searched for the next fifteen minutes, but the wagon was still nowhere to be seen.

"This is ridiculous all I need now is a bunch of nosey teenagers with their dog to make this day complete." Ted moaned to Gemma via his mobile phone as he circled the car around and continued with his search.

"Perhaps aliens have landed on the air base and the wagon passed through into another dimension!" Gemma replied, trying not to laugh out loud at Ted's miserable tone.

"I'm glad my disappointment seems to amuse you madam, tell me how's the cleanup duty going?" He replied sarcastically. Gemma snorted and abruptly ended the call leaving Ted smiling to himself as he pictured her pouting face while he drove slowly around in an ever-widening spiral, which luckily gave him time to spot something odd. Across the middle of the access road was a large puddle of standing water that both the wagon and Ted's car had driven through. From the water's edge it was plain to see Ted's car tracks steadily drying as he circled around the sun bleached tarmac, but the tracks from the wider wheels of the wagon were different. They continued in a straight line, and then cut off right in the middle of the runway. Ted stopped his car less than ten feet from where the tracks ended and got out to inspect the scene. It was fairly easy to see, even in darkness, that the wet tyre tracks ended exactly where two embedded parallel narrow metal rails cut across the runway, but what he did not know was why. Following the extremely narrow gauge track, he soon discovered that the rails traced a large rectangular shape slightly bigger than a tennis court and that was it. At a loss of what to do next, he began to walk back across the box to his waiting car when suddenly the ground beneath his feet began to shudder. Bracing himself, Ted watched the inner railed section of tarmac begin to rise upwards out of the ground, hinging from one end akin to one half of a cantilever bridge. Frozen in a state of shock and disbelief, Ted spread out his arms for balance as he rose higher and higher into the air until common sense prevailed and he trotted hurriedly down the ramp onto level ground. Limping back to the safety of his car ready to drive away at the first sign of danger, Ted sat and stared as the road continued to open like the jaws of a huge Boa constrictor ready to swallow its prey. From deep inside the monster's mouth, beams of bright light spewed out, dancing across the underbelly of low cloud that had drifted over the site, accompanied by an echoing monotone hum. The lights grew steadily stronger until the same, now empty delivery wagon re-emerged from what was obviously a subterranean road. As the truck cleared the exit, the rays projected by truck's headlights, bounced quickly back to ground level and it sped off back towards the perimeter gates. The instant the truck drove clear, huge hydraulic rams hissed as the tarmac ramp lowered and within a few seconds it lay as flat as it did before.

Ted followed the truck closely so as not to get locked inside the airfield, then headed back to the village nearest to the depot. A fish and chip supper, followed by a few beers and a hotel room booked for the night, ended with Ted semi-reclined on his bed. Propped up by his pillows against the headboard, he leaned his clipboard computer screen against his suitcase and adjusted the angle of the on-board webcam, so he could visually report his latest findings to Gemma.

"Tomorrow I'm going to hitch a ride aboard the next delivery wagon and find out what's happening down there." Ted raced through the last sentence regarding plans for the morning; bracing himself for expected objections to its content. Gemma expected this to happen and knew that she had to try and talk him out of it. But she also knew that when Ted's mind was set on an issue there was little chance of anyone changing it.

"Why don't you just call the police and let them investigate?"

"I can't trust anyone at the moment and with Philip's money you never know who might be on his payroll." Ted replied with a well-rehearsed answer that he hoped would close the matter.

"We're all on his payroll Ted, don't you trust even little old me?" Gemma whined, then pouted as she dropped her chin and looked under her perfectly plucked eyebrows back at Ted.

"You know full well what I mean Gemma and course I didn't mean you; you're the only one I can trust."

Ted knew that Gemma was teasing, but he took the bait anyway and as he stretched his arms, and stifled a yawn, he tried to wrap up the conversation.

"If there's nothing else to say, I'm very tired and am going to call it a night."

Gemma conceded defeat, then gave Ted a smile that said she was up to something. Leaning closer to the camera, so her face almost filled the screen, she winked then breathlessly whispered.

"I felt guilty for teasing you earlier so here is a little treat before you go to sleep."

To the grinding beat of slow rhythm and blues music, Gemma moved back from her webcam and began to move her body to the rhythm. To make sure she remained in full view of the camera, she had already swapped Ted's large screen image with that of her own, leaving his smaller overlay in the left hand top corner of the display. Satisfied with the result, she slowly caressed her body, and with a devilish glint in her eye began to unfasten the buttons down the front of her silk blouse. Looking back at the camera, she seductively licked her lips and with Ted staring fixatedly at the screen, Gemma continued to undo the cuffs and turned her back while letting the blouse fall softly to the floor. Teasingly slow, she continued by unhooking her black lacy bra and sexily slipped both shoulder straps down to the crook of her arms to stop the unwanted item falling away. Looking coyly over her left shoulder, she continued to gyrate her hips to the sexy beat of the music while slowly turning around.

"I hope you like what you see." Gemma purred while holding the bra cups in place with both hands. With a tease here and a flash of cleavage there, she carefully slipped her bra away from her breasts with one hand, while leaving the forearm of the other covering her naked form. As the music ended, she dramatically opened her arms wide, proudly revealing all for her man. Surprised and upset upon not receiving any type of reaction from Ted, Gemma moved closer and tapped the clipboard screen, swapping Ted's picture back to full size. To her indignation, his eyes were closed and he was snoring loud enough for her to hear now the music had stopped.

"This one's gonna cost you plenty lover boy!"

She wanted to be angry, but the sight of Ted already sleeping heavily was proof enough of how tired he must be. Lovingly she kissed the tips of her fingers then placed them over Ted's lips on the screen before ending the call.

* * *

The next morning the unusual sight of genuine sunlight shining brightly through the thin material of the floral patterned curtains, roused Ted early from his slumbers. Apart from his head lolling to one side as he slept, he had hardly moved, and his stiff muscles let him know. A hot shower eased his tired body, releasing the crick in his neck, and with a clean set of clothes followed by a hearty breakfast, he was ready for the day. He could not remember how the conversation with Gemma ended last night and the fact that his computer screen had gone into standby made him wonder if he had nodded off. The nagging ache in the pit of his stomach was usually a good indicator that he was probably in trouble and he knew that very soon he would painfully find out.

Armed with a six-pack of bottled water, two green apples, a cheese sandwich, and a packet of chocolate biscuits, Ted positioned his car in the same place as yesterday, in the shade of the wide spreading branches of an old oak tree. Following the same routine as before, he carefully watched every delivery come and go to the depot. It was not until late in the afternoon and Ted was fighting to keep his eyes open in the warm sun shining directly through the car window, when a much smaller flatbed van stopped at the depot gate. Recognising the android power unit logo, spray painted on the cab door that his company used, Ted guessed that the contents had to be going to the abandoned base. Checking first to see if anyone was watching, he quickly got out and trotted across the road, stopping next to the roller shutter door. Waiting breathlessly for it to open, Ted watched the automated scanner perform its allotted task and the door rolled up, allowing the van inside with Ted following closely behind.

The smug feeling of how easily he gained access to the warehouse was soon quashed, when his eyes adjusted to the dim interior. What he had not allowed for was the sheer size of the place. Running as fast as his damaged knee would allow, he was just in time to hitch a ride on the back of a motorised grabber arm and combination forklift that followed every delivery to unload the cargo in the allotted storage bay. Lucky there appeared to be no other humans around and if a security camera picked up the intrusion, he hoped to be long gone before anyone arrived. When the wagon reached the correct storage zone, it stopped, as did the grabber. Ted jumped off, watched carefully as the goods were unloaded and both vehicles drove away. Finding the ideal site, he climbed up and positioned himself atop of a large crate in the adjoining bay, ready for the second long boring part of the day. Guessing that it would probably be early evening again before the collection truck arrived, he armed himself with a good book and a drink, settled down and waited.

It was incredible how many deliveries and collections there were and to pass the time he tried to calculate how many jobs had been lost in this warehouse alone and then multiply the amount to a national and then to a worldwide figure, but this was instantly forgotten when suddenly he heard a loud human voice.

"I'm telling you Bob we should have taken a right turn down isle fifteen, we're going the wrong way!"

The vehicle turned the corner and in a panic, Ted rolled off his lofty perch and had just enough time to hide in the shadows. To his surprise, one of the wagons contained a driver and his mate who were arguing with each other about the location of their collection. Looking back, he was shocked to see that he had forgotten his jacket and a bottle of water. Both items were still sitting on top of the crate and in full view of the truck's headlights, that now projected a huge shadow of both items growing steadily up the far wall as the truck drew near.

"I told you this was the wrong way; you couldn't find your own backside in the dark! Do as you're told and back up to the main roadway."

Fortunately, both men were far more concerned with their own state of affairs to notice anything out of the ordinary as the aged truck stopped. Suddenly they both got out of the cab and walked round to the front of the truck, casting their own elongated shadows along the floor. They now stood face to face waiting for the other to move out of the way, until the larger of the two barged his way passed his companion and quickly settled himself into the driver's seat ready to take charge.

"Are you comin' or what?" He yelled, encouraging his partner to get in. Ted listened as the gearbox clunked into reverse and with both men on board, the engine whined as it moved slowly backwards to the main roadway. Breathing a sigh of relief, he watched the shadows quickly shrink down the wall until they disappeared completely when the truck turned the corner and drove away. Cautious of a repeat performance he moved to a much more secluded location and continued to wait.

The time slowly passed by and Ted's thoughts repeatedly returned to Philip's recent behaviour, leaving him to wonder if it was at all possible that his best friend could be embroiled in such a heinous crime. He always tried to see the good side in everybody and foolishly decided that until there appeared any evidence to the contrary; he would give Philip the benefit of the doubt.

Luckily, the remaining part of the afternoon passed completely uneventful until the correct wagon finally rolled up for its collection. As soon as it stopped in the correct parking bay, the laser guided loading machine following closely behind, quickly began to complete the order by filling up the empty space in the back of the truck. During this small window of time, Ted jumped down, forced open the passenger door of the cab and squeezed himself inside. There was very little space for a man of his size, but he somehow managed to wedge himself in-between the collection of computer navigation equipment and hydraulic machinery that helped to drive the truck. Uncomfortable, but determined to stick it out, he slammed the cab door and began to wait. As soon as the last crate lowered onto the wagon, Ted's ride it pulled away. Within minutes, the truck was back out onto the main road where Ted found to his relief that it was already dark, giving him the chance to look out of the cab window with little chance of being seen.

Mercifully the surrounding roads were fairly deserted and as expected the truck pulled up outside the perimeter gates to the abandoned air base, just a few miles outside the village. Cautiously peering out, he recognised the same two gates marking the base perimeter; they were still padlocked and there appeared to be no other way to get in. Coming from a small aluminium pod attached to the top of the dashboard, Ted was alerted to a high-pitched pulsing tone. Mounted on the pod's lid were two rows of tiny red LED lights flashing in sequence. When the beeping ceased, the lights changed colour from red to green and the double-padlocked gates hinged open from the right-hand side as one complete unit, allowing direct access onto the base.

Just like the night before, the truck headed off down the runway and the roadway opened, allowing entry under the ground. Dropping down into a low gear, the delivery wagon drove steadily down the tarmac incline, continuing its journey deeper into the earth. For now, all Ted could do was sit and wait as he watched the hypnotic flash of bulkhead safety lights passing by the side-window. Eventually the highway levelled out and his ride entered a vast cathedral sized cavern hewn from solid rock. Carefully easing up to spy over the dashboard Ted watched the truck follow a set of yellow parallel lines painted on the floor denoting a roadway. Keeping within the painted guides, the truck continued across to the far side of the cavern until it stopped alongside yet another automated crane that instantly began to unload the cargo. This time, the crane placed everything onto a moving conveyer belt, transporting the delivery through a door-sized hole cut into a re-enforced concrete wall.

Luckily, there appeared to be very few people inside this section of the facility and the few remaining were all preoccupied with their own tasks to notice the delivery vehicle cab door pop open. Scanning the area for a second time, Ted finally crept out, pushed the door almost closed, and then quickly took cover behind a pyramid of small crates piled high against the far wall. Taking immediate revision of his surroundings, he noted that the facility was probably the same size as the central atrium back at headquarters, but due to the lack of internal structures it looked much larger and every sound echoed across the cavernous roof space. Along the opposite wall and dominating the scene were two levels of offices carved directly into the solid rock. Access was via a series of fire escape type metal stairwells and walkways bolted on the outside like an enormous exoskeleton. The stadium sized concrete floor below was filled with assorted transport vehicles, machinery, and pallet stacked boxes, also two small twin-engine propeller driven aircraft were positioned near the bottom of another wider access road that Ted guessed was used by the planes to reach the runway above. Hurriedly trying to absorb every scrap of visual information, Ted found his attention taken by a small land train similar to the ones seen at holiday resorts. It emerged like a giant caterpillar from inside one of several well-lit tunnels that disappeared into the underground facility. The train stopped, allowing three uniformed men to get out before it disappeared just as quickly down another tunnel. At the foot of the secondary access ramp, Ted closely watched eight more guards armed with rifles, as they appeared to be dealing with a small group of very docile, scruffy looking women and men who had disembarked from one of the recently arrived aircraft. He stared in fascination, as a flexible collar as thick as his little finger, was in turn, placed unopposed around the necks of what were obviously fresh prisoners. With each collar secured, the guard forced the prisoner into something akin to a giant pet carrier, complete with a steel mesh entrance secured by a lock. The last detainee, a very tall man who at first looked as calm as the rest of his group took an immediate dislike to the sight of his new cramped surroundings and before his personal collar could be secured, he sprang into life, animatedly fighting off two men who were ready to herd him towards his pod. It was a futile resistance and for his sins a third guard dealt him a heavy blow between the shoulder blades with his rifle butt, instantly stopping the fight and bringing the prisoner crashing heavily to his knees. With the collar swiftly secured, almost immediately the man appeared to lose all bodily coordination. Twitching violently he fell face first onto the floor thumping his forehead loud enough onto the concrete that even from his distance Ted could hear the thud. Clutching desperately at his neck, the man continued to convulse from what Ted now realised was a shock collar, operated by one of the guards who repeatedly pressed a button mounted on his wrist-mounted unit. Simultaneously, Ted pressed a button on the side of his own wrist mounted communication device and the viewing screen hinged to the vertical. Looking through the transparent viewfinder, Ted touched the outer edge of the screen and it began to record everything in sight; including each pod as the crane lifted it onto a much larger conveyer belt, transporting the prisoners away down yet another tunnel.

Armed with all the evidence he needed, Ted shrank back into the shadows and waited for the next truck to switch on its headlights as it powered up ready to leave. It was blatantly obvious that the telephone call from the sheriff could not have been a hoax and as soon as he got out, his next move was to call national security. Something that Ted had failed to take into account during his surveillance mission was a security camera installed high in the cavern roof relaying all his actions directly to Philip Sanderson's desk.

CHAPTER TWENTY-EIGHT

The town of Holtsville was still coming to terms with yet another death. As is typical of many semi-rural communities scattered across the southern states, nearly every resident could claim some connection to the deceased, either by family or as a general acquaintance.

Another coincidental factor, due to the level of necessity and budget limitations, was that many public officials combined their occupation with other similar roles. Dr Morton Booth held the dual occupation of coroner and medical examiner for the area. As he was now the deceased, the county authorities ordered another doctor from the neighbouring town of Baker Ridge to attend. Also, being a close colleague of the late doctor, he reluctantly set to the unwelcome task of the post mortem examination, and with professional courtesy proceeded with an earnest intent.

Already dressed in industry standard white one-piece hooded coverall, rubber gloves, and heavy-duty apron to avoid any cross contamination, he made doubly sure that the regulation, overhead video recording equipment was on voice activated standby. He then donned a tiny high-resolution video camera onto the bridge of his spectacles. This item, although not required by law, allowed for greater detailed analysis, as it relayed a coroner's eye view of the entire operation.

Satisfied all was well he began his narration. Verbally recording the time, date, and identification code number, he proceeded with his observations.

"My name is Doctor Theodore Delancy, physician for the town of Baker Ridge, Louisiana and temporary coroner for Triplerock County. I am working on the presumption that the deceased is Doctor Morton Booth, Caucasian male, age eighty-one, resident and owner of Gardenia House and Doctor's Surgery, Holtsville, Triplerock County, Louisiana.

If I find evidence to the contrary, due diligence will be taken to assert correct identification. This body has been recovered from the burnt out remains of said surgery and initial observations indicate death by fire, unless a more detailed examination dictates otherwise. The badly charred flesh makes it extremely difficult to detect any evidence of foul play, but there appear to be depressions in the rib cage indicating two or possibly three broken ribs; this I will verify following a full internal investigation. Also on the same right-hand side of the torso, the clavicle bone is definitely broken as one section is visibly protruding through the blackened skin. The approximation of both injuries indicates a heavy fall, which is conducive with a report from the fire department that the breakers from the lighting circuit were tripped prior to the fire. This presumably left the deceased to stumble blindly in the dark. My concern at the moment, is that the late doctor was found in his surgery. The level of damage to the right clavicle indicates a fall from a greater height such as a stairwell or at least from the top of his desk, something I find highly unlikely. I can only surmise that the deceased fell down the stairs, then was able to make his way into the surgery to call for help. He may have fallen onto the corner of his desk as that was in the vicinity, but the impact would have pushed the bone inwards not out as the injury suggests. I am knowledgeable with the layout of the house and the front door was closer to the stairs offering a safer option for escape. It may be possible the fall could have left him in a confused state and disorientated, but at this juncture foul play cannot be ruled out."

The coroner had already requested Doctor Booth's dental records for formal identification, but according to regulation, he proceeded to examine both hands for the slim chance that fingerprints were retrievable from inside the tightly clenched fists.

"Right hand finger tips damaged beyond any retrieval of prints, left hand appears to be in a similar condition. The left arm is positioned across the front of the chest and is fused in place by heat-melted skin. I shall attempt to reposition said limb to facilitate opening up of the chest cavity."

Pausing to validate his observations with detailed handwritten notes, the examiner exchanged his pen for a scalpel, ready to open the doctor's rib cage to determine the actual cause of death. First, he carefully cut away the melded skin between the late doctor's hand and upper chest, to facilitate moving of the charred limb, when the telephone rang. Pausing the recording, the examiner swapped the scalpel into his opposite hand and reached for the telephone receiver hanging on the wall.

"Coroner's office, Doctor Delancy speaking. No sheriff, I haven't forgotten the report on the Jefferson shooting I'm rather busy at the moment, you'll have it by the morning. Yes, I know it's important, but I'm doing two jobs at the moment sheriff, and every time you call it only delays me further."

The Baker Ridge sheriff ignored the hint and continued with his conversation while the coroner stared idly at the late doctor's remains. As he reached out to place the scalpel back onto the tray, something gripped tightly in the deceased's grip caught his eye.

"Sorry Sheriff, I have to go."

Not waiting for a reply, the doctor replaced the receiver, restarted the recording and returned to the job in hand. Being as delicate as someone could be when working with fire-hardened fingers, the examiner managed to slide the tips of a pair of forceps between the index and middle finger and draw the object out with minimal damage. Holding it up to the light it appeared to be a serrated metal disc, slightly larger than an inch in diameter, with a hole bored through the centre. A quick wash and brush up with detergent in a nearby sink quickly removed the melted flesh and grime to reveal that is was in fact a flat, pointed star with the word ***'Elvis'*** engraved around its inner rim. Holtsville was only a small town and often being in close attendance with the sheriff's department, the examiner knew exactly to whom it belonged. He had heard the tale more than once how Officer Tom Maybury proudly wore a pair of engraved spurs he received from the late Sheriff Dodson and then foolishly lost them in a poker game. The examiner turned the now clean and shiny star over and over in his fingers, smiling to himself, as he knew exactly the current owner of the broken spur.

Within an hour, the medical examiner, his assistant and two more officers from the neighbouring county of Dulton, arrested Acting Sheriff Clifford 'Duke' Thornbuck on suspicion of murder.

Duke had not noticed the missing rowel and was still wearing the main yoke and strap of the broken spur that he unknowingly snapped off as he kicked the doorframe to the doctor's surgery. When the desperate doctor reached out for an anchor point, found the star embedded in the frame, and clutched it to his chest as Duke dragged him towards his death.

An initial search of Duke's house and patrol car, revealed blood soaked clothing that he had arrogantly tossed into the car's trunk. A week later, following a full and thorough forensic investigation, it revealed that the blood matched that of Doctor Booth. Also in the same trunk, investigators found another fortuitous piece of evidence, not related to the doctor's murder. The stinger device used to kill Elvis and Nathan Howton was missing one of its thumb-sized spikes that had snapped away from its mount. Cross referenced with documented evidence from the other recent case, revealed that it precisely matched the one found embedded into the wheel arch of Nathan Howton's burnt-out wreck of a car.

* * *

Within six months, Federal court found Clifford Thornbuck guilty on three counts of first-degree murder of Nathan Howton, Police Officer Tom Maybury, and Doctor Morton Booth. The sentence was life with no remission. There was no evidence to link him with the death of Sheriff Oberon P Dodson and the verdict remained one of accidental death. Three years later, workmen discovered the body of Lyle Simpkins and Duke was questioned regarding his death. He immediately confessed to his murder, also offering up that of Sheriff Oberon P Dodson.

Under a recently passed amendment, Duke believed he could then apply to his state senator, asking his approval for life termination via the assisted suicide initiative for lifetime prisoners. This would take the form of a painless lethal injection. He hoped that his confessions would sway the balance in his favour. Unfortunately, for Duke, the request was denied on the grounds that the confessions were only forthcoming with regard to personal gain and not as an expression of guilt or regret. Without the courage to take his own life, Clifford 'Duke' Thornbuck served the next forty-five years in jail.

CHAPTER TWENTY-NINE

Looking down from a high granite bluff, the panoramic view of the valley spreading out below was truly incredible. From one horizon to the other, tens of thousands of mature woodland trees, created a vast array of autumnal russets, old gold, and a myriad of verdant forest greens. This multi-hued leafy quilt contrasted harshly against the backdrop of a cold grey mountain range with its snow-capped peaks piercing the fiery orange twilight sky. Sited amid this dramatic setting an almost childlike triangular interpretation of an active volcano rose majestically toward the heavens, dominating the horizon. From its summit, fiery lava belched thousands of feet into the air, with the remaining liquid magma bubbling over the broken peak, creating a glowing amber tide oozing sedately down the steep gradients. Following the jagged watercourses and rifts, the cooling liquid rock divided naturally into thinner and thinner arterial tributaries of glowing treacle until it cooled enough to harden completely at the forest's edge. Completely incinerating all of the flora, and fauna within a three-quarter radius of the peak, the barren land beyond this mark slowly succumbed to a thickening coat of volcanic grey soot. Drifting steadily on a light southerly breeze, heavy ash filled clouds smudged a dirty veil across the dusky sky, moodily darkening the colours of a sunset that now resembled the glow of a forest fire on the western horizon, adding yet more vibrancy to the volcano's amber glow.

In the very centre of the forest, a single ancient oak tree stood in a natural clearing. In spite of the lateness of the year, the old timer's gnarly branches still lay heavily decked with semi-desiccated, lobed, ovate leaves arranged on short twigs and branches in an imbricate spiral design. This curious pattern provides excellent shade during the summer months, but when autumn comes, each dry golden leaf nestles against its neighbour to fill the air with a constant rustling, courtesy of even the gentlest breeze. Crowning the top of the oak's mighty trunk where the main branches begin, parasitic mistletoe had wound its narrow leaved, pale green, sinuous foliage into a large birdlike nest decorated with an abundance of poisonous, white, waxy berries.

Across the remaining forest canopy, dramatic colours of the equinox marked the approaching end of another year, when tens of millions of unwanted retainers now free from seasonal duty, flutter gently down to carpet the verdant forest floor.

At the far side of the clearing, a single file procession of around twenty men emerged from under the shelter of the woodland glen and headed directly towards the solitary oak. Leading the group walked a tall, slender, bald-headed man dressed head to foot in black floor length ceremonial robes edged with golden twisted brocade. Carried purposely before him, he held a large golden goblet in one hand and a jewelled handled stiletto dagger in the other. Immediately behind the leader, two men walked Indian file while carrying either end of a double wooden oar. Hanging from this makeshift litter hung the body of a comatose young woman. Her hands and feet, tied together over the single pole, where she hung similar to that of a rainforest sloth. Swinging gently from her captor's rhythmic gait, her head hung back at a painful angle through her arms and low enough to the ground that her lustrous mane of jet-black hair trailed through the long wet grass.

Cleansed with an infusion of rare and pungent oils and dressed in a pure white, sleeveless, ankle length robe. The woman was fortunate to have the hem of the dress pulled snugly between her thighs preserving at least some of her modesty. Immediately behind the two pole bearers the remainder of the male only procession, followed closely in single file.

Reaching the oak in the centre of the clearing, the men quickly formed a loose circle approximately twenty feet from the trunk's base and watched impassioned as the two pole bearers lowered their trophy gently to the floor ready to release her bindings. The sudden painful rush of blood to her extremities as the leader cut the leather thongs quickly awakened the woman from her stupor and in panic, she tried to jump up and run away. Unfortunately, a lack of proper circulation to her limbs nipped that idea in the bud and she fell helplessly to the ground. Crawling awkwardly to the foot of the tree she cowered against the trunk and frantically looked around, but hope quelled as she saw no obvious means of escape. Her succeeding thought was to raise the alarm and began with a piercing scream followed by defensive verbal abuse.

"I don't know what the hell is going on here, but if any of you bastards come near, I'll kill you, d'you hear me?"

Ignoring the terrified woman's diatribe, the men seemed much more interested in the guttural recitation of an ancient chant. The two who carried the woman into the clearing, re-approached their captive from either side and even though she found some strength to fight back, the men easily subdued their captive. Amid a timid bout of kicking and screaming as fear became fight, the men lifted the woman to her feet and forcibly pushed her back against the tree trunk. With relative ease, one man slipped a fresh leather strap onto her wrist, looped the remainder around the back of the tree, and secured the other end to the wrist of her free hand. The two men backed away, knelt side by side less than six feet away, and joined in with their own fervent intonation.

Wild-eyed in terror she repeatedly thrashed and pulled, chafing the rough leather deep into the skin around her wrists until it began to bleed. Near exhaustion, terror turned into despair as the terrifying mental imagery of what might happen flooded her brain and her piercing screams graduated quickly into wracking sobs as she tried to bargain for her release.

"I'll give you money if you just let me go, my brother's a multi-millionaire, he'll pay you as much as you want, no questions asked. I won't go to the police or anything. Please I'm begging you!"

Ignoring her desperate plea the chanting continued uninterrupted as the men repeated their archaic words. With tears pouring down her sweaty red face, she attempted a gut wrenching cry, hoping that someone would come to her aid. Deep down she knew that this was too well organised and the effort was futile; but she continued until she could scream no more. Quaking in terror the young woman's legs failed in their support and she collapsed heavily to her haunches, raising long welts up her back and tearing open the diaphanous robe as it snagged against the rough tree bark. The only thing keeping her from falling to the ground were the extremely taught bindings biting into her wrists, while painfully stretching her arms backwards against the trunk of the tree. Ignoring her pain and distress, the two helpers waited patiently until they received a nod from the group leader and then ran forwards, to once again, lift her back onto her feet. Remaining in place, they continued to hold the terrified woman upright as the ceremony reached its climax. The leader had now turned his back on the woman and raised his laden hands to the sky in sacrificial suppliancy as he began to offer his entreaty.

"I chief warlock Beriso, call upon the servant of Lucifer, high priestess Toomak to receive this blood sacrifice as a gift from your true acolytes, to give you the strength to one day return and walk amongst us once more."

The sky suddenly darkened and flashes of lightning accompanied by rumbles of distant thunder chilled the air. Harsh winds swept across the clearing, dislodging swarms of dry, brittle leaves stinging any exposed skin. The horrified woman's long black hair flapped wildly around her tear stained face, blinding her sight and refusing to budge no matter how hard she shook her head. At this point, the leader turned around and in a surprisingly caring gesture, he stepped closer and gently teased away the tear soaked strands, allowing the full body of her raven locks to unfurl in the strong gusts. Shocked by the unexpected show of compassion, her sobbing eased and she looked deeply into the pale blue mesmerising eyes of her captor. Smiling softly in return, he moved closer and even though she turned her head, shying away in fear, she allowed him to whisper a few words into her ear that were lost to the others in the rush of the wind. Instantly she became completely suggestive in his presence. Even if she had been fully alert there was no time to react as hidden from her vision, the leader gripped the handle of the stiletto dagger tightly in his fist and pointed it inwardly at his prey. Still holding the enamoured woman in his gaze, he watched avidly, waiting for her reaction, paying close attention to the widely dilated pupils of her startled eyes as he plunged the needle-thin point through the taught skin of her chest, aiming for the gap between the fifth and sixth ribs. With a surgeon's precision, he lightly slipped the narrow blade easily through the soft bronchial tissue of her lung before its tip pierced the right chamber of her wildly beating heart. Holding her tightly in his arms as the exquisitely sharp pain locked her chest muscles in a constricting rigour; the woman opened her mouth in an attempt to scream only to find it covered with his own in a fatal kiss. Her damaged heart continued to beat, but instead of pumping fresh red oxygenated blood out through the aorta, it pulsed into her right lung. Her soon to be assassin moaned with delight as her exhalation infused with the sanguine fluid rushing up to the back of her mouth and out into his. Gulping eagerly, he sated his blood lust, then released his grip and looked on lasciviously as the remainder pulsated out over her bottom lip, splashing heavily onto her pure white robe.

On this sign, the circle of acolytes closed in and watched him remove the blade. One of the aids, stepped up, slid two fingers through the tiny hole in the bloodstained robe, and tore the delicate fabric wide enough to expose the narrow incision ejaculating rhythmic crimson spurts with every heartbeat. The majority of the white cloth now imbrued glistening red, building the group into a dizzying rapture as the leader raised his goblet to the wound, filling it quickly with the frothy soup. Turning around, he screamed out his offering, raising the goblet to the thunderous skies as his men clamoured in to receive their share. With a blood stained mouth, he stared up at the heavens, deliriously screaming Toomak's name when the dramatic encircling diorama flickered and disappeared. In the confusion the baying mob ceased, wrenched from their blood lust, they stood bewildered as all around them the storm dropped and the entire forest vanished. The volcano, the sky, and even the leaf-strewn grass beneath their feet disappeared, leaving the men standing alone on a bare concrete floor. All of this due to a complete power failure on movie stage three.

The only real prop left behind was the oak tree, painstakingly created out of painted fibreglass and chicken wire. Apart from the hooded men, the other figure that was very real was the mortally wounded young woman, ignored by all as she hung limply at the limit of her bonds and still pumping out an incredible amount of blood as her life drained quickly away.

"What the hell happened?" The leader screamed, his face turning a rich shade of puce, exaggerating the thread veins on his neck and bald head. Snatching the goblet from one of the acolytes, he slammed it angrily onto the floor, painting an abstract pattern across the pale grey concrete with the splash of rapidly congealing blood that still held within. Ignoring the sticky mess beneath his feet the leader barged his way through the men, leaving a fading trail of footprints as he headed in the direction of the high bluff. This projection had also disappeared, revealing a glass fronted production booth sited up on the far wall of the hanger sized building. Before he could say another word, the studio echoed to a tooth-jarring squeal as the sound equipment responded to the supply of the backup generator, allowing the producer to offer his apology.

"Very sorry Mr Beriso sir, but we have just experienced an unexpected power failure that was completely beyond our control."

A small middle-aged man wearing black jeans and a white T-shirt trembled visibly as he leaned nervously into a desk mike and attempted to explain. However, it was impossible to placate the anger of the man standing below him and the reply was curt.

"I don't care for excuses, I only care for results. The sacrifice is ruined; we will have to go again tomorrow. Get me an identical woman with genuine long black hair, not dyed, genuine, do you hear me?"

Not waiting for an answer, Beriso kicked open the exit door and strode out into the sunlight. Sparked into action, the booth operator immediately began to feed the required information into the database of his clipboard computer and as *'searching for your request'* flashed repeatedly on the screen he crossed his fingers that a suitable replacement could be found before morning. Within a few tentatively long seconds a picture of the woman fitting the criteria, appeared on his screen and a relieved producer called up to make his request.

* * *

Deep in the underground prison, the remaining group of university friends had just finished their daily exercises and they were all heading back to their cell block, when one of the senior guards separated Kristy from the rear of the line.

"You on the end, stand your ground, the rest of the group can go."

Unable to do anything to stop the order, the remaining friends looked on anxiously at Kristy's brave smile before they all turned the corner. Each one wondering if they would never see each her again. As with Jacob, the guards escorted Kristy back onto the land train headed back down the tunnel into the cavernous main interior. This time instead of being loaded onto a plane and flown abroad, Kristy was placed into one of six individual prison cells contained inside a small driverless automated vehicle. As soon as her door was secured, the wagon started up and transported her up the access ramp and out onto the runway of the abandoned military base. Unable to see anything but skyline from the high tinted window above where she sat, Kristy tried to remain calm and concentrated on holding in the urine from her full bladder adding to the terror of the unknown gripping tightly at her bowels. For the next hour she closed her eyes and clasped her hands together, praying to any deity who might just be listening to her plight, but if truth be known, she did not believe existed. Dire situations call for desperate measures and for Kristy this was it.

An uneventful hour passed and the prisoner transport slowed as it turned through the gates of a small high walled compound consisting mainly of six identical film-studio shaped white walled buildings, arranged facing in two rows of three. Driving down to the last one on the right, the vehicle drove directly through the waiting open double doors and the old-fashioned petrol engine juddered to a halt as the ignition turned off. Trying hard to control the frantic beating of her heart, Kristy placed her ear against the outer metal panel and listened intently to the muffled sound of a male voice as he issued orders to an unknown number of people milling around outside the van. Apart from the odd word, she understood very little and all too soon, the voice faded into the distance, leaving everything mind-numbingly silent. Another twenty minutes passed by and as Kristy drifted away in exhaustion, the metal clang of something heavy, dropped onto the concrete floor jolted her back to her senses. This followed quickly by the sounds of the van's rear doors opening and some of the other doors inside the van being unlocked before Kristy's cell door finally opened. As she was the last to leave, her surprise showed as three other women of similar age and features stood outside silent and waiting. For the entire journey Kristy believed she was alone, there was no sound coming from any of the other cells, and the similar expression on the faces of the other women revealed that they shared a similar thought. Looking around they appeared to be in the loading bay of a factory or warehouse and thoughts of slave labour immediately sprang to mind. Waiting anxiously with the others, Kristy was quick to note that the two men guarding the group wore different uniforms to the underground prison, adding a belief that she had been sold on again. Her next thought was to wonder whether the collars that she and the other women wore were still active, and if the answer was no, it would improve any chance of escape. Without thought for her own safety, Kristy tried a quick test.

"Hey you, where have you taken all of us and what happens now?" Kristy yelled to the young man who appeared to be in command of the six other guards. He was a spotty youth who looked barely out of short trousers, let alone allowed to carry a rifle.

"Prisoners will remain quiet until further notice." He replied, looking a little nervous that the silence had been broken and seemed unsure how to handle the situation.

"Come on big boy, we've been locked up for hours and I desperately need a pee, so do the others." Kristy added feeling a little more confident now that her collar remained inert, so she decided to take her insolence even further. Even though armed with a rifle, the lead man looked and around hopefully for whoever was higher in command to make their appearance.

"I can't hold it any longer; if I don't go soon I'm going to piss myself, *please!*" Kristy exclaimed, exaggerating her plight by hunching forwards with her hands pressed to her privates, clamping her knees together, and dancing from one foot to the other. Embarrassed by the situation, the guard finally gave in and after issuing orders for the remaining guards to keep watch on the others; he grabbed Kristy roughly by the elbow and led her out through a side door.

"You're the one with the gun so get off me and show me which way to go. If I run away, how far do you think I'm going to get?" Kristy snapped as she yanked her arm free from the young man's grasp and tried to take a dominant hold of the situation. Surprisingly, he allowed her to walk unhindered and pointed silently to the toilet block sited across the yard. The warmth of the sun upon her face and the taste of clean, fresh air, made it hard to concentrate on a plan for escape, but Kristy quickly cantered on the job in hand. A quick scan of the compound revealed that there were very few people around, the surrounding high walls offered little chance of escape, and guards had already closed the gate. Unfortunately, there was no time to observe anything else as the guard hurriedly Kristy forced inside the small tin roofed building and followed her inside.

"Take your pick." he proffered, pointing to the five identical stalls, all with their doors wide open.

"Are you going to stand and watch me as well?" Kristy asked, successfully embarrassing the young man whose cheeks flushed at the implication.

"I, I'll stand outside the door." He stuttered, turning quickly away.

"You can stay if you want, you might see something you'd like." Kristy replied, coyly dragging in the left hand side of her bottom lip with her top set of perfectly shaped teeth and opening her eyes wide. The guard stood and stared, his innocence showed and he was unsure what to do. Shyness finally prevailed as he turned and took a few steps towards the door, but he could not help himself and looked back as Kristy walked into a stall. She knew that he was still there and shimmied slowly, easing down her trousers to expose tight white knickers clinging to the shapely contours of her pert behind to the excited guard.

"Come on then, we haven't got very long." Kristy instructed as she coyly looked back over her right shoulder while bending over and bracing her upper body on the low-level cistern in a blatantly sexual offer. The guard still did not move so Kristy saucily wiggled her behind and spoke again.

"This is your last chance tiger, it's been several weeks, and I need a man ***now***!"

The guard did not need any more prompting; forgetting all his training, he leaned his rifle against the wall by the exit and ran towards his prize while hastily trying to undo the front of his trousers. Drawing level with the cubicle door, he eagerly reached out both hands ready to grab hold of Kristy's hips, when a searing pain shot through his testicles and as she deftly swiftly jerked out her right foot and mule kicked him with all her strength in his groin. With his eyes closed tight from the pain, he doubled over as the chronic sickening ache spread across his lower abdomen leaving him blind to Kristy's next move. Quickly, she straightened up, turned around, and slammed his head sideways into the doorframe. The effect was instant and the unconscious guard dropped heavily to the floor. Hastily pulling up and refastening her own trousers, Kristy stepped over the comatose body, ran across to the exit, grabbed the rifle, and peered cautiously into the compound. Unbelievably the first thing she saw less than a hand's breadth away from her face was the muzzle of a gun pointing her way. The absence of Kristy had caused great concern when the production manager arrived and he had instructed another guard to go and check-up on his colleague. Upon hearing the sound of a fight coming from within the toilet block, he had waited patiently outside, waiting to see who emerged. Desperate for escape, Kristy walked straight into the trap and now with the rifle placed carefully on the ground and her hands in the air, she instinctively walked back towards the group. Furious her easy capture, Kristy tried to talk her way around the new guard, but he ignored her questions and silently pushed her roughly by the right shoulder to maintain the current pace. To Kristy's surprise, her fate changed yet again as the guard guided her away from the door and towards another transportation van parked out of sight around the corner. Guessing that he too might succumb to a sexual offer, Kristy decided to try once more to use her body as means to escape. Climbing the three steps into the rear of the truck, she immediately turned around and began caressing her shapely contours, hoping to entice the guard close enough to use her black belt karate skills and kick him in the face. To her surprise, he ignored the offer and slammed the door. Seconds later the engine fired up, forcing Kristy to brace herself against the sudden movement as the van pulled quickly away.

Fighting against the motion of the rapidly accelerating truck, Kristy tried to re-open the rear door, but there was no handle on the inside. Unable to see what was happening through the high windows she listened to several voices yelling loudly, then hastily dropped face down on the floor as shots rang out and bullets pinged off the metal frame at the rear of the van. More shouting followed and her ears rang to a deafening clang, followed by the sound of squealing metal as she guessed the van crashed through the main gates or maybe part of a fence. Very quickly, the debris fell behind as the van accelerated away, heading out into the open countryside. At the point of impact, the solitary interior light extinguished, leaving Kristy in semi-darkness and all she could do was wait patiently for this latest twist to play its self out. Around ten minutes passed and by jumping up and down, Kristy could see through the window mounted high in the rear door; thankfully, no one appeared to be following the escape. Suddenly the van dropped its speed, swerved alarmingly, and skidded to a halt in a layby. Bracing herself by the exit, Kristy listened to the sound of footsteps running from the cab and watched the back door swing open. She was ready to launch into an attack as he climbed in but he just shouted from outside.

"Hurry up and get out before they find out where we are." The guard exclaimed to Kristy, who stepped forwards then stood her ground, staring at the tall, handsome man who she now realised, was not dressed in the same uniform as the others.

"If you don't trust me, take the rifle, I'm not sure how to shoot one anyway, but please hurry up!"

Before she knew it, the guard thrust the loaded weapon into her hands and ran to the driver's side of a very expensive sports car parked in the layby not fifty feet away.

"***Come on!***" He yelled before climbing inside and starting the noiseless engine. Kristy tentatively climbed down the steps as the car drew closer and the gull-wing passenger door opened invitingly.

"I know you're scared and believe me, so am I. If those goons catch us up we'll both be history so *pleeease* get in."

Still pointing the rifle in the man's direction, Kristy climbed into the passenger seat and with a screech of smoking tyres they sped away out of sight, just seconds before the pursuing guards topped the brow of the previous rise and homed in on the now empty getaway van.

"I think now is a good time for you to tell me what the hell is going on?" Kristy asked her as yet unnamed companion as he hastily increased their speed to well over ninety miles an hour and climbing.

"My name is Ted Langton and I would feel much safer if you could point that thing away from my face before I continue."

Kristy lowered the muzzle of the rifle and pointed it more towards the dashboard, but still kept her finger resting on the trigger for her own comfort. Ted observed the limited actions and figured that if he were in her place, he would probably do the same thing. Easing off the accelerator to cope with the conditions of the road, and activating the independent driving and navigation system allowed Ted to concentrate precisely on what to say next.

"Before you jump to any conclusions, please hear me out while I explain how we have both ended up in my car driving at great speed across the countryside. I will answer any questions you have as honestly as I can as I hope you too will answer mine. Oh, and by the way I've told you my name but I still don't know yours."

"Kristy, and that's all you need for now!" She replied tersely. Ted thought it best not push for a surname so he began his story.

"As you already know, my name is Ted Langton and I am head of operations at the Hologram Dreams Corporation, The same company who I believe is behind your abduction and possibly many others."

Kristy tensed up, tightening her trigger finger at Ted's revelation, but he ignored the defensive act and continued.

"Not long ago I received a report via a private source based in the U.S.A. that human slaves were being used instead of androids at one of the company franchises. I promise you that I had no idea that this was going on, so I did a little digging of my own and personally discovered an underground prison where obviously you were held before being transported here. By coincidence, the van I chose to make my own escape happened to be the same one you were being transported in, bringing us both to the studio site. When the guards left the van for a tea break, I crept out and had a look around. I recognised the same equipment used by my company for filmmaking. Inside one of the empty hangers, there was evidence of bloodstains on the floor. I sneaked back outside and saw you being taken into the toilet block by one of the guards, then a minute later followed by another. I knocked out the second guard, took his rifle, and was just coming to rescue you from the first, when you reappeared without him. As we were now in full view of the crew, I pretended to keep you at gunpoint and guided us both into a vacant wagon. The rest you know yourself."

Kristy colour paled as she thought of the blood on the floor and she swallowed hard trying to regain her composure. She then remembered the three other women left behind. Before she could say a word, Ted continued.

"I know what you are thinking, but I couldn't rescue everyone. To buy some time, I broke into the main projection booth and smashed things up a bit. It will be at least a week before they can get everything working again. My guess is that all involved will have form of one sort or another, so a call to the local boys in blue will sort the rest out. Finally, I thought you were in danger from the guard, but when I got there you had apparently sorted it all out by yourself."

Kristy smiled at the compliment and relaxed her grip on the rifle as she asked her next question.

"How did you manage to have a car waiting for our escape?"

"I'm quite proud of that one actually. I have a device on my watch that can program the car to take it to any destination in the country. I didn't know how long the journey would take so every fifteen minutes or so I logged the coordinates and told the car to make its way there. The last one was in the layby where we just found it."

Ted smiled smugly at his own ingenuity and waited for a compliment, but none came.

"I've got friends in the prison; we need to get them out." Kristy snapped, ignoring Ted's ego and feeling sick in the stomach at what could be happening to the rest of the group; and what might have already happened to Jacob.

"I'm well aware that there are many more people in danger but…"

Cut off in the middle of his sentence, Ted listened as a recorded voice announced that Philip Sanderson was on the line. Ted held a finger up to his mouth signalling for to Kristy to remain silent then verbally accepted the call.

"Philip, what can I do for you on this beautiful day?" He began; feeling very ill at ease from the sudden intrusion and amateurishly over-acted his part. Philip ignored the pleasantries; he was in no mood for chitchat.

"Cut the crap Ted, we both know where you've been this morning. I've been watching your every movement via surveillance cameras in the distribution warehouse through to the underground camp. I've also just been informed about the sabotage to one of the film studios and subsequent escape of one of my guests. I am confident that you are behind this incident and must understand that I cannot let things like this happen, she must be returned."

Ted's knuckles turned white as he angrily increased his grip on the steering wheel, finding it hard to comprehend the matter of fact way that Philip discussed Kristy like domestic chattel. Following a short pause, he finally gained enough control of his temper to give a reply.

"I don't think that you have a grasp on the situation Philip. We are heading straight to the authorities who will you put away for the rest of your days. Do you understand that much?"

Philip replied almost immediately, as if he knew what Ted was about to say.

"I understand a lot more than you give me credit for Ted; but you must realise that I am prepared to do absolutely anything to avoid this consequence. Now, are you going to return the woman to me or do we play this the hard way?"

Ted refused to answer the question and a tense silence hung in the air. Philip finally spoke again with a sad finality in his voice.

"Your meddlesome ways give me no choice, you need to be shown first-hand how serious I am."

Ted wondered what Philip could do from such a distance, when Kristy suddenly began to shake and grab for her throat, trying desperately to rip away the shock collar still fastened around her neck. Slamming on the brakes, Ted hastily jumped out of the car and ran around to the passenger side to access Kristy, who was already beginning to foam at the mouth. He tried to slide his fingers under her collar in an attempt to prise it apart, but with her neck muscles swollen in spasm, the device lay buried deeply into the bulging flesh.

"Stop it Philip, you've made your point, I'm ordering you to stop it *now!*" Ted screamed as he helplessly watched Kristy's plight. Realising that her collar was well out of range of the underground prison, Ted wondered whether his car somehow acted as an amplifier. With nothing to lose, he dragged Kristy from her seat and carried her in his arms to the opposite side of the road. Positive that the signal was weakening, he continued to stagger as far away from the vehicle as his damaged knee would allow. The phone call automatically transferred to Ted's personal communication device and he continued his plea for clemency, but Philip refused to answer as Ted begged over and over again.

His intuition was proving correct, Kristy's muscles began to relax, and her breathing steadily improved the further

Ted carried her away. She even managed a smile as her focus cleared to see Ted's anxious face looking back. That was until Philip finally decided to break his silence.

"I admire the dogged determination Ted, but now you must pay the consequence for your interfering ways; you leave me with no other option."

Kristy's brief smile turned quickly into a grimace, as somehow Philip boosted the output to her collar even greater than before. With her body rigid in a spasm, her muscles swelled violently, attempting to absorb every single drop of blood, while deep inside her abdomen, similar vital organs began to shut down under the intense strain. She now found it impossible to breathe and her mouth clamped tightly shut, cracking some of her weaker teeth under the pressure.

"She's dying Philip if you have any compassion in your soul; I'm begging you, stop this!"

Ted tried to increase his speed as he desperately pleaded for Kristy's life, but the strain was too much for his partially crippled joint and he collapsed heavily onto the grassy verge. Even with only one fully operational leg, Ted tried to use it to push both of them along the damp grass, but the distance gained was pitiful, leaving him with nothing else to do except cradle Kristy in his arms and pray.

To his horror, Ted watched as the blood vessels beneath the collar on Kristy's neck tumefied then burst, producing fractal patterns of violet snowflakes under the impossibly taught skin. Following this, a narrow stream of blood poured from both of her ears as more internal membranes ruptured under the strain. Twitching violently as the sinews connecting her joints snapped, Ted thought his revulsion had reached new extremes until he witnessed the sight of Kristy's beautiful green eyes rotating back into their sockets, tearing the delicate optic nerves away at the root. The resulting ocular haemorrhage, spilled all the way down her face and onto Ted's lap.

Suddenly the power supply to the collar ceased and her rigid body relaxed, slumping lifeless in Ted's arms. In desperation, Ted gave Kristy the kiss of life and tried chest compressions, but it was obvious there was too much internal damage and his attempts were futile.

With tear filled eyes, Ted limped across the road and placed Kristy's dead body gently back onto the passenger seat, eased himself painfully into the driver's side of the car and drove away. Whether Philip did finally relent and turn off the power, or that he knew that Kristy was already dead and relieved the collar of its charge, Ted could not tell. Whatever the truth, he knew that he had never been so enraged in all his life and swore personal revenge. In a wretched duet, Ted screamed at the top of his lungs along with the screech of the car's tyres as he set out for the nearest hospital. It was then onward for a showdown with Philip at the main headquarters of Hologram Dreams.

CHAPTER THIRTY

"Gemma where are you?" Ted asked his girlfriend via the car phone, while he drove at breakneck speed through the countryside.

"I'm back inside my apartment; you sound tense, what's happened?"

"Too much to explain right now, but first I have to make a small detour, phone an old friend of mine, and then I'm heading back to the office to have a showdown with Philip. I don't think this is a safe place to be for anyone to be right now so I want you to organise a complete evacuation of all personnel, including yourself. I don't care how you do it, but I want everyone out. Do I make myself clear?"

There was a brief pause as Gemma fought the urge to bombard Ted with a raft of questions, but she crossed her fingers and agreed. Ted quickly ended the call, allowing Gemma to get on with the task in hand and the first thing she did was call Stan in the control centre to fill him in with everything that had happened since the day she received the telephone call from Sheriff Dodson. To her surprise, Stan took all the information in his stride as it only added to his personal misgivings whenever he was around Philip Sanderson, giving him all the excuses he needed to usurp his arrogant boss.

"Right, now I'm up to speed, what about an entire site shut down by claiming a poison gas leak?" Stan proffered, without really needing any approval from Gemma, but was polite enough to keep her in the loop. His actions would overrule any single section shutdown and the unpredictable nature of possible poison gas was the only time a complete evacuation without Ted or Philip's authorisation was permissible. Setting the ball in motion, Stan activated every tannoy, video screen, and messaging device in the entire complex to broadcast an evacuation alert.

This began with a ten-second blast from a police siren to initiate attention, followed immediately by a pre-recorded evacuation command repeated every thirty seconds through the public address system. The recording was in deep male reassuring tone, sounding very similar to a public service announcement by the home office played over the radio during the Second World War. The intention was not to induce panic and facilitate a calm participation of instructions.

'Please pay attention to the following message. You are all required to evacuate the facility immediately and without delay. This is not a drill, repeat this is not a drill. The nature of the incident allows full use of the transport system. Proceed to the nearest exit bay indicated by the flashing red information signs and board an outbound shuttle. Do not delay your evacuation by attempting to retrieve any belongings, continue immediately to the nearest exit.'

Everyone in the facility stopped what they were doing and proceeded to follow the well-rehearsed protocol. To satisfy health and safety, Stan cleared various individual sections cleared on many occasions, but this was the first time the whole site had a complete evacuation order. Within seconds, Philip Sanderson called Stan on his direct line.

"What on earth is going on Stan? I've checked every safety program on the system and everything appears to be in order."

Stan was expecting the call and he replied quickly and hopefully convincingly to Philip.

"Same thing here Mr Sanderson sir, but I've just received a report from mobile maintenance on the artificial lake side, that there are dangerously high levels of chlorine gas coming from the holding tanks buried near the edge of the site. Apparently the resident control device monitoring that part of the site is malfunctioning and it still reports a safe level."

The line fell silent as Philip analysed the information and decided on his next question.

Surely this doesn't require a complete evacuation Stan. The lake is miles away."

Stan smiled at Gemma sitting across the desk. He knew that Philip believed his story and was trying to find a solution that did not require shutting down the facility, costing the company millions of pounds in lost production. Stan instantly replied to Philip's question.

"Have you ever seen the effects of chlorine gas on a person Mr Sanderson sir? It is not pleasant I can assure you. An engineer cousin of mine was caught in the aftermath of the Winchester chemical plant explosion ten years ago. He inhaled the gaseous element and it reacted with the moist lining of his lungs, turning it into Hydrochloric acid. This new compound slowly burned away at his insides until a hole the size of a fist appeared through his ribs. He died a slow agonising death."

Stan choked on the last words of his sentence as he tried not to laugh, but Philip interpreted it as negative emotion and he quickly backed down.

"I fully understand how you feel Stan and I will leave you to sort the incident out. We don't want any lawsuits on our hands do we?"

Philip terminated the call leaving Gemma staring quizzically at Stan's face.

"Is any of your story true Stan?"

Taking a second to calm down from the obvious fact that Philip cared more about his money than public safety, Stan paused and cleared his throat.

"The effects of chlorine gas are correct, but the rest of the story was total hogwash. Now, according to your promise to Ted, I think it's time that you vacated the area as well."

Gemma smiled and shook her head at the request.

"We both know that it's not going to happen and I'm sure that you of all people have no intention of leaving either.

Ted is going to need as much help as he can get don't you agree?"

CHAPTER THIRTY-ONE

Preceding the telephone conversation with Stan in the control centre, Philip was preoccupied with dictating an urgent message to the voice recognition program on his computer. His audio memo was instantly converted into an electronically mailed order to the commander of the underground prison. He knew that Ted needed proof if he was to get a conviction, so without the slightest conscience; he issued an edict for the destruction of all evidence linking Hologram Dreams with the facility. This began with the evacuation of all personnel to the Eastern European base, and take with them as many of the prisoners as possible. For the ones left behind, and with blatant disregard for human life, he gave orders for their execution by whatever means necessary, followed by incineration of all bodily remains.

Philip knew that the commander would only be effectively able to evacuate less than twenty-five per cent of the current contingent and the hundreds that remained would have to be dealt with in such a way so as not to start a riot. The ideal solution would be to use the shock collars; but what the prisoners and the majority of the guards did not know, was that even though every inmate could be punished simultaneously, there was not enough power to kill more than one prisoner at a time. This made the collars virtually redundant for this purpose and another solution would have to be found.

While all this was happening, Adam Cartwright sat in the prison computer room, waiting patiently for Philip to make his move in an epic two-day and one morning game of chess that Adam had purposely padded out in order to probe deeper into the mainframe of the computer system. Displayed on his computer monitor, next to the animated image of a chessboard, was a blueprint of the facility that he was doing his best memorise in-between surreptitious glances towards the control room containing the guards.

Another page Adam had open on the visual display, was a personally programmed hack into all communications coming and going to Philip's office. In the pauses between moves, Adam scanned what was mostly mundane interdepartmental traffic, until he read two messages making him retch loudly. Clasping both hands across his mouth, he repeatedly re-read the latest Philip's orders. The first thing to come to mind was that Philip knew about the computer hack and was testing Adam's reaction. The second was the completely abhorrent possibility was that the information could actually be true. His unusual behaviour alerted the guard who looking annoyed, eyed Adam suspiciously from the control room. With a quickness of thought, he quickly swallowed down the eye-watering bile and managed to turn his reaction into an exaggerated stretch and yawn. Satisfied that all was well, the guard sat back down and resumed his lecherous browsing of a well-thumbed girly magazine.

Using his incredible memory for trivial detail, Adam recalled how he had frequently overheard his guards' gossip about how the commander was an extremely '*lecherous, lazy bastard*', and only bothered to leave his quarters when necessary as he was serviced with a constant supply of female prisoners to satisfy his needs. Adam had been well aware of this and had managed to spare both Kristy and Amy from this terrible fate by deleting their names from the availability list. Using the commanders slovenly work record it was unlikely that the message would be read by him immediately and if Adam had anything to do with it he never will.

Softly pressing the keys on his antiquated keyboard, he typed out a reply to acknowledge the information and then deleted both messages from the system. Due to the obvious nature of events, Philip terminated the game, leaving Adam only just enough time to close all other open programs before the guard came over to take him away. If he had been given just another minute, Adam would have seen an amendment to a second message that for him and his friends would change everything.

For the next hour, Adam was a troubled man. An electrician was working to repair a faulty power supply to the camera inside the cell, making it impossible to tell everyone at once. Starting with Neil, he ushered him into the bathroom. Using the sound of running water to muffle his voice, he relayed everything he knew, before they both returned and had to endure the prolonged wait to inform everybody else. Fortunately the task inside the cell was completed halfway through their lunch break, and luckily for Adam it recommenced with the droning of a power drill used directly outside the door, making it unable for anyone to eavesdrop on the conversation held within.

"I have some very serious information to pass on and I don't want you to overreact and alert the guards."

Adam's statement gained immediate attention of the remaining members of the group and his brief nod towards the surveillance cameras indicated his intent. Without cushioning the blow, he came straight to the point.

"There's been an order to evacuate the prison and kill anyone left behind."

They all did their best to mask their astonished faces, and as the exterior noise from the power drill continued, it allowed Adam a free flow of pre-prepared answers. He went on to explain that for now, he had deleted the message, but had no idea when any follow up orders might arrive. It was apparent to all, that an attempt to escape immediately was paramount and they all looked hopefully to their friend for an answer. To everyone's relief, Adam proceeded to explain how he had acquired the necessary information to draw up his master plan.

"As you all know I have been playing chess with an unknown opponent for the last few weeks, and during that time I have managed to hack into the computer system that includes blueprints of this prison."

Questions immediately began to fly in from all sides; Adam ignored all of them and held up his hand to silence the group.

"Please let me explain everything, and if any of you have questions I hope there will be time to answer them as long as the noise manages to muffle our voices."

Amid an almost religious fervour, Adam tried to remain calm while quickly explaining how he had discovered scale diagrams of the prison ventilation system, and they appeared big enough to crawl along, leading everyone directly to the surface.

"There is an access point at the back of the gymnasium store room. I have observed that the guards' pay little attention during the activities and the place is always crowded, so it shouldn't be too difficult to slip away unnoticed. If the daily routine doesn't change, we will all be in the gym within two hours."

It was impossible for them to hide their excitement and Adam hoped that the guards in the observation room were paying as little attention as they did with him when he played chess with Philip.

"What about the collars?" Amy suddenly asked, bringing and abrupt silence. One again the group looked hopefully to Adam for yet another solution. Looking a little unsure he scanned all of his friends' faces, while taking a deep breath, almost reluctant to reply. To add to the tension, the drilling suddenly stopped and everyone waited anxiously while waiting for the droning to resume. Luckily, less than a minute later, the familiar whine filled the room, and Adam continued.

"If my calculations are correct, the collars are already deactivated."

It was impossible not to react to the statement, and the surprise on everyone's faces was the last thing Adam needed.

"Can everyone calm down before the guards get suspicious and I will explain? I'm not a hundred per cent sure if it will work, but I planted a Trojan on the system that should disable the collars. I don't know if is going to work and there isn't any way to test it. I only hope that all the other prisoners behave themselves in the meantime, because if the collars are found not to be working it will not be difficult to fix and if it causes a riot, escape will be almost impossible."

Almost to the second that Adam finished his sentence, the drilling ceased and so as not to arouse suspicion some of the group left the table, trying their very best to act as calm as possible.

CHAPTER THIRTY-TWO

The lack of human habitation gave rise to an uneasy eerie silence throughout the underground complex. It seemed impossible to imagine that less than an hour ago, over fifty thousand people occupied the site, and now like ghosts in the machine they were all gone. Waiting patiently for Ted's arrival, Stan and Gemma constantly scanned the wall of video screens displaying real time images from the hundreds of surveillance cameras dotted in and around the site. Even though the campus was void of all human personnel, there was still plenty of visible activity coming from the small army of maintenance robot drones meticulously carrying out their designated pre-programmed tasks, making it a constant interference when trying to identify Ted. Added to this there were still a sizeable number of robotic personnel sited mainly in the main atrium arrival hall and they remained unnervingly static. Dressed in identical bellhop uniforms and lined up side by side like soldiers on parade, they stared vacantly into space while waiting patiently beside designated pick up points. The primary role of this second level robot is to act as an aid or assistant, responding solely to verbal human commands such as carrying bags or running menial errands. Hundreds of pairs of lidless eyes searching for human instruction would constantly scan their immediate surroundings, sometimes reacting to movement from their fellow automatons and stepping out of line to offer assistance, the confusion activating a return to post.

To make doubly sure that no human personnel re-entered the complex, Stan instigated a supplementary procedure. This involved initialisation of a pre-recorded message to alert all the evacuated staff via mobile communication, insisting that under no circumstance should anyone be allowed to return until the all clear is given. He even offered for the company to pay for any overnight accommodation required should the evacuation last beyond seven o'clock in the evening. He hoped that this would calm anxious nerves and leave the site completely clear for Ted.

"He can't be far away now." Gemma began, breaking a voluntary fifteen-minute silence. Stan grunted in agreement as he continued to press a massive array of control buttons, alternating the display of the main entrances relayed onto the large central viewing screen even though he guessed that these were an unlikely port of access. Ted followed up his last call with Gemma with a digital message to keep communication to a minimum in case the signal could be traced and his position found. This would reduce Philip to only being able to monitor his own smaller array of surveillance screens from inside his private office.

The monotony of the search dragged on; for nearly two hours Stan and Gemma stared anxiously at the screens looking for signs of life, when suddenly Ted's white sports car flashed into view. It appeared at the end of the road leading through the densely wooded south gate area, and at great speed headed directly for the closed wooden access gate. Normally the gate and security booth would have been made from high-density steel, but in keeping with the forestry commission guidelines for the aesthetic beauty of the area, a wooden alternative was installed and this was the reason for Ted's choice. Alerted to the proximity of the oncoming vehicle, the robot security guard stepped out from the confines of the booth and stood in front of the gate while holding forwards an outstretched right arm with its palm facing outwards visually informing the driver to stop the vehicle. This command had no effect at all and instead of slowing down, the car actually began to speed up. Undeterred, the robot maintained its position, even though it was obvious to anyone else that the car was not going to stop. There were safety systems built into the robot's programming, but in this event they were inadequate to cope with such a situation and it maintained its stance until it was much too late. Ted's beautifully crafted sports car ploughed directly into the guard, snapping the metal and plastic automaton clean in two. The top half impacted the car's windscreen, leaving behind a shattered crater of frosted glass before cartwheeling high into the air and then crashing down in almost the same spot where it began. The lower half of the robot's torso was instantly dragged under the car's low-slung sports chassis and squealed loudly as its metal legs twisted then jammed between the sub frame and the tarmac.

Gemma gasped as she watched the event unfold, and physically jolted when a fraction of a second later the wooden roadblock exploded into a thousand pieces of kindling as the car continued uninterrupted through the closed gate. Immediately sirens blared and rotating red lights mounted on the roof of the security booth flashed through the now dusty air to warn others of the intrusion. Security cameras continued to track the car's progress, relaying incredible images as bright gold and silver sparks sprayed out from between the car's back wheels, while the robot's legs glowed white hot from continuous friction. Eventually the car passed over a cattle grid and the unwanted metal hitchhiker jammed into the rails, grated along the remainder of the speeding car's undercarriage and shot out of the rear. With smoke pouring out of whatever remained, the twisted metal lump bounced over and over until it finally rolled to a stop at the side of the road.

"Come on Ted, answer the goddamn phone." Gemma yelled into the mouthpiece of her wrist communication device as she broke the rules and frantically made a call to see if Ted was unharmed, but the only thing she could hear was static crackle.

"I don't think that he's in the car at all, look!"

Stan pointed to the rhythmic pulse of a glowing green dot sited two miles inside the perimeter of the western gate. This marker appeared on what looked like a *'You are here'* map that was usually found in seaside towns to help direct tourists.

"Before you ask, I already know the frequency of Ted's phone signal, and provided that it is switched on I can locate him at a moment's notice anywhere on the site. It's obvious now that he is close enough to need our help, Ted must have turned it back on. So unless someone shares the same frequency or Ted has lost his phone; that is exactly where he is at the moment." Stan announced as they watched the dot move steadily closer towards the main complex.

"He must be using his car as a decoy." Gemma announced, stating the obvious to Stan, but he did not pass any comment. Instead, he tried to block all signals coming from security cameras at the western gate. In his attempt to help, all he succeeded in doing was possibly alert Philip as to where Ted really was.

It was obvious now that Philip was also aware of the car's intrusion and armed with every piece of holographic programming at his disposal, he set about producing a plethora of incredibly realistic objects that suddenly appeared out of thin air. The initial projections were a simple affair, ranging from realistic looking anamorphic images of massive holes appearing in the road, to raging swollen rivers that suddenly flowed across the car's path. Each projection was designed to alter Ted's perception of reality and make him crash the car, or at the very least slow him down, but unaffected by the visual interference, the car ploughed through every obstacle and somehow managed to stay on course, moving it ever closer towards the main complex. The image density profiler that gave the recipient a realistic feel to the latest hologram projections held little sway to the powerful car. For the driver, the feeling was little more than a heavy crosswind or the effect of driving through standing water, causing a slight drag to velocity. With minimal interruption to his progress, it looked that the first round was going to Ted; that was until Philip altered the rules.

Infuriated by his constant failure, he tapped away furiously at his keyboard, disengaging all the safety protocols of the groundbreaking program and boosted the profiler up way beyond its safe operational limit. Luckily for him, this massive drain on the system was only maintainable, as almost everything else on the site had been closed down due to the evacuation. This allowed Philip to redirect power from anywhere he liked. This uncharted territory, even though highly dangerous, created a hologram that somehow approached the density and mass of the image portrayed.

Pine trees shivered and the surrounding forest floor began to vibrate when from out of nowhere, a full size centurion tank bulldozed its way through the undergrowth and into a clearing. Jerkily altering its velocity, it rumbled heavily onto the main road and headed directly for Ted's car. As before, the projection was completely ignored and the expensive gleaming white vehicle maintained its present course. The general expectation was that it would pass directly and unaffected through the image, but this time the reality defied logic. When the front of the car impacted directly under the main turret of the tank, its bonnet crumpled in a similar fashion to hitting a brick wall. The huge tank on the other-hand; first appeared to buckle at the front from the huge impact, then shuddered as it regained shape by melding over the car like thick molasses. The deeper the car pushed into the projection, the tank's huge mass somehow intensified beyond all credible reasoning and it rolled over the top of the vehicle, crushing it into the tarmac like a steam roller flattening soft earth. Headlights popped and windows shattered, embedding tiny fragments of glass into the projection accompanied by strips of hardened rubber when all four tyres exploded from the immense pressure. When the remainder of the car finally curled out from under the rear of the of the massive caterpillar tracks, it had been flattened into an oblong slab of plastic, metal, and fabric less than twelve inches thick.

According to Sir Isaac Newton's third law of motion, every action has an equal and opposite reaction, and this amazing phenomenon was not going to be the exception. Deep underground less than a quarter of a mile away, all hell was breaking loose. The removal of all safety protocols and overclocking of the image density profiler was having a devastating effect. The several hundred racks containing the server units, called upon to provide the information to create the super dense image, were rapidly overheating, triggering a cascade effect with the rest of the main system. Philip was well aware of the situation as red warning triangles flashed repeatedly across his desktop, alerting him to the imminent danger; but he chose to ignore them all until he was completely satisfied. With the crushing of Ted's car, the desired result was complete and he attempted to shut down the program, but it was all too little too late. The server room was already filling with acrid black smoke as the paint coating the exterior panels began to bubble, along with the plastic blade housings melting in the intense heat. Alarms immediately sounded when thousands of ice cube processors bulged out of shape and erupted in a spectacular display of multi-coloured xenon sparks, showering everything in sight. This was quickly followed by a series of explosions rocking the facility, that were even felt by Gemma and Stan in the hub. It finally ended when the power supply to the image profiler finally ceased and fire-damping systems filled the lower levels with a cloud of Argon and carbon dioxide gas.

Outside in the forest, the tank quivered briefly, then popped like a soap bubble. Fragments of Ted's car previously embedded in the image, fell like confetti to the ground, showering the indentations in the tarmac that had been made by the caterpillar tracks. The twisted metal remains of Ted's car was the only other evidence that the super dense image of the tank had even been there at all.

The explosions jolted Gemma and Ted from their visual fixation of the bizarre tableaux and they looked in disbelief at one another trying to comprehend the impossible that had just happened right before their eyes.

"I didn't believe what I have just seen. Philip seems to have rewritten the laws of physics!" Stan exclaimed breaking the silence as he repeatedly rewound the surveillance video and double-checked all the monitoring equipment, trying to figure out how Philip had done it.

"Stan... *Stan...* ***Stan,*** leave that alone and concentrate finding Ted." Gemma chided as Stan ignored her request and continued to scour through the test results flashing across the visual display. Placing the tip of her thumb and index finger just far enough inside her mouth to curl the tip of her tongue, Gemma exhaled sharply, producing a piercing whistle that echoed around the empty control room, immediately gaining Stan's attention. Realising sheepishly that there were more pressing matters at hand, he swiftly pressed a couple of buttons, bringing up the familiar flashing green dot on the map screen.

"Can you get a visual?" Gemma asked, breaking the awkward silence in hope that she could see some evidence that Ted was still alive and not dead inside the flattened remains of his sports car. Stan thought for a moment, and then swore loudly as he switched to a one of his own pet programs giving him total control to every security camera on the entire base. Before responding to Gemma's request, he blocked all other access to the cameras, including Philip's office.

"Let's just hope that Philip has not been watching and monitoring any of our conversations or we might just have told him where to find Ted." Stan reported as he continued to curse himself under his breath for not thinking of this sooner. A knot formed in Gemma's stomach at the thought as she watched anxiously for a glimpse of Ted, while Stan cycled through dozens of active feeds.

"There, it's Ted, go back a bit Stan, no, not that far, forward a bit, stop, that's Ted right there."

Stan fixed the selected video camera on what appeared to be a small, nondescript clump of trees, but Gemma's younger and quicker eyes managed to pick out her man's profile behind an evergreen holly bush. As if by chance he turned and looked directly into the camera while he called Stan from his mobile device.

"Can I assume Stan, that everyone has been evacuated from the entire site and can I speak to Gemma?"

Ted began the conversation without the usual pleasantries. Stan answered in the affirmative as he turned to give Gemma the phone, but she shook her head and placed a vertical index finger to her pursed lips.

"I know that Gemma is in there with you Stan so please don't waste time by lying." Ted added, loud enough for all to hear. Gemma sighed, took the phone from Stan's outstretched hand, placed it to her ear, and began to speak.

"Are you ok Ted? We've just watched your car crash through the gates. It took a few seconds to realise that you weren't driving, gave us a real fright."

"Don't try to change the subject, why didn't you leave as promised? You could be in great danger."

Ted was trying to sound cross, but he admired the fact that Gemma would not leave him to face trouble alone, so he decided to put her to good use.

"We'll continue this conversation later; seeing that you are still here, I need you to pick me up at the access road tunnel at the end of highway seven. Can you do that?"

Gemma agreed, passed the phone back to Stan, and set off immediately to find a transportation buggy, while Ted relayed further information to the only other person he could trust.

"Listen Stan, I'm not sure how much Gemma has told you, but it is probably going to get messy in here and you should leave as soon as possible ok!"

Stan smiled to himself as he listened to his friend's worried tone. But he had no intention of leaving Ted and Gemma to face Philip alone and he made his point clear.

"Thanks for your concern old man, but I'm staying to the end of the ride. I know that he was your best friend, but I've never liked the smug little turd and if he's going to get his comeuppance, I for one wouldn't miss it for the world."

Ted smiled to himself as he listened to the reply; he would have been very surprised if Stan had said anything else.

"That's your choice Stan, I'm sure you know all the risks, but I'm very happy for your offer of help. The first thing I want you to do, is to completely seal off the control room, secure every window, door and access port into your domain ok."

Stan agreed to *'bomb proof'* the building and agreed to monitor Ted's progress, helping where he could from within.

From inside Philip Sanderson's office, plans were also being made as he listened to every word of Ted and Stan's conversation via a microchip-bugging device built into almost every public area of the complex. The device allowed him to eavesdrop into any conversation or tap into any communication device within a twenty-yard radius. This illegal procedure had allowed him to keep one-step ahead of all his employees, including Ted whom he now tried and failed to pick up on the security cameras near to the access tunnel at the end of highway seven. Realising what Stan had done, Philip decided that if he could not receive any visual input he would revert to an output program that he had created to strike fear into his employees. One moment Stan was cycling through images from video surveillance feeds, the next thing Philip's hawkish features adorned every screen in the hub.

"Jesus Christ Philip, what the bloody hell are you playing at?" Stan exclaimed, almost choking on a mouthful of hot coffee.

Encouraged by Stan's reaction, Philip smiled unctuously and leaned even closer to the webcam positioned above his desk.

"You know exactly what I'm doing Stan and I insist that you immediately return control of all the security cameras to me or suffer the consequences."

Now it was Stan's turn to smile. Even though Philip was the chairman of the organisation and a very powerful man to try and cross swords with he knew that it was nothing more than an empty threat.

"Sorry boss, no can do. You're nothing more than a jumped up computer geek who scares no one. I think you know the game's over and you've lost, so why don't you just give yourself up and make things easier for everyone."

It was well known that Philip hated personal confrontation, especially with Stan. Even though Stan was one of his employees, he never acted subservient in Philip's presence; in fact he sometimes went out of his way to be noncompliant, but always in private, never in public. This pseudo compromise was accepted by Philip because he knew that Stan was by far the best man for the job. Before Stan could continue with his insults, Philip terminated the broadcast, replacing every one of his images with the current security camera input.

Furious at being intimidated by someone whom he regarded as a subspecies compared to his own intelligence, Philip used his intercom to call in his two personal bodyguards who waited patiently in a small sitting room just outside his office. Philip hated being reliant on thuggery rather than his superior intelligence to settle his problems, but at the moment there was little time to waste. One thing Philip did share with his bodyguards was that they had both been responsible for incredible cruelty without conscience on many occasions.

Two heavy-set, identically suited employees walked into Philip's office, but they both could not be more different. One was an ex royal marine who had seen action all over the world, but had now moved into the lucrative world of personal security. The other, although highly trained in several martial arts and all aspects of security was actually a custom designed android. Philip wasted no time in issuing his orders.

"I have two tasks for you both to complete so listen carefully."

Neither bodyguard replied, allowing Philip to continue.

"First, I need you both to collect an item recently deposited inside my private delivery room, just off highway nine. It is the usual package and I want it brought to me here immediately. Second, I need you to find a way to access to the central command room; Stanley Gibson has locked himself inside and he refuses to leave. I need you to evict him as soon as possible and I don't care how you get the job done, but in doing so you must not damage any of the equipment within. Do you both understand?"

The bodyguards nodded their heads in unison, turned silently away, and headed for the door.

CHAPTER THIRTY-THREE

The five-minute warning bell sounded and several groups of prisoners gathered behind their cell doors ready to be escorted to the gymnasium. As each cell unlocked, the inmates filed out into the corridor and joined the ever increasing snake of up to two-hundred and fifty people ready for their morning exercise. When they reached the facility, every inmate passed single file through the narrow gymnasium door allowing a scanner mounted on the lintel above, to register their relevant serial number and relay the gathered information onto a clipboard computer pad held by the head guard. When Adam reached the doorway a buzzer sounded halting the queue and he was forcibly pulled to one side, much to the consternation of his friends. Jason opened his mouth ready to complain but a swift poke in the ribs from his sister reminded him that the shock collars had been hopefully deactivated and now was not the time for the guards to find out. Anxious but unable to do nothing else but leave Adam behind, the remainder of the group filed passed their friend to each receive a nod and meaningful stare from Adam, telling them all silently that they should adhere to his plan.

Inside the gymnasium they followed Adam's instructions and purposely forced their way to the back to stand directly outside the door to the apparatus storeroom in anticipation for their escape. With every prisoner inside and ready to go, a bell sounded and the warm up stretching program began. Amy being the shortest stood directly behind Neil and John, who shielded her from prying eyes as she cautiously turned the bulb shaped door handle, expecting an alarm to sound at any second. As usual, Adam was one-step ahead; he had already isolated the power supply to the door. With no obvious signs of the guards being alerted, Amy ducked down and slipped quickly inside unnoticed. Motion sensors in the ceiling detected her presence and immediately the overhead lights flickered into life, casting elaborate shadows across the room.

The heady aroma of sweat, varnish, and old leather, assaulted her nostrils in the claustrophobic environment, but desperation overshadowed her fears as she headed directly for the back of the room. Luckily, there was only a pommel horse blocking her way and dragging it to one side, she easily located the air vent. The grill protecting the hole was exactly where Adam said it would be, but it was considerably smaller than he had described. Fearful that the taller men of the group would struggle to fit she said a silent prayer that the air ducting was larger on the inside. Crouching down in the half-light behind a huge pile of crash mats, Amy slid her fingers into the large mesh, lifted the grill panel upwards, and away from its slots in the wall then placed it on the floor nearby. The low angle to the overhead light made it impossible to see more than a few feet into the hole, but mercifully it looked much more accommodating behind than the opening itself suggested. Relieved, she returned to the storeroom door, opened it a crack and beckoned the next one in. At this point, the entire gymnasium echoed to the sound of two-hundred and fifty pairs of feet running on the spot in a group exercise as one by one, Amy's would-be escapees ducked down and crept through the door until every member stood inside the small room.

Before anyone had a chance to raise the subject of Adam's removal from the group, Neil jumped in with a brief statement.

"I know exactly what we all need to discuss, but the best thing to do right now is to get out of sight. I'll go first and you will all have to follow my lead."

Neil did not wait for a reply as he was already kneeling down ready to squeeze into the hole. Before he could leave, Oliver stepped forwards, slipped a hand up his own sleeve, and retrieved a small high-powered torch that he offered up for Neil's use.

"You'll probably need this; I stole it from the doctor when I had my check-up yesterday afternoon." Oliver announced shyly, and then blushed heavily when Amy kissed him on the cheek for his bravery. Neil turned on the torch and problem free, he slid into the air vent followed quickly by the others. Luckily behind the vent there appeared to be a large box junction connecting several pipes where they could all congregate. Jason was the last man through, and he slid in backwards, dragging the pommel horse with him as close to the vent as possible before taking hold and clipping the mesh cover back into place from the inside. Immediately everything was secure, Neil made his speech.

"I know that everyone is upset that Adam has been separated from us and will feel reluctant to attempt this escape without him. We are all aware that our lives are in immediate peril and to abandon everything right now would be nothing short of stupid. Adam is an extremely resourceful man and I'm sure he will find some other way to escape without having the rest of us to consider in the process. I know the diagrams of the air ducts were all contained inside his head, but he explained everything to me in the bathroom yesterday and I am confident that I can get us all to the surface so who's with me?"

Grunts of reluctant acceptance were all he received, but no one disagreed so Neil closed his eyes for a second, and then silently set off leaving the others to follow. Luckily the diameter of the aluminium tubing allowed everyone to crawl childlike and in elephant fashion, as they followed the soft light from the bobbing torch into the unknown.

For the next twenty to thirty minutes they covered several hundred metres and everything seemed to go to plan, until a siren alerted the entire complex that they were missing. The head count in the gymnasium at the end of the exercise regime fell five persons short and in the excitement of the event a fight had broken out. In his frustration a guard had pushed over the wife of one of the inmates and her husband had retaliated by hitting him in the face. The immediate reaction was for the head guard to shock everyone into submission that to his surprise had zero effect. It did not take long for the inmates to realise that the collars were now defunct, and by sheer will of numbers, the gymnasium guards were overpowered and a mass riot began. Under threat of personal violence, the guards were frogmarched back to the prison accommodation blocks and forced to unlock every cell door releasing hundreds more excited and angry inmates. As usual, the commander was ignoring all forms of communication, and at a loss of how to proceed, his subordinate rang Philip Sanderson directly.

"I don't have time for this now, talk fast." Philip began, wondering what else could possibly go wrong.

"I'm sorry to disturb you, Mr Sanderson sir, but there is a riot at the facility and the shock collars aren't working." The commander's assistant garbled frantically, almost shaking in fear. Philip immediately stopped what he was doing and gave the issue his full attention.

"There's a *what* happening? I thought I sent a memo to evacuate the place and now you're telling me you have a riot on your hands. Put the commander on the line."

"Not sure where he is at the moment sir; it's possible he may be off site or something."

It was the truth, the assistant had no idea where the commander was at the moment and hedged his bets to try and keep out of trouble. Philip swore loudly and slammed a fist onto his desk in frustration. Through gritted teeth, but apparently no pain, he issued his reply.

"Do not under any circumstances allow anyone to reach the surface. Kill them all if necessary, are we clear on that? I will check the collar control program for a glitch and see if I can fix it from here."

Philip abruptly ended the phone call without waiting for an answer and then immediately accessed the relevant program to scan the coding for what may have caused the malfunction. For Philip this was a simple task and it did not take him long to find and delete Adam's line of rogue data, resume the program to its full capacity and then re-contact the prison.

"The program is now back online, use according to operational parameters to restore order, then complete the task."

Philip again did not wait for a reply and he hung up, leaving the junior officer wondering what according to operational parameters referred to, as his lazy commanding officer had failed to inform anyone else of the collar's limitations. Too afraid to call back and ask what Philip meant, he flicked every switch on the main control panel activating all the collars at once. The immediate effect was startling for the prisoners and it caused a brief halt to the fighting, but within seconds they all realised that the effect was not completely debilitating and fuelled by adrenaline the riot resumed.

Deep in the ventilation ducts, the small group of friends froze as they heard the sound of the alarm and tensed their muscles ready for the shock to follow. Seconds passed and much to their relief nothing happened. With a communal sigh and several silent promises to thank Adam should they be reunited, they continued to wend their way slowly towards the surface and freedom. Adam's eidetic memory was incredible, not only had he memorised a three-dimensional layout of the ventilation ducts, he also planned and passed on to Neil, a simple to follow route avoiding any major vertical shafts or fan assisted junctions. For the first fifteen minutes everything was going to plan with good progress made, until Philip repaired the program and everyone received the inevitable shock. With every bodily muscle seized tight, the group were unable to move and all they could do was silently endure the pain. To their surprise this was not quite as bad as in previous occasions and to everyone's relief their tense muscles relaxed as the current steadily faltered. The capacitors quickly drained and the aged generators were unable to maintain the power output for so many people at once. Eventually the cramps subsided, restoring near normal muscular function for all, except Oliver. The shock triggered an asthma attack and as he fumbled in the dark for his inhaler, his trembling fingers dropped the canister and it slid away down a side tunnel into the darkness.

"What's the hold up?" Neil shouted in a stage whisper from the front of the procession.

"It's Oliver, he's having an attack and dropped his inhaler down a side vent. Pass the torch back so we can look for it." Jason replied, who was positioned directly behind Oliver and bringing up the rear of the ragtag group. The torch was duly passed back and everyone waited anxiously in the cloying dusty heat as Jason shone the torch beam down the shaft. At first he believed it to have rolled completely out of sight until he spotted the familiar canister shape sitting atop a wide mesh horizontal grid sited directly above one of the upper corridors of the prison.

"For God's sake Oliver why can't you be more careful?" John Turner hissed, as his frustrations from their painfully slow progress began to boil over. Ignoring the urge to respond directly to the outburst and defend Oliver, Jason channelled his anger into forcing his frame around the narrow junction and down the smaller side duct until he reached the grid and the lost item. Without too much difficulty, he reached his goal, but just as his fingertips touched the canister, the corridor lights directly below him suddenly lit up, bathing the underneath of Jason's body in a checkerboard of light. Rigid with fear, he watched horrified as more than twenty armed men marched hurriedly along the corridor directly below his semiprostrate, trembling, frame. Luckily they were all too preoccupied with the task that lay ahead to notice Jason as they headed towards the riot. In the relieved silence that followed, Jason slowly eased himself back onto his hands and knees ready to reverse when the door at the far end of the corridor clicked again and two senior officers walked casually by. This time their approach was much quieter than the squad of soldiers and Jason held his breath, hoping that neither man could hear Oliver as his wheezing became progressively louder and he struggled to breathe. If either one had glimpsed skywards looking for the sound, they would have seen Jason's skinny form clearly visible through the grid sited in the ceiling above. Luckily they had more pressing matters and walked swiftly away. The corridor light automatically switched off, leaving a thoroughly relieved young man time to stuff Oliver's inhaler inside his shirt and then reverse his course. Jason awkwardly squirmed his way back into the main air duct, passed over the inhaler, and much to everyone's relief Oliver soon breathed freely again, allowing the escape attempt to resume. It was not long before the mild shock from the collars dissipated even further and then ceased completely as the generators providing the pulse, overheated and shut down one by one. This worked in direct correlation with the continuing echo of fighting and sporadic gunfire as the riot intensified. Praying that the worst was now behind them, the young group inched their way to safety, unaware that they were not the sole occupants of the air ducts. There was something behind that was considerably quicker, and it was closing in fast.

CHAPTER THIRTY-FOUR

As soon as she left the control centre, Gemma took a shuttle pod down several levels, then horizontally into the central plaza of the complex. The sight facing her on arrival gave a very unnerving sensation as she walked across the completely abandoned concourse with its empty shops, bars, and restaurants. Feeling like the last woman on earth, the high domed ceiling echoed exclusively to the sound of her footsteps. Unnerved, she picked up the pace, heading directly towards the electric buggy charging zone. Eerily, every operational helper drone looked up and slowly turned its head, silently checking her progress as she walked by. Passing too close to one of the holding pens, Gemma screamed in fright as several robots simultaneously jumped out of their queue.

"Good afternoon madam, I am a helper drone, my primary function is to offer assistance in whatever form you require. Is there anything I can do for you today?"

The close proximity of the drones invading her personal space, combined with an out of sync chorus of the preprogramed sentence, set an immediate panic.

"Get away from me, you metal headed groupies."

The fearful grip in her belly made Gemma yell far too loudly and her voice resounded through the vast open space as the robots immediately backed away and resumed their position in the holding pen. Feeling a little shaken, she settled herself with a few deep breaths and then resumed her march to the far end of the plaza.

Slipping hastily into the driver's seat of a fully charged open sided buggy, Gemma slammed her foot hard down on the accelerator pedal, circled around and set off down highway seven. The altercation with the helper drones still played on her mind, and less than fifty yards into the journey her lack of concentration nearly caused a crash. Luckily a violent swerve helped her to avoid three empty barrels that had been dumped from another buggy onto the highway and replaced by human passengers who were eager to evacuate the site. Slewing sideways to a halt and almost facing the opposite way, Gemma paused as she stared back down the narrow tunnel when an idea came to mind. Heading straight back into the central plaza, she aimed for the waiting group of helper drones.

"You, you, you, and you get in the buggy now!"

She ordered, pointing to the first four robots standing in the line. Duly obeying her command, three climbed onto the rear bench seat and the remainder took its place in the front next to Gemma. To her amusement, they all secured themselves in with a lap belt and stared back at Gemma's face, eager for the next instruction.

"Eyes front and be quiet!" Was Gemma's succeeding order; with the command obeyed, the journey resumed to collect Ted at the end of highway number seven

At this point in time, Philip's bodyguards had completed their first assigned task and now arrived outside the closed and locked metal security door of the control room containing Stanley Gibson. Their first obvious attempt at entry consisted of repeated swipes of master-pass card through the reader to the left of the door, all resulting with the same flashing red light and '*Entry Denied*' illuminating the adjacent display panel. Philip had guessed that this might be the case, so he had recited from memory his personal list of special private access codes to the android half of the duo, who recorded them all into his memory bank. This thirty-plus list of special five digit key codes were designed to override any current security protocol, but repeated attempts using the adjacent number pad still bore the same negative result. Stan, who had been in Philip's employ since its launch, had been one of the instigators of the security settings throughout the entire system. During his regular 'personal' security sweeps, Stan had found, and purposely deleted all of Philip's lines of backdoor entry keys. Third on the list of attempts was a complete reconnaissance of the immediate area surrounding the control hub. Using the android's hardwired navigational three-dimensional blueprint of the complex, they wasted the next twenty minutes, trying every supply corridor and escape hatch in an attempt to gain entry. However, Stan was always one-step ahead and the result ended in defeat. At a loss of now how to proceed, the human half of the duo called Philip for help.

"I'm sorry Mr Sanderson sir, but the place is completely secure. What do you want us to do now?"

Philip, finding it very hard to keep his patience at the lack of ingenuity and apparent incompetence of his men, paced the room trying to remain calm. He had to realise that his options were very limited, but frustration got the better of him and he yelled his reply.

"As I have already told the both of you, do whatever it takes. Smash down the door and kill him if you have to, but keep damage to the control room down to a minimum. Do you understand?"

"Yessir, leave it to us."

Slightly unnerved by the outburst, the guard hastily ended the call, leaving Philip to try to quell his frustrations on battling with Stan for control of the security cameras in the western sector. Philip realised now that he had underestimated Ted's cunning and it was only through listening to Stan and Gemma via his bugging device that he realised that Ted was not killed inside his car near the south gate entrance and was now on foot heading in from the west. It would take a team of engineers a week to repair the image density profiler, leaving Philip unable to create anything more solid than realistic looking visual effects that would only fool Ted for a few seconds before he realised that he could walk right through them. The next line of defence had to be something considerably more solid than a few gimmicks. After a brief bout of head scratching Philip finally settled on what he considered to be the ideal solution.

With his latest delivery unpacked and prepped for installation, Philip returned to his private quarters and sat behind the massive control desk. Utilising his touch screen keyboard, he typed in the activation codes for his pride and joy, and nearly half a mile away in a quiet corner of the complex, a hermetically clean storeroom came to life. Under the soft glow of the solar powered overhead security lights, several rows of coffin shaped crates slowly hinged open their lids.

Following the company's inception and subsequent introduction of the mark one robotic humanoid model, Philip had retained a working example of every new version designed and upgraded by the company. He would eventually donate them to the British Museum of Invention for them to display his collection. His fantasy was that the world renowned institution would create a tableaux display of his incredible creations, thereby announcing his genius to the world, ranking him shoulder to shoulder with the most famous inventors in history. Until this momentous imagined event could take place, the entire collection was regularly inspected and maintained, including all the power packs that were periodically recharged to preserve the longevity of the batteries, providing several hours of heavy use. Now for the first time ever, every single one of Philip's prized collection simultaneously jerked into life. Amid a carpet of loose packing foam, the robotic army climbed out of their crates.

The progression in design and quality from the earliest to the latest model was truly amazing. The first model, PS-1 looked nothing more than a shiny chrome skeleton adorned with tiny servomotors at every moveable joint, controlled via masses of ribbon cable secured loosely to the metallic limbs. All of these linked back into the chest cavity containing the motherboard, battery, gyroscope, and a central processing unit. Even though basic by today's standards, this model marked a milestone in independent thinking for advanced robotics. Incorporated into the software was Philip's incredible new awareness program, allowing units to think independently for the first time and to learn from previous mistakes in order to safely achieve the ordered goal. As Philip introduced subsequent versions, improvements in programmable capability, body structure, mobility, and human appearance showed a natural progression that ended currently with PS-46, a model that had yet to be used in a public environment. This unit moved with the grace of a dancer, had the strength of an athlete, and bore such a resemblance to a human, it was almost impossible to believe that it was not real flesh and blood.

Depending on the mobility of each unit, the automatons filed silently through the storeroom door, and in accordance to individual speed, the bizarre procession gradually spread out along the length of the corridor. A side on view of this incredible site resembled the robotic version of the ascent of man, with the most developed and able bodied at the front, and the older slower versions steadily bringing up the rear. Unfortunately for Philip, he was unable to arm his private army with anything more dangerous than a spanner or screwdriver from the tool cupboards in the workshop. Fortunately, some of the later models possessed a far superior strength and were considerably nimble, compared to the average human, and he was convinced that they were more than capable of completing the job of stopping Ted. If this required killing his best friend, then so be it.

CHAPTER THIRTY-FIVE

Even though they were making good progress towards the surface, heat and smoke extracted from the lower levels caused by the intense fighting was making the journey unbearable. The air ducts were doing exactly what they were designed for and vacuumed up the choking fumes, hampering everyone's breathing as they continued with their escape. The light from the stolen torch was also quickly fading, leaving Neil fumbling almost blindly in the darkness, leading to a change of plan.

"It's no use; we can't carry on like this. As soon as we reach the next air flow grid we are going to have to kick it open, climb out, and find another way."

A universal murmur of approval, returned from the group, and Neil set about looking for a suitable exit. He was actually pleased to be leaving the confines of the ducting because he was not entirely sure where they all were. He did not have the heart to inform his friends that Adam's description of the blueprint had been long forgotten and it was only luck that had allowed them to get this far. He hoped they would now be many floors above the fighting that hopefully would occupy the guards, so all they would now have to do was keep on heading upwards until they reached the surface.

"Can anybody hear that noise?" Jason shouted hoarsely, from where he maintained his position at the rear of the group. No one paid any attention apart from Oliver, who stopped immediately and listened intently for any change in the current background noise. He was unable to hear any variation apart from the drone of assorted generators and sporadic gunfire coming from many floors below, but now a different noise added to the mix. At first it sounded just like hailstones on a windowpane, but it combined with a sporadic nerve-jangling squeal, akin to the sound of fingernails being dragged down a blackboard. The toe curling screak grew increasingly loud, until his tired and fuddled brain identified the sound and a horrified realisation kicked in.

Long forgotten childhood memories flooded into his cerebral cortex, instantly returning him to the long summer holidays on his uncle's farm in the Cotswolds. For a city boy like Oliver, this was an incredible adventure land and he quickly became adept at rural life. One memory however, was not as idyllic as the rest. He recalled playing ball with the family sheepdog Bobby, when something caught the old dog's eye. Defying his age, he dashed across the farmyard and disappeared through a gap in the barnyard door. A blood-chilling squeal followed and fearing that the dog had hurt himself, Oliver ran over only to see Bobby promptly return with a large brown rat clamped securely between his teeth. The rat was still very much alive, and between frantic bouts of violent squirming, the rat screamed constantly as it tried unsuccessfully to wriggle free. This only encouraged Bobby and in his excitement he shook his head frantically from side to side until the rat cried no more. The pitiful sound haunted Oliver's nightmares for many weeks and now the same baleful memory echoed from deep within the darkness as he pictured hundreds of rodents utilising the same air ducts in search of their own escape.

"Everybody wait!" Oliver wheezed as loud as he could, stopping everyone dead in their tracts as they all wondered what could possibly be wrong now.

"I'm positive that I can hear rats in the ducts. I don't know how many, but it sounds like a hell of a lot. What I do know is that they're not far behind us and closing in fast." He added, breathlessly forcing him to use his already semi-depleted inhaler to ease his burning lungs.

"I'm damned if I can hear anything, it's probably just the sound of your chest wheezing in your own head. I for one would like to see daylight once more, so can we all just get a move on?"

John added sarcastically and sighed audibly at yet another hold up. Oliver remained silent to allow the inhaled gas to take maximum effect and then completely out of his normal character, he answered back.

"For once in your life just shut up and listen. If there are rats behind us you *do not* want to get in their way as they make their escape. As there isn't time to get out of here I need all of you to lie flat and keep to as still as possible so they can get through. Does everyone understand?"

There was not enough time for John to argue as suddenly out of the darkness the squealing intensified when around a dozen of large brown rats dropped down heavily from an overhead vent, and with their claws scrabbling for purchase on the shiny aluminium duct casing, they began to close in quickly on the stricken group. Amy screamed in unison with the furry visitors, but she had no other options to consider except follow orders along with everyone else and lay flat, while covering exposed faces behind grubby hands. Shaking in terror at the sensation of flea-ridden, stinking rodents, scrambling over her quaking frame, Amy tried desperately to remain still, but she squealed again and began to thrash about as one rat released a squirt of hot urine on the back of her neck and then stopped to inspect his work.

"Amy for Christ's sake, keep still!" Jason yelled from the rear of the group, but his desperate plea was lost in the deafening thunder, as hundreds more thudded down into a metal air-duct behind him. There was not anywhere near enough room for the rats and Jason to occupy the same space and his body bore the brunt of razor sharp teeth and claws trying to dig through his soft flesh hoping to find another exit. Amy heard nothing from her brother, she was already lost in her own personal hell, leaving Jason to suffer the torture from the growing multitude. The temperature in the air ducts rose dramatically, forcing the rats to even greater desperation in their attempt to get through, but they were still held back by Amy's frantic blockade. Still the vermin continued to pour in, squealing and squeezing into every available space. Because of Amy, the rodent bottleneck on Jason's chest soon became unbearable. Every time he breathed out it was almost impossible to breathe in. Trapped in the darkness of his aluminium coffin, he tried to call for his sister's help one last time, but he had no air left and he could feel his life ebbing away. Suddenly fate intervened; out of sheer terror Amy blacked out and her body fell flat, allowing the rats a simple exit over her limp body that wriggled and twitched as tiny clawed feet gained purchase on skin and clothing in haste for escape. Relieved of the pressure, Jason took in a gulp of somewhat rank, but life giving air and waited as the rats continued on their way.

It was all over in a matter of seconds, but the stench remained, also nightmares that would last a lifetime as everyone breathlessly listened to the sound of their uninvited guests fade into the distance. Luckily, Amy and Jason recovered quickly and apart from the sting of numerous bites and scratches, they wearily followed Neil's lead as he continued to seek a suitable way out.

Within thirty yards, security lights in a room below, offered a soft hazy glow bright enough to guide Neil through the smoke. Listening intently for any sounds of fighting or disturbance, he decided all was well, and a swift kick, flipped open the grid. One by one, the small, filthy group followed the big man out, until everyone cleared the confines of the duct into what appeared to be an empty room.

"Where are we now?" Amy asked, who was still visibly shaken but was naively confident that Neil had everything under control and it would only be a matter of time before they would all reach the surface and freedom. Neil ignored the question and placed a vertical index finger to his lips to quieten her before he carefully turned the door knob and peered through the tiny crack formed as he opened the door. Luckily the short corridor that the doorway opened onto was deserted and the only sound of any fighting or other activity appeared to be a long way away. Cautiously everyone stayed close and snaked their way towards the nearest stairwell ready to begin their ascent. Smoke rising from fires raging down in the lower levels still hung heavily in the air, making breathing a little difficult, but it was considerably better than staying inside the air ducts. This was of significant benefit for Oliver's asthma, but the hurried climb soon took its toll on his weakened state and another enforced rest was required.

"You... don't... have... to... wait... for... me." He wheezed before closing his eyes and hurriedly taking the last remaining puff from his inhaler. Seconds later he breathed a little easier and continued his short speech.

"We can't be far from the surface now; leave me to follow on at my own pace."

Oliver still wheezed heavily, but not quite as bad as before. It was a noble 'Captain Oats' type of gesture, and for the majority of the group they gave little thought to leaving him behind. Suddenly, much to everyone's surprise, John Turner accepted Oliver's suggestion and before anyone else could offer any sort of disapproval for his selfish actions, he was running up the stairs and soon out of sight, leaving only the echo of his footsteps coming down the upper stairwell as a sign that he had been there at all.

"Of all the selfish, self-centred, conceited, arrogant..." Neil began as he broke the short silence and voiced what everybody else was thinking. But his tirade was abruptly cut short and everyone stared upwards, flinching to the sound of raised voices shortly followed by the rataplan of semi-automatic gunfire. Amy screamed and her brother clapped his hand across her mouth to stop the noise but he was too late. For a second everything was quiet as their ears rang to the deafening acoustics, then the group turned and ran for their lives at the heavy thud of at least ten pairs of booted feet running down the stairs.

Instead of allowing the group to descend back down the way they had just come, Jason took the lead and guided everyone through the exit onto one of the many floors. They hid behind the first available door leading into another store room that they all prayed would be enough to avoid capture or more likely execution.

The heavy footsteps grew louder as three uniformed and armed men burst through the access door onto their level, ran past the hiding place to the far dead-end of the corridor, then began to test every door on their return. Muffled orders and replies grew steadily closer, until one of the guards stood directly outside the terrified gang's hideout. Neil and Jason had already braced their shoulders against the inside of the door and gripped the handle as tightly as possible to refuse entry from anyone on the outside. The remainder of the group stared intently at the shadows cast by the guard's boots, blocking the only available source of light coming through the gap under the door of the darkened storeroom. Amy physically flinched when the door handle creaked from the strain as her two friends held tight. The guard tried three or four more times to operate the handle, but his endeavour was no match for desperation. In his frustration the guard let go and stepped back, slid his M16 assault rifle from his shoulder and aimed the nozzle at the lock, ready to release a few rounds and blast his way in. Bracing himself from the recoil of the weapon, he wrapped the shoulder strap around his arm and slowly squeezed the trigger. Unaware of the guard's intent, Neil and Jason continued to brace themselves against the door. The rifle's trigger was almost at the point of release when a loud crash coming from much lower down the stairwell grabbed the guard's attention. This was quickly followed by shouted orders from his commander for everyone to continue with their descent. Releasing his finger, he turned away and quickly ran to the exit.

It was a full five minutes of nerve jangling silence before any of the gang dare open the door and venture out back out into the corridor. Luckily for them, the small group of armed guards were now several flights down the stairs, leaving the way clear for their continued ascent.

According to fitness, the group steadily stretched out into single file, with the more able bodied taking the lead, but only two more levels had been cleared when the rear of the group bumped into their friends at the front who had stopped dead in their tracks and stared open mouthed upon the crumpled, blood soaked body of John. He lay face down with his head twisted painfully to one side and forced backwards against the wall, with his limbs jutting out at painful angles to his torso. His gruesome appearance took the form of a blooded and broken marionette abandoned in an untidy heap at the turn of the stair run. Tragically, he had run into a squad of surface security guards who were under orders to assist with quelling the riot. John had turned to run back down the stairs, but before he had made it to the second step, a short burst of automatic gunfire fired at point blank range had catapulted the poor man from the top step down the flight of the stairs to crash face first into the walled turn at the bottom. The tight grouping of bullets fired into his lower back had passed easily through the soft abdominal flesh and gouged fist size chunks of plaster from the wall directly above John's bloodied body, that now decanted a crimson waterfall of rapidly cooling, congealing blood down the succeeding run of precast concrete steps. With his eyes still open and face still bearing his final terrified expression, Neil stepped forwards and gently closed the dead man's eyelids for the last time.

"There's nothing we can do for him now so quickly say your goodbyes then we can all go." Neil announced sternly as he straightened up, turned away, and purposely climbed the next flight of stairs two at a time. With their goodbyes hastily proffered, it was not too far up the next level before the rest of the group caught up with Neil, who was stooped over the handrail and weeping openly for the loss of his friend.

"I… I should have stopped him from running off like that. How am I going to look his family in the eye and tell them he's dead?"

Neil burbled through gut wrenching gasps for air and gagging on his own rapid production of phlegm. Jason put a consoling hand across his friend's shoulders and whispered a few words of comfort that Neil barely heard as he embarrassedly wiped the excess snot onto his sleeve and sniffed the remainder back into his considerably large nose. The rest of the gang filed by, silently lost in private grief, but knew only too well that they could also share the same fate unless the ascent continued.

Neil and Jason continued to bring up the rear, when the sound of a slamming door, followed by and heavy footfalls from the armed guards spurred them back into action. John's plight fuelled an adrenaline rush, and the group quickly opened up a comfortable distance between themselves and the pursuing armed men. Flight after flight of a lung busting stair climb finally took its toll on Oliver and he collapsed yet again, fighting for breath. Before he knew it, Jason and Neil had hooked their elbows under his armpits, physically lifted Oliver up off his knees, and half carried him up the stairs with his flailing feet catching only one out of three steps as he air-walked in his attempt to help his cause.

To their surprise, the stairwell suddenly came to an abrupt end, leaving them with a single exit door at the top landing.

"It's locked." Amy gasped; trying not to burst into tears from exhaustion and frustration as she desperately rattled the door handle again and again. At this point Jason and Neil, with Oliver still suspended between them, reached the top of the stairs, and dropped the poor man unceremoniously to his knees while they both tried the door with the same negative result. Neil turned around to face his friends and then leaned over the top safety railing, listening intently to the sound of the approaching guards. He knew they were desperately running out of time, so he turned around and tried to shoulder charge the door, with little effect.

"Let me have a go." Jason stepped up to try his luck as Neil gingerly rubbed his shoulder and moved out of the way. Bracing himself against the railing, he lashed out his right foot against the door. The wood cracked, but it still remained in place. Jason tried again and the door split a little more.

"It needs both of you!" Amy ordered, Pushing Neil towards Jason who was still against the rail. Side by side, both men raised one leg and on Jason's mark, lashed out at the door. The lock housing tore apart the frame and the splintered door flew open, but that was barely noticed as everyone ran through into what looked like the dead-end of an underground car park. The lowered ramp over their heads was constructed of riveted metal H-beams, supported by two huge hydraulic rams sited on either side of the tunnel, all of which fitted exactly against the acute angle of the roadway. It was obvious that freedom lay just above their heads, but having no means of powering the mechanism, escape was impossible. As the dust filled air from the broken door settled in the glow of the bulkhead lights, the group realised that they had only one option, and that was to follow the access road deeper underground, and hope to find another way out.

As Jason and Neil resumed their positions either side of Oliver, ready to aid him for the long descent; He looked over his shoulder for Amy, to find her listening intently at the doorway, trying to estimate how much time they had before the guards arrived. Silent tears of fear and frustration rolled from her eyes and he tried to offer a reassuring smile, when something shiny and partially hidden behind the broken door caught his eye. Freeing himself from the grip of his friends, Oliver wrenched the door back against its sprained hinges to expose a small aluminium hinge fronted box attached to the wall. Neil immediately took charge and opened the tiny door cover, to reveal a numbered keypad and two buttons individually coloured red and green.

"This has got to operate the exit ramp; it can't just stop here can it?" Jason gasped as he stared at the keypad with a religious zeal. Neil was the first to respond, pushing Jason out of the way and began to input random number combinations, followed by a press of the green button. Anxious faces watched as he tried dozens of different combinations, but every attempt ended in failure. While she waited, Amy returned to the stairwell to listen for the sound of approaching guards and quickly reported back with an estimate that they were less than a minute away. Neil cleared his throat and without check from his constant attempts he made a quick speech.

"We have to make a very important decision right now. We either wait to see if I can open the ramp in the next thirty seconds or we have to leave immediately. The descending roadway appears to have no other visible exits as far as the eye can see, and there will be nowhere to hide when the guards reach the top of the stairs. So what's it gonna be folks?"

A brief silence followed until Jason decided for everyone.

"I for one have no intention of descending back into that hell hole as I can taste freedom is just above our heads, therefore I put my trust in Neil. He has already managed to get us this far and I am sure he will finish the job; any other objections?"

Everyone silently shook their heads, leaving Neil with the added pressure of saving the group once again.

He knew that the majority of keyless systems operated on a four-digit input because that offered enough variation of number sequences, balanced against the human brain's capacity to remember a code. So he continued with this strategy until to everyone's horror, he just stopped and stared intently at the numbers on the pad. Amy drew breath to question why, but held her tongue as Oliver raised his hand for silence, allowing Neil to keep his full concentration. Half closing the shiny aluminium door cover, he reflected the limited light source across the number pad to reveal that only three of the numbers were slightly dirtier than the rest, due to the residue of oily fingerprints and dirt laden gloves. This narrowed the number combinations down considerably, and with feverish speed he resumed his attempt, incorporating the possible variables of a three number code. Valuable seconds ticked agonisingly by, but if group willpower could be harnessed, the ramp would have opened instantly and everyone would soon be on their way, but still it refused to budge. Just as Neil believed that he had reached the point of completing every possible combination, he pressed the green button for the umpteenth time and heard a loud clunk followed by the groaning of hydraulic rams hinged open the roof. Dust rained gently down on their upturned faces, and for the first time in several weeks, painful eye-watering sunlight streamed through the ever widening gap as the depleted group of friends made a final bid for freedom.

The gentle breeze blowing across the newly created exit, acted like wind over a chimney stack, sucking ever increasing clouds of smoke rising from deep underground. Through this man-made fog, the exhausted group emerged and broke into a run for freedom. Rejuvenated from the fresher if somewhat still tainted air, Oliver managed to keep up with the rest of his friends for a good fifty yards until the clearing echoed to the crack of a single gunshot and Oliver's skinny body acrobatically cartwheeled to the ground. Throwing themselves down onto the tarmac, the remaining group peered back through the rising smoke curtain to see the sunlit silhouettes of three armed guards and their commanding officer standing at the tunnel entrance. Not too far away, Oliver lay moaning on face down on the tarmac. He was lucky to be alive, the bullet had pinged off the top of his shoulder blade and clipped his earlobe, missing his skull by less than half an inch. The damage, although extremely painful was not life threatening and a few stitches would soon have the bleeding under control. But that was the last thing on everyone's mind as the guards closed in ready for the kill. As if to prolong the agony they marched slowly, taking careful aim to guarantee a clean shot. Jason reached out and found Amy's hand, gripping it tightly as they waited for death to come. Neil rolled onto his side, ready to stand up and reason with the armed men, but before he could make his move a volley of gunfire rang out.

"Remain where you are."

A loud and authoritative voice announced. Almost crying in relief, Neil and his friends turned their heads slowly to see a platoon of British soldiers and their commanding officer, emerge from behind the prison guards and into the clear air. The soldiers quickly secured the position, training their weapons on the prison guards, who lay dead or dying amid splatters of their own blood on the runway. In a blur of activity, a medic applied a field dressing to Oliver's wound and the exhausted friends tasted their first minutes of freedom.

As self-appointed spokesperson, Neil wearily got to his feet and introduced everyone to the officer in charge. He then explained the recent events as accurately as possible and the fact that some of their group had already been taken from the facility and needed to be found as quickly as possible. The commander listened intently, issued extra orders to his second in command, and watched as hundreds of armed troops wearing breathing apparatus, climbed back into their personnel carriers and headed down underground in the hope of rescuing many more prisoners trapped below. He then turned back to the group and explained how they happened to be there.

"We were alerted to your possible plight by an old friend of mine Teddy Langton. He is second in command at the Hologram Dreams Corporation who happen to own this site. Normally I wouldn't respond to this type of thing, but if Teddy boy says something's amiss, I'm damn well going to believe him. We began with a close inspection of the abandoned military buildings, which incidentally showed no apparent signs of life. The search continued along the runway in regard for a bally hidden tunnel. Not finding anything of consequence, we were on the point of abandoning the operation as a complete wild goose chase."

The officer stopped to receive combat information from his adjutant, and then concluded his brief speech.

"Where did I get to, oh yes, we were conducting a final sweep and heading for the exit when blow me down, the bally tarmac began to open up like some enormous great serpent's mouth, and low and behold you chaps come running out. A few minutes later and we would have missed you all completely. Jolly good stroke of luck what?"

Not waiting to receive any questions, the commanding officer slapped Neil heavily on his shoulder, then strode purposefully away to accept a call from headquarters. Two army ambulances arrived on the scene and the exhausted but relieved group split into two groups and climbed in.

CHAPTER THIRTY-SIX

Ted Langton waited anxiously as he hid in a small copse, sited within visual range of the entrance to highway seven in the western sector. It was almost impossible to avoid the myriad of security cameras dotted all over the site and he hoped that Stan was doing his best in keeping control away from Philip. Just in case, he kept perfectly still and hoped that if Philip was still searching for him, he would prove very difficult to find.

The sun was beginning to set and his stomach growled for sustenance that it had not received since early this morning. Worried that something had gone wrong, he was just about to risk another chat with Stan when less than fifty feet away, a small patch of rough undergrowth began to tremble and split down the middle as two hydraulically operated camouflaged access doors slowly hinged apart. For a few seconds nothing emerged and Ted wondered if it was Philip baiting a trap, when all of a sudden an electric buggy with Gemma at the wheel came barrelling into view. To his surprise the passenger seats were occupied by four helper drones who bounced violently up and down as the buggy traversed the rough ground heading directly towards Ted. As Gemma approached, Ted emerged from his hiding place and waited while she circled around and stopped the buggy.

"Right, you get in the back with the others."

Gemma instructed the drone sitting in the front, allowing Ted a seat. With everyone safely ensconced she floored the accelerator pedal and the rear of the vehicle slewed from left to right as the wheels fought for purchase in the soft ground. Finally, back inside the tunnel, and with the access door closed behind them, they finally had time to talk.

"What's with the drones in the back?" Ted asked, feeling like he was out on a date and they had chaperones sitting behind.

"We have no idea what Philip's going to throw at us and these bad boys just might come in useful." Gemma replied, and then wondered about the sanity of the idea as she glanced in her rear view mirror to see the drone that she had evicted from the front, trying to adhere to its programmed safety protocol and was wrestling with one of his colleagues in the back for the use of a lap belt. They finally compromised by sitting tightly together, extending the belt to its limit and just managing to clip the buckle into its housing.

Gemma's doubts did not have time to linger as they approached the halfway mark on the tunnel and caught sight of what appeared to be a small group of people heading in their direction.

"What the hell? I gave specific orders for everyone to evacuate immediately." Ted exclaimed as he leaned forwards in his seat trying to focus on the group ahead. Just as confused, Gemma stopped the buggy and they both stared open mouthed at the bizarre sight. Less than one-hundred feet away, approximately ten of what appeared to be a collection of some of Philip's first generation robots shuffled ungainly towards them. They were some of the oldest models Ted could remember and had not seen for years, and he watched with fascination as the silent group moved steadily closer. Some were literally shiny metal skeletons adorned with wires and servo motors, while others had limbs that were covered in a solid white moulded plastic shell. Controlled remotely by Philip, the motley crew had armed themselves with whatever implements were at hand, including spanners, a hammer, and even a length of chain taken from around a display in the main plaza. Using the relayed signal from the robotic on-board visuals combined with an overhead view from security cameras, Philip attempted to control this pathetic robot gang to attack. The limited speed and dexterity of these obsolete models was no match for a fit and agile human, but all Philip required at the moment, was to delay Ted long enough to complete his latest assimilation protocol.

The whole thing began as a joke; all Ted had to do was duck or sidestep from every attack, circle around behind and push the assailant over. Some of the pathetic attempts to attack were enough to do the job for him, as the robot's archaic internal gyroscopes were unable to counteract the forward momentum, stumble forwards or lose its balance completely and thud heavily to the floor. Within a few short minutes Ted bobbed and weaved through the entire gang and in spite of their menacing appearance the fight was over, leaving every robot sprawling helplessly on the ground. With the assistance of the helper drones, Ted and Gemma dragged the defeated gang to one side of the highway, clearing just enough space for Ted to drive the buggy through. The helper drones climbed back on board and were soon squabbling again over the allocation of available seat belts while Gemma walked around to resume her seat at the front. But with one foot placed onto the running board, ready to climb into the front passenger seat, she stopped and screamed from a searing pain in her trailing leg. The last robot to be cleared out of the way had reached out its shiny white plastic covered hand, clamped it tightly around her ankle, and pulled. Heavily winded as she fell to the ground, Gemma remained motionless for a second until the robot twisted its grip. Jolted immediately from her stupor and lashing out with her free leg, she repeatedly kicked the attacking robot in its face, but with little effect. Ted ran to Gemma's aid and tried to prise open the metal fingers, but his strength was no match for the robot's high power servo, controlled remotely by Philip back in his office.

"This is what happens when you come to grips with Philip Sanderson." Philip's announced, his voice booming out through the speakers of the tunnel's tannoy system.

The bad attempt at humour was completely lost on Ted, who repeatedly swore under his breath, trying to block out the announcement. Redoubling his efforts at the sound of Gemma's distress, Ted ripped open the soft plastic covering of the robotic arm and tried to claw away the protective rubber sheath covering the wires hidden beneath.

Gemma tried to be brave, but even the slightest movement caused terrible pain and she squealed pitifully, forcing Ted to stop and try to think of another plan as the tunnel once again echoed to the sound of Philip's maniacal tone.

"Give up now Ted, or I will increase the pressure until the bone is crushed and Miss Cassidy loses her foot."

Ted paused a little too long and was rewarded with more of Gemma's screams as the metal hand clamped even tighter. Deep purple lesions developed just above the ankle bone and the taught skin began to split. Reaching for his shoulder holster, Ted removed his gun and took aim at the robot's chest where he knew the central processing unit was housed.

"Shield your face. I'm going to kill the son of a bitch!" Ted snarled, cocking the weapon and waiting for Gemma to raise her forearm across her eyes. The video feed from the robot's ophthalmic receptors linked directly into Philip's office, and it looked like Ted was pointing the gun directly at him and in a panic, Philip tightened the robot's grip even more. Gemma was now in so much pain that she did not care how Ted got the job done.

"Get this effing thing off me now!" She snarled through gritted teeth while doing her best not to cry; suddenly to everyone's surprise, one of the helper drones jumped out of the buggy and crouched down at the robot's side, blocking Ted's view. It looked like it was protecting the threatened robot, but nothing could be further from the truth.

"Get out of the way!" Ted Yelled as he held fast his finger on the trigger while circling around in an attempt to get a clean shot. Before he had a chance to re-aim, he watched amazed as the helper effortlessly pulled apart the metal ribs of the prostrate robot's carcass then ripped out a handful of wires, killing all power to the body. Without any electrical input, the hand relaxed and opened flower-like from its grip. Quickly holstering the gun, Ted tenderly picked Gemma up from the floor and placed her into the passenger side of the waiting buggy, ran around and jumped into the other side and drove away before any more damage could be done.

"How is it?" Ted asked brusquely, furious at allowing Gemma to get hurt and equally embarrassed at his inadequate help.

"Perhaps I should be dating my hero the handsome robot." Gemma replied, trying to make light of the situation, hoping to block out the throbbing pain coming from her damaged ankle. As fast as the buggy could go, Ted drove to the nearest first aid post for a pain killing injection and treatment for Gemma's injury. Luckily, there were no more robots waiting in the deserted plaza, so Ted ordered the drones to guard the door while he carried Gemma into the surgery, laying her carefully onto the examination table.

Using his limited knowledge of sports injuries, Ted assessed the damage and decided that apart from superficial skin damage and severe bruising, Gemma was still able to rotate her foot so he guessed that it was not broken.

"Can we play doctors and nurses now?" Gemma purred huskily, trying to break the serious scowl fixed upon Ted's face. Ignoring her request, he turned away and anxiously rummaged through the supply fridge hoping to find an ice pack.

"Brace yourself, this might sting a bit." Ted offered dryly as he chanced upon a *'Chilly Wrap'*. This looked like a normal sterile bandage, but as it is removed from its hermetically sealed packaging, reactive chemicals lowered the temperature of the fabric to just above freezing. Without warning Ted slapped the dressing around Gemma's ankle, to a barrage of loud accusations about his parenthood and where else he should put the bandage.

"Undo your belt and lower your trousers a little." Ted ordered as he prepared the latest applicator of Morphine.

"Shouldn't you take me to dinner and buy me flowers first?" Gemma quipped before gingerly rolling onto her side, exposing the left cheek of her backside. Ted continued to ignore the comments and maintained his curt manner as he wiped a small patch of skin with a dab of cleaning alcohol, swiftly administered the pain relieving dose, and turned away. Instead of the traditional hollow needle injection, this applicator produced an ultra-fine mist of the required chemical that could be blasted through the outer dermis of the skin and immediately absorbed into the body without pain. Feeling almost instantaneous relief as the throbbing in her leg quickly subsided, Gemma endeavoured to cover her fear with yet more saucy innuendo.

"If this is your idea of foreplay you need to improve your technique!"

Ted failed to reply while Gemma rolled over and re-buckled her belt, she tried again.

"Anyway, never mind all that, what's the next part of our plan to get Philip?"

Ted finally turned around with a serious look on his face. This quickly softened to concern accompanied by a quickly rehearsed speech.

"I'm sorry Gemma but for you this is the end of the line. I know that you can handle yourself and are eager to see Philip pay for what he's done, but I won't risk your life any more. Only this morning I watched a young woman very much like you, murdered by Philip's hand right before my eyes, so I know that he won't think twice about taking yours. I hope you'll forgive me!"

Gemma wondered what on earth Ted was talking about as she opened her mouth to reply, but suddenly felt woozy and his face began to fade from view. Feeling very weak, Gemma laid her head back and instantly fell asleep from the tranquilliser that Ted had administered instead. Gently lifting Gemma into his arms, Ted carried her out to the buggy and lay her down across the back seat, securing her in place with the lap belts. Pointing to the nearest helper drone waiting nearby, he issued precise orders.

"You are instructed to protect Miss Cassidy at all costs, drive her away from the complex, and wait with her in the buggy park just outside the main northern entrance until help arrives. Do I make myself clear?"

The drone repeated Ted's instructions verbatim to prove understanding of the order. With a few additional directives regarding Gemma's safety, Ted watched anxiously as the buggy disappeared from view down highway one to the north gate. Looking around for any other surprises that Philip may have in store, and satisfied that for the time being he was relatively safe; he set off in the opposite direction with the three remaining drones. The plan was to take the transportation shuttle directly to Philip's front door.

CHAPTER THIRTY-SEVEN

"Come on Stan, do your magic." Ted mumbled under his breath, while nervously chewing at the thumbnail of his free hand. This prompted curious looks from the remaining three helper drones standing patiently on the platform, waiting for the transportation shuttle to arrive. The ongoing battle for technical control of the complex had ebbed and flowed for over an hour and for the time being, Stan's experience and institution had managed to thwart Philip's bodyguards gaining access to the control room. The main reason for his success was that on a regular basis, Stan initiated security sweeps of the entire system, constantly removing any trace of Philip's interference.

One failure however, was control of the transportation network, leaving his friend stranded. Ted could see the shuttle about a hundred yards away inside a tunnel and it would suddenly come to life and head his way, then suddenly it would stop and the internal lights would extinguish as the power ceased. Frustrated by the lack of progress, Ted was on the verge of setting off on foot when the shuttle once again illuminated and an accompanying message from Stan informed him that control was finally his and it was safe to board.

"Right you three; I want you all to refer to me as Ted, and to avoid confusion, I'm going to give you each a name that will be yours to respond to when I give an order. Do you understand?"

All three drones nodded in unison and listened attentively for Ted to issue them with a name.

"Right I've got it; you're Jack, you're Charlie and you're Mandy. Sorry the last one is a girl's name, but there're of my two nephews and niece. It's all I can think of right now and someone had to draw the short straw."

Apart from repeating their given titles out loud as Ted pointed to each one in turn, the three drones showed little reaction to their new monikers, and also Ted's necessity to explain how his sister had given birth to triplets following years of fertility treatment. With formalities complete they all boarded the waiting shuttle. Allowing his left hand to be scanned on the shuttle's wall-mounted device, it gave Ted clearance to access the most exclusive living quarters of the complex, nicknamed *'White collar Manor'* by Gemma. This is where Philip lived as well as worked, and where Ted was sure he would be found.

Using the touch screen interface, Ted tapped in the desired destination, sat down with the three drones as the pod doors closed, and the shuttle moved swiftly away. Ted smiled inwardly at the bizarre sight of himself and three helper droids, who with a childlike innocence were oblivious to the seriousness of the situation and sat calmly staring ahead and occasionally glancing in Ted's direction, eager and ready to receive further instruction. Uninterrupted, the journey along the main looped service line from the central plaza to Philip's front door usually takes five minutes, and as Ted nervously checked and rechecked his gun to pass the time, he realised that several minutes had already elapsed and the pod did not appear to be decelerating as it approached the stop. In fact the opposite seemed to be happening and the pod continued to pick up speed. Ted stood up and studied the interactive map on the pod wall that gave constant updates of speed and location, only to find that they were already well beyond the chosen destination; with no sign of stopping. Calling via the emergency intercom, Ted spoke to Stan immediately.

"Talk to me Stan, what's going on?"

There was a slight delay before Stan replied and all Ted could hear was the high pitched whine of a drilling sound coming down the phone.

"Sorry about that, but at the moment I appear to have visitors, Philip's two henchmen to be precise. They are very determined to get into the command booth and stop me from helping you with your quest."

Ted swallowed hard at the information. He had no intention of putting anyone else in danger apart from himself, and that included Stan.

"I have no idea what's going on buddy, but's too dangerous for you to be in there so get yourself out now!" Ted ordered, but Stan did not reply, as he was too busy trying to stop the shuttle from hurtling completely off the rails.

"Stan, Stan, I don't know if you can hear me, but do not put your life in danger, please get out."

Stan continued to ignore his friend as he was too caught up in a battle that he initially thought to have had control, but Philip determinedly refused to give in.

Following several failed attempts to gain access to the command booth, the two bodyguards had now acquired an industrial sized drill that they were using to bore holes through the security locks in the outer door. Putting Ted on speaker, Stan attempted to talk and type at the same time but it was no use.

"I'm sorry Ted but it's too late to get out, I'm trapped in here so I might as well be useful. Anyway, these doors are bomb proof, there's no way anyone can get in here without my permission, so stop worrying."

Stan's bravado far outweighed his confidence as he glanced over his shoulder to see slivers of twisted metal fall to the floor as the diamond tipped drill-bit wormed its way through the first lock at the top of the door, then retreat to recommence on the lock in the middle.

"If there's anything I can do from this end let me know."

Ted added, feeling completely impotent as the shuttle hurled faster and faster around the looped circuit. All he could do was listen to the teeth-jarring whine of the drilling, masking the rapid key taps of Stan in his life threatening battle.

It was at this point that the bodyguards drilled through the second lock and in the welcome silence that followed, Stan managed to hone his concentration bringing him to the point of victory. What he did not see was the android half of the two bodyguards, kneeling down and peering through the second hole directly at the back of Stan's head, when an idea came to mind. Built into his left hand was a little gizmo invention of Philip's that gave him personal satisfaction when attending functions with his bodyguards where weapons were not permitted. Built inside the index finger of the android, was a small yet powerful gas cylinder that looked like any other servo unit built into the robot when examined by x-ray. Attached to the front of the cylinder, Philip had installed a narrow bore steel tube the length of the first metacarpal bone. Should the necessity arrive, the android can swiftly snap off the tip of the finger and fire a series of steel ball bearings at almost the same velocity as any common handgun, with the same deadly result. With this in mind, the android carefully aligned the now open end of the barrel with the hole in the door and activated the bright red laser pointer from the built-in diode allowing pinpoint accuracy when aiming the gun. Guided by the sight of other bodyguard peering through the first hole drilled in the top of the door, the android traced the red dot along the floor, up the back of a chair and stopped directly on the back of Stan's head. Without warning or even having to pull a trigger, the mechanical assassin released the pressurised gas and fired the deadly cargo.

"Hold tight Ted, this may be a little violent, but I'm about to cut the power."

They were the last words Stan uttered before the high velocity projectile smashed through the base of his skull, severed the top of the spinal column and bounced around the inside of his cranium, killing him instantly and leaving his limp body slumped over the main console. Ted began to panic from the sudden lack of response from Stan and fired numerous questions down the intercom.

"Stan what happened? Stan, are you alright? Can you hear me, ***Staaan?"*** Ted screamed for an answer for several seconds, praying that Stan was alright and maybe it was just a communication failure. Unable to do anything else he now had to put his own precarious state to the top of the agenda and hope to get to Stan before anything untoward happened to his friend.

Inside the shuttle pod, Ted first tried to force open the sliding doors hoping to activate the emergency braking system but it was hydraulically sealed shut. Watching curiously from his seat, the drone Ted christened Mandy, suddenly stood up to offer its assistance.

"Excuse me sir, but you will find that the doors on this transport system are impossible to open while the shuttle is in motion. If you wish is to stop the vehicle, there is an emergency isolation switch located under a flap outside the rear window. It is designed to protect occupants from danger of electrocution. I believe this will cut the power and bring the vehicle to a halt immediately."

Mandy had hardly finished talking when Ted pushed the two remaining drones aside, stood on the rear seat, kicked out the clear Perspex panel from its rubber edged mount, and watched it bounce away along the tracks into the darkness. This was quickly forgotten as the screaming rush of air almost burst Ted's eardrums from the sudden pressure change in the former insulated comfort of the shuttle. The inside of the pod now sounded like a jet engine ready for take-off. Swallowing hard to ease the pain, Ted leaned out through the now open window and peered into the semi-darkness looking for the cover of the switch. Shouting over the deafening rush of the passing air flow, Ted instructed the three drones to hold onto his legs while he leaned further out in an increasingly desperate attempt to halt the runaway pod. Luckily there were few bends in the track that slowed things down, but they soon passed and the speed increased as they reached the long gradual sweep around in a full circle and flashed by their starting point yet again. But it was no use, the pain from the old injury to Ted's knee made it impossible to lean out far enough and he ordered the drones to pull him in.

"Do you know what to do if you are lowered over the side?"

Ted asked Mandy; following its affirmative reply, Ted wasted little time in lowering the surprisingly lightweight android out through the back window. Holding the robot in place was another matter, as the rushing wind flow battered Mandy from side to side as it attempted to reach for the switch. To his horror the buffeting became increasingly violent and before he could pull the drone inside, it swung heavily into the tunnel wall, tearing away its forearm from the elbow joint accompanied by a shower of sparks coming from what remained of the twisted metal protruding from the shoulder. Finally managing to pull the drone back into the shuttle pod Ted questioned an unemotional looking Mandy if it was alright and could he do anything to help.

"I feel no pain sir, and I am still fully operational with my remaining limbs." Mandy replied while already being inspected by the other two drones and patched up as best they could. Feeling a little sheepish, Ted quickly selected Jack, and with the help of the other androids, they lowered him carefully over the side. The linear motors powering the shuttle were already starting to overheat producing a plume of thick black smoke from underneath the pod. This hampered the information supplied to the visual cortex of the drone's artificial brain and it grasped blindly about. The delay lasted for three-quarters of a circuit, until Jack finally located the small plastic flap covering the isolation switch. With this easily opened, it pulled the red emergency stop handle, cutting the power and throwing its occupants onto the front seat as the shuttle rapidly decelerated to a complete stop. Jack was still hanging out through the rear window until Ted dragged the soot covered drone back into the cab. He watched with fascination how Jack unscrewed the lens from each eye socket, licked the dirty surface clean with an extremely realistic looking tongue, before replacing the now clear object back into its optical housing, restoring vision.

Now the shuttle pod was stationary, Ted finally managed to force open the sliding doors and avoiding stepping onto the live rails, the rag tag gang set off along the dimly lit tunnel towards the nearest station. Unfortunately for Ted, he no longer had Stan's assistance and Philip was slowly gaining control of the complex, although still playing in Ted's favour was the fact that Stan had locked Philip out of some of the systems and until access could be made directly into the control booth, Ted and the three drones could continue unobserved and relatively unhindered.

CHAPTER THIRTY-EIGHT

"I'm still waiting! How long are you imbeciles going to be?" Philip berated the human half of his bodyguard duo as they were still having trouble gaining access to the control room. Philip believed that he always had complete control of the system from his own private office, but this was not the case. Over the years, Stan had become increasingly concerned with Philip's behaviour and had taken it upon himself to place several Trojan programs throughout the entire computer network, that when implemented, isolated complete command to his desk. Even though he now lay dead with his body slumped over the controls Stan still held the upper hand over Philip.

"It's taking much longer than we anticipated sir. Even though all the security locks have been drilled out, several additional sliding bolts are still in place. My best guess is at least another half an hour, maybe more."

The bodyguard flinched as he ended the sentence, waiting for the barrage of abuse to come his way, but Philip's attention was taken by the fact that his visual interface displaying Ted's shuttle, showed it to have stopped midway between stations.

"Let me know as soon as you are in." Then abruptly ended the call and returned to the job in hand. One of the few systems that Philip still maintained complete control was the transportation system, and as the shuttle carrying Ted was now at a complete standstill, it was obvious that somehow he had managed to stop the pod and escape. Quickly displaying a three-dimensional map of the entire complex, Philip calculated the most probable route Ted would take and instigated the remainder of his private robot army to go out and stop him. These were the most advanced robots ever created and it was his last throw of the dice. Philip did not care whether Ted lived or died, as long as he gleaned enough time to complete his master plan.

CHAPTER THIRTY-NINE

Helping one another to climb up onto the deserted platform, Ted and his three android helpers found themselves at the guest entrance to the indoor film production stages, leaving them not too far from Philip's private residence. A clever short cut through a couple more film sets and Ted would soon become face to face with his new nemesis.

The mass evacuation protocol had ensured enough light was available to navigate through the vast complex, but the limited illumination from the security lights casting ugly shadows across the film studios, did nothing to ease Ted's fear and trepidation. Even though the majority of the latest film backgrounds were computer generated, there were still many lower budget productions using real sets. This particular middle-age market scene, set in the shadow of an imposing grey stone castle, contained several traditional stalls, and their associated wares. To save time and preserve continuity between takes, the android extras employed as merchants and townsfolk were powered down in situ, and now dozens of mannequins stood or sat silently, ready to continue from the same position on the next day of filming.

As the small group snaked their way through the market square, Ted had a feeling that something was wrong. He had already guessed where the first batch of robots had come from and it was only a small mental leap to assume that the more advanced models were probably already on the way. Reaching the exact centre of the film set, a gust of wind fluttered the scalloped edge fabric of a stall's rain awning when a security door somewhere at the back of the studio opened wide and then slammed shut, producing a deafening echo across the site. Suddenly the entire market place came to life, conscripting Ted and his three robot companions as unwilling cast members to this medieval set. Ted began fighting his way through the milling crowd, looking for a way out, only to find that he had been separated from the others and stumbled into the path of the latest batch from Philip's robotic army. This new group were all mid to high-generation models and wore matching black boiler suits with identifying numbers printed across their shoulders. These additions to Philip's family were the best examples to be found anywhere, all with lifelike features and realistic looking skin, that from a distance made them hard to distinguish from a real human. The thing that separated these models was a perfect human gait, accompanied by fluidity of movement that was still difficult to conquer. But it mattered little at the moment as they advanced en masse at Ted.

In all the best action movies where the hero is surrounded by the bad guys, they always seem to take turns and attack one at a time, but this was not the case. Unluckily for Ted, the five swiftest robots closed in trying to grab hold of any part of his body, ready to crush his flesh or tear him apart. Luckily Ted was still a little more agile, and for a time, a sinister game of tag ensued.

"Jack, Charlie, Mandy; if you can hear me, I could really do with some help right now." Ted yelled in-between tripping up one robot and giving another a swift clout around the back of the head with a cooking pot snatched hastily from one of the market stalls. Even though he had a gun, Ted was reluctant to waste any bullets unnecessarily as he knew that the showdown with Philip would require everything his personal arsenal possessed. That was if he made it that far as these robots were nothing like the older models encountered on highway seven, and required more than being pushed over to put them out of action. Luckily for him the maze of stalls and extra numbers of drones programmed just to mill about, helped to separate the gang members, allowing Ted a more even fight, and using a carthorse as cover, he crept up behind one of the slowest in the gang ready to strike. Using his acquired knowledge of robot anatomy, Ted knew that the most vulnerable part of this level of humanoid model was the back of the neck. This is where the largest range of head movement is required and it exposes some of the internal wiring exposed to damage, even when hidden under synthetic skin. Aiming to use this to his advantage he grabbed an imitation arrow from a quiver hanging next to a hunter's tent and from behind, plunged the sharp tip into the soft area next to the android's spinal column. In an instant the robotic motor skills failed and it collapsed heavily onto the floor, flailing its arms and legs around randomly as its system short circuited. Ted was satisfied that the unit was now completely out of action and did not want to wait around to see the remainder of the performance, so he disappeared back into the crowd ready to choose another victim. Behind an auction stage where a few village whores were touting their wares, Ted spotted another and was ready to advance when from behind a powerful hand grabbed the collar of his jacket, lifting him clean off the floor.

"Get off me, you metal ape." He yelled while trying to unzip the jacket front and slip his arms from the sleeves in an attempt to escape. Before he had a chance to do anything the robot reached out with its free hand and tried to clamp it around Ted's throat. With extremely limited movement due to his own weight being suspended in the arms of his clothing, Ted could only feebly block and parry before the inevitable happened and the android's cold synthetic fingers clamped around his neck. Within seconds Ted's vision began to fill with black spots and all focus blurred into darkness. Slowly but surely the metallic hand tightened, painfully blocking off the blood supply to Ted's brain. With the little strength that he had left, Ted kicked his legs into the robot's rigid torso, but it was like kicking the side of a rubber dingy and his foot rebounded, inflicting minimal damage. Now completely unable to move and breathing becoming impossible, Ted's world faded to black.

The darkness cleared and Ted bizarrely found himself dressed as an England footballer. He was playing on the right wing in an international match against Brazil. Booming loudly from the stadium tannoy system, the voice of Philip Sanderson commentated on the play.

'I'm sure you will agree viewers that this is a thrilling conclusion to the inaugural final of the cybernetic world football tournament. It has been a fascinating event and it sets a benchmark for future competitions for all artificially enhanced humans. I for one look forward to the world's sports forum this summer.

Victory for either side sits on a knife edge as play resumes near the end of a thrilling match. England have a free kick near the halfway line, and it's a long ball to Ted Langton. As usual, he begins a flying run down the right, pursued by two of South America's finest, but they are left trailing in his wake as he jinks left and right heading directly for Brazil's penalty box. With only seconds left on the clock and the game tied at two goals apiece, both England goals scored by Langton, this must be the final attack of the game before it goes to the dreaded penalties. Could we all be witnessing history in the making and hopefully see the first Englishman to score a cup final hat-trick on foreign soil? With only one defender to beat, Langton drops his shoulder feigning a move to the left and dodges to the right. The Brazilian captain slips and falls flat on his backside in confusion. A hundred thousand people are now on their feet as Langton hoofs the ball high into the sky over the fast approaching goalkeeper, who in his desperate attempt to stop him, crashes heavily into Langton's leg. The whole stadium is now holding its breath as the golden ball arcs magnificently through the air, lands squarely on the touchline and bounces into the back of the net. The ref blows his whistle and Langton wins the match for England.

The scenes inside the stadium are totally unbelievable as the crowd roars to a deafening crescendo, but instead of jumping up to celebrate his goal, Ted Langton is left clutching his leg and rolling about on the floor. The crowd gasps as the cameras zoom in to his damaged kneecap, custom made by the boffins at the Hologram Dreams Corporation. It has torn through his skin, revealing the bionic components hidden within. The android referee approaches, kneels down, and cradles Ted Langton's shoulders as he waits for the robot medic to arrive, but everyone knows that Langton's career is over viewers, his lower leg has now fallen off and lies twitching on the ground. I don't believe it football fans, the floodlights have just failed and the stadium is in complete darkness, but the crowd still politely cheers his name, Mis-ter Ted, Mis-ter Ted, Mis-ter Ted…'

"Mr Ted, Mr Ted, are you alright?"

Ted awoke from his bizarre dream to find himself lying on the straw and dirt ground of the marketplace with his upper half cradled in the arms of the helper droid Mandy. Trying to breath in, ready to speak, Ted choked on his own spittle, lodged in his now swollen throat. With the tenderness of a nursing mother, the droid sat him up and gently patted Ted on his back until the convulsion stopped.

"What happened?" Ted finally managed to whisper hoarsely, massaging his neck until the pain subsided.

"You were attacked by another droid Mr Ted, and that is forbidden in our programming. Myself and the other two droids have disabled the rogue unit and also all the other units in the immediate vicinity who intend you harm."

Ted looked about him to see pieces of robotic limbs and torsos showered all across the main square and the other two drones standing waiting patiently at his side. Apart from the droid who ended up filthy from stopping the runaway shuttle, the helper droids seemed none the worse for wear.

"Remind me never to piss off any of you guys." Ted whispered and tried to chuckle at his own joke, only to choke yet again on yet more spittle lodged in his swollen throat. The three droids, not understanding Ted's black humour, helped him to his feet. Limping from the pain inflicted on his already damaged knee, Ted worked his way through the now once again eerily static crowd as he headed for the exit door.

CHAPTER FORTY

Philip Sanderson wrung his hands together over and over as he paced the floor in front of his desk. He had finally completed the installation of his latest acquisition and with little else to do, he waited impatiently for his men to access the control hub. He had done everything he could possibly think of to gain control and shut down the entire complex, but Stan's hidden programs had thwarted nearly all of his efforts. Trying to steady his nerves, he crossed over to the drinks cabinet ready to pour himself a shot of malt whisky when he realised his faux pas and was about to set it down when at that precise moment the telephone rang. In his haste Philip dropped the bottle and several glugs of single malt spilled out over the front of the cabinet and ran onto the floor. Anxious at the sound of the telephone ringing in his ears, making his hands shake, he clumsily snatched repeatedly at the bottle's neck as it spun around filling the silver drinks tray in the clear coppery liquid. Finally, with the bottle retrieved and upright, Philip wiped his sticky hands down the front of his trousers as he crossed the room to answer the phone.

"This had better be good news or you are going to be very sorry." Philip snapped before he identified who was on the other end of the line.

"I don't know who you think this is Philip, but it's me Ted."

Philip was stunned and he had to support himself against his desk as the room began to spin. He could not believe that his old friend and now adversary was still alive after all that he had thrown at him and now had the gall to call directly on the phone.

"Philip, are you still there, it's Ted, can you hear me?"

Philip tried to speak, but he seemed to have lost communication with his mouth. Ted was on the verge of ending the call, guessing that he was being ignored on purpose, when Philip finally found his voice.

"Wha', what do you want?" He whispered softly, but it was the best he could muster. Ted paused and swallowed hard before he replied.

"I am appealing to you as my best friend Philip. A man of your intelligence must know that there is no way out, so I'm giving you one last chance to give yourself up before anyone else gets hurt."

Philip remained silent as he listened to the comforting familiar tones. In the short time that everything had fallen apart and his only real friend had turned against him, he had felt alone and insecure without Ted's morale support. The thought of doing what was asked suddenly had great appeal. The fear of confronting Ted face to face scared him more than anything, and without full control over the complex, his greatest fear could actually happen. In Philip's twisted mind, the man who saved his life all those years ago had now somehow come to the rescue once again and would solve everything.

Sited in an emergency stairwell two floors directly under Philip's private suite, Ted pressed his mobile phone close to his ear and waited patiently on the other end of the line. To pass the time, he sat massaging his throat and flexing his constantly sore knee. The drone named Mandy kept watch on the corridor while Jack and Charlie split up and positioned themselves one flight up and one flight down on the stairs ready for any attack from other levels.

As Ted waited, he pictured the scene in his mind's eye, of Philip sitting at his desk, staring blankly into space with his hands placed as if in prayer with fingertips pressing under his chin as he cogitated over a problem. This was a familiar scene that Ted had become used to over the years, and he found the only way to a definitive answer was to wait. Philip was just about to agree with Ted and give himself in when a call came in on the other line. Recognising the caller identification jolted him away from his current train of thought and Philip put Ted on hold while he answered the other line.

"What do you want now?" He yelled, losing whatever patience he had left for his imbecile bodyguard.

"Sorry to disturb you again, sir, but you did say to inform you immediately when we have gained entry to the command centre."

"Do you have definite access to the central control desk? Does it look operational?" Philip asked, his heart racing at the sudden change of events.

"Yes sir, There are lights and switches flashing all over it and all the monitors appear to be working. I can even see you standing in front of your desk."

Philip's immediate anger was lost on the irony of the situation as he frantically looked around trying to find the hidden camera that Stan had obviously installed to keep an eye on his boss. Philip always believed that he had sole control of the equipment in his office, but once again Stan was one step ahead.

"Clear away the body and don't touch anything." Philip instructed before abruptly ending the call. Feeling vulnerable at the thought of what Stan may have witnessed when he thought he was alone, and the possibility that there may be recordings that others could view, cleared the conflict in his mind. Now with total control of the complex he knew that he could seal himself off indefinitely from the world outside and nothing short of a nuclear strike could remove him from this one time cold war underground facility.

"Philip, are you still there?" Ted finally asked as the pain in his damaged knee wore his patience thin. A soft click on the other end of the line signalled a voiceless end to the call. Ted closed his eyes and hung his head, realising that he had no other option but to do what was necessary, putting an end to this nightmare.

CHAPTER FORTY-ONE

Gathering up every piece of necessary equipment he could carry, Philip Sanderson headed off down the short glass walled aquarium corridor to the private shuttle pod station outside his front door. Luckily the shuttle transport was one of the few systems of which he had total control, and within a few minutes he was exiting his own personalised pod that brought him swiftly to the command centre.

"You get the rest of my things from the shuttle, and *you* find me a chair that isn't covered in blood." Philip instructed his two bodyguards after quickly surveying the damage to the control room door before hurrying into Stan's booth. He immediately initialised the lockdown sequence for the entire complex, sealing every conceivable entrance from attack.

Sitting bolt upright in a new chair that had been acquired from an adjoining office, Philip began the painstaking task of rebooting all the surveillance cameras in an attempt to find Ted Langton.

"Both of you stand guard outside the door and don't disturb me while I sort out this mess; do you understand?" Philip snapped the two guards who obediently cleared the room and waited on the platform next to Philip's private shuttle pod. With the speed of thought and dexterity of finger work only a genius such as Philip possessed, he soon had all of the hundreds of operational surveillance cameras up and working, leaving him the much more mundane task of scanning the bank of video screens for signs of Ted, when something else of equal interest caught his eye. Without removing his fascinated gaze from the screen, Philip shouted his latest order.

"One of you get back in here, there is another job to be done."

CHAPTER FORTY-TWO

With a heavy heart and tired mind, Ted called in the three helper drones and limped his weary way up the flights of stairs leading directly to Philip's private quarters. To his surprise, he found the metal security door already open and after a tentative peek down the illuminated aquarium corridor, it revealed that the heavy wooden inner door was also ajar, allowing Ted a direct view into Philip's den. Fearing a trap, Ted ordered the robot Charlie, to venture into the inner sanctum and reconnoitre the situation before allowing himself and the two other helper drones to enter the room. Expecting a long wait, Ted settled himself down on the edge of the platform near the outer door and hung his weary legs over the short drop to the rails that accommodated the transport shuttles. Pained and despondent, Ted rested his chin on his chest and screwed his eyes tightly shut, trying to reconcile how his near perfect world had turned on its head and that he now hunted his former best friend, ready to kill him if necessary. Images of the last few days flashed repeatedly through his troubled mind until suddenly he felt the cold hard grip of a hand on his shoulder. Jolted violently from his waking nightmare, Ted lashed out from the unexpected attack and rolled away ready to defend himself from whatever was to come next, only to see Charlie jump backwards out of reach with a very human expression of surprise on his face.

"Sorry about that Charlie boy, you caught me off guard for a minute. What did you find?"

Feeling a little embarrassed, Ted staggered clumsily to his feet and shunning any offers of help, brushed away imaginary dirt from his trousers. The droid had already regained his usual programmed composure to report that nothing appeared to be out of the ordinary and that it was safe to enter. Leading the way, Charlie ventured back into Philip's office, with Ted following behind, and the two remaining drones standing guard at the outer door. To Ted's disappointment there was no sign of Philip, and apart from what appeared to be a drinks tray full of glasses sitting in a puddle of expensive whisky, there was little else of interest. This left only one other place that Philip could be, and that was the control room. Philip was already watching via the security camera feed and decided to make contact. Sending a signal to his projection desk it suddenly lit up and Philip's gaunt image rose up from the glass surface, looked directly at Ted, and began to speak.

"You're running out of time and luck Ted. I have gained access to the command centre and now have full control of the facility. It's a pity Stan had to die because he could have been very useful in the months ahead. But at least you're still here. The complex is now completely locked down and nothing can get in or out. There are enough food supplies for over a hundred years, so why not give up now and we can grow old together."

Ted stared open mouthed at Philip's brief speech. The confirmation of Stan's death reported so nonchalantly by Philip took him to a level of anger he did not know he possessed. In a blind fury, Ted grabbed hold of the nearest thing to hand, which happened to be an ornate brass paperweight from a side table, and hurled it at Philip's head. The object flew harmlessly through the flickering image, causing only a slight tremor in the projection before it crashed noisily into a full sized antique suit of armour decorating the far wall behind the desk. As Philip could see every movement Ted made, he instinctively tried to dodge the projectile, but having a complete lack of athletic skill, the object still managed to pass through the left hand side of his forehead.

"Nothing's going to stop me Philip; I'm coming to get you!" Ted roared with all his might, as he turned to head back towards the shuttle pod.

"Perhaps you will change your mind when you see this."

Ted stopped in his tracks and turned to see Philip's image replaced with that of Gemma Cassidy being dragged across the living room of Ted's quarters by the android half of Philip's bodyguard duo.

"I think Ted that you will do whatever I say from now on. Unless of course you like to hear the sound of Miss Cassidy's screams as she is dismembered by my personal assistant. What I want from you is to meet me in the control room immediately."

Philip's voice ceased, but the image of Gemma being dragged across the room remained. Ted stared incredulously for just a few seconds, then he turned and ran as quickly as his damaged knee could carry him towards the shuttle. Accompanied by his three android helpers, he boarded the pod and set off.

CHAPTER FORTY-THREE

The tranquilliser Ted had administered to Gemma was nowhere as potent as he thought, and as the helper droid waited patiently with its human cargo, just outside the north entrance, Gemma woke up. She carefully undid the security straps holding her in place and was just about to make a move when Philip initiated a complete base lockdown. At every entrance to the complex, massive hydraulic rams screamed under their intense workload as they began to raise the reinforced concrete blast shields out of the ground and into position. Camouflaged by the noise and vibration, she rolled stiffly from the back seat of the buggy and dived back over the rising concrete wall, securing herself inside the sealed base before the droid realised she was gone. Facing a long painful walk back to the main hub and then on to Ted's apartment, her idea was to contact him via his private line to let him know that his plan to remove her from the base had failed and she was back to help out.

* * *

"What the.... Get your filthy hands off me, you lumbering great oaf!" Gemma screamed at Philip's bodyguard when she was rudely awoken. Convinced it had only been a few minutes, but an hour had passed since she collapsed wearily onto Ted's sofa in an attempt to regain some strength. With her eyes closed, trying to gather her thoughts, the sedative in her system was still taking its toll and she had fallen asleep. With a solid grip on the collar of her jacket the android had jerked Gemma's sleeping body clear over the back of the sofa and allowed her to drop heavily onto the floor. Ignoring the barrage of insults, the android maintained its hold and unceremoniously dragged her backwards towards the entrance to Ted's apartment.

"I said, let me go!" Gemma snarled gritting her teeth in anger and pain. Suddenly fully wide awake, she managed to roll over and scramble ungainly to her feet. Embarrassed an angry, she channelled all her emotions ready for the fight. Wildly, punching and kicking out at her assailant was the initial attempt, but it had little effect. Her next reaction was to pull her damndest in the opposite direction, trying to slow the android's progress, but it was really no contest and it continued unhindered towards the door.

Suddenly deciding to change tack, Gemma stopped resisting and quickly threw all her weight towards her foe. Her impact managed to upset the android's internal gyroscope and it began to stagger forwards at an increasing rate. Gemma continued to push hard as the android tried to regain its balance, but it was too late. It all stopped with a sickening thud as three-hundred pounds of metal, fabric, and toughened polyurethane charged head first into Ted's cylinder shaped aquarium sited in the middle of the room. To Gemma's amazement the Perspex column cracked and a thick jet of salty water sprayed out, soaking into the suit of the robot as it lay face down on the floor. In the several seconds it took the android's system to reboot it released its grip, giving her more than enough time to run from the apartment, but instead she stood her ground. Realising that she had limited mobility, attack now seemed to be the best form of defence. Looking quickly around the room, she spied Ted's collection of prized samurai swords and hastily grabbed the nearest from a display against the wall. With her feet either side of the mechanical man, Gemma held the sword's hilt in both hands and stabbed the razor sharp tip of the Katana blade downwards through the soft part of the android's midriff, pinning the sword's tip, deep into the hardwood floor. Standing back, she watched fascinated as the robotic body twitched and convulsed from the damage at it tried to break free, but the sword held fast until the android lay still. Thinking that the fight was over, Gemma took another sword from the display and turned to head for the door, when suddenly the android came back to life. A system overload had forced a reboot and to Gemma's amazement she watched the robot's arms turn around in their shoulder sockets well beyond any human limitation until they had rotated 180 degrees and operated as easily around its back as it did at the front. The movement was considerably less fluid than before, but it still managed to clamp both hands around the blade and worry it free. But the to and fro motion widened the puncture wound, allowing even more water to run down into the abdominal cavity. Eventually the floor released its grip on the sword's tip and the robot re-aligned its arms and staggered drunkenly to its feet heading directly for Gemma. Bracing for the attack, she dropped back into the classic defensive stance, raised the blade to the horizontal, and waited. Still holding the Katana sword, the android circled around to block the exit, then began to advance.

Gemma screamed and prepared to make the first strike, but things did not proceed as expected. With the android standing upright, gravity allowed the water, already inside its body cavity to run down into several vital components, shorting out the circuits. Every internal servo affected within the complex automaton began to operate at once, making it twitch and vibrate like it was having an epileptic a fit. Simultaneously, it began to recite Philip's last command over and over with steadily increasing speed until all that could be heard was a high pitched whine as the mouth flapped open and closed. Fascinated by what she had done, Gemma lowered her sword and watched the system overload yet again, until a cracking sound came from within the chest region as the central processor failed and the android fell to the floor. Satisfied with the result, she stepped gingerly over the now defunct robotic man, and headed for the door.

CHAPTER FORTY-FOUR

Within minutes, Ted and his three companions arrived in the transportation pod outside the control room main entrance. Philip had allowed the shuttle to travel unaffected and he now eagerly awaited the arrival of Ted whom in his deranged mind still believed to be his friend.

The remaining armed bodyguard approached Ted as he cautiously emerged out onto the platform and conveyed orders from Philip of his insistence that the helper droids remain inside the shuttle. Reluctantly Ted agreed and with his gun handed over, he stood nervously on the brightly lit concourse. Without warning the pod doors closed and he turned to watch as it silently whisked his droid triplets away into the darkness of the nearest tunnel. Feeling very much alone, Ted limped painfully into the main hub of the control room to come face to face with the man he used to call his friend. Sickened to the core and gagging at the sight of Stan's blood decorating the floor and half of a subsidiary control desk, it took every fibre in Ted's being, not to launch himself at Philip's throat. Shaking with rage, he walked up as close to his ex-friend as the bodyguard would allow and said his piece.

"I'm here now so let Gemma go." Ted began while trying to hide the anger in his voice and hoping to sound as calm as possible so as not to upset Philip's disturbed mind. Philip took a deep breath and forced a rare, but insidious smile before giving his reply.

"Ted please don't be like that, we can still be friends. I'm sure that Miss Cassidy is being well taken care off and will be with us very soon. In the meantime, we need to discuss the future."

"There is no future for Hologram Dreams Philip. Don't you see it's over? Now when Gemma gets here you are going to let her go and I will do my best to protect you when the authorities arrive. Do we have a deal?"

Philip's smile continued and he shook his head like he was trying to reason with a recalcitrant child. The enormity of the situation still did not register in his unique brain.

"The whole place is locked down Ted, it is impervious to everyone. Nothing can get in or out. Don't you understand, you can never leave!"

Philip turned his back to continue with his operations at the control desk, leaving Ted still held at gunpoint. All he could do now was to sit and rest his knee while he waited for Gemma and the other bodyguard to arrive. Turning his chair slowly around, Ted scanned the room looking for a means of escape when he spotted the sharp end of one of his swords emerge from one side of the outer doorway followed by Gemma's hands gripping tightly to the hilt. Immediately Ted stood up to gain the bodyguard's attention, allowing Gemma to advance on the man who luckily had his back to the door.

"Keep your hands where I can see them! Now, nice and slow I want you to lower your weapon and pass it handle first to Ted." Gemma ordered the extremely tense guard as she placed the tip of the cold forged steel blade firmly into the nape of his neck. Philip stopped what he was doing and jumped up from his seat wondering where Gemma's voice was coming from, until he saw her much smaller frame emerge from behind the guard's imposing bulk when he reached out to pass over the gun. Before the weapon reached Ted's hand, Philip leaped out of his seat and made a grab for the pistol, only to knock it from the guard's grip and watch it slide out of harm's way under a cabinet across the far side of the room. Safe from immediate harm, Ted threw himself at Philip, who to his amazement dodged the move with the agility of a cat and made a run for the door. Gemma had already caught sight of Stan's body lying on the floor and in her anger the response was clinical. As Philip attempted to dash by, she took a high en guard stance and swung the blade in a decisive high mezzane strike, lopping Philip's head neatly from his shoulders in a single stroke. To everyone's amazement the remaining body continued unaffected and it ran through the outer door onto the concourse until it fell off the edge of the platform and into the rail track gully. This was followed by a puff of white smoke and the acrid smell of melting plastic as the body touched both rails simultaneously. Internal lights dimmed and surveillance screens faded for a few seconds as Ted, Gemma and the guard watched silently as the thick black smoke began to rise when combustible materials within the body started to ignite. Next they all turned back to stare at the severed head of Philip. Even after death, his eyes blinked and mouth continued to open and close as if it was trying to speak. The grotesque image was all the more bizarre as there was no blood pouring from the massive wound. Swallowing down an urge to vomit, Ted crossed to where the head lay, gingerly picked it up at arms-length, and then turned it over to reveal nothing more than neatly sliced circuits and wires bristling alongside a three dimensionally printed spinal column.

"Jesus Christ, he's an android." Gemma exclaimed, stating the obvious once more but feeling that something had to be said. Ted carefully placed the animated cranium on top of a control desk and stepped back as it began to blink rapidly and stare alternately from Ted to Gemma and back again as somewhere deep inside the complex Philip watched through the still operating visual cortex.

"Look, I don't quite know what's going on here, but I didn't think I was working for a robot." The guard blurted out as he switched his glances between Gemma holding the sword and the severed head blinking on the desk. Before there was time to answer, the guard turned and ran, almost sliding onto the tracks himself, as he turned the corner and headed for the stairs. With no heart for a pursuit they listened to the sound of the stairwell access door slam shut behind the confused man as he made his long run for freedom.

"Get rid of it Ted, it's creeping me out." Gemma announced and turned away. Ted gingerly picked up the head and carried it out onto the concourse where he dropped it over the edge onto the top of what remained of the rest of its smoking body.

Silent in shock and disbelief, Ted stared hard at the molten mess when he was hit by a sudden realisation and limped hurriedly back into the command hub to share his thoughts. Before he had chance he found Gemma down on her knees, sobbing next to Stan's dead body that had been dumped unceremoniously in the far corner of the room. Straightening out the already cold body of his friend, Ted removed his jacket and placed over Stan's head before helping Gemma to her feet.

"I don't care what it takes but Philip's going to pay for this if it's the last thing I do." Gemma growled as she allowed Ted to use his thumb to wipe away the streaks of mascara from her tear stained face. Kissing her tenderly on her forehead, Ted sat Gemma down ready to explain his idea.

"There's nothing we can do for Stan now, apart from focus on the job in hand and bring Philip to justice. As we have just witnessed, that wasn't Philip at all, but an incredibly realistic looking android. The thing is that no matter how complex these machines are, they cannot run with complete autonomy; Philip has to be holed up somewhere directing all of this."

Gemma looked nervously around wondering if she was still being watched.

"Do you think that Philip is still inside the complex?" She asked. Ted nodded silently as an idea formed and he turned to face the main console.

"Philip is definitely here, otherwise why would he lock the place down? There must be a massive power supply needed to connect remotely and provide his doppelgänger with enough information to interact convincingly with everyone and everything else around him. Pull up a map of the complex containing all the biggest electrical drains on the system and we will see where the most unusual power spike is coming from."

Gemma did as instructed and within seconds the entire bank of surveillance screens had been converted into a large scale map of the central zone. This contained the top fifty electrical power supply conduits in the complex.

"Right now let me see." Ted began, as he scanned the screens before him and pointed to the sites to disregard.

"That's heating, lighting, and air conditioning, so delete those; that one belongs to the transportation system so that's a no-no. The supply to the third quadrant belongs to guest accommodation and recreation. With everything else shut down following the evacuation, it leaves nothing of significant value worth investigating, except for this one. The power consumption is far in excess of the norm; Ha, I might have guessed, Philip's office."

Gemma retained hold of the sword and Ted retrieved the discarded pistol before they both boarded Philip's shuttle. He was very happy to find that it was still operational as the last thing he wanted now was another long walk with a very sore knee. Within five minutes he stood once again inside Philip Sanderson's private quarters.

"What are we looking for?" Gemma asked in a breathy stage whisper. It was the first time she had set foot in this room and had a feeling like she was standing in church or something equally sacred.

"I don't really know and I wish Stan was here with us, he'd have it sorted in no time." Ted replied as he searched for clues. Gemma only half listened to Ted's reply as she eagerly snooped around what was the most technologically sophisticated room on the planet. It was something she had dreamed about for years, and now given the opportunity she was not going to let go to waste. After five minutes of prodding and poking through some of the rarest artefacts known to man, Ted's comment about Stan continued to repeat inside her head.

"That's it! Stan can still help us. He once confided in me that he had placed hidden security cameras inside this office. He said that if the brown stuff ever hit the fan, he had recorded evidence of some of the bizarre things Philip was getting up to."

Ted immediately stopped what he was doing and turned to face Gemma.

"He had what? Why have you never told me this before?"

Gemma blushed and suddenly found her fingernails very interesting as she stalled while conjuring up suitable answer.

"Stan made me promise not to tell anyone and I always keep my promises." She replied followed by a pout and shy glance from under whatever mascara remained on her heavily made-up eyelashes. Ted's anger melted quickly away and sighing heavily, he posed with hands on hips while waiting for Gemma's explanation.

"Stanley told me that he had hidden a file on the system labelled Ellie or Elsie something like that."

"Do you mean Elsa?" Ted interrupted, suddenly latching on to something from Stan's past and Gemma's train of thought. Surprised that Ted knew the correct name, Gemma stared puzzled, but remained silent as he sat down behind Philip's touch screen desk and tapped out a system wide search request via the visual interface displayed on the brightly lit surface. As they waited for the program to sift through the exbibytes of information stored in the vast underground server rooms, Ted explained how he knew.

"I have had the honour to be a friend and colleague of Stan for many years. He was always a private man, but on one drunken stag night, he told me of the time when he was in the army and was unfortunate to be on the receiving end of a roadside terrorist bomb. It blew him twenty feet through the air and shattered both legs below the knee. With the damage to my own knee, we formed an even closer kinship. The army did its best for him of course and when fully recovered, he was the recipient of a pair of the best bionic legs money could buy."

"Nice story Ted, but where does Elsa fit into all of this?" Gemma cut in then wished she had not as Ted scowled at the interruption.

"I was just coming to that if you'd just wait. Anyway, where was I, oh yes Elsa; in-between the bomb blast and his new legs, there was a great deal of care and rehabilitation, dealing with Stan's mental health as well as his physical. To keep a continuity of care, a single nurse is put in charge of each individual case, staying the course from start to finish. The one assigned to care for Stan was a pretty young woman called Elsa. As is fairly common in such cases, Stan misinterpreted Elsa's caring manner for affection and soon developed an emotional bond, eventually falling in love. When the treatment came to an end and his life was back on track, Stan asked her to marry him only to be shattered emotionally again when she turned him down. It was nearly a year and several drunken episodes later before he recovered from the rebuttal, but he never forgot the care she gave him and a hope that she would one day change her mind."

"You sound like the afternoon movie for bored housewives." Gemma quipped, trying to hide the fact that her eyes were again welling up with tears and threatening to spill down her pretty face. Ted did his best to avoid eye contact and concentrated instead on staring at the progress bar as it grew steadily across the screen. Eventually a secure file appeared and when prompted for the password, Ted shamefully had to admit that he knew what it was after he watched Stan many years ago working at his desk in the hub. Praying silently that Stan had not bothered to change it, Ted typed in the eight-figure code and waited. To his relief the file opened and over fifty film clips listed within. The only thing to do now was to sit back and watch each one in turn; hoping that one of them would cast light on Philip's whereabouts.

It was obvious from the beginning that Stan had viewed and saved only the videos that he considered important, including meetings with a selection of famous and infamous clientele. Ted quickly dismissed anything with similar content and it was not too long before they were down to the last half dozen candidates. The first showed Philip opening the door of a large black safe that Ted was surprised to see rise up from the floor from under the coffee table sited in the middle of the room. It was a sight he had never seen before and was hurt, but not at all surprised that Philip had never allowed him to see it in his presence. The angle of the hidden cameras did not allow any view directly into the giant safe, so when Philip stepped inside it was impossible to see what he was doing and that troubled Ted.

"There can only be so many things that someone can do in there and Philip is taking a very long time doing it." He said, voicing his thoughts out loud, not really wanting an answer as he touched the fast forward icon and the video whizzed through at twenty-five times normal speed until Philip re-emerged and appeared to be drying his hair with a towel. Amid the silence of wide-eyed astonishment, Gemma spoke first.

"Unless he's had a shower installed, there's more to this metal box than meets the eye. Rewind back to just before it rises from the floor and let's see how he does it."

Ted did as instructed and they both stared intently at Philip's actions until several runs through later, Gemma spotted a deliberate unnatural movement of his left hand. Verbally calling a pause to the playback, she reached her open hand into the scene distorting the shimmering image as it interfered with the projection. Closing her fist at the required locale, Gemma appeared to grab part of the illusion then slowly withdrew her hand. This action enlarged the image of the edge of the desk into a clearer more well-defined view. Not satisfied with the aspect, Gemma rotated her hand at the wrist and the projection reciprocated the movement until the underneath of the left hand side of the desk became more visible. It was now clear that half way along the underside, Philip had purposely placed his index finger into a small indentation sited underneath the glass topped ridge, With his opposing thumb placed directly above, sandwiching the sensory glass in-between. With his right hand, a simple double finger tap of a desktop icon that looked like a blue star, elevated the safe upwards from the floor and into the room. Eager to try it out, Ted terminated the playback and then duplicated Philip's actions exactly. To his amazement, the coffee table in the centre of the room raised skywards on top of a battleship grey, hardened steel box complete with a full sized doorway at the front.

"They say if you live long enough, you'll see everything." He quipped nervously as they both stood facing the seven foot high metal box. The only thing missing was a handle and numbered dial that usually operated the locking mechanism of this type of device, but this was devoid of both. Fearful of activating an alarm or triggering an electric shock for his interference, Ted carefully reached out and gently pushed against the door with the toe end of his shoe. To their surprise, there was a soft click and the door swung wide open. Cautiously looking inside, all they could see was a flight of stairs leading down to what appeared to be a large well illuminated room at the bottom. Gemma stepped forwards ready to descend, but Ted blocked her path ready to take the lead.

"Age before beauty in this case I think!" He announced, encouraging Gemma to stay behind him as he released his pistol from its holster, raised it in both hands to chest height and took his first step, ready to face whatever lay at the bottom of the stairs.

"You are both perfectly safe, I mean you no harm." Philip's voice boomed loudly from somewhere down below. Ted subconsciously tightened his grip around the pistol, swallowed hard, and with his heart pounding, he cautiously descended the short flight. They both stepped out at the bottom into what appeared to be a well illuminated, white walled animatronic construction room identical to many dotted about the main complex, however this one was slightly different. The far wall appeared to be made of toughened glass or Perspex and it was impossible to see what lay beyond. In the standard workshop, robotic body parts are repaired when possible, and only assembled as and when required. This keeps costs down, improving company profits. This usually would leave the workshops fairly sparse of spares, but this room contained enough pieces of hi-tech hardware to construct at least eight or more fully functioning human replicas. Identical, arms, legs, and pale-skinned male torsos adorned the walls jostling with every other conceivable humanoid body part except for heads, that were obvious in their absence. Gemma stood close to Ted's side and jumped physically as Philip's voice boomed even louder inside the confines of the room.

"If I wanted you dead I could have killed you both as you rifled through my office. Now put your gun away Ted and we can talk." Philip's bodiless voice announced. Ted ignored the request and continued to scout around, finally attempting to peer through a wall of glass into the darkness of what appeared to be another room.

"If it makes you feel more secure you can keep your little toy, but once again, I can assure that you are perfectly safe."

Ted ignored Philip, continuing to shield his eyes with his free hand and stared into the darkness of the second room as Philip spoke yet again.

"It is obvious that you have been clever enough to reach my inner sanctum, and I applaud you for that. But do you really want to know what comes next? Are you ready to step up and see what lies behind the curtain*? Are you really sure Ted? Can you ever be prepared for a view of immortality?"*

The pitch of Philip's voice became higher and more excitable as he reached the end of the sentence, adding to the tension and Ted stepped back, bumping into Gemma who had moved in for a closer look. As the lights suddenly dimmed, they both instinctively began to reverse towards the foot of the stairs when a single floodlight sited in the floor behind the glass wall, illuminated an object within a huge liquid filled tank. Their reaction was probably not what Philip wanted, as they both stood frozen to the spot in equal measures of complete shock and utter revulsion. Nearly a minute passed until Ted finally found a whispered voice.

"Jesus Christ Philip, what have you done?"

Suspended in the slightly green-tinted, but still fairly transparent solution was the semi-naked body of Philip Sanderson. Attached to his ankles, a pair of adjustable buckled straps connected to a length of chain, that in turn was secured to a large metal ring bolted him to the floor of the tank. This stopped him from floating up to the surface while allowing him to remain upright. The image portrayed before them was not too dissimilar to that of an organised crime execution, where unfortunate murder victims were often thrown into the sea with heavy weights or lumps of concrete attached to their feet. But it was here that the similarity ended; Philip was still alive. On his clean shaven head he wore a close fitting neural sensor skull cap complete with a wig of coloured optical fibres leading up through the water, transmitting brain signals directly to an interface sited somewhere outside the tank. He had flexible plastic tubing slid over and secured to the root of his penis, with another tube of similar dimensions inserted snugly into his anus, both presumably designed for the removal of waste products that could be clearly seen passing through the pipe walls and down through a drain hole sited in the floor. The final piece of medical equipment on show was a feeding tube that screwed onto a surgically manufactured cone shaped orifice bonded to his outer skin and passed directly through into Philip's stomach. Both Ted and Gemma continued to stare in wonder, trying to comprehend how a body could still be kept alive in such conditions with no visibly apparent aids, but they watched his chest steadily rise and fall apparently able to breathe underwater. Even though his mouth remained closed, Philip's voice boomed out again.

"Ted my friend; I am pleased that you are the first to bear witness to the next great leap forwards in the evolution of mankind. As you can see I am no longer restricted to the pathetic limitations of the human body as my entire existence is now experienced remotely via my neural interface. Using the power of my mind, I am able to control and receive sensory feedback from any number of my latest personal android facsimiles, all capable of achieving feats of strength and dexterity that previously mankind could only dream of."

Gemma gasped and stepped back when suddenly Philip's eyes opened and stared intently at the two of them. A second shock quickly followed when something large splashed into the water on the far side of the tank. The air bubbles created, quickly cleared to reveal what appeared to be a second Philip Sanderson in the water, although this one wore a red neoprene wet suit. Obviously this was another of Philip's androids identical to the one Gemma decapitated back in the control room.

The outlandish scene soon resembled a voyeuristic freak show as the android flittered around like a pilot fish carrying out its assigned cleaning regime and physically checking the many tubes and cables attached to Philip's body. Philip actually smiled, apparently enjoying the attention from his bizarre display, a rare event from such a normally dour faced man. As the maintenance continued, Philip's voice boomed out yet again.

"I am sure that you are both wondering how I am managing to breathe in such an environment so please let me explain. The water around me is not your usual run of the mill H_2O. This is a molecular engineered super saturated liquid, giving me the ability to breathe underwater like a fish, with my human lungs more than able to absorb all the increased levels of oxygenated molecules that my body requires. Also the android you see before you is identical to the one you have both already met, although this one is designed to function fully underwater. One of many I have produced to satisfy my every need and each one is so advanced it can build itself a replacement even better than the first."

The original quest to bring Philip to justice was temporarily sidetracked as both Ted and Gemma listened in stupefied amazement to the information until Ted finally came back to his senses.

"I don't care what you have achieved Philip but I am still going to bring you to justice for Stan's murder and probably for hundreds more so get out of the tank before I come in and get you."

The small underground room echoed to the throbbing resonance of Philip's laughter, and even the apparent lifeless body in the tank twitched in time to his mocking peals.

"I don't think you have a grasp on the enormity of the situation Ted. The man that has lived amongst you all for the last four years has actually been one of my android clones controlled by myself from this very tank. If you attempt to permanently remove me from my new environment I will die."

Furious and humiliated by Philip's laughter, Ted's response was swift and cold.

"I don't believe you, or even care what you have to say Philip, get out now or I'm coming in."

Even from the comparative safety of the fluid filled tank, Philip still feared Ted's anger, so he tried a different tack.

"Please listen to me Ted, I am offering you and Miss Cassidy the chance of immortality. We can live like Gods controlling a new evolutionary race to inhabit the earth, all from the safety of this underground dominion, completely sealed off from the rest of the world."

Trying to ignore the egotistic dissertation, Ted began to search the room for an exit and gain access to the tank. Philip immediately began to panic, swiftly escalating his delivery from intellectual reasoning into a full diatribe, deafening the occupants in the confines of the room.

"You still don't understand do you, the entire site is completely sealed off from the rest of humanity. I have already informed the world security network, after I battened down the hatches. They have been informed that the entire complex is booby-trapped and that any attempt to break in will result in considerable loss of life. Also that I have androids sited worldwide, patiently waiting for my command to release pressurised canisters of sarin gas in densely populated districts sited more than fifty cities dotted around the globe. I can assure you that the League of Nations will take years to decide on the most appropriate form of action and they will realise the folly of risking the lives of millions just to make the attempt to reach the three of us in here. We will all be left well alone."

Ted stopped for a second and stared hard at the bloated face of the man he used to call his friend. He could not decide if Philip was telling the truth or it was an elaborate bluff designed to keep him at bay, but he knew the world would not be held to ransom. Deeply mixed emotions of anger at Philip's blatant disregard for human life contrasted sharply with feelings of guilt at the numerous times he had witnessed the man's genius cause problems with almost all social interaction. Philip's condescending manor with people whom he regarded as intellectually inferior and the simple inability to distinguish the difference between the etiquette of polite conversation and the childlike rudeness of sometimes brutal, but honest truth, caused great animosity amongst work colleagues and clients alike, so it was with little wonder he frequently requested Ted to be by his side. He regretted not pushing Philip harder to seek psychological support as it might have saved them all from the dire situation they now faced.

"You can't change the past." Ted muttered to himself under his breath, hastily dismissing his oneirism and realising now was not a good time for sentiment. Turning away from the tank, Ted tried the handle to the door marking the only other exit to the room. As expected, it was locked, so he stepped back ready to kick it open. Realising that his threat was not going to work Philip changed tack.

"Ted, Ted please listen to me; I know you mean well, but this is a battle you cannot win. I still have two places remaining that can be taken up by you and Miss Cassidy; please Ted I wish you no harm."

Ted paused for a moment, and then turned to face Philip floating in the tank.

"What exactly do you mean two places left? Who else is with you on this?"

Philip fell silent and Ted wondered if his aggressive manner had pushed him too far. Fearful of some kind of violent reaction, Ted urged Gemma to move away from the glass and drew her near as he stared down Philip's gaze.

Suddenly, row by row, several banks of under-floor spotlights powered up, illuminating the previously impenetrable darkness at the rear of the tank. To Ted's and Gemma's horror each beam of light illuminated an adult human, restrained inside a three-quarter length straight jacket and swaying slowly in the tinted water. There were women as well as men, all with shaved heads and wearing a smaller skullcap containing only half as many neural connecting cables as the one Philip wore. Every poor soul appeared to be asleep or in some type of medically induced coma as their bodies floated lifelessly in the oxygen rich solution. Philip smiled and his voice resounded in triumph at the revelation.

"Behold, you are the first people to witness the new generation of humankind! On display before you are some of the finest minds in the world. World renowned scientists, mathematicians and even Noble prize winners from across the globe; I even added this one today. He has a fine intellect and is also a remarkable chess player. I anticipate a great challenge."

Sited just behind and to Philip's left, the restrained and near naked body of a young man looking considerably fresher than the rest, stared plaintively into space until his blue eyes blinked in the sharp light and he focused directly upon Gemma. She immediately recognised the face of Adam Cartwright, whose picture had been posted on all the media news feeds announcing the possible kidnap of this young genius and his group of friends during a yachting holiday in the Red Sea. This latest addition to the tank appeared to be very much awake even though he too wore the neural skull cap, but unlike the rest of the pitiful group had yet to be attached to feeding or bodily waste tubes floating at his side. With a direful gaze, he mouthed a silent plea for help from his watery hell. Unaware of this reaction, Philip continued with the macabre presentation.

"Each specimen is sedated and then introduced to their new habitat. Once the body has acclimatised, the neural interface is connected, allowing me complete access to their brain functions where I slowly reduce the body into a permanent comatose state. This collective hive mind controlled by me has an intellectual capacity beyond your wildest dreams, and with it I can control the world!"

Philip paused, expecting some kind of ecstatic reaction to his speech, but Ted and Gemma remained stunned into silence; undeterred, Philip continued.

"But that is not all, everything here does not have be so political and academic; companionship is also important and as I have stated, two places remain therefore I am giving you both the incredible opportunity to join us."

Immediately to Philips left, two more spotlights illuminated similar sets of apparel swaying lifelessly in the water; it was obvious that Philip had no intention of being alone. Aghast, Ted backed away from the glass trying to contain his revulsion. Gemma remained, transfixed by the sight of the young man mouthing his silent cry for help, until his spotlight turned off and he disappeared once more into the darkness.

Ted was already facing the assembly bench sited in the middle of the room. He was hoping that one of the buttons located on the adjacent control panel, operated the lock on the exit door allowing access to Philip. Unable to fathom the layout, he pressed buttons at random. To his surprise, one of the animatronic hands began to claw its way across the work surface and fell onto the floor. Unfazed, Ted pressed several buttons in an attempt to turn it off, only to activate three panels in the right hand wall, which slid down to reveal more than a dozen of Philip's android heads sitting on glass shelves behind. Some were complete facsimiles of Philip's image, others were hairless or still required a coating of synthetic skin. As one, they all opened their eyes and every pair stared directly at Ted and Gemma in the middle of the room. Gemma screamed and ran into Ted's arms, when everyone began to talk. Every word Philip spoke multiplied a dozen times, filling the small room with his maniacal chorus line.

Ted had had enough, moving away from Gemma, he took a few steps back and then launched himself at the locked wooden panelled door. To his relief the thin partition splintered and he sprawled full length into another stairwell. Philip finally lost his patience and angrily issued a final mandate.

"Ted this is your last warning; desist from your attempt or you will leave me no other choice."

If Ted did hear Philip's last words he showed no reaction as he picked himself up from amongst the pile of debris and began to climb the stairs. In retaliation at Ted's obstinacy, Philip initiated phase one of his threat.

The recently deceased Stanley Gibson believed that he knew every covert operation Philip happened to be involved with, but he could not be further from the truth. Apart from the worldwide people trafficking, slavery and murder, he also had no idea that Philip's ground breaking autonomy platform, hardwired into all of his robotic creations, included a remote override. This allowed Philip total control of every android his company created. Globally, every artificial operative now danced to Philip's tune, with the initial intention of mayhem.

At Philip's command, tens of thousands of robot actors, helpers, and even worker drones all around the world, suddenly behaved as if possessed; failing in any way to respond to verbal, or computer programmed command.

Across the globe, in response to the panic, every line manager, technical director, and supervising officer responsible for said drones supplied by the Hologram

Dreams Corporation, read with disbelief as they received the same emergency message.

'Red alert: this is not a drill: Major malfunction of every robot, android and autonomous system: Emergency shutdown protocol inactive: Assistance required immediately:'

While all hell broke loose, Philip initiated phase two. Amongst this vast robotic riot, one-hundred and fifty of the most lifelike and advanced androids appeared to remain unaffected, continuing with their duties as normal, thus completely invisible in the surrounding chaos. Each one of these adapted units contained a deadly payload that had been purposely shipped to a franchise in every major city across the world. Behaving normally, rendering them invisible in relation to their counterparts, the walking assassins ceased their designated task, and began a deadly journey towards a pre-programmed target, ready to release enough sarin gas in total, to kill over one-hundred million innocent souls.

At the top of the stairs, Ted reached a dead-end corridor with four unmarked doors leading off. Before he could open the one that he hoped would lead to the water tank, Gemma came running up behind him curiously holding the robotic forearm. In her haste to stay with Ted when they descended the stairs from Philip's office, she forgot to bring the samurai sword and was just going back to retrieve it when the sound of footsteps coming down the stairwell quickly changed her mind.

"We've got company, move!"

Ted did not need telling twice and they both bundled through the nearest door, hoping to hide from what they were sure was another remotely controlled android, only to come face to face with the neoprene clad maintenance droid from Philip's water tank. With the speed of a leopard, the robot launched into an attack, clamping its wet hands around Ted's throat faster than he had time to react. Gemma's immediate reaction was to use the artificial forearm as a club, but the effect was superficial. The strength of the unit was far too powerful, even for both of them, and Ted quickly sank to his knees as for the second time today his life force quickly faded. Using up what little energy he had left, he rolled onto his back hoping to flip the robot over his head, but the machine was much too heavy and he ended up pinned to the floor. Frantically looking around for another weapon, Gemma spotted a metal framed chair in the corner of the room. She took two steps towards it when the world appeared to shift on its axis. Almost floored by the sudden deafening noise, Gemma's ears pained to the close quarter crack of a gunshot. Dizzily, she looked back to see tiny fragments of metal, fabric, and plastic, spraying high into the air, and rain down like pieces of confetti. A bullet fired from Ted's pistol had torn up through the robot's chest, disappeared through the suspended ceiling, pinged loudly from the union of a pressurised copper recycling tube carrying waste water from Philip's aquarium, and finally came to rest inside a piece of foam insulation.

Gemma dizzily held her head while trying to focus on the battling duo. Ted was still pinned under the injured robot that was already twitching erratically. Ignoring her own problems, she staggered across the room and managed to roll the lump of damaged hardware onto the floor, leaving Ted free to sit up and massage his bruised throat.

"Ted, are you ok?"

Ted could not hear Gemma's voice, but the concern etched on her face said it all, without any need to understand the question. He remained mute and nodded slowly assuming that Gemma could not hear him either, as she probably shared the painful high pitched tuning fork ringing in her ears. One thing they did notice was the outer door handle turning violently and an attempt at opening the door only to be thwarted by the dead weight of the now defunct android blocking the way. Helping Ted to his feet,

Gemma grabbed the spare android forearm and they headed through the only other exit to the room, that they hoped would lead to Philip's water tank. They were in luck, the next room contained several pressurised gas cylinders, and assorted filters that Ted guessed provided the oxygen saturated water that Philip used to keep alive. In the corner, a trapdoor sized hole, complete with an aluminium ladder secured to one side, led down into Philip's watery abode. Thinking quickly, Gemma closed the door behind them and jammed the artificial forearm into the gap behind the door handle hoping to buy some time.

"What do we do now?" She shouted, louder than was necessary, as nearly all of their hearing had now returned.

"We get out of here before whatever is after us comes through that door, that's what." Ted replied, looking desperately around for another exit and realising there was none. Thinking to herself for a few seconds, Gemma came up with a possible solution.

"This looks like some kind of water treatment room so I'm guessing that there must be another server type room dealing with all the interface cables coming up from everyone down there."

Ted nodded; still not sure where Gemma was going with her train of thought, but waited while she took a breath to continue.

"Perhaps there is another trapdoor leading from the tank into that room where we can find a way out."

Ted was not really convinced by the logic of Gemma's argument and considered shooting whatever came through the door, but he was uncertain how many there were. Suddenly the heavy thudding outside became frantic and rapid turning of the door handle burying deeper into the latex flesh of the android body part, quickly helped Ted make up his mind.

"Ladies first!" He announced as he forced Gemma across the floor. Without ceremony, he pushed her off the edge and down into the warm, faint green-tinted solution. Looking back as the door burst open, Ted could see two partially completed androids charge into the room. One was completely devoid of any type of humanoid skin and comprised of an anodised metal skeleton held together with high impact plastics, all controlled by internal computerised circuitry. The other looked identical to Philip and was almost complete, apart from the lack of a right arm. The gruesome pair swiftly covered the short distance across the room, but not quickly enough as Ted held his breath and stepped off the ledge into what he hoped was not a watery grave.

Ted had always held a fearful respect for deep water, and not being much of a swimmer had rarely travelled out of his depth. The shock of having nothing solid to hold on to, coupled with throat pain, and the limited mobility of his left knee, quickly had him in distress. Finding it difficult for his eyes to focus under the water, Ted began to panic as Gemma's forecast of a secondary exit failed to materialise. The only thing visible through the watery fog were the amorphous blobs of semi-naked bodies bobbing ghostlike only a few feet away, illuminated in part by the light from the now empty observation room sited behind the glass. Looking back up through the hole into the room he had just left Ted was thankful to see that the two androids had not followed him into the water and he wondered if it was safe to return the way he came when suddenly a hand came from out of nowhere and grabbed firmly at his left wrist. Instinctively Ted turned his head and opened his mouth to scream, releasing nearly all of the air from his lungs in a huge chain of bubbles blocking the view of his foe. Freezing in terror, his over active mind expected to see Philip's pale, bloated visage grinning maniacally back at him as he tried to secure Ted to the floor of the tank. But as his vision cleared, he was thankful to see that it was the anxious face of Gemma desperately trying to pull his cramping body up from the depths as she had already found the other exit. It was less than twenty feet away, but it might as well have been a mile as Ted's breathless state sent his muscles in a painful spasm. Gemma kicked hard through the water, but the few seconds it took to reach the surface seemed to last an eternity. Cramp developed into serious pain and not for the first time today, Ted believed he was going to die. Surprisingly, this time it was not what he expected. All he now wanted to do was close his eyes and fall asleep, but as the thought developed into a strong possibility, a swift kick in the shin from Gemma painfully released him from his trance. Ted could now see a high-tech beanstalk of fibre optic wires tracing back up from every prisoner in the tank. The tight bundle, held together with cable ties, trailed upwards through the water, to a small hole next to the hatch leading into the computer room. Desperately he grabbed hold, and using them to aid his ascent he made rapid progress to the water's surface. With searing chest pain Ted coughed heavily and clung weakly onto the side of the ladder leading up into yet another hidden lab. Gemma was already out of the warm, slightly sticky liquid and trailed water from her saturated body across the floor as she looked to secure the room. As in the previous laboratory on the far side of the tank, there was only one exit door, but this time she had nothing at hand with to jam the door handle.

"It won't be long before Philip sends his henchmen round to get us so we'd better make haste, so how about a little help here?" Ted rasped in-between pain relieving gulps of air while he clung exhausted to the ladder.

"Sorry, old man, I thought you were fitter than that." Gemma replied as she grunted and strained to help Ted lift his aching body clear of the water.

"Less of the old if you don't mind." Ted chided as he collapsed on the floor, then forced a breathless smile as Gemma winked and blew him a kiss. Looking around, he could see that the room was not too dissimilar to a small server room, with the requisite aluminium computer units whirring away and occupying half of the available space. The far wall served as a monitoring and distribution unit connected to nearly every person interred in the water below. The only exception was a large cluster of fibre optic cables connected to Philip. His neural feed plugged into a floor mounted central housing allowing him direct contact, and complete control of the abducted hive intelligence. Positioning himself wearily in front of the clipboard control panel, Ted slid out the touch screen and tried to gain entry to the system, but even in his hidden bunker, Philip had secured the program from any unauthorised access.

"I really don't have a clue here Gemma; see if it's possible to disconnect any of the feeds coming directly from Philip."

Gemma followed orders and began to detach random connections, while Ted gave up on his attempt and limped painfully for the exit. Before he could reach for the handle, the door flew open and thudded into Ted's outstretched arm, knocking him off balance as the one armed, Philip Sanderson doppelgänger burst into the room. With Ted temporarily out of action, it ran straight for Gemma. Before she knew what was happening, a flash of white light blinded her sight as the android slammed its fist into the side of her head, leaving the poor woman unconscious as she crumpled to the floor.

"You bastard Philip!"

Fuelled by anger Ted screamed as he jumped up and launched an immediate counterattack. Throwing himself bodily at the android he hoped to push it towards the trapdoor and into the water but the attempt was useless. This model was stronger and faster than anything Ted had ever seen before and in the blink of an eye the fight was over. One second he was in facing the android, the next he was flat on his back, nursing two cracked ribs, and the android was already correcting the sabotage. Any hope of assistance from Gemma was futile as she continued to lay comatose, but the steady rise and fall of her chest indicated that she was alive and breathing normally.

All seemed lost as repairs were quickly made and the remaining skeletal android marched quickly into the room. The one handed droid easily threw Ted's pained and exhausted frame over its shoulder and headed through the door. The other skinless model crossed the room to where Gemma lay, dropping to one knee, ready to scoop her into its arms. To its surprise, Gemma rolled over, curled her knees up into her chest and using what little strength remained, lash out both feet, planting them squarely into the android's chest, catapulting the mechanical biped backwards across the room into the exposed distribution board.

Overhead lights fluttered and dimmed as its metal frame short circuited several systems. Sparks flew as the android slid heavily to the floor, severing even more vital connections on the way. Without realising it, Gemma had saved the lives of millions of people when the neural induced connection to the hive mind ceased to function. Every android around the world, including the separate cohort programmed to release the sarin gas, halted in mid-operation.

"Ted where are you?" Gemma shouted as she dashed out into the corridor and almost ran into him, still hanging off the android's shoulder, as it stood frozen in mid-stride.

"Get me off him!" Ted yelled breathlessly. Gemma grimaced in pain as she slowly prised away the android's arm, still pinned around Ted's waist, allowing him to slide painfully to the floor. Before he had a chance to see if Gemma was unharmed, she was already heading back into the server room. Ted followed, to bear witness the damage Gemma had caused and satisfied that the battle was over, they soon found the correct route back into the observation room to see what effect it had had on Philip and the others.

But when they descended the stairs, it was not what they expected.

"He's gone!" Gemma exclaimed, once again stating the obvious as they both stared at the shaft of light illuminating Philip's feeding and waste tubes bobbing about in the water. The remaining prisoners still appeared to be in situ, but their fate was unknown as it was much too dark to see to the back of the tank. The only exception was the latest addition, Adam, who was still very much alive and fought vainly with the restraints binding him to the floor of the tank. The desperation in his eyes was more than Gemma could take, and in an instant she turned away and was running as fast as her injured leg would allow, up the stairs and back into the server room.

"What the hell are you doing?" Ted shouted as Gemma turned the corner onto the upper level.

"I can't leave him to die!" Gemma's voice echoed back down the stairs. This left Ted little option but to follow wearily, as he too limped back up the stairwell. When he reached the top he almost bumped into Gemma as she stood just inside the doorway, staring open mouthed at an incredible sight.

Just a few feet away, Philip Sanderson had climbed out of the tank and while down on all fours, he vomited copiously, producing bile that was similar in colour but more viscous than the oxygenated solution where he was recently suspended. Completely naked and detached from all of his life sustaining apparatus, his body appeared to deflate as honey coloured liquid oozed profusely from the distended pores of his sodden wrinkled skin. When the majority had all but drained away, Philip staggered to his feet, took hold of the android, and with considerable effort rolled it away from the circuit board before returning to make a repair.

"The game's over Philip; step away and I will stay by your side to make sure you get the best medical treatment possible. What do you say?" Ted offered up in his best calm and reassuring voice. Up to that point Philip had been oblivious to any company as he stopped the repair and now appeared to show more concern with an annoying drip of water repeatedly tapping his head. Looking up, his breathing gurgled noisily as he stared at the root of the problem. There had obviously been a leak of some sorts and it had been absorbed by a large portion of increasingly sodden fibre ceiling tiles. Believing Philip's change of focus to be a good sign, Ted began to approach, but the reaction was not what he expected. Philip snapped his head around, snarling like a rabid dog, baring the grey mouldy stubs of what remained of his teeth, eroded by the chemicals contained within his life sustaining solution. This contrasted violently with the sickly hue of a limp mustard-yellow tongue lolling in the corner of his mouth. Ted immediately raised his hands and backed away as Philip resumed his repairs.

"What do we do now?" Gemma whispered, wrinkling her nose as steam began to rise from Philip's imbued body and the pungent smell of wet dog wafted in their direction. Ted remained silent, trying to decide on the best course of action, but found it hard to concentrate as he stared at the grotesque form standing just a few feet away. He watched fascinated as Philip continued to affect a remedy, but the muscles in his arms had atrophied, leaving them in a string-like state and hard to control. When he raised his hands to the circuit board, the skinny limbs quivered and bobbed like a loosely jointed marionette. This severely slowed down Philip's attempt to rectify the damage; but that was only one part of the problem. As his body was now clear of the water's support, the joints in his legs slowly began to buckle from the increased load accompanied by the sight of his softened bones visibly beginning to warp, twisting out of their original shape. All of this exaggerated the overlapping folds of slimy flesh now hanging like curtains of molten wax from Philip's raddled frame.

"We can't let him repair the connection to his droids or we're all done for." Ted whispered behind his raised hand, before making a second attempt to reason with Philip. Ignoring the approach, Philip stood back, quickly scanned his work, and satisfied with the result he jumped back into the tank. Without warning Gemma ran across the room and followed suit, disappearing headfirst into the warm pale green liquid. Ted ran to the water's edge wondering if he should follow, but quickly decided that he would be more hindrance than help, so he turned to the control panel and tried valiantly to close down the system. It may have only been a few seconds, but Philip had already reconnected himself and his maniacal voice echoed across the room.

"This is your final warning, any further interference and I will reactivate my robotic army that will poison millions. Do you hear me?"

Ted ignored the order, believing it to be an empty threat and continued with his task, but he was wrong. Across the world chaos resumed and thousands of Philip's inactive androids received fresh input and burst into life, including the one-hundred programmed to release the sarin gas. Gemma suddenly reappeared at the hatch and to Ted's relief she was holding tightly to the body of Adam Cartwright. Ted hauled him clear of the water, quickly undid the arm restraining straps, and then placed him onto his side to cough up the oxygen enriched solution, while he helped Gemma back into the room.

"Everyone else apart from Philip are chained to the floor and impossible to release right now, so I will have to return later when we've dealt with Philip; give me a hand." Gemma gasped as she staggered to her feet and stood next to the defunct android waiting for Ted's help to throw it back onto the distribution board. Ted grabbed hold of the android's shoulders and Gemma its legs, ready to drag it across the room and hurl it into the panel when the one armed android marched back into the room. Ted immediately dropped his end and charged at the robot, His momentum this time managing to bulldoze the mechanical man backwards into the hallway, where they both landed in an untidy heap. Ted was first to his feet, removed his gun from its holster, took aim, and pulled the trigger. Unfortunately, instead of the deafening crack of a gunshot, the click of the firing pin was all he heard. Again and again he pulled the trigger, but the effect was the same. The ammunition in the magazine was waterlogged, leaving the gun completely useless. Gemma moved to help Ted, but Adam held up a hand and gargled a few words.

"Wait! I can help. Get me to the control panel and I can end all of this"

Gemma stopped, unsure what to do first, but she could see Ted was already on his feet and reaching for his gun so she helped Adam him to the operator's chair. Being upright induced another coughing fit and a secondary pool of watery phlegm hit the floor, before he could explain how.

"My name is Adam Cartwright and I was kidnapped several weeks ago along with a group of my friends. To cut a long story short, I understand computing. My mind has been connected to this system, I know what's at stake, and I'm sure I can safely shut it down."

Adam's modest declaration of his computing skills made Gemma smile, but it quickly changed into jaw dropping amazement as she observed the speed of his manual dexterity on the computer. Gemma turned away to go and help Ted when Philip's voice boomed out once again.

"Remove Mr Cartwright from the terminal or I will shut down air supply for this level."

Adam smiled briefly at the bluff and his fingers moved even faster because he knew that he had Philip on the ropes. There was more than enough oxygen evaporating from Philip's super saturated solution to last for weeks.

"Don't believe a word of it, he's lying; go and help your friend."

Adam had barely finished his sentence before Gemma turned and ran into the corridor to see Ted still aiming his gun and pulling the trigger but to no avail. Completely out of options Ted was already backing down the corridor, hoping the android would follow him. His idea was to keep Gemma and Adam from danger, but unfortunately it turned back to the server room door. What it did not expect, was to see Gemma armed with a fire extinguisher, smash the base into its face, knocking it back to the floor. Before the android had time to initiate a reboot, Gemma forced the end of the extinguisher hose into the open shoulder socket and pulled the trigger. White fire suppressant foam blasted from the nozzle, instantly filling the chest cavity and poured into every internal orifice. Unbelievably the android still attempted to regain its feet, but now every movement appeared to be in slow motion. Foam poured copiously from its mouth, eye sockets and even through the fine mesh protecting the command recognition pods sited inside the ears. The extinguisher eventually emptied and Gemma stepped back. Somehow the android managed to stand upright and take one stride, then suddenly a loud crack emanated from somewhere inside the chest and it stood completely still. Not waiting for an encore, Ted and Gemma ran back into the computer control room to find Adam still hard at work. Ted began to question what was going on only for Gemma to squeeze his arm, allowing the young man to maintain his concentration. Philip had been unable to reintegrate the hive mind and now had to pit his wits against someone of equal intelligence, but also had youth on his side. As fast as he believed to have locked Adam out, the young genius found another way to circumvent Philip's digital blockade. Ted and Gemma watched in amazement as one by one, Adam gained access to the major systems, but Philip still maintained control of the androids across the globe, and some were now only minutes away from their target. Adam realised this and decided that there was only one solution left, and that was to connect with Philip directly. Switching neural control to a multiple input system, Adam jumped from his seat, and without explanation, he ran across the floor, and jumped back into the tank. He could hear muffled yelling coming from the room above and looked up to see Ted holding Gemma back from jumping in for a second time.

Wrapping his leg around the anchor chain to stop his body from floating to the top of the tank, Adam opened his mouth and resisting the vomit reflex, he breathed in the oxygen rich solution. Luckily, as he had not been long out of his watery prison, he readapted quickly and managed to replace the neural skull cap. In the server room Ted and Gemma watched with fascination as the terminal screen blurred from the rapid display of computer code, scrolling rapidly up the screen as time and time again Philip wrestled with Adam's mental invasion. Every time Adam believed that he had taken command, Philip somehow managed to claw his way back and the androids edged closer to their target.

The stalemate continued until something completely unexpected changed everything. The pressurised aquarium water pipe, cracked by the bullet from Ted's gun had sprayed a fine mist across the entire suspended ceiling cavity, that steadily absorbed the warm liquid. Eventually it could hold no more and portions began to collapse onto the floor below. The constant flow of saline solution through the hairline crack further weakened the pipe until suddenly it snapped and thousands of gallons of chemically enriched aquarium saltwater cascaded like a waterfall into every room, shorting out the system once more as it flooded into Philip's tank.

"Let's get out of here before we drown." Ted yelled above the noise of gushing water and the sound of even more ceiling panels slapping heavily onto the floor. "What about Adam, he's still down there?" Gemma replied and ran to the edge of the hatch.

"I can't see anything Ted, go down to the observation room, and see if you see him."

Reluctant to leave Gemma alone, Ted did as asked and limped carefully down the flooded stairs to take a look. The previously clear tank now compared to a consommé soup as the chemicals formulated for tropical fish, swirled in oily rainbow patterns trying to combine with Philip's dense oxygenated water. Random shapes of compressed paper ceiling tiles washed into the open hatch and slowly descended to the bottom of the tank, settling like filthy snowflakes around Philip's and Adam's feet as both men writhed and convulsed trying to breathe in the dirty cocktail. Adam was doing his best to release the anchor chain that had somehow tightened around his leg, but Philip made no attempt for his own release.

"Get out you fool!" Ted screamed, banging his fists on the glass in frustration. For a second Philip looked up and wiped his hand through the grime building up on the inside of the tank so he could focus on his friend. Ted could now see the mad glint in Philip's eye had changed to one of resignation and he had no intention of releasing his ankle straps securing him to the bottom. He knew that it was too late and his life was nearly over. Ignoring Ted's repeated pleas for him to get out, Philip woefully turned his gaze upon Adam fighting frantically for his own life.

In most forms of sport and pastimes there are rules that must be adhered to if the game is to be played in the correct manner. There is also an unwritten rule of etiquette that any competitor who is serious about their chosen passion must follow, and the game of chess is no exception. If a player finds himself in such a predicament that success is impossible it is considered very bad form to prolong the game, therefore he should tip his king and resign. Even though Philip Sanderson must be considered on almost every level completely insane, deep down he still held within him a common sense of fair play. Realising that defeat was imminent, he reached out, untangled Adam Cartwright's leg from the snarled up anchor chain and watched stoically as the young man kicked desperately for the surface. Returning his gaze to the front, Philip stared hard at Ted and tried to communicate, but there was too much damage to the system for any coherent speech to get through. At one point Ted believed that Philip had changed his mind when he removed his skull cap, but he just closed his eyes and it ended there.

With rapidly increasing effort, Philip's chest rose and fell as his lungs tried harder and harder to filter the oxygen from this new deadly solution, and even though it was horrific to watch, the visceral fascination to witness the final moments made it impossible for Ted to look away. When the end finally came, Philip's body arched backwards as his stomach distended to an almost impossible size, and then in an instant it deflated. Blood drenched ribbons of shredded lung tissue spurted forth from his nose and mouth, pushing back the lifeless body to the limit of its anchor point in a deep crimson cloud, defiling the water as it rolled out along the glass wall of the tank. Ted's gaze remained transfixed on the hideous diorama as the elongated crimson bronchial strands egressed from Philip's open mouth akin to red sea whip wafting gently back and forth under the sea.

He had no idea how long he had been standing staring through the glass, or whether Gemma had been there to witness Philip's demise, but the gentle touch of her hand on his, was enough to break his trance.

"How do we get out of here?" She yelled over the noise of gushing water while wondering how he would react over Philip's death. Holding her tightly in his arms, Ted looked up and was relieved to see Adam was alive, although looking very sick indeed as he descended the stairwell. Nodding over Gemma's shoulder, Ted smiled and said,

"Perhaps we should ask him!"

THE END

EPILOGUE

High up on the edge of a bluff overhanging a well-guarded valley, Ivan Stefanovich watched with stomach churning revulsion and anger at the carnage being measured out in the arena below. His conscience had got the better of him, and instead of continuing his bid for freedom, he had spent the night tracking the progress of his comrades. He now stood less than fifty yards away from the bizarre façade of a roman gladiatorial event. Completely impotent to do anything to affect proceedings, he continued to witness the controlled savage murder of his friends and fellow prisoners, all in the name of entertainment. The entire event appeared to be for the enjoyment of one man, living out a twisted fantasy of being an emperor for a day. Tears rolled steadily from his pale blue eyes, leaving streaks in his sallow cheeks as the salty liquid picked up the dust on his skin, then dripped silently from the tips of his pepper pot beard onto the earth below.

The living nightmare seemed to continue without end, as one by one his friends and colleagues succumbed to the slaughter, until finally he spotted Jacob fighting gamely for his life. Using all the correct techniques, some of which he taught Jacob himself, he watched with a twisted sense of pride at how well Jacob fought, until he too lay dead on the arena floor.

Doggedly resisting the urge to make a charge from where he stood and not caring about the consequence, Ivan swore a silent oath that everyone involved in the nightmare would pay the price; starting with the head man. Drawing on all of his Ukrainian army experience, found a good place to hide, and made a plan.

There was only one road leading down the mountainside from the complex and using this to his advantage, he lay in wait at the roadside for the right victim to come along.

The sun was high in the sky and as he rested in the shade of the scrub he soon fell asleep, but awoke sharply as the rumble of an approaching truck jolted him to his senses. From his cover deep in the undergrowth he could see that it was a uniformed guard driving a small truck down into town for supplies. By rolling a small boulder into the middle of the road, blocking the truck's path, Ivan waited until the driver climbed down from his vehicle to roll the rock out of the way and then launched his one man ambush. His military training had served him well, and before the driver had a chance to make any sound, he lay dead with a broken neck. Quickly stripping the victim of his weapons and uniform, Ivan hid the partially clothed body in the nearest ditch and secreted the truck behind a dilapidated goat herder's shack, ready to use it for a getaway later.

It was obvious that he would not pass even the lightest scrutiny from any other personnel, but he hoped if spotted, the uniform would work from a distance. To his surprise, as well as a small hunting knife, the dead man carried a Makarov pistol in his shoulder holster. This standard issue Russian sidearm was discontinued before the end of the last century, but still proved effective if properly maintained. Unfortunately this one had seen better days and would need to be stripped down and examined if it was going to save his life. First, he unloaded the full eight round detachable magazine, and then tested the mechanism. Surprisingly, everything worked well apart from the actuator return spring that appeared very weak. He found that before the gun was able to fire a second time, the trigger had to be manually clicked back into place, and this could prove critical should he get into a fire fight. The second problem was the uniform; even though the driver was considerably overweight, making the clothing baggy enough to fit Ivan's imposing frame, he stood over a foot taller, and when he put it on he looked like an overgrown schoolboy.

"Beggars can't be choosers." He muttered to himself as he reloaded the pistol, threw his old clothes into the truck, and waited for nightfall. Although baking hot during the daytime, the clear skies and high mountain altitude allowed the temperature to fall often down to freezing after the sun has set. Luckily, this happened to be tonight, playing to Ivan's advantage as the compound guards were mainly huddled around flaming braziers dotted throughout the site. Although more than twenty men were on duty that night, security was pretty lax as fear of the head man, living inside, was usually enough to keep people at bay. This made it fairly easy for Ivan to climb an old olive tree growing against the south wall, drop onto a walkway and slip inside the main building completely unnoticed. The late hour meant that nearly everyone was in bed and he soon reached the head man, sleeping alone in the master bedroom. It was hard to believe that this bald, obese man of about sixty years of age, who looked like a mild mannered shop keeper sleeping soundly in his bed, could be responsible for such pain and death. But Ivan held no qualms as to what he looked like as the debt had to be paid.

Using the belt from a silk bathrobe found hanging on the back of the door, He woke up his sleeping target with the cold muzzle of the gun pressed hard into the man's flabby cheek. To his surprise, he remained surprisingly calm and nodded silently in response to Ivan's instruction of an index finger placed upon his lips. Rolling him roughly onto his stomach, he expertly hog-tied the man's hands and feet behind his back, then pushed him back onto his side so they could talk. In the rush of the attack, he forgot which language to use and began in his native Russian. The confusion on the man's face made him realise his mistake, so Ivan whispered his threats in English, and his captive appeared to understand.

"What is your name? Answer softly or I will gut you where you lay."

Drawing a deep breath, ready to shout for help, the old man quickly dismissed the idea from his mind at the point of the cold dagger pressing into the skin directly below his left eyeball.

"My name is Don Roberto Delmar, also known as Little Emperor. I control this entire region and you will never make it out alive. If you let me go I will grant you safe passage."

Ivan smiled at the bravado.

"I suppose you are wondering who I am? My name is Ivan Stefanovich and I am the missing prisoner who should have died in your arena today. I hold you responsible for the death of my friends and I want to know who is behind this operation or you are going to pay."

To play for time, Don Roberto decided to tell his captor whatever he wanted because he knew he would not live long enough to tell his tale.

"The man who supplied the extra people for this event is Philip Sanderson, chairman of Hologram Dreams. If you think that you will get anywhere near a man like that, then you are very much mistaken."

The mention of Sanderson's name triggered the recent memory of the sallow looking man who chose him and the others from the line-up less the two days ago.

"It is not my fault, I'm not the one you need to blame, it is Sanderson you really want, and I can help you get him."

Ivan stared incredulously at the nonchalant way Don Roberto dismissed his responsibility. What he really wanted to do was scream at the top of his lungs and break every bone in the man's body as punishment for what he had witnessed that very afternoon, but time was not on his side.

"You talk too much old man."

With deep forethought on the most satisfying silent death, Ivan cut short his whispered curses and began. Pinning Roberto's head under a pillow, he used the freshly sharpened tip of the truck driver's, hunting knife, to jab through the loose folds of flesh hanging from under his chin. Ignoring the twitches and muffled squeals of pain, he soon found the ridge at the top of the larynx and with the precision of a surgeon; he forced the pointed tip through into the trachea, completely severing the vocal chords. Satisfied with the result, he removed the pillow and stepped back.

Eyes wide with terror as blood bubbled from his mouth and neck wound, Don Roberto, spluttered on just enough life giving oxygen to remain conscious and suffer his executioner's final blow. Ivan was about to slit open the old man's stomach and leave him the rest of the evening to bleed to death, when a guttural growl from one of the starving lions carried up from the arena floor.

The balcony adjoining the master bedroom overlooked the gladiatorial floor and served a dual purpose as the emperor's rostrum from which where could observe the events. Padding around below, inside the perimeter wall and moaning for food were the three lions used earlier in the games. They had been denied the chance to feed for long on the murdered prisoners, with the intention to keep them eager for even more entertainment tomorrow. Seizing the opportunity, Ivan carefully opened the double doors leading out onto the balcony, checked that the coast was clear, and then returned to drag his victim from the bed. Realising what now was to be his fate, the old man twisted and turned, fighting hard against the silk bindings biting painfully deep into his corpulent flesh. Instantly smelling the scent of fresh blood carried down on the cool night air, the hungry lions turned anxious circles in the sand and roared for the anticipated feast.

Smiling for the first time in nearly a year, Ivan lifted the old man to his feet and leaned him over the balcony wall. His neck wound dripped onto the faces of the hungry lions below, whipping them up into a blood-crazed frenzy and they roared incessantly. Ivan hoped to prolong the terror, stabbing Don Roberto in the gut as he recited the name of each friend, but the noise coming from the lions had alerted the guards and the floodlights came on.

"For my comrades." Ivan snarled as he heaved the trussed up bulk over the wall into the arena and watched with satisfaction as it thumped heavily onto the sand below. Pausing for a few seconds he leaned over the balustrade, watching the defenceless man scream silently and try to roll away before the lions pounced. Fighting for a share, each lion tore away great lumps of flesh from Don Roberto's still conscious body.

"Your death will be one of many!" Ivan growled under his breath. Satisfied that he had made a good start, the big man disappeared into the night.

* * *

* * *

Have you enjoyed the book? Hope so! If you did and are feeling generous, please leave a review on ***Amazon / AmazonKindle***.

If you are looking for something new – check out my first novel – Timelock – a chilling horror.

* * *

TIMELOCK

"You have no right to use this heresy."
"Your curiosities into the realms of the hereafter are forbidden to the living world, and your association with evil will deliver dire consequences"

When a close-knit group of university students conduct an experimental look into the afterlife, the joy at their success turns to disaster when their curious endeavours release an evil entity back into the living world.
In a desperate attempt to put things right, the group now face their greatest fears. Racing against time, they must pass through a purgatorial realm and prepare to do battle with the ultimate evil. Standing in their way and hell bent on revenge is Toomak, an undead ancient sorceress who has placed a curse on all mankind and will stop at nothing to make good her oath.

"My spirit will never die; I swear that I will
someday find the amulet of the ancients,
unite with the underworld and return to wreak
vengeance on you and the rest of the living world."
"You will all die screaming!"

One central character, two stories, each one set nearly two thousand years apart. When the two timelines collide, a cataclysmic showdown begins.

If you would like a digital half book sample of my first novel Timelock, then send a request to Russ-knighton@sky.com (please state the format required)